HEADPRESS

**A HEADPRESS BOOK**
First published by Headpress in 2023, Oxford, United Kingdom
headoffice@headpress.com

**B-SIDE**
**A Flipsided History of Pop**


Book layout: MARK CRITCHELL mark.critchell@gmail.com
Cover art and cover design: KID ACNE
Illustrations: KID ACNE
The Publisher wishes to thank Gareth Wilson

10 9 8 7 6 5 4 3 2



A CIP catalogue record for this book is available from the British Library

ISBN 978-1-915316-13-4 paperback
ISBN 978-1-915316-14-1 ebook
ISBN NO-ISBN hardback

HEADPRESS. POP AND UNPOP CULTURE



**B-Side Playlists**

To enhance your reading pleasure, a series of YouTube playlists have been created for B-Side. Access here: **www.youtube.com/@B-Sidebook/playlists**

**Get in touch**

Can't believe your favourite B-side is missing? Have a cool B-side tale to tell? Please get in touch. All suggestions will be taken into account for future editions.

Email: **andycowanbside@gmail.com**

# B-SIDE

"A FLIPSIDED HISTORY OF POP."

# CONTENTS

# CONTENTS

# INTRODUCTION

*Break on through to the other side...*

"She keeps on playing those B-side records," cried Adam Ant on 'B-Side Baby', just before his pop career hit the skids. Yet if anyone knew the subversive value of a great flipside it was the self-styled king of the wild frontier. Not only did Ant impishly save up some of his strongest material for B-sides, he used the pantomime of his biggest hit 'Stand And Deliver!' as a trojan horse to flog sadomasochism to his fans, many too young to know better, via the unremitting filth of its other side, 'Beat My Guest'.

Ant was not the first nor last to use the B-side as Mr Hyde to his Dr Jekyll. This book is riven with the bad young brothers and evil twins of pop's greatest hits (and misses) — songs deemed unworthy of the main spotlight that would somehow revolt against their lowly status and refuse to be denied.

But what exactly is a B-side? How did they start? For answers we need to go way back to the late 1890s.

That was when Emile Berliner built upon the innovations of Edouard-Leon Scott and Thomas Edison to create the first manually-operated gramophone. Yet the first recorded discs were single-sided affairs, carrying just four minutes of sound. The Victor Company's launch of its Red Seal line in 1901 to play 10-inch, 78 rpm records brought fresh momentum to the nascent industry — establishing a format that would endure another 47 years — as did the advent of double-sided recordings in 1910, allowing labels to add a second offering on the other side. Via that quirk of formatting, the B-side was born.

While the cheery farmyard impersonations of Original Dixieland Jass Band's 'Livery Stable Blues' — the first notable B-side, included here — did much to establish jazz as popular music in 1917, the lines between A and B-side were at first blurred. The B-side's importance only sharpened into focus in the 30s, with the arrival of the charts.

Just as early recording stars Louis Armstrong, Robert Johnson and Count Basie made commercial hay on 78s, other innovations were at play behind the scenes. These peaked in the great 'War of the Speeds'. It kicked off in 1948 when CBS launched the world's first LP (Long Play) record — twelve inches wide, 331/3 rpm — creating the album format still dominant today. However, the long-play disc was a pricey flop at retail — victim of a shortage of affordable players and intense consumer scepticism. Into the void leapt RCA Victor in December 1948 with their own LP — a kittenish little chancer, just seven inches in size, rotating at 45 rpm. It would soon be rebranded the single, typically with one song per side.

The 50s proved revolutionary for both formats, as consumers basked in the afterglow of post-war prosperity. Not only did the album finally come into its own as the chief focus for the serious artist — with Duke Ellington pioneering the long-form jazz suite — the single tapped into the pop culture of the here and now and was embraced by radio stations. The A-sides of singles were prioritised to feature the most radio-friendly track — the 'hit' — while that extra bit of bang for your buck, the B-side, was less straightjacketed, open to more hazy interpretation.

Not that labels always guessed the hit right. Many B-side bridesmaids would outstrip the fortunes of the favoured A-side when flip-curious DJs and radio programmers got hip to their potential. It's nigh impossible to envisage the 50s rock 'n' roll revolution being kicked off by Bill Haley & His Comets had radio paid fidelity to A-Side 'Thirteen Women (And Only One Man In Town)' and not the sweaty call to arms of '(We're Gonna) Rock Around The Clock'. Likewise, Britain's attempt at a half-decent response would have crashed and burned had the dippy teenage lusts of Cliff Richard & the Drifters' 'Schoolboy Crush' not been flipped to the edgy command 'Move It!' at the eleventh hour.

The 60s was the pop single's definitive era as classic labels such as Motown, Atlantic and Capitol held sway. The top singles prima-donnas were of course the Beatles — arguably the first group to really treat the B-side with reverence, often filling their other sides with superior songs to many acts' A-sides. The Fabs used it to stray into untrodden lands, a baton picked up by fellow travellers including Donovan, the Kinks and the Yardbirds. The 60s cemented the notion that the B-side was multifarious — capable of bringing great joy, bitter disappointment and total befuddlement — a gift and a curse to the guileless buyer with limited funds.

Pop history is littered with the forgotten corpses of half-baked, rushed, cheaply recorded B-sides knocked off to support an obvious money-maker

A-side (some making the point explicit with jokey titles like 'A Quick B'). At worst, the B-side is an unloved studio offcut; a dashed-off makeweight not good enough to grace an album. There are other 'variations' that rarely set the pulse racing — the acoustic version, the remix, the live take, the different language version, the one to appease the band's lesser songwriter.

And while such B-sides are ten-a-penny, there's a small but committed legion that rank as all-killer-no-filler, songs that took on a life of their own and etched the B-side deep into music history.

Depending on their approach to its blank canvas, the B-side allowed artists to let their hair down, have fun, toy with off-key ideas and venture into unexplored creative universes. The best B-sides often occupy a neutral space — between single and album — that enabled artists to experiment in the truest sense, mercifully free of the pressure to deliver a hit, and as an aesthetic counterweight to an A-Side with its hands already firmly in the till.

What's less known is that the B-side carried a keen financial imperative. While 70s superstars like Elton John, the Who and Queen were hard-grafters that rarely skimped on providing maximum VFM with quality non-album flips, the B-side proved a vital lifeline to some of the more acutely manufactured 70s bands (a case in point being glam clotheshorses the Sweet). A single's publishing royalties were split 50:50 — regardless of A or B-side — allowing the B-side's writers to cash-in on the publishing spoils, even if they'd surrendered the A-side to their mentors in a Faustian trade-off for fame.

B-sides were revelatory too — you could divine a lot about an act by how they approached it. The advent of the 12-inch single in the 80s — allowing for up to four extra tracks — gave great B-side embracers such as Depeche Mode, the Cure, Prince and the Smiths plenty of rope to reveal unseen sides of their musical psyche. It's tempting to wonder whether 'How Soon Is Now?' — one of the latter's greatest moments, if not their defining one — would exist without the freedom the expanded 12-inch format allowed. Many bands developed a special affinity for the B-side in the 80s, when knowing a band's more hidden sides was a way fans could signal the depth of their devotion.

The rise of the CD single and devil-may-care multi-formatting in the 90s put the dampeners on this golden age. With labels doubling or tripling the number of B-side tracks required — effectively demanding an extra album's worth of material for each long-playing campaign — quality control went south. There were a few exceptions to the rule — Oasis, Blur, Pulp, Suede and Radiohead still made B-sides that showed they cared.

The advent of streaming and downloads in the 21st century would ultimately do for the B-side — now less an endangered species than one barely twitching in the coffin. And while new vinyl releases still thrive among collectors, most are re-releases or limited editions, issued in relatively small numbers. The term B-side has also been widely misappropriated, reconfigured as a catch-all for non-album or bonus tracks.

Of course, when push comes to shove, the B-side is effectively a by-product of a by-product — vinyl only existing as a cheap adjunct of capitalism. However empirically true that is, the loss of the B-side is something far more dramatic and unfathomable for several generations of pop devotees, where standard metrics simply don't apply.

Rather than mourn the B-side's demise, I have come to praise it. *B-Side* is intended as both a loose reference book and an open celebration, jammed tight with more than 500 good reasons to toast pop's hidden game-changers.

***Inclusion Criteria***

To claim that narrowing down the A-Z of this B-side selection has been a headache would be an understatement. It's also been a great adventure, with one B-side rabbit-hole invariably leading to the next. Two simple criteria have persisted throughout:

1. Only one song per artist — a tricky tightrope to walk with some of the more prolific B-siders here, the choices subjective. This doesn't apply to solo turns. For example, all the Beatles also have individual entries under their own names.
2. Most songs here are stand-alone releases — songs that were originally only available as a B-side, not on any contemporaneous album. The odd exception has been made for those flipsides whose cultural import far outweighs any middling protests over format.

**'1963'**
New Order
FACTORY 1987
A-Side: 'True Faith'

**Post-punk Mancs rewrite US political history.**

From the moment Bernard Sumner put his hesitant but discrete vocal stamp on 'In A Lonely Place' — B-side of 'Ceremony', two of Joy Division's last songs before Ian Curtis killed himself — New Order began to live up to their name. While Curtis's shadow would inevitably haunt their cautious first steps, they amassed more than a dozen singles to their name, had embraced cutting-edge dance music and were poised to crack America when 'True Faith' trickled out with sassy self-assurance in 1987. Written alongside producer Stephen Hague during the same sessions, '1963' was unusual from the start — a wild conspiracy theory about a bizarre love triangle between John F. Kennedy, his assassin Lee Harvey Oswald and Marilyn Monroe that paid scant regard to facts or dates. Disputed subject matter aside, the song stood powerfully on its own, with Peter Hook's pealing bass and Stephen Morris's brutal hi-hats driving a melancholic chorus coda with tears still in its eyes. While Hook would mither in the press that his full contribution was ignored, recompense arrived seven years later when an Arthur Baker remix was released as an A-side that restored the bass to its original glory. Alongside it an intriguing, band-free video directed by the Raincoats' Gina Birch.

**'10 Guitars'**
Englebert Humperdinck
DECCA 1967
A-Side: 'Release Me'

**Luckless UK crooner scores Patea's national anthem.**

Best known as Gerry, Arnold Dorsey's struggles to break into the music industry continued into his thirties. The dark-eyed, easy listening crooner's fortunes changed when his manager, Gordon Mills, suggested he adopt a more interesting stage name. Dorsey plumped for the mantle of the German composer of Hansel and Gretel — impossible to forget, intrinsically funny — and after standing in for Dickie Valentine on the TV variety show *Sunday Night At The London Palladium*, the new Humperdinck suddenly had a huge hit on his hands. While it held off the Beatles' double A-side of 'Penny Lane' and 'Strawberry Fields

Forever', it stayed in the charts for a record 56 consecutive weeks, the single's B-side enjoyed an unexpected second life in New Zealand. Written by Mills — a not inconsiderable pop songsmith who also notched with Tom Jones' 'It's Not Unusual' — '10 Guitars' tale of a band of six-stringers serenading women with their mystical musical skills resonated heavily thanks, in part, to the dampened sound of its Maori guitar strum. Warmly embraced by Rotorua-based DJ Eddie O'Strange, it became an instant Kiwi favourite and even known as the national anthem of Patea. Yet, as Geoff Cawthorn recalled in his 1996 documentary *Ten Guitars*, Humperdinck was totally oblivious to the song's success. So much so that when he toured New Zealand in the 1970s he didn't play it at his first show in Christchurch — causing an outcry so strong his band had to hastily learn its three-chord motif. Humperdinck would later be mentioned in a 1970 Monty Python election night sketch (with John Cleese breathlessly reporting about "Engelbert Humperdinck taking Barrow and Furness") and even represent the UK at Eurovision with 2012's 'Love Will Set You Free'.

### '14 Hour Technicolour Dream'

The Syn
DERAM 1967
A-Side: 'Flowerman'

**Yes men capture Summer of Love's formative happening.**

The Syn's reputation went before them. The short-lived London band managed just two singles for Deram, but totally captured the mood of the prevailing counterculture. While 1967's first, 'Created By Clive', was a modish, Carnaby Street rip-off that the band tolerated just to see their name on wax, they moved seamlessly into the psychedelic zone with its breezy follow-up 'Flowerman', replete with "fla-la-las" and cooing backing harmonies. Yet it was its B-side that captured the spirit of the age. A wide-eyed account of the 14 Hour Technicolour Dream at Alexandra Palace — a benefit show for the highly respected underground rag *International Times* — it was a dizzy distillation of pop psychedelia whose powerful drums and mannered distortion carried melodic references to movies, smoking bananas and Suzy Creamcheese (Frank Zappa's generic term for an underage groupie) that summoned the Summer of Love's far-out vibes. A regular presence at the Marquee club on Wardour Street, the Syn were beloved of pirate radio DJ John Peel, who broadcast both sides on the valedictory edition of his coveted *Perfumed Garden* show. Yet by the following year they had left the building, morphing into Mabel Greer's Toyshop and, in the case of guitarist Peter Banks and bassist Chris Squire, Yes. Remarkably, Squire revived the Syn in 2004 for a comeback album *Syndestructible*.

### '20/20'

Alanis Morissette
MAVERICK 2008
A-Side: 'Underneath'

**Canadian navel-gazer's uber candid confessional.**

"I'm very pregnant with songs," Morissette told *Billboard* in the run-up to her seventh studio album *Flavors Of Entanglement*. The ever-angsty Canadian songwriter — forever working in the shadow of 1995's 30-million-selling debut *Jagged Little Pill* — had struggled to maintain its coursing momentum, the hits slowing to the extent that she had just completed an acoustic tour reprising it in full (selling the attendant album exclusively through Starbucks, itself a heavy nod to her audience demographic). While this lead single's A-side dealt in universal platitudes — a soul-searching warning that you can only change the world after you change yourself — its flip was far more personal, directly dealing with the emotional fallout of her broken engagement with clean-cut sitcom actor Ryan Reynolds. Morissette's pained mentions of 'fear lenses', 'fountain of regret', 'torturous hindsight' and a 'mountain of remorse' — prime therapy-speak riddled into pop poetry — over spare metallic drums, gabbling electronic bass and high-drama strings, marked it as a return to the uber-confessional style of her earlier work. '20/20' duly became a firm fan favourite.

### '2000 Seasons'

Reflection Eternal
RAWKUS 1997
A-Side: 'Fortified Live'

**Hook-free show of nascent rapper's lyrical prowess.**

Although rapper Talib Kweli and producer Hi-Tek first met up in Cincinnati, Ohio, both their careers gained traction on New York's late 90s underground scene. Snapped up by the freshly minted Rawkus imprint in the wake of their short contribution to Mood's debut LP *Doom* ('Industry Lies'), their first single was a bona fide no-frills independent record, the sound of two unpolished demos bristling with the vinyl static that was Hi-Tek's early trademark. While 'Fortified Live' was a braggadocio three-way with Kweli's future Black Star mate Mos Def and Da Bush Babees' Mr Man — bigging-up their microphone abilities while namechecking Keyser Soze, Lionel Ritchie and Richard Gere — it was the B-side that saw Kweli live up to his name as "seeker of truth". Using Hi-Tek's laidback rhythm and a twinkly jazz piano rip as foundation, the wordsmith boxed clever with metaphors and poetic allusions while radiating a political awareness largely lacking from his bling-obsessed counterparts during those materially-driven times. As beautiful and challenging as the Ayi Kwei Arma novel it took its name from (Keli even quoted the intro in the prologue), the densely written '2000 Seasons' quickly became an underground sensation, reaching wider ears on the scene-defining *Soundbombing* compilation.

### '20th Century'

John Foxx
METAL BEAT/VIRGIN 1980
A-Side: 'Burning Car'

**Futuristic machine rock, hand-tooled for the haunted fish tank.**

Having witnessed Gary Numan steal his thunder with the success of *Replicas* and *The Pleasure Principle* — albums that hid their debt to Foxx's first band Ultravox! in plain sight — the founding father of UK synth pop belatedly managed a degree of success with 1980's purely electronic *Metamatic*. Deliberately created using a restricted palette of instruments (notably the ARP Odyssey, Elka 'String Machine' and Roland CR-78 Compurhythm), the resulting steeliness suited the typically prickly Ballardian psychodramas the Lancashire-born auteur was so fond of — epitomised on the A-side here. The analogue oddness of its B-side was far more direct and strangely danceable, as it repeated the title in haughty fashion. First commissioned as the theme to Janet Street-Porter's early TV youth vehicle *20th Century Box* — which gave a critical platform for the then unsigned Spandau Ballet — '20th Century' also signalled the end of the mechanical phase of Foxx's earlier career as softer, lighter, more conventional pastures loomed.

## '51st Anniversary'

The Jimi Hendrix Experience
TRACK 1967
A-Side: 'Purple Haze'

**Guitarist gets *au fait* with the latest studio technology.**

Jimi Hendrix mesmerised fans and left fellow musicians fearing for their livelihoods. While the left-handed Seattle six-stringer's virtuosic, other-worldly guitar sounds first fired people's imaginations, it was the nonchalance of his delivery — the playing of intricate passages with his teeth while throwing out yoga poses or lazily chewing gum — that sealed his real-deal status. The mythical voodoo vibes of the Experience's second single 'Purple Haze' confirmed Hendrix as a first-rate songwriter to boot, as its ambiguous subject matter (maybe a nod to a short sci-fi story by Philip José Farmer, perhaps a description of an acid trip), its throbbing double-E bassline and fuzzy backbeat laid down the inspiration for stoner rock bands to come. Its UK-only B-side '51st Anniversary' was a rambling, R&B inspired rocker that saw him deconstructing a marriage backwards, all the way to its point of dissolution. If that venting about a venerable institution sounded rather dry on paper, the song was anything but — the suitably furious racket conjured by his rhythmic aides Noel Redding and Mitch Mitchell accompanied by Hendrix's valiant first attempt at studio overdubbing. The five different guitar performances it captured — all masterful miniatures in themselves — rightly gave his 60s peers an instant inferiority complex.

## '6 In The Mornin''

Ice-T
TECHNO HOP 1986
A-Side: 'Dog 'N The Wax (Ya Don't Quit-Part II)'

**Cold rhymer lays down gangsta rap template.**

There's a good reason why no one ever mentions the A-side here — the B-side was a revolution on wax. One of the first and most singularly defining tracks of the gangsta rap era — still to bear that name — penned by one its most articulate and intelligent early stars, it found the Crenshaw High School graduate building on the rap profile he had established in low-budget B-movies *Rappin'* and *Breakin'*. In contrast to the long-forgotten party-oriented A-side, '6 In The Mornin'' spoke directly about the crime and violence rife in his South Central Los Angeles neighbourhood. Ice-T's calm, distinctive diction combined authenticity with humour and an acute grasp of cinematic imagery as he depicted his strange plight, being "remotely controlled by hard hip-hop beats". Essentially an escape fable — penned in the wake of an early morning police visit — his continued success at evading the law's long arms, while buffering his criminal profile and getting jiggy on the side, proved how much he had absorbed the storytelling skills of pimp-turned-author Iceberg Slim. While it proved hugely impactful on the surrounding LA rap culture, its magnanimous creator freely admitted its prime inspiration was Schoolly D's 'PSK What Does It Mean?' single from the previous year. And although he adopted the exact same flow, the Unknown DJ's deft deployment of a Roland TR-808 drum machine made for great sonic dissonance between the two. It's a measure of the vaunted position this song has in his canon that Ice-T would later write a prequel, 'Midnight', for 1991's *OG Original Gangster*. That ended where this picks up.

**'£. s. d.'**
The Pretty Things
FONTANA 1966
A-Side: 'Come See Me'

**Doomed attempt to smuggle drugs into the charts.**
Calamity followed calamity for the Pretty Things. Formed by guitarist Dick Taylor after he left the Rolling Stones — just as huge success beckoned — they were briefly Britain's wildest, longest-haired upstarts, positioned at the frontier of psychedelia. Fuzzy and direct early R&B-influenced singles such as 'Rosalyn', 'Don't Bring Me Down' (both covered by David Bowie on *Pin Ups*) and 'Midnight To Six Man' garnered a glut of exposure, with TV appearances and gigs in Europe, making even the Stones sound reserved and polite. However, their seventh single 'Come See Me' — an anguished, punky take on an obscure J. J. Barnes soul trooper — proved a little too extreme for radio, and it landed well outside the target zone at number forty-three. That failure was compounded by the twangy garage rock of its B-side '£. s. d.' being banned by the BBC for its not so subtle drug connotations. Despite its writers Phil May and Taylor countering that it was about pounds, shillings and pence, the middle's eight call and response section ("Yes I need/LSD!") undermined their pre-decimal coinage defence. Indeed, LSD

would prove a recurring motif in their freakily zig-zagging career. A decision to mime the sophisticated complexities of 1969's *SF Sorrow* — the world's first rock opera, six months ahead of the Who's *Tommy* — onstage at Abbey Road fell flat when an under-the-influence soundman proved too incapacitated to press the play button. It somehow felt par for the course.

### 'A Bitch Iz A Bitch'

N.W.A.

RUTHLESS 1989

A-Side: 'Express Yourself'

**Mum was not the word for elite gangsta rap troupe.**

N.W.A gave voice to unheard stories from America's west coast. Since its inception hip-hop had been conceived of as an east coast phenomenon, but N.W.A changed that perception for good on 1989's incendiary debut *Straight Outta Compton*, powerfully conveying real life themes that resonated with black audiences across America. The only openly commercial moment on that resolutely hardcore, profanity-stuffed calling card was 'Express Yourself', a Dr. Dre-led funky appropriation of Charles Wright & The Watts 103rd Street Rhythm Band's song of the same name. Its single version came backed by a track that caused just as much furore as the album's 'Fuck The Police' did — prompting an FBI warning letter that proved the best free publicity coup in town. Yet while 'Fuck The Police' has maintained its relevance down the years — a sad barometer of the gulf between law enforcement and the black community — the sound of Ice Cube claiming "all women have a little bitch in 'em" and are money-grabbing sex fiends who can "eat shit and die" has fared less well. It's a moot point whether N.W.A were being openly provocative or not, but it's telling that 'A Bitch Iz A Bitch' was positioned as non-album B-side, leaving the rest of their debut's revolutionary fervour unsullied.

### 'A Boy Without A Girl'

Frankie Avalon

CHANCELLOR 1959

A-Side: 'Bobby Sox To Stockings'

**Yearning fare from Elvis and Beatles-bridging teen idol.**

Among the first manufactured teenage idols to cut through to the box office, Frankie Avalon had the credentials to back it up. A child trumpet prodigy — whose talents won a slot on *The Jackie Gleason Show* — budding impresario Bob Marucci discovered the quiff-rocking ace face tooting his horn backing local band Rocco & The Saints, and swiftly peeled him away. A swift swish of his magic wand, and several appearances on *Dick Clark's American Bandstand* later, Avalon was topping the US charts with 'Venus'. The flip of his third Top 10 single, the lilting 'A Boy Without A Girl' did the simple things best, his yearning delivery melting teenage hearts within the space of a few minutes. Although Avalon's pop career drifted into more insipid waters by the early 60s, he was thrown a lifeline by the movie biz, reinventing himself as a suntanned surfer in the *Beach Party* franchise alongside Annette Funicello. It was there he revived this B-side in 1964 movie *Muscle Beach Party* — a brattish yet fun fable about a preferred surfing spot being usurped by preposterously buff bodybuilders — ensuring its elevated position in his relatively slender catalogue.

**'A Change Is Gonna Come'**
Sam Cooke
RCA VICTOR 1965
A-Side: 'Shake'

**Civil rights anthem, borne from real life strife.**

'A Change Is Gonna Come' ranks as the greatest ever song of hope. Equally inspired by an altercation in Louisiana, where a righteously aggrieved Cooke and his entourage were turned away from a whites-only motel, and the anti-racist sentiments of 'Blowin' In The Wind' (after Cooke heard Peter, Paul And Mary singing Bob Dylan's song on the radio), it's arguably the most important song in a repertoire bulging with greatness. One that bridged the gap between Cooke's gospel roots and his status as a soul superstar. According to one biographer, Peter Guralnick, Cooke's grand paean to transformation came to him almost fully formed, despite its relative complexity. The marriage of his soaring delivery and René Hall's theatrical string assemblage seemed to deliberately hark back to Kern-Hammerstein's *Showboat* classic 'Ol' Man River' (as neatly paraphrased in the lyrics), yet Cooke's bold lines about segregation ("I go downtown/Somebody keep telling me don't hang around") would be chopped out of the single version, when it eventually appeared on the back of 'Shake' — a joyous party rocker that more closely signalled his direction of travel. Or it would have done, had Cooke not been ruthlessly gunned down by a Los Angeles motel manager — in a chilling echo of the events that inspired this B-side's creation — months before its official release. Extensively sampled by rappers and covered with notable brio by everyone from Billy Bragg and Baby Huey to Beyoncé, Barack Obama embraced its sentiments in 2008's presidential victory speech, proclaiming "a change *has* come to America". The song has gained more than its lost in enduring social relevance since.

**'A Fork In The Road'**
The Miracles
TAMLA 1965
A-Side: 'The Tracks Of My Tears'

**A cautionary tale as devastating as its A-side.**
By the time the million-selling heartbreak of its A-side had cried its way up the US charts, Smokey Robinson was facing stiff competition as Motown's most brilliant songwriter, with Holland-Dozier-Holland revving up close in his rear-view mirror. This equally distinguished B-side reproved his genius. With Robinson's tender yet wounded falsetto sugar-coating the bad news across one of the Miracles' deepest, mostly subtly devastating ballads, he advised listeners not to make the same mistakes as him. While its sumptuous strings and Marvin Tarplin's fluid guitar lines established a trance-like mood, danger reared its ugly head in the middle eight, where love could perish over a seemingly minor tiff — given weight and substance by the Miracles' full Greek backing chorus. A favoured part of their live show at the time, it gave more than a passing nod to previous single 'Ooh Baby Baby', while refining the class and craft of early dreamy Tamla B-side ballads '(You Can) Depend On Me' ['This Feeling Is So Fine', 1959] and 'I Can't Believe' ['Everybody's Gotta Pay Some Dues', 1961].

**'A Man Called Sun'**
The Verve
HUT 1992
'The Verve EP'

**Trippy 60s psych and shoegaze unite.**

With typical hyperbole, the Verve's gangly frontman Richard Ashcroft declared 'A Man Called Sun' "the greatest B-side ever released", cementing his hard-won *NME* reputation as 'Mad Richard' and doubtless raising an arch mono-brow or two among his Mancunian Britpop comrades. A band that combined 60s psychedelia with shimmering 90s shoegaze atmospherics, the Verve built a solid reputation beyond their Wigan base with long, spaced-out jams that relied heavily on improvisation. 'A Man Called Sun', one of five tracks on their first EP, captured that essence to a tee, with Nick McCabe's echoing freeform guitars riding Simon Jones' loping bass groove and Peter Salisbury's sensitive drums, topped by Ashcroft's ruminative wordplay, somehow floating *within* its soundscape. That gentle bluesy tension, combined with John Leckie's understated production, would prove a far cry from the anthemic strings that defined their true moment in the sun. It would have sat nicely amid the more ambient comedowns that closed 1993's debut *A Storm In Heaven*. This B-side gained meta indie traction in 1995 when Chester band Mansun informed the music press that the song was the inspiration for their name, as they tried to deflect legal action from the Charles Manson Estate.

## 'A Shot Of Rhythm And Blues'

Arthur Alexander

DOT 1961

A-Side: 'You Better Move On'

**Ill-starred R&B/country star Beatles' endorsed 12-bar blues.**

One of the few songwriters covered by the Beatles, the Rolling Stones and Bob Dylan, Arthur Alexander's musical legacy was vast. The son of a bottleneck blues guitarist, Alexander graduated from singing in gospel group the Heartstrings to co-write 'She Wanna Rock' for country singer Arnie Derksen. He used its proceeds to fund the fledgling Muscle Shoals FAME studio in his native Alabama. 'You Better Move On' was the first hit to emerge, his heartfelt R&B/country fusion anticipating much of the Memphis deep soul that followed. Its B-side would also prove hugely influential as Alexander powerfully rendered Terry Thompson's inverted 12-bar blues in his commanding baritone. Adored by John Lennon, the Beatles performed a slightly slower arrangement on their 1963 BBC radio show *Pop Go The Beatles* (later included on 1994's *Live At The BBC*), while

Johnny Kidd & the Pirates, Gerry & the Pacemakers and Dave Edmunds also had royal bashes at it. Sadly, Alexander's meteoric rise was sorely mismanaged, a situation compounded by sustained drug and alcohol abuse, and he quit the business in 1977. He died from a heart attack in 1993, just three months after his comeback LP *Lonely Just Like Me* hit the stores.

**'Acquiesce'**
Oasis
CREATION 1995
A-Side: 'Some Might Say'

**Lighters-in-air favourite at the peak of Oasis mania.**

It's tempting to wonder whether Noel Gallagher rued his songwriting prolificacy — packing early Oasis B-sides with A-worthy bounty — when the big tunes started to run dry around 1997's *Be Here Now*, an album patched together amid a blizzard of cocaine, with no studio mirror safe. While not all those early B-sides were stadium call-to-arms, Noel-sung efforts such as 'Take Me Away' ['Supersonic', 1994], 'Half The World Away' ['Whatever', 1994] and 'Talk Tonight' [also backing 'Some Might Say'] showed a softer white underbelly at odds with the pugilistic rock 'n' roll posturing Liam specialised in. A song embodying deep friendship, 'Acquiesce' combined elements of both, Liam savaging the verses with his trademark sneer and Noel belting out its triumphant chorus ("We believe in one another"), allegedly because Liam couldn't hit its high notes. Written by Noel while stuck on a broken down train to Wales for sessions on their debut *Definitely Maybe*, he told *The Sun* in 2006: "Someone had said acquiesce on the phone and I'd written it down. Liam still doesn't know what it means!" He was also adamant that the chorus refrain was categorically not about Liam or their ongoing sibling rivalry — modern pop's most explosive love/hate saga. A near-perfect representation of everything Oasis stood for at the time, their Creation label boss Alan McGee campaigned for it to be the A-side. Gallagher demurred, his position vindicated when 'Some Might Say' entered the charts at number 1, with all previous Oasis singles re-entering in its wake. Later issued as a US A-Side to promote 1988 compilation *The Masterplan*, 'Acquiesce' may be the most quintessential Oasis track, let alone their most killer B.

## 'Ages Of You'

R.E.M.
IRS 1985
A-Side: 'Wendell Gee'

**Song that straddled R.E.M.'s growth into an alternative force.**

"A 45 is still essentially a piece of crap usually purchased by teenagers," wrote R.E.M. guitarist Peter Buck in the liner notes to 1987 compilation *Dead Letter Office*. "This is why musicians feel free to put just about anything on the B-side; nobody will listen to it anyway, so why not have some fun?" While that *laissez-faire* approach can yield the odd surprise diamond — Michael Stipe's improvised lyric on 'The Voice Of Harold' ['So. Central Rain (I'm Sorry)', 1994] or their haunting take on Syd Barrett's 'Dark Globe' ['Orange Crush', 1988] — more often than not he and his jangly Georgia bandmates came up with something more underwhelming. 'Ages Of You' was an exception. A rewritten version of early demo 'Burning Down', it was first recorded for 1984's *Reckoning* but somehow missed the cut. In those same notes, Buck implies the band simply got sick of it, but its strong hooks and cascading guitars were perfectly in keeping with their best work at the time. It remained a firm fan favourite and uninvited sing-along on the very rare occasions R.E.M. deigned to play it live.

## 'Ain't No Sunshine'

Bill Withers
SUSSEX 1971
A-Side: 'Harlem'

**Break-up classic elevates aircraft engineer to stellar heights.**

Bill Withers was working at a factory making toilet seats for Boeing 747s when he wrote 'Ain't No Sunshine'. The son of a West Virginia coal miner, Withers had spent nine years in the US Navy before accepting the role, trying his luck as a singer on the Los Angeles club circuit in his spare time. Inspired, in part, by Jack Lemmon and Lee Remick's descent into alcoholism in Blake Edwards' 1962 movie *Days Of Wine And Roses*, his easy ability to articulate emotion and smooth, soulful baritone made it one of the all-time greatest break-up tracks. The song has its own quirks — the third verse just goes "I know" 26 times — which Withers had intended to correct but bowed to the wisdom of the elite session musicians he played with in Memphis (Stephen Stills, Graham Nash and Booker T.) and the beauty of their tenderly orchestrated backing. Although he wrote other enduring standards including 'Lean On Me' and 'Just The Two of Us', 'Ain't No Sunshine' proved unfadeable throughout his career. Mystifyingly first issued as the B-side to 'Harlem' after Sussex's label reps failed to grasp its potential — a fact that rankled with Withers to the end — he was saved from the shitty day job by radio DJs flipping it on air, despite the lack of an intro for them to talk over. It catapulted him into a million-selling, Grammy-winning artist within a year, and the prickly recipient of a golden toilet from his new employers.

### 'Ain't Gonna Move'

Sam The Sham & The Pharaohs
XL 1965
A-Side: 'Wooly Bully'

**Serious side of wannabes' shock novelty hit.**

Sam the Sham's Tex-Mex-infused tunes boasted a completely unique sound. The self-styled 'Tijuana Troublemaker' — born in Dallas to Mexican parents — acted as an MC during US Navy dances, before switching to rock 'n' roll on his return to civilian life. Named Sam the Sham after a joke about his vocal limitations, several failed stabs at pop stardom led to all-out image change, with Sam lifting his band's Egyptian stylings wholesale from the costumes in Cecil B. DeMille's epic religious drama *The Ten Commandments*. Newly attired, his band summoned the delightfully strange Tex-Mex stomp 'Wooly Bully' — named after his cat, inspired by the Hully Gully dance craze — at Sam Phillips' new Memphis studio. With its unadulterated nonsense lyrics, it took off as a prime party track, becoming the first US record to sell a million copies amid the British Invasion. Many fans also flocked to the uptempo Chuck Berry-inspired 'Ain't Gonna Move'. Boasting the kind of scruffy garage rock sound that the Animals and the Rolling Stones were both gamely striving for, it undermined the notion that the Pharaohs were nothing more than a novelty act.

### 'Ain't No Nigga'

Jay-Z

ROC-A-FELLA 1996

A-Side: 'Dead Presidents'

**Duet presages Brooklyn rapper's future dominance.**

The street hustler from Brooklyn's notorious Marcy Projects had notched a small rap profile as Jaz-O's onstage hypeman when he made the hard-headed move to start his own Roc-A-Fella label, initially flaunting his wares from the trunk of his car. The most shamelessly commercial track on his debut *Reasonable Doubt* — an album funded from ill-gotten gains long before the world was listening — Jay-Z's quick-fire, quick witted rhymes, couched above the super rubbery bassline from the Whole Darn Family's 'Seven Minutes Of Funk', were met with equally fiery ripostes from 16-year-old rapper Foxy Brown (then juggling studio assignments with school time). Bewilderingly first released as the B-side to the Nas-sampling 'Dead Presidents' — surely a rookie marketeer's mistake — it took off when Roc-A-Fella switched distribution from Freeze/Priority to Def Jam. They quickly picked it as a single for Eddie Murphy's sci-fi comedy *The Nutty Professor* and watched it brine its way through New York's hot dog streets. Jay-Z told anyone who would listen that he only ever intended to make one album, but soon reneged on that, becoming the rap god of his dreams. This iconic B-side put him there.

### 'Alfie'

Dionne Warwick

SCEPTER 1967

A-Side: 'The Beginning Of Loneliness'

**Definitive reading of Bacharach and David classic.**

London was in full swing when *Alfie* hit the flicks in 1966. For the big screen adaption of Bill Naughton's racy play about a womanising chauffeur's promiscuous travails, with its star Michael Caine frequently breaking the fourth wall, its distributors gave Burt Bacharach and Hal David just three weeks to devise a theme. Among Bacharach's all-time favourite songs, they campaigned for their favoured interpreter — New Jersey diva Dionne Warwick — to sing it, only for Paramount to object, feeling the film's London setting demanded a British voice. Sandie Shaw declined and Cilla Black also had reservations — "Alfie is what you call your dog, or your budgie," she scoffed in 2019 ITV documentary *Cilla: The Lost Tapes* — but mindful she had previously had a hit with the composers' 'Anyone Who Had A Heart' (as indeed had Warwick), she accepted. Although Black's take just scraped the UK Top 10, cover versions proliferated, with over forty doing the rounds, Cher's husband Sonny Bono doing his best Phil Spector impression on her brassy cover for US movie theatres. Despite a reluctance to join the pack, Warwick eventually recorded an all-conquering take of 'Alfie', at the suggestion of Scepter A&R man Steve Tyrell, during a lull in another studio session. Cut in-the-moment, with no follow-up fiddle-faddle, she captured the essence of David's searching lyric about love being something "even non-believers can believe in". Issued on the back of melancholy Bacharach/David weepy 'The Beginning Of Loneliness', US disc jockeys made one of their most timely interventions and flipped for B-side gold, boosted by Warwick's anthemic reading at the 39th Academy Awards.

## 'All I Do Is Think Of You'

The Jackson 5
MOTOWN 1975
A-Side: 'Forever Came Today'

**Motown's famous brothers hit a fork in the road.**

Everything came to a head for one of the one of pop's biggest phenomena in 1975. Despite six consistent years of hit-making for Motown, both label and the Jackson 5 were at loggerheads. The label refused to let Indiana's favourite sons choose their own material, or even play their own instruments, and continued to push them in a bubblegum direction they felt they had outgrown. Badgered into recording a disco update of Diana Ross & the Supremes' 'Forever Came Today' for their last Motown hit, the group at least shared a mutual affection for its B-side. A simmering quiet storm ballad, 'All I Do Is Think Of You' stood apart from standard Jackson 5 fare as a twangy sitar paved the way for Michael's soaring tenor and rose-tinted longing — his most powerful lead to date. He claimed it was one of the band's personal favourites when they performed it on *The Mike Douglas Show* later that year, while the brothers also lip-synced it sporting natty powder blue suits on *Soul Train*. An intense legal battle followed, with all but Jermaine — who had married into Motown founder Berry Gordy's family — moving to Epic, youngest brother Randy taking his place. The

B-side later became a second-generation boy band hit for Californian quintet Troop, who topped 1990's R&B charts with their gauzy hi-tech update. Sampled by Drake, the Roots and Frank Ocean, its most audacious repurposing was by Detroit hip-hop producer J Dilla, who warped it forever on 2006's 'Time: The Donut Of The Heart'.

### 'Alltime Needletime Loser'

Radio Active

BEEB 1977

A-Side: 'Ten Years After'

**Hidden jewel backs salute to Radio 1's tenth anniversary.**

TV licence money has rarely been worse spent than on Radio Active's one and only single. Rendered by a grab-bag of BBC studio staff — including Assistant Controller Bryant Marriot, BBC Radiophonic Workshop's Paddy Kingsland and Radio 1 producers Malcolm Brown and Mike Harding — the execrable results trumpeted the station's dominance with cheesy, chest-beating lyrics seemingly scrawled on the back of a fag packet at closing time. A wildly optimistic release to say the least, notably ignored by the station's gurning cabal of egocentric sleazeball DJs (usually not averse to be a bit of flagrant self-aggrandisement), but par for the course from the regularly misfiring, hopelessly erratic BBC label. Salvation came from one of the station's few truly credible presenters, John Peel, who ignored the A-side completely and embraced 'Alltime Needletime Loser' instead. An intended punk parody, knocked off with indecent haste, its curdled sneer was welcomed by genuine punk fans, albeit those raised on the basic meat and potatoes rations of pub rock. Long after the fact, it became a collector's item.

### 'Amen Brother'

The Winstons

METROMEDIA 1969

A-Side: 'Color Him Father'

**Six-second drum break that shaped the future of pop.**

A bit of late-night studio improvisation would define the Winstons' career. The rousing Washington D.C. soul outfit had nailed swooning A-side 'Color Him Father' — a sentimental ode to a big shouldered stepfather, that went on to win a Grammy for Best R&B Song — but had nothing for the other side as the studio clock ticked loudly. With few available options, they knocked up a makeshift instrumental. Loosely based on old gospel number 'Amen, Brother', they added a guitar lick Curtis Mayfield had once played to singer Richard Spencer and Gregory Coleman's six-second four-bar drum solo. Unnoticed at the time, 'Amen Brother' was included on 1986's *Ultimate Breaks & Beats* compilation — manna for a new breed of sample-loving hip-hop producers — with Salt-N-Pepa incorporating Coleman's solo into 1986's 'I Desire'. Mantronix followed next, lacing it into 'King Of The Beats', but its most overt showing came as the foundation of N.W.A's 'Straight Outta Compton'. Quickly adopted by UK dance producers, it was sped up and unleashed into raves, before going mainstream with Oasis ('D'You Know What I Mean'), David Bowie ('Little Wonder') and Amy Winehouse ('You Know I'm No Good'). Although it became among the most sampled drum breaks of all time — used in over 1,500 songs — the Winstons were never rewarded for their creation. In a tragic coda, Coleman died homeless and destitute in Atlanta in 2006.

### 'And What You Give Is What You Get'

The Beastie Boys
CAPITOL 1989
A-Side: 'Shadrach'

**Rare, brilliant sonic experiment.**

Hip-hop's first credible white group would take a small age to dislodge an unwanted reputation as sex and booze fixated frat boys after 1986's rock-blasted debut *Licensed to Ill* became the first hip-hop album to top the US charts. Punks-turned-rhymers Mike D, Ad-Rock and MCA took a delicious left turn on 1989's follow-up *Paul's Boutique*, decamping to Los Angeles to work with little-known production duo the Dust Brothers, whose mix-and-match approach to the art of sampling proved revolutionary. The album's second single 'Shadrach' was a case in point, its title drawn from Sly & the Family Stone's 'Loose Booty' but augmented by seven more interweaving lifts (from James Brown, Rose Royce, Black Oak Arkansas, Funky 4+1, the Sugarhill Gang, Ballin' Jack, Juice) and wild lyrical interplay that brought AC/DC, Batman, Charles Dickens, J. D. Salinger and Alfred E. Neuman into the party. Its B-side was an incredible extension of the form, dropping the vocals but adding many more samples and effects from the Jam (whose 'Start!' provided the title), the Treacherous Three, Steve Miller, George Carlin, Black Flag and Prince. A relative flop at the time, its cavalier approach ensured this B-side has never appeared on an official release since, making it something of a holy grail for Beastie nerds. It's also part of a long list of killer Beastie Bs that include '33% God' ['Hey Ladies', 1989], 'The Skills To Pay The Bills' ['So What 'Cha Want', 1992] and 'Dope Little Song' ['Get It Together', 1994].

## 'Aneurysm'

Nirvana
GEFFEN 1991
A-Side: 'Smells Like Teen Spirit'

**Flip of the surprise success that legitimised grunge.**

The hyper intense, riff-heavy B-side of Nirvana's big breakthrough 'Smells Like Teen Spirit' was as brutal as its name suggested. A tune that witnessed Kurt Cobain picking over the wounds of his break-up with Bikini Kill founder and original riot grrl Tobi Vail — whose chosen brand of deodorant gave the A-side its distinctive title — it found him venting without barriers and screaming conviction. Recorded on the first day of 1991 at their first tub-thumping studio session with new drummer Dave Grohl, none of the band would have guessed that within nine months they would be on heavy MTV rotation or that second album *Nevermind* would topple Michael Jackson from the top of the US charts. A live staple easily on par with that album's best moments, 'Aneurysm' was revived for Nirvana's induction into the Rock & Roll Hall of Fame in 2014, as Sonic Youth's Kim Gordon — a key mentor who recommended the band to Geffen — dished up a blistering take alongside surviving members Grohl and Krist Novoselic.

## 'Angels And Devils'

Echo & The Bunnymen
KOROVA 1984
A-Side: 'Silver'

**Liverpool big mouths transform into VU.**

Among the decade's most tenacious 60s rock students, Echo & The Bunnymen were simultaneously a singles and albums band. Committed to putting out cohesive long-playing statements, it meant that when great songs didn't fit they would be repurposed — often as singles or, as here, on B-sides. While 1984's rainy weekend fourth album *Ocean Rain* was the Liverpool quartet's most romantic and ornamental, hauntingly rich pop songs like 'Silver' and 'The Killing Moon' augmented by a 35-piece orchestra, 'Angels And Devils' showed their ability to emulate the Velvet Underground almost to a tee. Veering dangerously close to full-on pastiche with Will Sergeant's ostrich guitar tunings, Pete DeFreitas's Mo Tucker-like tom-toms and Les Pattinson's John Cale-ish bass counter melody, McCulloch's poetic lyrics about a 'mad escape' took it into the Bunnymen's own zone, the ghost of the Doors' Jim Morrison fluttering close by. While *Ocean Rain* cracked the US Top 100 and should have paved the way to bigger riches, 'Angels and Devils' reminded what canny operators they were.

## 'Any Man Of Mine'

Shania Twain
POLYGRAM/MERCURY NASHVILLE 1995
A-Side: 'Whose Bed Have Your Boots Been Under'

**Fiery Canadian songstress reverses the country code.**

Shania Twain was one of the first country artists to fully exploit the potential of MTV. Having witnessed the somewhat safe, middle-of-the-road attractions of 1993's self-titled first album flop, a working and romantic hook-up with celebrated AC/DC producer Robert John 'Mutt' Lange opened fresh doors for the Canadian singer-songwriter. If there was still a cheesy whiff of 90s schmaltz to their first single outing 'Whose Bed Have Your Boots Been Under', its other side's utterly infectious hi-tech hoedown let it be known that Twain would not passively take anything lying down. The antithesis of all those country songs that cast the woman as a willing victim, Twain's fiddle-driven boot-stomper made no bones about what she was looking for in a partner. Reissued as an A-side in its own right three months later, Twain sealed its appeal with a double denim, horse hustling video that made her an instant country pop queen.

## 'Anything You Wanna Do'

The Marvelettes
TAMLA 1966
A-Side: 'Don't Mess With Bill'

**Letterbox lovers post come-and-get-me plea.**

Pop came naturally to Inkster Glee Club graduates the Marvelettes. Having started their career on an effortless high with 1961's pleading 'Please Mr Postman' — Motown's first number-one single — the group powered by the vocal talents of Gladys Horton and Wanda Young found their fame quickly usurped and upstaged by labelmates such as the Velvelettes, the Vandellas and the Supremes. After a string of near misses, early mentor Smokey Robinson helped them stage a comeback with the intricate sophisticated soul of 'Don't Mess With Bill', a kitchen sink drama that met its match in Young's emotive vocal strengths. A no less affecting, if more off-the-peg '60s girl group stomper from the pen of Stevie Wonder, the submissive lyrical conceits of 'Anything You Wanna Do' might have aged badly, but its shared harmonies and handclaps sound as box fresh as ever. Worth it for the condensed emotion of Norris Patterson's saxophone solo alone, it remains a high within the Marvelettes' often overlooked catalogue.

## 'Anytime, Anyplace'

Stetsasonic
TOMMY BOY 1991
A-Side: 'Speaking Of A Girl Named Suzy'

**World's first hip-hop band trade party flows.**

Stetsasonic were so far ahead of the game that their legacy often gets lost in the mix. Precursors to the Roots as the world's first actively styled hip-hop band, their combination of fluid rappers, capable musicians and innovative sampling (much by Prince Paul's sleight of hand) made the Brooklyn tag team a heady onstage experience. While their harmonised bombardment of styles arguably peaked on 1988's golden era classic *In Full Gear* — a set that anticipated the jazz rap explosion — it was Paul's production charges De Le Soul who took their promotion of positive black consciousness to the masses with *3 Feet High And Rising*. In stark contrast to the A-side's squelchy, against-the-grain fable of groupie love, 'Anytime, Anyplace' borrowed its opening flurry of horns and chunky Hammond riff from Syl Johnson's 'The Love You Left Behind', establishing an agreeable looseness for the energetic emceeing of Daddy-O, Delite and Crown Supreme. It was Stetsasonic at their least inhibited and more riveting than most of the fare on valedictory offering *Blood, Sweat & No Tears*.

# B-SIDES ABOUT B-SIDES

*When ideas are running low, is writing one of these a last resort? Not always...*

Like the author's fear of a blank page, the need to summon up a quick flip has often led acts to spiral into a panic, get meta about their craft and write a B-side about writing a B-side. Jokes that seemed to resonate with their situation at the time, they often fail to relate to fans or age particularly well. It's a B-side conundrum that seems particularly acute among comedians — whether shooting for credible pop careers or muddying the chart waters with novelty spin-offs.

**Tracey Ullman**, who came to prominence on BBC TV sketch show *Three Of A Kind* (alongside Lenny Henry and David Copperfield) before going supernova with *A Kick Up The Eighties*, seemed to be showing off her serious face when she issued her kitchen sink take on Kirsty MacColl's first single and, very nearly, topped the UK charts. Its more bizarre counterpart, **'The B Side'** ['They Don't Know', STIFF 1983] was a better glimpse into Ullman's numerous personas, as she unleashed a battery of monologues — random excerpt: "B-sides! Oh, go way! I don't know why they have them" — bemoaning the uselessness of B-sides. Needless to say, it only added to the pile.

**Harry Enfield** took a very similar approach to **'The B-Side'** ['Loadsamoney (Doin' Up The House)', MERCURY 1988] as, between belches, his loud, obnoxious and cash-obsessed fictional plasterer Loadsamoney questioned why he had to record a B-side for his single. Reassured that he'd get paid "loads of money" for any old tat — a knowing reference to the 50:50 singles royalty split sometimes dubbed 'the flipside racket' — he unleashed an unintelligible sub-football chant. Jazzed up, just about, with some final minute synth squiggles, its sole redeeming feature was the sound of

Enfield desperately trying not to crack up halfway through.

As with Loadsamoney, one hit wonders **Morris Minor and the Majors** managed to extract the maximum mileage from the ill-formed bones of their creation, somehow parlaying the success of their inane Beastie Boys parody into a primetime BBC1 comedy vehicle *Morris Minor's Marvellous Motors* (a show that everyone seems to have collectively wiped from their memories) and topping the charts in Australia. '**Another Boring 'B'-Side**' ['Stutter Rap (No Sleep Til Bedtime)', TEN 1988] rather laboured the point about filling up the other side with "the product of considerable neglect" with a repeated chorus refrain that, by its own admission, "goes on a bit".

Self-consciously wacky New Yorkers **Blotto** took it one step further on '**The B-side**' ['When The Second Feature Starts', BLOTTO 1981], contending that "you're probably not even listening to this right now". It was possibly nearer the knuckle than they intended — their popularity quickly plummeted when MTV grew tired of playing their escapist fable 'I Wanna Be A Lifeguard'.

Using the B-side as a dumping ground for problematic songs or ill-formed ideas is nothing new. Songwriter Ross Bagdasarian was a regular abuser, who was paid rather handsomely for knocked-off B-sides after his stage alias David Seville scored a 1958 hit with 'Witch Doctor' — paving the way for his animated band **the Chipmunks** to take over. And while the sound of his sped-up, high-pitched warbling helped his furry troubadours Alvin, Simon and Theodore became the most popular musical cartoon of all time, a consistent thread ran through B-side instrumental ditties 'Almost Good' ['The Chipmunk Song', 1958] and 'Mediocre' ['Alvin's Harmonica', 1959] that peaked with '**Flip Side**' ['Ragtime Cowboy Joe', LIBERTY 1959]. Brief, at under 90 seconds, its whistled coda, simple drumbeat, handclaps and repeated piano melody had the feel of demo sketch, at best, but still resonated with Chipmunks' vast pre-teen audience.

When New Order linked with the England football team to record a self-congratulatory anthem for 1990's World Cup in Italy their intended

demographic was probably not ageing Joy Division fans. While the A-side avoided most of the obvious pratfalls and chimed with the loved-up club culture of the time, **Englandneworder**'s **'The B-Side'** ['World In Motion...', FACTORY 1990] presented the song's original demo (once cheekily titled 'E For England') with much harder percussion (courtesy of ex-Swans man Roli Mossiman) and an additional verse, but mercifully free of the "Eng-ger-land" chants that marred the A-side.

Love And Rockets decided to explore their whimsical side as the **Bubblemen** by playing against type, advising listeners to wobble over slinky basslines and nonsense rhymes. The 12-inch **'B-Side'** ['The Bubblemen Are Coming!', BEGGARS BANQUET 1988] took the advice of its third track 'Bubblemen Rap' — to "make like a bee in a commotion" — totally to heart, offering just under four minutes of buzzing sounds.

Paul McCartney was open about the financial incentive behind the sole single by **Suzy and the Red Stripes** ['Seaside Woman', A&M 1978]. A throwaway reggae number, written by his photographer wife Linda during a family visit to Jamaica, it was designed to prove to ATV, his suspicious publishers, that she deserved to share in his recent songwriting credits for Wings. If anything, its throwaway flip, **'B-Side To Seaside'**, might have made them pause about the wisdom of that arrangement.

Its title was nonetheless given a further twist by the Scottish Springsteen with the Forsyth chin, **BA Robertson**, on a slightly sticky wicket after his first major label single badly bombed. The slightly impenetrable **'2(b) B Side The C Side'** ['Bang Bang', A&M 1979] seemed closer to its curious creator's heart than the strangely cockney flavoured A-side and was the Glasgow bard's second consecutive self-referential flip, albeit a much better one than the luck lustre Elvis impersonations of 'The B-Side' ['Goosebumps', 1979].

Not all B-sides about B-sides are the poorest runts in the litter, however. On the back of their first US number 1 after leaving producer Phil Spector (with Bill Medley retaining the grand ambience of Spector's wall-of-sound production

style) the **Righteous Brothers' 'B Side Blues'** ['(You're My) Soul And Inspiration', VERVE 1966], found the Californian duo of Bobby Hadfield and Medley channelling Ray Charles and showing off the power of their voices. As Hatfield's soaring tenor matched Medley's deeply soulful baritone punch for punch over a 12-bar bass figure and bluesy piano run, its suitably crunchy and gritty sound nodded way back to their formative motions in the Paramours.

The Hendrix-loving **Lenny Kravitz**'s own take on **'B Side Blues'** ['Heaven Help', VIRGIN AMERICA 1993] arrived in the midst of a creative purple patch, with MTV constantly rotating the title track of his classic rock oriented third LP *Are You Gonna Go My Way*. It nonetheless proved a bare-faced dig at his label's A&R department. "They say I got to write some new songs," he complained over a great scuzzy blues riff. The feeling that its lyrics had been improvised in-the-now were enhanced when Kravitz declaimed "Take this song and shove it up your ass" and by the sound of in-studio laughter at its denouement. Nonetheless its openly hostile and wonkily menacing guitar solo made it feel far more essential than the A-side's sweet-voiced but inconsequential Curtis Mayfield tribute.

With their calling card three-part harmonies, genre-fluid Californians **Three Dog Night** snagged 22 US hits, thanks to a sixth sense for picking the right songs. Lambasted in the press for not bothering to pen their own material, they avenged that notion forever with **'Our 'B' Side'** ['Shambala', DUNHILL 1973] — a single-fingered salute that skipped between rock, blues and reggae and let their families and children into the recording booth. However, its shaky promise "Someday we'll write an A-side, maybe" never came to pass, after their chart fortunes tapered off in the mid-70s.

In the right hands, the very concept of the B-side could prove a super cool allegorical tool. "No one takes me seriously/I'm the B-side," snarled **Charlotte Cornwell** on the **'B-Side'** to her offshoot single from pioneering TV musical drama *Rock Follies* alongside Julie Covington, Rula

Lenska and Sue Jones Davis ['OK?', POLYDOR 1977]. "One day they will rate me," she continued as, in a case of life imitating art, its tale of struggling actresses in London's west end turned the quartet into bona fide UK charts stars (despite being denied the oxygen of a *Top Of The Pops* slot).

San Francisco new wavers **Pearl Harbor and the Explosions** knew how to pen a pop hook (as evidenced by 1979's big indie hit 'Drivin'') and garner press attention (*that* deliberately provocative name), although their fortunes fared less well when they hooked up to the major label machine. **'Busy Little B Side'** ['You Got It (Release It)', WARNER BROS 1979], a knowing rock 'n' roll ditty about putting out a single, having it fail, before watching its B-side take off — a narrative evidenced several times elsewhere in this book — showed they deserved much better.

**Public Enemy** made no bones about their preference for harder, non-radio-friendly flipsides with the sentiments of **'B-Side Wins Again'** ['Black Steel In The Hour Of Chaos', DEF JAM 1988], a track whose simple raw beats and purposefully distorted vocals were meant to emulate the Prophets of Rage's formative years rapping in parks, ballcourts and basement jams in their native Long Island. It was a fitting contrast to the A-side's nerve-shredding flip of Isaac Hayes' piano solo in 'Hyperbolicsyllabicsesquedalymistic' — sampling at its most artful and inventive.

The first audible hint that **Robbie Williams** solo career might be one in the eye for Gary Barlow arrived with **'Average B-Side'** ['Old Before I Die', CHRYSALIS 1997]. A far more sophisticated affair than the A-side's stodgy pub rock, Williams' clever and knowing dissection of a romance that had long ago withered on the vine suggested he might survive the transition from MOR boy band star into a nuanced rock entertainer after all — as long as he stopped effectively tossing his best songs into the bin.

There was little allegory but a whole sky full of promise to **Shyheim AKA The Rugged Child**'s **'The B Side (Bring The Drama)'** ['On And On', VIRGIN 1993]. The 15-year old rap wonderkid from Staten Island showed a looser contrast to the A-side's dissection of crack ills on a rugged posse cut with Down Low Recka, K-Tez and Rubbabandz that seemed to confirm his abundant potential over producer RNS's

sinister jazz horns and dusty boom bap beats (replete with a fantastic sudden ending). Just to confuse matters, Shyheim also titled the flip of his next single 'The B Side (Licka Shot)' ['Pass It Off', 1994].

**Manfred Mann** were making increasingly complex forays into psychedelic and progressive rock as the 70s hovered on the horizon. The wonderfully evocative but woefully titled **'A 'B' Side'** ['Ragamuffin Man', FONTANA 1969] found the sometimes moody multi-instrumentalists getting louche and loose over a low organ drone, wilding flutes and brooding guitars as they evoked a travelling lady "who comes and goes like the wind and rain" on the back of their final chart hit. A primer for their fully jazzed-out next incarnation, it enjoyed a longer shelf life soundtracking a risqué ad for Manikin Cigars.

**Adam Ant** saved some of his grittiest material for his B-sides — the likes of 'Press Darlings' ['Kings Of The Wild Frontier', 1980] and 'Red Scab' ['Goody Two Shoes', 1982] becoming long-established live favourites. Ant archly greeted listeners to **'B-Side Baby'** ['Apollo 9', CBS 1985] using spoken words to set the scene "in sunny Soho on a Thursday afternoon" before his long-serving guitarist Marco Pirroni let loose one of his most dirty, distorted and swaggering riffs. Bowling in on the back of a show-off harmonica solo, Ant delivered a nonchalant vocal turn about his girlfriend playing obscure B-sides and made bare threats towards Joey Ramone, seemingly upset at hearing Ramones' B-side 'Beat On The Brat' ['Rockaway Beach', 1977] "all day long in the flat". A vibrant slice of old school rawness that made the most of Bowie/Bolan producer Tony Visconti's talents, this stadium anthem that never was sounded infinitely fresher than its overthought, overwrought and programmed half to death A-side.

### 'Baby I've Got It'

Jimmy Ruffin
SOUL 1966
A-Side: 'What Becomes Of The Brokenhearted'

**Motown heart-tugger plays against type.**
Jimmy Ruffin handled adversity with grace. Hot in the running to join Motown's male vocal group the Temptations in 1964, he was beaten at the last by his younger brother David, thanks to a slightly grittier tone. Jimmy bore his sibling no malice. Rather than just chalk it down to experience, he used it as a catalyst for a solo career whose blue touch paper was lit when Motown writers William Weatherspoon, Paul Riser and James Dean let him have first dibs on a song they'd written for the Spinners. The dramatic 'What Becomes Of The Brokenhearted' was gut-wrenching in its evocation of pain and loneliness, Ruffin's supple, expressive tenor soaring above the melodic instrumentation of Motown house band the Funk Brothers. If the A-side all but guaranteed him a vaulted position amid soul music's greats, the ex-gospel singer from rural Collinsville let his full range out on its swinging, horn-blasted B-side — a celebration of the giddiness of love achieved against all odds and the A-side's polar opposite. It would prove a largely forgotten nugget as Ruffin struggled to escape being typecast as a lonely balladeer.

## 'Back For Good (Live Version)'

Robbie Williams
CHRYSALIS 1997
A-Side: 'Angels'

**Take That refugee cocks snook at his past.**
Two years after he left Take That's protective bosom, Robbie Williams still had a point to prove. Seemingly in thrall to Britpop kings Oasis, who he partied with backstage at 1995's Glastonbury Festival, early singles such as his cover of Wham's 'Freedom' and 'Lazy Days' were slight, stodgy fare, suggesting Take That's refusal to take his creative ideas seriously had some foundation, exacerbated by an unseemly diet of beer, pies and cocaine. Pressganged into rehab before promotional activities for 1997 debut *Life Thru A Lens* began in earnest, a trimmer, more focused Williams emerged clutching a career-changing single to his heart. A guaranteed wedding weepie first thrust into his palm in a Dublin bar by songwriter Ray Heffernan, 'Angels' changed everything, pushing Williams up the pop totem pole as Take That slid down the other end. As if to rub salt into a gaping wound, he backed it with a punk-inspired hatchet job on his last significant outing with the boy band. Captured live in Manchester, his take

on 'Back For Good' switched from lachrymose to thrash in a knowing blink and quickly became a live standard. They had publicly reconciled when Take That joined in the pogoing fun as Williams accepted a Brit Icon Award in 2016.

### 'Bad Side Of The Moon'

Elton John
DJM 1970
A-Side: 'Border Song'

**Reg's heavily orchestrated space oddity.**

Reginald Kenneth Dwight secured his unlikely ascension to pop royalty in 1970. The ivory tinkling son of a Royal Air Force trumpeter shrugged off failed auditions with King Crimson and Gentle Giant to forge a formidable compositional partnership with lyricist Bernie Taupin that found them penning hits for Roger Cook and Lulu as DJM's staff songwriters. Even the failure of 1969's solo debut *Empty Sky* failed to dampen John's ardour, his persistence finally paying off when the plangent call for racial harmony of 'Border Song' made chart inroads in the States. While he capitalised with the evergreen 'Your Song' and a show-stealing turn at Los Angeles' Troubadour Club (faithfully recreated in 2019 biopic *Rocketman*), many fans had fallen for the more off-kilter charms of 'Bad Side Of The Moon' — an almost military snare drum leading into a whacked-out, sci-fi inspired Taupin lyric that descended into an intergalactic rave-up. John would take it even further out there, pounding his piano's keys without mercy on 1971's live album *17-11-70*. While his unparalleled early 70s output saw him amass an enviable array of killer Bs including 'Take Me To The Pilot' ['Your Song', 1970], 'Skyline Pigeon' ['Daniel', 1973] and 'Bennie & The Jets' ['Candle In The Wind', 1974], 'Bad Side...' became a staple of American classic rock stations in another guise, thanks to Canadian hard-rockers April Wine's 1972 cover.

### 'Badgeman Brown'

Blur
FOOD 1992
A-Side: 'Popscene'

**Freewheeling Syd Barrett homage.**

Dismissed as manufactured teen idols and a second-rate baggy band in some press quarters, Blur's problems were mounting in 1992. Already in significant debt, an American tour was arranged to help alleviate that burden, accompanied by a brash, rocky new single, 'Popscene', that mangled up horn-fired 60s mod with punk. A pivotal release in many ways, it fell on deaf ears at the time, the ex-Goldsmiths guttersnipes carping that grunge's popularity had scuppered its chances. All but stashed away on the CD single was 'Badgeman Brown' — an explicit homage to Syd Barrett-era Pink Floyd. Blur had a little form here. Albarn's lazy drawl owed a debt to Floyd's chief madcap, while 'Mr Briggs' and 'Uncle Love' on previous year's debut *Leisure* made his influence explicit. 'Badgeman Brown' took it to another level, guitarist Graham Coxon's slashing riffs nodding to 'Interstellar Overdrive' as Albarn recalled Barrett's little-boy-lost delivery from 'Scream Thy Last Scream'. The song was despised by Blur's label bosses Andy Ross and Dave Balfe, a situation that deteriorated when it was mooted for inclusion in a film directed by Barrett's old artist friend Storm Thorgerson.

### 'Badges, Posters, Stickers, T-Shirts'

Dire Straits
VERTIGO 1982
A-Side: 'Private Investigations'

**Star mocks his most obsessive fans.**

Sizeable transatlantic success in the early 80s gave Dire Straits *carte blanche* to do what they wished on their 4th studio album *Love Over Gold*. A sprawling, indulgent affair, it was characterised by lengthy experimental passages and languid atmospherics. But with only five long tracks, obvious radio-friendly hits were in short supply. That didn't prevent a slightly appended though still almost six-minute edit of its unorthodox Raymond Chandler-inspired ballad 'Private Investigations' winding its way to number 2 in the UK charts, Mark Knopfler's gruff voice dropping in private-eye clichés by the pound. Among several offcuts from the album sessions — another would become the title track of Tina Turner's comeback LP *Private Dancer* — 'Badges, Posters, Stickers, T-Shirts' witnessed Knopfler adopt a not totally convincing Yorkshire accent for its sarcastic mickey take on intense fandom and collectorism. It peaked as this increasingly needy and emboldened protagonist leapt from requests for items of the band's merchandise to snaffling the backstage rider over a skippy, ten-a-penny jazz/blues routine. Knopfler would successfully reprise its skewed sentiments on 1985's overplayed chart-busting Sting duet 'Money For Nothing'.

## 'The Ballad Of Michael Valentine'

The Killers
LIZARD KING 2004
A-Side: 'Somebody Told Me'

**Vegas band's mysterious road trip.**

The Killers' seamless blend of 80s synth pop, art rock, new wave and Springsteen-inspired Americana proved an irresistible pop confection. The Las Vegas band fronted with no little charm and abundant sex appeal by Brandon Flowers quickly proved that they possessed catchy hooks by the bucket-load, cheer-led by chunky riffage of singles 'Mr Brightside' and 'Somebody Told Me'. The latter's almost unstoppable adrenalin wooed a ready and primed MTV audience and proved, to those who checked its widescreen B-side, the genuine depth in their songwriting ranks. A chugging, filmic, hugely romantic Stateside travelogue that took in Dallas, New Orleans, Memphis, North Dakota and namechecked Marlon Brando and Greta Garbo, the gambling man referenced in 'The Ballad Of Michael Valentine' was later revealed to be the alter ego of their long-time friend Rod Pardey — a professional poker player, whose own alt-rock band Romance Fantasy previously featured the Killers' drummer Ronnie Vannucci. Many fans remain bewildered that it was excluded from 2004's heavily manicured debut *Hot Fuss*.

## 'Beat My Guest'

Adam and the Ants
CBS 1980
A-Side: 'Stand And Deliver!'

**Ant music for sex people.**

"A good beating's really where it's at," asserted punk's Peter Pan, Adam Ant, his tongue lodged firmly in cheek, on the flip of his band's first UK number 1 hit. Restyled as a 'dandy' highwayman and channelling the look of ITV's *Dick*

*Turpin* in the enticing video shot at Hertfordshire's Hatfield House, the single built on the thunderous Burundi drums that drove *Kings Of The Wild Frontier* to sustained success (replete with curious chorus yells of "Huh!" and "O-yo-yo-yoy!"). Gleefully smuggled onto the other side was a fresh, cartoonish update of an old Ant song hymning the joys of sadomasochistic sex, first debuted at their inaugural gig at London's ICA restaurant in May 1977 and later featured in Derek Jarman's *Jubilee*. Very much at odds with their new Royal Variety Performance status, Ant urged a dominatrix to "use a truncheon or a household brick" and promised to "be your dog for just one flog" over a rollercoaster-paced glam/punk amalgam. Its sneering, pleading lyrics either sailed over the heads of their young fan base or caused them to snicker knowingly amongst their mates, making it quite the secret commodity.

**'Be-Bop-A-Lula'**
Gene Vincent and His Blue Caps
CAPITOL 1956
A-Side: 'Woman Love'

**Ill-fated rock 'n' roller's defining moment.**

Leather-clad Virginian Gene Vincent was one of rock 'n' roll's first mythic figures, but an unlikely star. An ex-Marine who spent more than a year in a naval hospital following a severe motorcycle accident, the ever-limping rockabilly rebel used his convalescence to his advantage, working up the bones of 'Be-Bop-A-Lula' with fellow patient Donald Graves, their words inspired by comic strip Little Lulu. The song proved instrumental in winning a contract with Capitol — then looking for a slice of the emerging rock 'n' roll pie — prompting Vincent's wily business manager Bill 'Sheriff Tex' Davis to buy-out Graves' share for a desultory $25 (and nab himself a lucrative co-writing credit). Yet when Vincent and his crack band of Blue Caps (Cliff Gallup, 'Wee' Willie Williams, 'Jumpin'' Jack Neal and Dickie 'Be Bop' Harrell) first laid it down at Owen Bradley's legendary Barn studio in Nashville, it was for the B-side of the largely forgotten 'Woman Love'. Where that floundered 'Be-Bop-A-Lula' succeeded, the slap-back echo on Vincent's swooping vocals reminding listeners of Elvis after disc jockeys finally decided to flip the single. It would sadly prove to be the original bad boy's only major hit — a string of similarly powerful sequels failed to capture the public's imagination. Bedevilled by relationship woes, medical issues and his love of heavy drinking, Vincent nonetheless left an exquisite corpse when he passed from a ruptured stomach ulcer in 1969. He bequeathed a standard that has been revived by the Everly Brothers, Jerry Lee Lewis, Cliff Richard and the Beatles, among many others.

**'Begin The Beguine'**
Artie Shaw and His Orchestra
BLUEBIRD 1938
A-Side: 'Indian Love Call'

**'Complicated' Cole Porter cover makes career.**
'Begin The Beguine' spirited jazz clarinettist Artie Shaw into a celebrity status he found deeply uncomfortable. The New Yorker got his first breaks playing with Austin Wylie, Irving Aaronson and Willie 'the Lion' Smith before becoming a busy studio session player in the 30s. He had a brief retirement and a failed novel behind him when he launched his latest big band project in 1936, combining a string quartet with a rhythm section to create a swinging dance ensemble that found steady if not always profitable work. His fortunes picked up when he signed to RCA Victor's budget label Bluebird and recorded a cover of Cole Porter's 'Begin The Beguine', a relatively untampered tune from the Broadway show *Jubilee*. Based on a Jerry Gray arrangement that Shaw had tried and tested in many New York ballrooms, it made prominent use of his warm-toned clarinet, John Best's cupped trumpet, Les Robinson's smooth saxophone quartet and George Arus' trombone trio. Despite delivering a piece where the song, arrangement and ensemble effortlessly combined, his label's pessimism about a long tune "nobody could remember from beginning to end" saw it relegated to the B-side of Shaw's almost parodic take on 'Indian Love Call'. The struggling bandleader would laugh the loudest when the A-side was roundly ignored and its flip became a World War II classic, defining the swing era and selling more than any instrumental recording in history. The pressure of being a bandleader, combined with a succession of marital woes got to Shaw though — he wed eight times, including unions to Hollywood stars Lana Turner and Ava Gardner. He frequently broke up his successful orchestras and later moved into classical music.

## 'The Bells Of Avignon'

Françoise Hardy
UNITED ARTISTS 1970
A-Side: 'Soon Is Slipping Away'

**Signature fringe singer's schlager rarity.**

The face of 1960s French pop, Françoise Hardy proved a highly exportable style icon with enduring cult appeal in the English-speaking world. A reluctant pop star from the start, who hated her early recordings, Hardy shot to fame in 1962 with the million-selling yé-yé of 'Tous Les Garçons Et Les Filles', the start of a seemingly ceaseless string of 60s hits. After becoming a sultry, unsmiling cover girl she attracted the attentions of Bob Dylan and Mick Jagger, but married the similarly debonair French singer and songwriter Jacques Dutronc instead. She opened the 70s by issuing a one-off German-language schlager album, *Träume*, to appease fans there and in Switzerland. Recorded in those same sessions, but issued on the British B-side of 'Soon Is Slipping Away', 'The Bells Of Avignon' was an enigmatic rarity written by Long John Baldry, Scott Walker and the Hollies' hit-maker Tony Macaulay. While it cast Hardy on a "long and dusty road" where her "suitcase weighs a load", it was much cheerier than the other side, evoking memories of its titular French town and a regretful yearning for the lover she left behind.

## 'Bend Over Beethoven'

Wizzard
HARVEST 1973
A-Side: 'See My Baby Jive'

**A rude riposte to former bandmates.**

Self-exiled from the Electric Light Orchestra (ELO) following a rift with his old Move bandmate Jeff Lynne, Roy Wood created an even more dramatic outfit that matched his futuristic onstage garb and multi-coloured mane. While Wood mixed a glittering array of strings, brass and backing vocals with generous ladleful of Spector's wall-of-sound to their first UK number 1 'See My Baby Jive', its B-side was an openly provocative pastiche of ELO's recent cover of Chuck Berry's 'Roll Over Beethoven', telling them exactly where to stick it. A Zappa-like, cello-powered jazz-rock instrumental, with sinuous saxophone/piano interplay and a hefty groove by fellow ELO renegade Hugh McDowell, it revealed a deeper side to what critics had already pegged as a light and fluffy singles band (as duly confirmed by the likes of 'Angel Fingers' and the perennial 'I Wish It Could Be Christmas Everyday'). Although Wood and McDowell refused to air more dirty linen in public, the fact that McDowell re-joined ELO later that year suggested any real rancour was short-lived.

### 'Bernardine'

Pat Boone

DOT 1957

A-Side: 'Love Letters In The Sand'

**Clean-cut Elvis rival's sentimental soother.**

Pat Boone was America's biggest music star bar Elvis Presley when he landed a role in Henry Levin's teen film musical *Bernardine*. Boone was very much the slick-quiffed, hip-swivelling, lip-sneering Presley's antithesis — a sunny, clean-cut, good-natured Christian, his all-American smile revealing a streak of gleaming pearly whites and a suitably wholesome voice. As his equally likeable screen partners and high-school pals Ronnie Burns and Dick Sargent pined for the perfect girl — a fictional paramour they named Bernardine Mudd of Sneaky Falls, Idaho — the General Motors-endorsed Boone got to show off two sides of his soothing pop repertoire on its accompanying single. And while his whistling US number 1 take on Ted Black's 1931 hit 'Love Letters In The Sand' was an almost cynical study in teen heart manipulation, 'Bernardine' was genuinely tender. His abject yearning for a dream girl from another planet also garnered an unexpected second chart wind after he used his ABC television series *The Pat Boone-Chevy Showroom* to promote it.

### 'Beth'

Kiss

CASABLANCA 1976

A-Side: 'Detroit Rock City'

**Drummer's solo turn alienates bandmates and hardcore fans.**

Kiss's highest-ever charting song had a complicated genesis. Based on 'Beck', a more mean-spirited ditty by Peter Criss's previous band Chelsea — effectively a hen-pecked hubby's riposte to his nagging wife — the drummer suggested it to cement his place in the fire-breathing New York hard rockers as they started recording their fifth studio album *Destroyer*. It didn't go smoothly. Bandmates Gene Simmons and Paul Stanley turned him down flat, insisting they were not *that* type of band. Their manager, Bill Aucoin, had other ideas, however, and directed Criss towards producer Bob Ezrin, who helped flesh it out. Even when it was given a more recognisable woman's name, honouring Casablanca label head Neil Bogart's wife, few in the camp recognised the sentimental piano ballad's true potential, with some still actively campaigning against its inclusion. Later issued as B-side to the album's high-octane third single 'Detroit Rock City', FM deejays gave 'Beth' significantly more airplay. Reissued with the sides reversed, it took *Destroyer* platinum and helped spark genuine Kiss mania across America, with every possible merchandising permutation (comics, coffins, cologne, condoms) duly exploited. A tricky proposition to play live without an orchestra, Criss would often perform it solo to its original backing track — a coded signal to the Kiss Army's most devoted ballad-dodging members to hit the bar.

## 'Beware Of The Flowers (Cos I'm Sure They're Gonna Get You Yeah!)'

John Otway and Wild Willy Barrett
POLYDOR 1977

A-Side: 'Really Free'

**British eccentric's warning shot to Percy Thrower.**

One of British rock's great pioneering spirits, 'Really Free' was a critical two-track dip into the wild labyrinths of John Otway's involved inner world. Alongside the guitar-wielding Barrett, the devil-may-care duo were dead bent on making music of their own design — no formula, no obvious genre, no straight lines. That was all channelled into a manic performance of the semi-spoken A-side on BBC2's *The Old Grey Whistle Test* that helped it broach the charts and gave the Aylesbury-born dreamer a fleeting taste of the success he had always craved. B-side 'Beware Of The Flowers...' was better still — a deep-pile sneering boogie laced with Barrett's leaden guitar and a hooky stop/start chorus. While its creators conceded that it should have been saved for the follow-up, it gained attention anew when it was voted Britain's seventh most popular lyric in a 1999 BBC online poll (topped by John Lennon's 'Imagine'). That was largely due to the well-coordinated efforts of Otway's committed fan base — kept regularly sated by unpredictable live shows that witnessed Otway leaping off tables, turning somersaults, beating up guitars, headbutting microphones and playing wild Theremin solos. Their efforts also heaved 2002's Trammps-sampling 'Bunsen Burner' into the Top 10, allowing the man who had revelled in the running joke of being 'rock 'n' roll's greatest failure' the late luxury of a *Greatest Hits* album.

**'BFDRF Blues'**
Paul Revere and the Raiders
COLUMBIA 1965
A-Side: 'Just Like Me'

**They won't play this on the radio.**
Paul Revere and the Raiders developed an image problem. A straight-up rock 'n' roll band that gigged their way to fortune on the garage circuit, they were considered up there with the best of the British Invasion, outsold by only the Beatles and the Rolling Stones. Nonetheless their decision to promote 1965's 'Steppin' Out' on Dick Clark's TV show *Where The Action Is* in matching revolutionary war costumes became an albatross they struggled to shake. While the targeted hooks and raw power of its follow-up 'Just Like Me' cemented their popularity, they made a point of making its B-side longer and looser so there was no chance it could challenge the A for airplay. After making hay with a harpsichord left in the studio, Revere started to sputter risqué lyrics about a bald girlfriend that only just hinted at the title's edgy defiance ('BFDRF' standing for 'Big Fucking Deal, Rat Fuck'). Despite constantly moving upwards in a sustained period of US chart domination that peaked with 1971's number 1 cover of John D. Loudermilk's 'Indian Reservation', the band's innate slipperiness worked against them as the 70s wore on.

**'The Big Boss Groove'**
The Style Council
POLYDOR 1984
A-Side: 'You're The Best Thing'

**Paul Weller rides the power of his new big band.**

Having split the Jam at the height of their powers, Paul Weller started to embrace a wider world view beyond the disaffected suburbs from which he came. Working alongside ex-Merton Parkas' keyboardist Mick Talbot plus an ever-changing cast of musicians, the Style Council gave Woking's answer to Curtis Mayfield licence to roam all over the musical map in open defiance of a power pop trio's restrictions, incorporating elements of soul, R&B and jazz. The A-side of their 6th single, 'You're the Best Thing', was Weller at his most tender and cuddly, a superlative slice of soul-tinged, ear-tickling pop that made waves in the USA and stood apart on their surprisingly eclectic and experimental debut *Café Bleu* (not least due to Weller deigning to sing on less than half its tracks). A man whose Jam B-sides were never mere throwaways continued that tradition above the punchy horns of 'The Big Boss Groove', building on the album's jazzy stylings to create a living, breathing, swinging fan favourite that still made an explicit political point about the "holy Tory government" and showed off his previously hidden harmonica skills.

## 'Billie's Blues'

Billie Holiday and Her Orchestra
VOCALION 1936
A-Side: 'Summertime'

**Bone-chilling Lady Day improvisation.**

Billie Holiday was the first jazz singer to popularise the blues. To back her agelessly cool take on Gershwin's 'Summertime' — which helped it chart for the first time — came her first copyrighted composition. While ostensibly signed to parent label Brunswick to feed the omnivorous jukebox trade, the pressing need to fill up the B-side's grooves found her producer Bernie Hanighen suggesting she improvise a blues on the spot. Yet what began as an age-old lament of marital strife over Joe Bushkin's contrastingly jaunty dinner jazz piano also hid a darker intent — the sultry Baltimore bluestress Trojan-horsing in threats to kill her man rather than be made a slave. It all turned good by its final verse, with Holiday declaring herself "everything a good man needs" against superlative riffing from trumpeter Bunny Berrigan and clarinettist Artie Shaw, pinned into precision by Cozy Cole's assured brush rolls. Wildly prolific throughout the following decade, Holiday B-sides frequently turned up unexpected treasures, not least her gloriously understated refiguring of Duke Ellington's 'Solitude' ['God Bless The Child', 1946] ten years later.

### 'Birdses'

Dino Valente
ELEKTRA 1964
A-Side: 'Don't Let It Down'

**Shady folk traveller summons the Byrds.**

Dino Valente was one of the first folk singers to turn electric. The mysterious Connecticut songwriter had an east coast carny past — trapeze flyer, alligator runner, sideshow operator — before he apprenticed playing with small rock bands in New England lounges. New York came next, Valente becoming an ever present on the early 60s folk circuit where he was branded 'the underground Bob Dylan' due to his lack of a record deal. That changed when Elektra financed one-off single 'Don't Let It Down' — a mercifully brief hit of lumpen bluesy rock. Its more acoustic B-side 'Birdses' was a stark improvement, Valente's pastoral lyric augmented by a thumbed bassline and Leon Russell's baroque harpsichord motif. It also inspired the name of a group that melded folk and rock together far more memorably, the Byrds, the following year. Although Valente declined David Crosby's offer to join the band, he gained success writing the Youngbloods' hippy anthem 'Get Together' and Quicksilver Messenger Service's 'Fresh Air', joining the San Francisco psychedelic rockers in 1970.

### 'Bitches Ain't Shit'

Ben Folds
EPIC 2005
A-Side: 'Landed'

**Underground Dr. Dre hit repurposed as sweary ballad.**

Blessed with an abundance of geeky charm and goofball charisma, Ben Folds made a habit of defying expectations, playing "punk rock for sissies". When the bespectacled North Carolina songwriter emerged in the mid-90s with the sarcastically-named Ben Folds Five — in fact a trio — he was playing piano-led pop with an ache of Billy Joel and Elton John just as grunge dominated the US mainstream. And while his contemporaries sang about personal angst, Folds wrote character studies about life in suburbia, jilted boyfriends and, on his sole significant hit 'Brick', his high school girlfriend's abortion. The B-side of his tender mid-00s single 'Landed' was an equally uninhibited and poignant piano take on Dr. Dre's 'Bitches Ain't Shit' that didn't suppress any of its expletives (Folds reputation for near-the-knuckle onstage banter preceded him) and underlined its innate pop sensibility. While it quickly became a word-of-mouth crowd favourite, even pushing his stalled single back up the charts, Folds excised it from the stage in the 10s, conscious of the offence his use of the 'n' word might provoke in the woke generation.

**'Black And Tan Fantasie'**
Duke Ellington and His Orchestra
VICTOR 1928
A-Side: 'Creole Love Call'

**Bracing showcase of 'Bubber' Miley's trumpet prowess.**
Duke Ellington and his Orchestra's ceaseless supply of entertainment in the prohibition era matched the fast-changing times. The Washington D.C.-born son of a White House butler dropped out of high school to follow his muse, creating an ever-growing ensemble and originating the heavily drummed jungle style typified by trumpeter James 'Bubber' Miley's distinctive growling delivery. An experiment with its lead instrument's tonal qualities, his first hit 'Creole Love Call' featured Miley as his performative best. He was equally prominent on its 12-bar structured B-side 'Black And Tan Fantasie' (a reference to races mixing), deploying dramatic plunger tactics that contrasted with Ellington's stride-style piano solo and trombonist Joe Nanton's high glissandi. Among Ellington's early masterpieces, written in the back of a cab for a review at Harlem's Cotton Club, its coda even made a sly nod to Chopin's 'Funeral March'. It was restaged at the climax of Daniel Murphy's gritty short musical film *Black And Tan* about the Harlem renaissance the following year (with Ellington playing an exaggerated version of himself), but lacked the B-side's dynamism, chiefly because Miley had defected into a losing battle with alcoholism.

### 'Black Water'

The Doobie Brothers
WARNER BROS 1974
A-Side: 'Another Park, Another Sunday'

**Accidental anthem that slowly rose to the top.**

The Doobie Brothers first million-selling number 1 arrived fortuitously. Loosely based on singer's Tom Johnston latest relationship break-up and a riff guitarist Patrick Simmons had left over from 1973's *The Captain And Me* sessions, its decidedly laid-back vibe, bluegrass licks and Appalachian strings matched its tale of floating down the Mississippi on a homemade raft, while its multi-tracked a cappella breakdown echoed a cover of Simon & Garfunkel's 'The 59th Street Bridge Song (Feelin' Groovy)' by Harpers Bizarre. Yet given its acoustic nature, 'Black Water' was not even considered a potential A-side, debuting on the flip of the more obviously commercial 'Another Park, Another Sunday' — a song whose fortunes were seemingly jinxed by Johnston's lyric about radio bringing him down. It stalled at number 32 on the *Billboard* chart, twenty places above the follow-up 'Silver', with an increasingly all-at-sea Warner Bros resorting to supplying radio with the three-year-old 'Nobody' to try and reverse the band's ailing fortunes. Those desperate tactics were forgotten when DJs unexpectedly embraced 'Black Water', taking it on an unforeseen ride to the top. The California band celebrated their 50th anniversary in 2020 by serving up an online self-isolated version to aid the Feeding America network.

### 'The Black Widow'

Link Wray & His Ray Men
SWAN 1963
A-Side: 'Jack The Ripper'

**Brutal rock stylist gets hot and bothered.**

Link Wray proved the power of raw simplicity. When he started to gain popularity at the tail-end of the rock 'n' roll era, the North Carolina Shawnee made the most of his limited musical ability — taking basic melodies and cranking up the reverb and tremolo to create an extremely stylised sound. It pushed the electric guitar into places it had never been before and matched his brilliantly spare, rudimentary arrangements. Recorded at his producer brother Ray Vernon's studio in Washington D.C., Wray's first single for Philadelphia's tiny Swan label 'Jack The Ripper' set his singularly aggressive course, its innate menace chiming with its creator's beloved black leather and sunglasses attire. Despite its title 'The Black Widow' was a much more upbeat counterpart, a scuffed and harried party-starter that displayed Wray's brutal virtuosity at fever pitch and reflected his seemingly telepathic empathy with his long-serving Ray Men (drummer and younger brother Doug, bassist Shorty Horton). Still thrilling to this day, the power chord inventor's influence on guitar pop remains incalculable.

### 'Blood Money'

Sisters of Mercy

MERCIFUL RELEASE 1985

A-Side: 'No Time To Cry'

**Mystic fan invitation to kiss rings and blades.**

Doom and gloom purveyors from nasty Leeds, Sisters of Mercy created their own dark planet. A flange of short, impossibly skinny men in long black coats and cowboy hats, self-financed and self-produced early 80s singles such as 'The Damage Done' and 'Body Electric' retained a demo-ish quality just a notch above the primitivism of black metal. By 1995 they had experienced a sonic upgrade, ex-Dead or Alive man Wayne Hussey adding his chiming 12-string acoustic guitar to Gary Marx's edgy electric arpeggios and the mutant disco beats of Doktor Avalanche (their beloved Boss DR-55 drum machine). One of two strong B-sides on the lead single from *First And Last And Always*, 'Blood Money' was a camp blast of outrageous doom pop whose totally nonsense lyrics were portentously delivered in Andrew Eldritch's graveyard baritone. As miasmic as the best of that album — a document that finally delivered on the raw promise of their early independent releases and John Peel radio sessions — it creaked its way into the light of the day just seconds before its creators decided to part ways.

### 'Bloody Well Right'

Supertramp

A&M 1974

A-Side: 'Dreamer'

**Thumbs down to 'phoney' British school system.**
Supertramp's distinct blend of pop, progressive rock, blues and jazz finally turned them into global hit-makers in the mid-70s. Defined by the semi-bickering lyrical dialogue between founders Roger Hodgson and Rick Davies, their creative core had toned down a penchant for prog-overload when recording 1974's make-or-break third album *Crime Of The Century* — a loose concept set about mental instability. In contrast to the almost trance-layered harmonies and swirling organs of the philosophically-musing 'Dreamer' — an A-Side rooted in Hodgson's teenage demos — American radio jocks favoured the grinding power chords of 'Bloody Well Right', despite its unique structure and two-minute intro (or perhaps *because* of the talk-over scope it provided). Stitched between Davies's music hall Wurlitzer and Hodgeson's sturdy riffs was a peeved indictment of the British school system — written long before Pink Floyd started putting bricks in *The Wall* — that, once flipped, became their breakthrough American hit. A major staple of Stateside shows thereafter, often in wildly extended form, 'Bloody Well Right' reaffirmed Supertramp's reputation as off-the-wall songwriters.

**'Blue (Armed)'**
Wham!
INNERVISION 1983
A-Side: 'Club Tropicana'

**Semi-hidden clue to Wham!'s next destination.**
Hertfordshire's unlikely pop revivalists showed more of their hand on their third single. Having scored instant hits with the semi-rapped "soul on the dole" sentiments of 'Wham! Rap' and leather jacket posturing of 'Bad Boys' and 'Young Guns (Go For It)', chubby songwriter George Michael and wan ace-face Andrew Ridgeley renounced any vague pretensions of street credibility for a lunge at the pop jugular on 'Club Tropicana'. A satirical celebration of Club 18-30 idealism that chimed with the glossy aspirations of their fan base, the out-and-out holiday tune danced the conga into the UK Top 5. All but parcelled away on its flip was 'Blue (Armed)', an enigmatic semi-instrumental whose introspective soul-searching, colour-coded lyrics and synth-led production betrayed a heavy US R&B influence. An early signal of the direction of travel Wham! would pursue

on 1984's second album *Make It Big*, it received a single TV airing when Michael lip-synched to an alternative take on *The Russell Harty Show*. It featured far more prominently on their mid-80s tour of China, with a live version surfacing on 1986 swansong *Music From The Edge Of Heaven*.

## 'The Boat Of A Millions Years'

Van Der Graaf Generator
CHARISMA 1970
A-Side: 'The Refugees'

**Hifalutin prog of the highest calibre.**

Cult art-rockers Van Der Graaf Generator's reputation first spread by word of mouth. After 1969's largely disowned debut LP *The Aerosol Grey Machine*, intended as a solo vehicle for singer Peter Hammill, they headed deep into the post-apocalyptic darkness on *The Least We Can Do Is Wave To Each Other*, their well-nurtured avant-garde tendencies also bringing free jazz into the equation. The album's only single proved double-bubble for fans. On the A-side was a unique mix of their stirring cello and woodwind-laced prog ballad 'Refugees', on the B-side a non-album cut almost as dark and deep as album high 'White Hammer'. A reference to the Egyptian solar barque *wjꜣ-n-ḥḥw* — the sacred sailing ship that rides across the sky, lighting up the world — its lyrics were equally pretentious with their wide-eyed talk of High God Ra, Horus the Good and Lord of the Dead Osiris in a wracked land of drought and perversity. It was hailed by fans, among them future Sex Pistol Johnny Rotten, as one of their greatest early outings.

## 'Bonanzoid Deathgrip'

Biffy Clyro
BEGGARS BANQUET 2004
A-Side: 'Glitter and Trauma'

**There will be blood.**

A band that always regarded the B-side as an artform, Biffy Clyro forever concealed gems in its grooves and rarely sold their fans short. The anthemic Kilmarnock trio were already well on their way to finishing their third album

— the sprawling, complex and kaleidoscopic *Infinity Land* — when 'Bonanzoid Deathgrip' (a title as fetching as 2005 'Folding Stars' flip 'Asexual Meat Kitchen') surfaced, a song that only missed the final cut at the eleventh hour. Single purchasers were instead treated to one of their most outwardly enraged and deeply twisted travails. It kept them guessing though. The restrained shuffle beat, soft vocals and haunting guitar lines of its first couple of minutes were a decoy for the full-on feral nightmare that would suddenly erupt — frontman Simon Neil screaming manically about vampires at a 'blood bonanza' over brutal riffs and powerhouse percussion, prior to its unrestrained finale. Biffy Clyro B-sides are a cult in themselves, but this is their bile-soaked leader, capturing all their famed duality in under five minutes.

**'Boogie Chillen'**
John Lee Hooker
MODERN 1948
A-Side: 'Sally May'

**Blues avatar's brilliantly basic breakthrough.**

John Lee Hooker's first ever B-side stands as his greatest work. The seeds for the Mississippi plantation-born blues avatar's mournful guitar sound were sown by stepfather Will Moore, and cemented by visits from legends such as Charley Patten and Blind Lemon Jefferson. Soon afterwards Hooker moved to Detroit and started making his name on the Hastings Street circuit, where he hooked up with record store and label owner Bernard Besman. They worked together for several years, Hooker clocking into the studio shortly after clocking out of his day job as a janitor in the Chrysler factory. As with its long-forgotten A-side, 'Boogie Chillen' was as primitive as any blues out there — just Hooker's distinctive voice, chugging guitar and endlessly stomping feet. Leased to Modern Records, it became a true blues sensation, shifting over a million copies while its insistent rhythm became a stylistic spar for a fresh generation of six-stringers and an epiphany for future rock 'n' roll songwriter Jerry Leiber. A profligate artist in its wake, with a shaky grip on quality control, Hooker remade his first hit again in 1970 alongside Canned Heat. ZZ Top later used its two chords to propel 1973's breakthrough tale of notorious knocking shop 'La Grange'.

### 'Boogie Shoes'

KC & the Sunshine Band
TK 1976
A-Side: '(Shake Shake Shake) Shake Your Booty'

**Pre-twerk anthem liberated by the movies.**

Only the Bee Gees beat KC & the Sunshine Band in notching up disco's most memorable dance hits. The B-side of their third US number 1 single, 'Shake Your Booty', was a case in point, its tight addictive funk guitars, punchy horns, nudge-nudge lyrics and 16-bar structure playing to the superior songwriting, production and arranging strengths of leaders Harry Wayne Casey and Richard Finch. Seemingly tossed away as a B-side, 'Boogie Shoes' enjoyed an unexpected second life when it was included in John Badham's 1977 film blockbuster *Saturday Night Fever*, the band even enjoying a brief cameo in full glimmering disco regalia and high-heeled rhinestone shoes. Reissued as a single in 1978, it shuffled to a respectable number 35 on the US charts. While the full force of the disco backlash would cause the band to split in 1985, they returned to the revival circuit in the 90s and continued to cut new material. Film producers have kept returning to 'Boogie Shoes' too, the song also surfacing in *Mallrats*, *Boogie Nights* and *Detroit Rock City*.

### 'Born On The Bayou'

Creedence Clearwater Revival
FANTASY 1968
A-Side: 'Proud Mary'

**Songwriter proves Einstein's edict about imagination.**

There's little doubt that 'Proud Mary' did wonders for Creedence Clearwater Revival's career. It laid to waste the notion that the Southern roots rocker were just a glorified covers band and missed the US number 1 slot by a whisker. But it was the swampy, otherworldly B-side 'Born On The Bayou', filled with plenty of soul and grit by the rasping vocals of frontman John Fogerty, that confirmed their authorial vision. If what sounded like him pining for his childhood was fake news — Fogerty had never visited the Louisiana Bayou, where it was set — the words came naturally. "Somehow it all just seemed familiar to me," he wrote in 2015 memoir *Fortunate Son: My Life, My Music*. Inspired by his love of gospel, its musical genesis went back to a bottom of the bill show at San Francisco's Avalon

Ballroom in 1968. Last to soundcheck but first to play, he gave his bandmates its distinctive guitar riff to follow and they jammed it out (he got the words down later, along with 'Proud Mary', in his tiny Californian apartment). Creedence Clearwater Revival's opener at Woodstock in a year they notched no less than three US Top 10 albums, it remains Fogerty's favourite CCR song.

### 'Born Slippy .NUXX'

Underworld
JUNIOR BOY'S OWN 1995
A-Side: 'Born Slippy'

**The start of a beautiful friendship.**

Underworld became an unlikely electronic force on the back of a throwaway B-side. Needing something to fill the grooves of 'Born Slippy' — a shivery, high-tempo breakbeat-led instrumental named after a winning greyhound — they speedily fashioned the unrelated 'Born Slippy .NUXX', inspired by singer Karl Hyde's struggles to catch the last train home to Romford after a squiffy night in London's Soho. "A drunk sees the world in fragments and I wanted to recreate that," he told *The Guardian* in 2006, further describing it as a cry for help when he "was still deep into alcoholism." Recorded in a single frenetic take, with Hyde resorting to its infamous "Lager, lager, lager, lager..." refrain whenever he lost his place, it became a club hit that reached the ears of film director Danny Boyle, working on his adaptation of Irvine Welsh's heroin fable *Trainspotting*. Keen to use it for the movie's climactic scene — when Renton wakes early and disappears with his friends' ill-gotten gains — Underworld initially baulked, keen to dodge any druggy associations. They changed their mind when Boyle persuaded them to watch *Trainspotting* in the edit suite. While its reissue went number 2 in the UK charts, their association with Boyle extended to the opening ceremony for 2012's Summer Olympics. They also supplied an updated version, 'Slow Slippy', for 2017 sequel *Trainspotting T2*.

### 'Both Sides Now'

Viola Wills
STREETWAVE 1985
A-Side: 'Dare To Dream'

**Refashioned Joni Mitchell song attracts pink pound.**

Music saved Viola Wills from the poverty line. Born into hardship in Watts, Los Angeles, her dreams of escape came true when she started singing backing vocals for Barry White. While a few early solo singles for Bronco became local hits, resonating wider on the UK's northern soul scene, it was a turn backing Joe Cocker that brought her to London, even though 1974's first album *Soft Centres* sank without trace. Wills kept plugging away regardless and by 1979 her hi-NRG update of the Patience And Prudence 50s hit 'Gonna Get Along Without You Now' took her into the UK Top 10. As follow-ups flopped, Wills seemed set for a permanent place in the one-hit-wonders hall of fame. That changed when 1986's self-written 'Dare To Dream' inveigled its way into the Top 40. Much of the heavy-lifting had been done by its B-side, an emotive take on Joni Mitchell's signature song that club DJs favoured for its clipped, chugging synths. Beloved on the Brighton gay scene, where she briefly resided, Wills regularly played it alongside fellow hi-NRG sirens Miquel Brown and Hazell Dean before returning to America to study music therapy in the 00s.

## 'Bottle To The Baby'

Charlie Feathers

KING 1956

A-Side: 'One Hand Loose'

**Rockabilly rebel's untrustworthy child-rearing tips.**

Charlie Feathers was overtly aware of his importance to American pop. While the controversial Mississippi musician's wild claim that he taught Elvis Presly to sing rockabilly was debunked, the power of his early 50s recordings for both Sam Phillips' Sun and Cincinnati's King labels can't be so easily denied. Feathers used his light, bouncy vocal style to launch two of rockabilly's purest, most unadulterated songs on this 1956 keeper, packed with powerful string play from guitarist Jerry Huffman, slapping bass from Jody Chastain and the thwacking percussion of Jimmy Swords. If the A-side's cryptic lyrics leaned towards the sleazy side, superior B-side 'Bottle To The Baby''s casual talk of jacking juice from a liquor still added dark undertones of alcoholism to the mix, without sounding anything but remorselessly cheerful. Despite ailing sales, the stubborn Feathers kept faith in his music and continued to play the Memphis circuit while recording for increasingly obscure labels. As such he was perfectly poised to exploit the 70s rockabilly revival, his increasingly delusional interviews offset by his enduring ability to deliver the goods.

## 'Boys'

The Shirelles
SCEPTER 1960
A-Side: 'Will You Love Me Tomorrow'

**Beatles-loved tale of romantic expectations.**

The Shirelles' biggest hit was a sloppy kiss goodbye to 50s romantic ideals. The first of many masterpieces from the pens of Carol King and Gerry Goffin, it bridged the keening tension between romantic rapture and bitter heartbreak, while establishing the 60s girl group format — Shirley Owens' plaintive lead vocal cushioned by charming counter-melodies from her New Jersey schoolmates. Despite the prudish resistance of certain radio stations, it became the first single by an all-girl black group to top the American charts. Their string-loving producer Luther Dixon went back to basics on B-side 'Boys'. A bouncily brief, hormone-heavy encapsulation of pubescent obsession with the opposite sex, co-written with Wes Farrell, its fevered imaginings of deep sensual thrills from these 'bundles of joy' was palpable throughout. Genders even remained unchanged when Ringo Starr made it his solo turn in Rory Storm and the Hurricanes' skiffle repertoire, sometimes alongside Cilla Black. That translated into his Beatles role too, Starr making it his first official lead vocal on 1963's 'Please Please Me' (which added another Shirelles cover in 'Baby It's You').

## 'Brain Salad Surgery'

Emerson, Lake & Palmer
ATLANTIC 1977
A-Side: 'Fanfare For The Common Man'

**Early outing for world's first polyphonic synth.**

Emerson, Lake & Palmer were progressive rock's first supergroup. Pooling its members from the Nice (Keith Emerson), King Crimson (Greg Lake) and Atomic Rooster (Carl Palmer), their instrumental prowess and complex bombastic sound was allied to onstage flamboyance defined by Emerson's show-stealing pyrotechnics and the speedy-fisted Palmer's giant rotating drum kit. To back their fiercely edited take on Aaron Copland's 1942 classical piece 'Fanfare For The Common Man' — written to exalt patriotism and democracy — they pillaged sessions from 1973's 4th studio album *Brain Salad Surgery*. One of the last songs they recorded, distinguished by Emerson's jolting forays on the Moog Apollo, its title track had previously surfaced as a free flexi-disc with music paper *NME*. Another studio outtake, 'When The Apple Blossoms Bloom In The Windmills Of Your Mind I'll Be Your Valentine', first appeared on the back of their soaring adaptation of a William Blake hymn ['Jerusalem', 1973], although its chart fortunes perished when the BBC banned it for potential blasphemy.

### 'Brand New Cadillac'

Vince Taylor & His Playboys
PARLOPHONE 1959
A-Side: 'Pledgin' My Love'

**Ill-fated singer turns the wheel of fortune.**

Vince Taylor became David Bowie's inspiration for Ziggy Stardust. One spin of the unfadeable, greased lightning squeal of 'Brand New Cadillac' and it's easy to hear why. The original live-fast-die-young wild man of British rock 'n' roll, Taylor was inspired by Elvis and Gene Vincent after his family moved from Middlesex to California in his teens. Bundled on the B-side of his second single, sappy sub-Elvis ballad 'Pledgin' My Love', came the handsome singer's first original composition — a hard-edged, rip-snorting show of strength that ranks among first wave rock 'n' roll's greatest originals. Taylor's snottily delivered tale of his girl abandoning him in favour of fresh hot wheels boasted the Shadows' Brian Locking and Brian Bennett holding down the rhythm and hyper-tense, fast-fingered guitar from the Pirates' Joe Moretti. A massive hit in France and the Netherlands, propelling the leather-clad Taylor to genuine stardom there, the indifference at home hurt him badly, and by the 60s he was a broke, drug-addled and deluded figure, obsessed with UFOs and convinced of his messianic powers — perfect for Bowie's dissolute stage creation. 'Brand New Cadillac' continued to weave its magic without him, becoming a Swedish number 1 for the Hep Stars in 1965 (featuring a very young, pre-ABBA Benny Andersson). It was also the first song the Clash recorded for *London Calling*, setting its prevailing mood.

### 'Breadfan'

Metallica
ELEKTRA 1988
A-Side: 'Harvester Of Sorrow'

**Thrash legends reanimate lost Welsh band's career.**

Metallica often used their B-sides to pay homage. Never shy of tipping their caps to their heroes, the Californian thrash titans put everything from NWOBHM stalwarts Diamond Head's 'Am I Evil?' ['Creeping Death', 1984] to Queen's 'Stone Cold Crazy' ['Enter Sandman', 1991] through the ringer, including a rare B-side cover of a B-side in Anti-Nowhere League's 'So What' ['The Unforgiven', 1991]. The pinnacle was a powerful take on Budgie's 1973 anthem 'Breadfan' — a riff-heavy, money-is-the-root-of-evil warning that first surfaced on the Welsh prog-rockers' 3rd album *Never Turn Your Back On A Friend* (whose early pressings included an excerpt from Winston Churchill's "Blood, tears, toil and sweat" speech). While Metallica's cover didn't budge from its established structure it did upgrade it, showcasing their mastery of speed and volume, with guitarist Kirk Hammett in blistering solo form. A production error ensured it ended with a distorted voice asking "Mommy, where's Fluffy?" — a unique marker that was repeated when it was used again as the B-side of Metallica's next single 'Eye Of The Beholder'. A regular encore when touring 1988's conceptually dense 4th LP *...And Justice For All*, it was also their opener at Woodstock in 1994.

### 'Breakaway'

The Cars
ELEKTRA 1985
A-Side: 'Why Can't I Have You'

**Druggy allusions sabotage hit potential.**

With their chart fortunes on the slide, Boston's proudest wearers of skinny ties and shades brought in outside help for their 5th studio epistle. The one-time vanguard of the US new wave spent over six months in the studio with AC/DC and Def Leppard producer Mutt Lange, trying to perfect a sleek MOR sound that their last album *Shake It Up* had only hinted at. The resulting *Heartbeat City* allied Lange's gleaming perfectionist touch to songwriter Ric Ocasek's primal power pop instincts, resulting in instant fan favourites 'Magic' and 'You

Might Think', plus the track that would prove to be *Live Aid*'s ultimate tear-jearker. While bassist Ben Orr's aching delivery on 'Drive' helped it go triple platinum, the Cars all but buried the LP's brightest offcut 'Breakaway' on the B-side of the album's 5th single. Riding in above a fleet of Moogs and a great bouncing bassline, Ocasek's brooding vocal and Greg Hawkes chorus keyboard riff put it on par with anything on the album, although explicit references to heroin ("chasing the dragon... china white... Persian dreams") presumably nuked its mainstream potential.

### 'The Bridge'

MC Shan
BRIDGE 1986
A-Side: 'Beat Biter'

**B-side starts bitter friction between New York boroughs.**

'The Bridge' sparked one of the greatest hip-hop battles of all time. A B-side no less powerful than its largely passed-over A-side, it found Marley Marl's raw and explosive James Brown-sampling beat topped by his cousin Shan's already nostalgic rhymes about early night time hip-hop jams when they'd "do it out in the park" in their native Queensbridge. One of the first songs to really represent their home borough — tipping the wink to mythical figures like Cousin Bruce, Jabby Jack, Larry Laughter and Gas — 'The Bridge' espoused the joys of making something out of nothing and rising above your station. Not that everyone heard it with those ears. Boogie Down Productions' rapper KRS-One interpreted it as a boast that hip-hop had started out in Queensbridge. He was furious about it. And to prove that he wasn't having it he launched his highly aggrieved answer-dis 'South Bronx' with the far from coded warning: "If you popped that junk up in the Bronx you might not live." A full-blown regional war erupted in its wake, with Shan's associates in the Juice Crew also becoming involved. A plea to desist on 'Kill That Noise' from Shan's 1987 debut *Down By Law* made matters worse, as BDP returned fire with mega-diss 'The Bridge Is Over'. And while Shan's career faded rapidly in its aftermath, the dispute launched KRS-One into the hip-hop limelight. It was a role he took to with relish, repositioning himself a highly quotable 'Teacha' and later founding his own ministry, the Temple of Hip Hop.

### 'Broad Old Woman (6 AM Insanity)'

Neil Diamond

UNI 1968

A-Side: 'Two-Bit Manchild'

**Pop crooner's band fail to nail it in one.**

Essentially a jam session gone very publicly wrong, 'Broad Old Woman' let fans into the mechanics of a recording sessions — bum notes, stray coughs and on-the-fly instructions included. While the New Yorker's measured croon was as velveteen as ever as he evoked a mysterious woman with heavily mascaraed eyes, his band's collective failure to nail its stopping sections found him almost giving up the ghost on the second verse, strangling his own laughter and issuing the slightly piqued complaint: "If you think I'm putting my name on this you're out of your mind!" Fortunately for Diamond, many fans weren't listening. After two years of sustained success, solo and as a writer for the Monkees, the Brill Building graduate was having a mini career blip, after falling out with Bert Berns' teenybopper-oriented producers at BANG. This more mature single, from third LP *Velvet Gloves And Spit*, did little to reverse his fortunes. Diamond had previously enjoyed much more success with another B-side 'The Boat That I Row' ['I Got The Feelin' (Oh No No)', 1966] after Lulu's quick-off-the-mark cover topped the Canadian charts.

### 'Brothers From Brentwood L.I.'

EPMD

DEF JAM 1992

A-Side: 'Crossover'

**Other side of commercial breakthrough appeases fans.**

By 1992's 4th album *Business Never Personal*, EPMD had hit a dilemma: how to retain their hardcore hip-hop credibility while living up to their acronym — Erick and Parrish Making Dollars. They managed it by creating the double-edged 'Crossover', a Zapp-sampling headnodder that allied a catchy sung chorus with scathing lyrics that attacked any of their rapping peers prepared to "sell their souls to go gold". Job cleverly done. And if there were any hardcore doubters still in the house, they were thoroughly appeased by its superior self-aggrandising B-side 'Brothers From Brentwood L.I.', which sparked off the same clicky sample from the Emotions' 'Blind Alley' that Big Daddy Kane used on 'Ain't No Half Steppin''. For some the best EPMD song in an august canon, it brought many of the fans' favourite elements together in one production — loud banging beats, layered effects, sped-up vocals and a classic hook: "We make the sounds that make you 'Ow!'" While it helped make 'Crossover' their first gold single, that success was mercifully fleeting — the pair split up shortly afterwards due, almost inevitably, to fiscal tensions.

### 'Brown Girl In The Ring'

Boney M
HANSA 1978
A-Side: 'Rivers Of Babylon'

**Great pop swindle that became a 70s party constant.**

Decked out in gold lamé costumes, chains and exotic lingerie, Boney M quickly became a slightly risqué chart fixture. Essentially the miming puppets of singer and producer Frank Farian — first brought in as stand-ins to perform his surprise 1975 Dutch hit 'Baby Do You Wanna Bump?' on TV — he ran with the concept until they became a bona fide European phenomenon. By 1978 the manufactured disco stars were at the height of their popularity, having just spent five weeks at the top of the UK charts with their cover of the Melodians' 'Rivers Of Babylon'. The single had slipped to the fringes of the Top 20 when radio DJs started playing B-side 'Brown Girl In The Ring', a riff on a traditional Caribbean nursery rhyme and playground game. Its insistent "Tra-la-la-la-las" soon engineered a happy chart reversal, with the single re-entering the Top 10 for two months — peaking at number 2 — with few mainstream buyers aware that they had bought the exact same 45 twice (and made it the second highest-selling single of all time). It was not the first time their singer Liz Mitchell had recorded 'Brown Girl...' as a B-side. The previous year she duetted it with boyfriend Malcolm Magaron on the flip of Malcolm's Locks' single 'Caribbean Rock'. That didn't escape Farian's all-seeing eyes, and he was later accused by trombonist Peter Herbolzheimer of copycatting his arrangement. Farian would pull similar Svengali moves in the 80s as the mastermind behind Milli Vanilli.

### 'Buffalo Ghosts'

Elbow
FICTION/POLYDOR 2011
A-Side: 'Open Arms'

**Bury stadium fillers show intimate side.**

Right from their inception, Elbow considered B-sides as a serious business — songs that didn't have to be poor relations to the A-side. Even during their early days on Island Records, Bury's misfit art-rockers could barely wait for their producer to go home. It gave them free studio reign that they often use to explore their more experimental and downbeat side. Their intimate B-side work helped keyboardist Craig Potter teach himself the necessary studio skills to become their in-house producer, belated vindication arriving with 2008's Mercury Prize for *The Seldom Seen Kid* a full 20 years into their career. 'Buffalo Ghosts' was very much a continuum of Elbow tradition — a gentle hidden treasure that many fans preferred to its Coldplay-sounding A-side. It majored on Guy Garvey's tender voice, the everyday people's laureate whisperingly evoking a teller of porkie pies amid a huge blue sky. "None of our B-sides are album rejects," Garvey wrote on their website when they launched 2012 compilation *Dead In The Boot*. "It's a different space, usually... when all the members of Elbow are chiming and feeling very creative."

### 'The Bump'

Bay City Rollers
BELL 1974
A-Side: 'All Of Me Loves All Of You'

**Tartan tykes' two hits for the price of one.**

Teen sensations the Bay City Rollers were a run-of-the-mill Beatles covers band before the Edinburgh quintet fell into the musty palms of entrepreneur Tam Paton. After touring the Scottish circuit and scoring a minor hit with a cover of the Gentrys' 'Keep On Dancing', he reshuffled the line-up, its founders Derek and Alan Longmuir now joined by pretty boys Stuart 'Woody' Wood, Eric Faulkner and singer Les McKeown. Faulkner's suggestion that they go tartan was a marketing masterstroke on par with their partnership with songwriters/producers Bill Martin and Phil Coulter, as the ever-ready pin-ups dominated the mid-70s pop marketplace. The Rollers already had four Top 10 hits in the bag when the nonsense-glam of 'All of Me Loves All Of You' surfaced in 1974. Its equally accessible flip 'The Bump' didn't disappoint their hysterical fan base, its Glitter Band beat and numbered chant accompanied by an easy to copy dance move. Its popularity was affirmed when Mickie Most-managed London hopefuls Kenny nicked it for their first single later that year and steamrolled straight into the Top 3.

**'Buried Treasure'**
Kenny Rogers
RCA 1983
A-Side: 'This Woman'

**Country legend throws bone to early followers.**
Kenny Rogers' laidback Texan charm took him a long way. A versatile singer and songwriter from the poor side of the tracks, he had tried his hand at doo-wop, jazz, folk and psychedelic rock (as part of First Edition) before a solo career beckoned in his late thirties, his trademark beard and amenable stagecraft now in place. Having made his name with MOR country tracks like 'The Gambler' and 'The Coward Of The County', songs whose outward softness concealed much harsher truths, he reinvented himself as a mainstream pop-rocker in the 80s, starting with a cover of Lionel Richie's 'Lady'. Fellow disco stars the Bee Gees took authorial control on 1983's *Eyes That See In The Dark*, a set kicked off with his platinum duet with Dolly Parton 'Islands In the Stream' (a song fans forced him to repeat at Glastonbury 30 years later). Tucked on the B-side of its high harmony follow-up 'This Woman' was 'Buried Treasure', a palpable return to Rogers' country roots gilded by the tidy licks of guitarist George Terry and soothing guest vocals of the Gatlin Brothers. American country radio lapped it up, ignoring the A-side and skimming it to number three in the country charts.

**'Burning Ambition'**
Iron Maiden
EMI 1980
A-Side: 'Running Free'

**British metallers prove that they're not for turning.**

The mother of all Iron Maiden B-sides was also the first song their bassist Steve Harris composed. Written while in previous outfit Gypsy's Kiss, the east-ender's slightly hackneyed tale of not being tied down by relationships was elevated by the rare energy of his rookie brothers in arms: singer Paul Di'Anno, guitarist Dave Murray and drummer Doug Sampson. Despite a proggy intro that hinted at Rush and Genesis, the rest was a punk-infused three-chord rocker with Di'Anno's rasping, snarling warning about "something burning inside" matched by Sampson's choppy fretwork and an unhinged midsection solo that hinted at the duelling Wishbone Ash-on-cheap-speed madness set to unfold when second guitarist Derek Stratton joined the band. Forcefully dispatched in less than three minutes, it was every bit the equal of the A-side's semi-autobiographical tale of teenage escape. While the single just missed the Top 40 — great shakes for an untried band then largely trading on word of mouth — Derek Riggs' artwork was also the first depiction of their talisman Eddie, captured lurking menacingly in the shadows.

## 'The Butterfly Collector'

The Jam
POLYDOR 1979
A-Side: 'Strange Town'

**Modfather resists attentions of scarlet woman.**

Suited, sartorially acute 60s mod revivalists the Jam were very much the round pegs in punk's square holes. Even so, they were one of the few acts to pledge fidelity to its founding ideals, never reforming after they split in 1982 (although bassist Bruce Foxton and drummer Rick Butler continued to put bread on the table by playing in a Jam tribute act). The Woking band's ability to knock out potent three-minute singles continued on the flip side of their 7th single — a slowly unfurling psychedelic folk reel with bitter lyrics about a fame-hungry seductress. Variously interpreted as a scathing groupie put-down, a rejection of Soo Catwoman (kittenishly coiffured part of the Sex Pistols' Bromley contingent) or a revenge diss of *NME* writer Julie Burchill, whoever the target was, their 'second-rate' fashion sense (no Union Jack blazers then) clearly riled singer/songwriter Paul Weller. While there was a slight compositional debt to the Kinks'

'Shangri La', the way its verses seethed with quiet anger pointed to the acerbic bleakness of 1980's incoming *Sound Affects* album. Further Jam flipside thrills could be found on the Beatles-nodding 'Liza Radley' ['Start!', 1980] or the pastel-tinged nostalgia of 'Tales From The Riverbank' ['Absolute Beginners', 1981].

## 'Can-I-Bust'

Common Sense
RELATIVITY 1993
A-Side: 'Soul By The Pound'

**Strictly street bragging rights.**

Long before he lost his Sense and evolved into an Emmy-winning actor and one of rap's most woke commentators, Lonnie Rashid Lynn was honing his skills in the hardscrabble clubs on Chicago's South Side. Having supported N.W.A and Big Daddy Kane while still in high school, his coronation in *The Source* magazine's coveted Unsigned Hype column led to a deal with aspirant independent Relativity. After setting out his playful and densely referenced stall over minimalist production on 1982's under-radar debut *Can I Borrow A Dollar*, this two-way skills showcase with Ynot (now better known as The Twilite Tone) was an old-fashioned challenge to his peers — a warning that any opposition would be lyrically lynched. While the A-side's plea for brotherly solidarity was criticised for its depiction of women, its hiccupping B-side mixed so-so rhymes like "I'm the pimp of hip-hop" with smart-bombs such as "I'm not Jehovah/But can I get a witness?" A true time capsule, the lack of worldly sophistication to 'Can-I-Bust' nonetheless sealed Common Sense's reputation as one of the rap underground's hungriest wordsmiths.

## 'Can't Find My Way Home'

Blind Faith
POLYDOR 1969
A-Side: 'Presence Of The Lord'

**Short-lived supergroup's paean to misadventure.**

Blind Faith brought together several stellar talents in pursuit of the perfect blues/rock fusion. Formed by Eric Clapton as an escape from the biting inter-band politics of Cream — caught in a vicious feud between drummer Ginger Baker and bassist Jack Bruce — the guitarist recruited former Spencer Davis Group boy wonder Steve Winwood (on temporary hiatus from Traffic), ex-Family bassist Ric Grech and, reluctantly, Baker. Having made a far from low profile live debut at London's Hyde Park in June 1969, they shot into wider ears with the surging gospel rock of the Clapton-penned 'Presence Of The Lord', driven by Winwood's wild electric piano. The singer was in more winsome form on its self-written B-side. A gentle Celtic folk evocation of someone going off the rails, possibly through drink or drugs, it was carried by Clapton's gentle acoustic fingerpicking and Baker's jazzy drum licks. While Blind Faith folded soon after their self-titled debut — a rare transatlantic number 1 — this B-side has lived several new lives, reprised on record by Winwood and Clapton in 2009 and covered by everyone from Joe Cocker, John Mayer and Bonnie Raitt to Styx and Swans.

## 'Can't Get Over Losing You'

The Delfonics
PHILLY GROOVE 1968
A-Side: 'La-La (Means I Love You)'

**The rough that goes with the smooth.**

By the late 60s soul was headed in a far grittier direction: James Brown was celebrating his blackness loud and proud, Aretha Franklin was trading on her gospel roots, while Sly & the Family Stone were bringing psychedelia to the dancefloor. Little-known Philadelphians the Delfonics — brothers William and Wilbert Hart alongside Randy Cain, a friend who sang doo-wop with them at school dances — bucked the trend for rawer harder sounds. Impeccably smooth, the feather-lite 'La-La (Means I Love You)' witnessed William's ecstatic falsetto coast away on waves of his partners' gossamer harmonies above the stringy glissandos studiously fashioned by producer Thom Bell. Those who flipped the single were in for an equally powerful surprise — a fleet-footed, almost Motown-ish arrangement that showed the bitterer side of love's coin flip, with those who leant towards grittier arrangements marking 'Can't Get Over Losing You' as the Delfonics' definitive joint. Both sides of this supremely well-judged single set the template for the Delfonics' hit-making marathon and helped define the early parameters of Philly soul.

## 'Can't Get It Out Of My Head'

Fountains of Wayne
ATLANTIC 1997
A-Side: 'Sink To The Bottom'

**Pop satirists' ELO cover plays it straight.**

Long before their early 00s hit with 'Stacy's Mom', Fountains of Wayne had snared the affections of clever-clever power pop fans. The New Jersey Beatles freaks — pivoted around the songwriting frisson between Chris Collingwood and Adam Schlesinger — showed their compositional smarts on 1996's wry, charming self-titled debut, its punchily arranged miniatures riven with telling details. While their compatible talents surged through the bittersweet romance of 'Sink To The Bottom', they displayed more interpretative vim on its B-side's cover of Electric Light Orchestra's stringy US breakthrough. Stripped right back to its essence, with regret palpable in Collingwood's heaving tones, this live take (from a Florida show) was worlds adrift from later, knowing covers of Britney Spears and Burt Bacharach. Their long-standing fidelity to the B-side art was also evident amid the knotty relationship cut and thrust of 'I'll Do The Driving' ['Denise', 1999], 'Baby I've Changed' ['Hey Julie', 2004] and the squiffy festive regret of 'The Man In The Santa Suit' ['I Want An Alien For Christmas', 1999].

## 'Can't Hurry Love'

Stray Cats
ARISTA 1982
A-Side: 'Rock This Town'

**Supremes' soul doozy given rockin' re-lick.**

Rockabilly was dead on its feet when the Long Island trio of Brian Setzer, Lee Rocker and Slim Jim Phantom sought to revive it. In love with the vehicles, music, fashion and lifestyle, but finding few peers at home, they inveigled their way into the UK rockabilly revival. Thanks to crucial help from the Faces' Ronnie Lane (who put them up) and Rockpile's Dave Edmunds (who offered to produce them), they pulled off an unexpected chart coup. Backing the high-energy thrust of their second single 'Rock This Town' was a cover of Holland-Dozier-Holland's Motown masterpiece that majored on its bouncing bassline and showed a more vulnerable side to Setzer's voice, becoming increasingly impassioned as it progressed. Ruffed up a little, but with obvious affection, Setzer's trademark guitar break was a rock 'n' roll miniature of intense beauty that pointed towards the genre experiments they'd risk on second LP *Gonna Ball*, even though many had ceased listening. If nothing else, it knocked Phil Collins' needy murmuring into the shade.

### 'Candy And A Currant Bun'

The Pink Floyd
COLUMBIA 1967
A-Side: 'Arnold Layne'

**Sweet-toothed drug anthem refix conceals a naughty word.**

If some radio stations didn't take kindly to the cross-dressing narrative of the Pink Floyd's first single 'Arnold Layne', they were thrown another bouncer by its off-kilter B-side. 'Candy And A Currant Bun' was a potent display of songwriter Syd Barrett's easy way with a hook and very English otherness, before his prodigious LSD consumption took its toll. Its gleeful tale of getting wasted in the summer sun also showcased the Cambridge band's peculiarity — Roger Waters' groovy bassline and Nick Mason's offbeat drums offset by Rick Wright's snarling organ bursts. A long-standing staple of the early Floyd's live sets (then titled 'Let's Roll Another One'), Barrett ultimately ceded to Waters' suggestion he tone down the drug references. Instead he nodded to the sweets ban then in place in English public schools (currant buns were considered acceptable tuck), omitting the original line "I'm high/Don't spoil my fun" while smuggling an easily missed profanity into its first bridge. It ranks among the most elusive entries in the heavily recycled Floyd catalogue, alongside other 1967 flipside renegades 'The Scarecrow' ['See Emily Play'] and 'The Gnome' ['Flaming'].

### 'The Canyons Of Your Mind'

Bonzo Dog Doo-Dah Band
LIBERTY 1968
A-Side: 'I'm The Urban Spaceman'

**British pop's original nutty boys open their minds.**

"This is the B-side of our platter, sports fans," announced Vivian Stanshall at the start of their parody of Noel Harrison hit 'The Windmills Of Your Mind', "I hope it makes you sick..." Art students Bonzo allied Stanshall's outlandish plummy wit with the songwriting class of Neil Innes, building an avid pub following with their penchant for satire and silliness. Having briefly starred in the Beatles' 1967 film *Magical Mystery Tour*, performing 'Death Cab for Cutie' in the style of Elvis, Paul McCartney (trading as Apollo C Vermouth) was on hand to produce their only UK hit, 'I'm The Urban Spaceman'. Rather strait-laced by their standards, Bonzo fanatics preferred the Las Vegas-style croon of its flipside as Stanshall declaimed a love that caused him pain in "The wardrobes of my soul/In the section labelled shirts" while future Rutles mastermind Innes cranked out one of the most deliberately terrible guitar solos before punk rock. It was taken at face value by the manager of real-life crooner Matt Monro, who asked Stanshall to write his charge something similar. The inevitably rejected 'Blind Date' — about a mismatched tryst between an escaped gorilla and a pygmy — eventually surfaced as the B-side of Gargantuan Chums' only single 'Suspicion' in 1970.

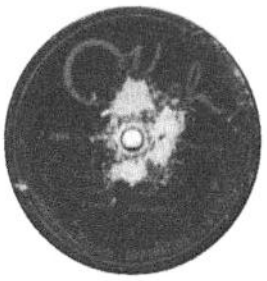

## 'Carolina Shout'

James P. Johnson
OKEH 1922
A-Side: 'Keep Off The Grass'

**Jazz stylist lays down gauntlet to stride piano rivals.**

James P. Johnson earned his reputation as 'the father of the stride piano'. The New Jersey-born jazz stylist and composer became a fixture of New York clubs in the 1910s, regularly showing off his speed, skill and flair at the hardcore piano cutting contests conducted in Harlem apartments. Writer of 'The Charleston', which inspired the 20s dance craze, the technically gifted Johnson was among the first soloists to make it onto record, gloriously capturing stride's signature blend of swing, power and rhythm on 'Carolina Shout'. A challenging number that nodded to ragtime but majored on its performer's improvised solo skills, it became the signature test piece for upcoming pianists, with Johnson's prodigy Fats Waller often coming out top and even besting his mentor. Its style also paved the way for the later innovations of Count Basie and Duke Ellington. While Johnson went on to accompany singers such as Bessie Smith and Ethel Waters, he re-recorded his signature piece many times. However, most agree that his original flip to 'Keep Off The Grass' is its definitive take.

## 'Caroline Wheeler's Birthday Present'

The Jazz Butcher
GLASS 1984
A-Side: 'Marnie'

**Bedroom songwriter's all-revealing hissy fit.**

To accompany the A-side's tale of the perils of keeping tigers in confined spaces, the Jazz Butcher chose to expose himself, revealing part of the decidedly non-Dolby bedroom demo tape that won him a record deal. Those demos came about by accident, borne from a design flaw in his Amstrad 7090 twin cassette deck. While it made copying tapes troublesome — its internal mics captured the user's every cough, slurp or splutter — it was a boon for the nascent songwriter. By continually swapping cassettes and repeating the process, the Butcher could now multi-track his parts, even if they were played on just a nylon string guitar, toy xylophone and an electric heater. As such the "definitely not produced" 'Caroline Wheeler's Birthday Present' was a super fascinating, super lo-fi insight into an artist exploring his craft without boundaries. The hissy charm offensive was a many-splendored beast too, with mentions of sasquatches, monsters and Alice Cooper colliding with simulated dog woofs, maniacal laughter and a heavy nod to the Velvet Underground's 'Murder Mystery'. As for the present itself? Referred to here as "a little piece of chocolate and a Grace Jones tape", it became something far more sinister and putrescent when re-recorded above a wall of bass guitars for 1984's second LP *A Scandal In Bohemia*.

## 'Carry Me Home'

AC/DC
ALBERT PRODUCTIONS 1977
A-Side: 'Dog Eat Dog'

**Good time boogie chillingly predicts singer's death.**

AC/DC were still on their uppers when they recorded 1977's third LP *Let There Be Rock*. It crystalised their stripped back yet stylised high-voltage mix of bludgeoning guitar power chords, pounding drums and Bon Scott's hysterical vocals as it made crucial inroads into the UK and US heavy rock markets. To back its Australian-only single 'Dog Eat Dog' they dusted off the much looser high-energy stomp-along 'Carry Me Home', recorded in London the previous year. A good time boogie about a night on the tiles 'sinking whisky', it found Scott's vocal becoming more and more theatrically slurred as his drunken revels progressed. Yet it also had a sinister edge. The lines "You're getting up and leaving/You think I'm gonna drown" pretty much foreshadowed Scott's death in 1980, when he choked on his own vomit in a friend's car after a night out in the Big Smoke. The many layers to that mystery were explored in forensic depth in Jesse Fink's 2017 biography *Bon: The Last Highway*.

**'Cassandra'**

ABBA

EPIC 1982

A-Side: 'The Day Before You Came'

**Swedish pop icons veer towards the stage musical.**

ABBA had a chequered relationship with B-sides. The 70s most successful pop group appeared reluctant to indulge their legions of fans regularly, usually drawing no-nonsense flips from the same parent album. 'Cassandra' was an exception. Recorded during studio sessions in 1982, as they tried and failed to summon a successor to *The Visitors* — *that* would finally arrive 40 years later with *Voyage* — it backed what was then regarded as their penultimate group effort. The foreboding, chorus-free 'The Day Before You Came', a song that finally gave the lie to their all-smiling Eurovision image, was filled with ill portents that continued amid its flipside's sparse scuttle of synths. A cryptic lyric about the prophetess of the Trojan War (one of the most tragic figures in Greek mythology) imbued with deep suffering and sadness by Anni-Frid Lyngstad, it suggested songwriters Benny Andersson and Bjorn Ulvaeus were starting to write with musical theatre in mind (and marked a baby step towards *Chess*). A boon for long-starved ABBA singles buyers, it even became the preferred A-side in Yugoslavia. There was further rare ABBA B-side gold in the unreconstructed Swedish schlager of 'Åh Vilka Tider' ['Ring Ring', 1973], 'Happy Hawaii', their work-in-progress version of 'Why Did It Have To Be Me' ['Knowing Me, Knowing You', 1977] and the unabashed synth-pop of 'Elaine' ['The Winner Takes It All', 1980].

## 'Castles In The Air'

Don McLean

LIBERTY 1972

A-Side: 'Vincent'

**'American Pie' hitmaker refers fans to less starry past.**

Before his nine-minute tale of the death of rock 'n' roll became a freak hit, Don McLean trod the fine line between confessional singer/songwriter and confectioner of radio-friendly pop. To back 'American Pie' follow-up single 'Vincent' — a poignant tribute to the life of Van Gogh — the New Yorker took his instant fan base back to his roots. Back to the time he was writing voraciously in search of that elusive record deal while doing the rounds on the folk circuit, back to the time the crushing hand of rejection always came his way before Mediarts took a punt on his 1969's debut LP *Tapestry*, back to the time his first single 'Castles In The Air' flopped. The tale of a disillusioned city dweller who leaves his partner because he's tired of the 'cocktail generation' and their superficial lifestyle, it once again found the preternaturally nostalgic McLean pining for older, more meaningful times. Played enough as a radio flip to climb into the *Billboard* Hot 100 under its own merits, McLean issued a slower, far more sorrowful version in 1981, just before the hits dried up for good.

## 'The Celts'

Enya

BBC 1987

A-Side: 'I Want Tomorrow'

**Celtic chanteuse discovers her solo groove.**

Once a keyboardist with Irish neo-folksters Clannad, Eithne Pádraigín Ní Bhraonáin eschewed their new pop direction to try her solo luck as Enya in the early 80s. The County Donegal singer and composer's contribution to rom-com soundtrack *The Frog Prince* prompted TV producer Tony McAyey to ask her to score the BBC's deep documentary delve into Irish mythology, *The Celts*. Having summoned a bespoke blend of synth madrigals, folk melodies and classical motifs for its incidental music, Enya attempted to come up with something altogether catchier and original for its signature tune. She settled on a forthright repetitive synth refrain that chimed with her heavily overdubbed vocals and

Roma Ryan's minimal Gaelic lyrics on the joy of life. Inexplicably shunted onto the reverse of 'I Want Tomorrow', the title theme seemed lost to history when the album only tickled the Irish charts. That changed after the surprise international success of 1988's 'Orinocco Flow' and the *Watermark* album, Enya's new label WEA plugging a product gap by repurposing 'The Celts' as an A-side and repackaging her debut (also retitled *The Celts*) to Top 10 UK success. It was helped along by an equally mythical video of the camera-shy singer riding a white horse around Bodiam Castle.

### 'Centerfield'

John Fogerty

WARNER BROS 1985

A-Side: 'Rock And Roll Girls'

**Comeback B-side knocks it out the park.**

John Fogerty warmed the bench for the best part of a decade. Battered and bruised from losing a lengthy legal tussle for the rights to songs he wrote for Creedence Clearwater Revival, his disappointment spiralled into a bad case of writer's block. Having broken his dry spell with 'I Saw it on TV', the California native and lifelong New York Yankees fan witnessed his comeback album's title track arrive with stealth. "I came up with that guitar riff..." he told *ESPN*, "went into the studio with a drumbeat and it just came out." And if you ignored the synthesised handclaps, it sounded a lot like a CCR record. It came with affectionate namedrops to old school legends Mighty Casey, Babe Ruth, Willie Mays, Ty Cobb and Joe DiMaggio, while Fogerty beat his brow and demanded that his coach put him into battle. There's little doubt its easy appeal helped A-Side 'Rock And Roll Girls' climb into the US Top 20, with Fogerty's flipside later honoured at New York's Baseball Hall of Fame. He commemorated its 25th anniversary at their Cooperstown museum in July 2010, performing it on a baseball bat-shaped guitar.

### 'The Chauffeur (Blue Silver)'

Duran Duran

EMI 1982

A-Side: 'Rio'

**Camera-hogging new romantics show hidden side.**
Duran Duran's embrace of the pop video was a gamble that paid dividends again and again. Recast as jet-setting international playboys in thin-lapelled Antony Price suits, the Roxy Music-nodding art rock of their tentative new romantic debut was replaced by something far more stylishly confident on its sequel *Rio*, a retro-futuristic feast that meshed synthy pop thrills with John and Roger Taylor's Chic-inspired rhythm section. In arch contrast to a single whose video captured them coursing Antiguan waves atop a 70-foot yacht was a revelatory acoustic version of 'The Chauffeur' (a close relation to Roxy's eerie 1973 offering 'The Bogus Man') that replaced the album version's silvery synth shimmers with Spanish acoustic guitars and majored on Le Bon's foreboding lyrics (written as poetry long before the band was a reality). A long-term band favourite, they even commissioned a moody video homage to Liliana Cavani's erotic psychodrama *The Night Porter* for it. Yet this peculiar B-side rendering was badly neglected by their handlers, who lost the original master tapes and had to dub it straight from the single when *Rio* was awarded the deluxe reissue treatment.

**'Child Of The Moon'**
The Rolling Stones
DECCA 1968
A-Side: 'Jumpin' Jack Flash'

**Psychedelic farewell as The Stones return to their roots.**
Tensions were high when the Rolling Stone sought to avert the relative failure of their chaotically recorded, acid-drenched 6th album *Their Satanic Majesties Request* — an overly ornamental dalliance with psychedelia that non-plussed original fans. Keith Richards' iconic riff on 'Jumpin' Jack' Flash' rewarded them a hot shot of the blues-based rock 'n' roll they had been missing and would ultimately finesse on the four album stretch from that year's *Beggars Banquet* to 1972's *Exile On Main St.* Its gothic B-side was a further representation of the Stones' trippy dark side — made flesh in Michael Lindsay-Hogg's giallo-inspired promo film — with a subtle nod to Beatles' B-side 'Rain' along the way. Introduced by an unearthly country blues riff and producer Jimmy Miller's unsettling shouts, the sax-droning, organ-drenched groover was a paganistic love letter from Mick Jagger to his then lover Marianne Faithfull as the lippy

singer patiently awaited her "wide-awake crescent-shaped smile". The Stones' last true psychedelic gasp and one of their lesser known and least compiled B-sides, it's fully on par with other flipside highs 'I'm Free' ['Get Off Of My Cloud', 1965], 'Who's Driving Your Plane' ['Have You Seen Your Mother, Baby, Standing In The Shadows', 1973] and 'Everything Is Turning To Gold' ['Shattered', 1978].

### 'Cold As Ice'

Foreigner
ATLANTIC 1977
A-Side: 'Feels Like The First Time'

**MOR behemoths dampen down the histrionics.**

One of the 70s most recognisable rock songs was nearly lost to the B-side. The chilling signature riff to 'Cold As Ice' was summoned by ex-Spooky Tooth guitarist Mick Jones on a mini-piano one snowy night, after he'd just watched a Joan Crawford movie in his New York flat, while singer Lou Gramm's recriminating lyric drew from recent romantic disappointments. Among the earliest songs written for Foreigner's arena-filling debut, it doubled down on the pair's compositional chemistry, whose glossy, airbrushed fare (and throwback fashion sense) was anathema to the punk rock revolution happening across the ocean. For reasons that remain obscure, 'Cold As Ice' was originally appended to the slick radio-friendly rock of their first single 'Feels Like The First Time', albeit only on early pressings (later ones went with 'Woman, Oh Woman'), before becoming its follow-up and Foreigner's second US Top 10 hit. It enjoyed an unlikely second hip-hop life too, as both the basis of Brooklyn hard nuts M.O.P.'s 2001 stompathon and Kanye West's introduction to 'Cold' at 2015's Glastonbury Festival.

### 'The Colour And The Shape'

Foo Fighters
ROSWELL/CAPITOL 1997
A-Side: 'Monkey Wrench'

**Last rites for the gods of hardcore noise.**

That Dave Grohl managed to step out of Kurt Cobain's shadow was a minor miracle in itself. Having established a new identity as Foo Fighters with a collection of demos the drummer worked up during Nirvana's dissolute final days, the project became much more than mere catharsis when he enlisted the Germs' guitarist Pat Smear and Sunny Day Real Estate's bassist Nate Mendel to join him on its follow-up. And while they eventually found their collective feet with the spit-polished *The Colour And The Shape* it wasn't without detours. Fraught early sessions at Washington's Bear Creek studio were discarded, along with drum parts played by William Goldsmith, before the trio convened with Pixies producer Gil Norton in Hollywood and hit that previously elusive midpoint between hardcore roots rock and arena-sized pop. Omitted from the album because Grohl felt "We've done that already", what would have been the album's title track nonetheless turned into Foo Fighters' most invigorating B-side — the last time they kept Nirvana's shrieking aggression aflame. It was also the sole refugee from those Bear Creek sessions.

**'Colour My World'**
Chicago
COLUMBIA 1970
A-Side: 'Make Me Smile'

**Bach-inspired slowie that put Ol' Blue Eyes in a spin.**
Long before they became a saccharine staple of oldies radio stations, Chicago was on rock's cutting edge. Set apart from the pack by their integrated horn section and tricksy jazz rhythms, the ex-DePaul University music students boasted stronger chops than most as they blended outré styles into an affecting pop cocktail. They were ambitious too, launching their career with two fusion-heavy double albums. Lifted from 1970's second self-titled LP, both sides of this breakthrough single came from trombonist James Panko's 13-minute suite 'Ballet For A Girl In Buchannon', inspired by Bach's *Brandenburg Concertos*. Unlike the sunny upbeat pop of 'Make Me Smile' — their first Top 10 US hit — 'Colour My World' was a slow piano shuffle that allowed the soulful voice of guitarist Terry Kath full reign on its single verse, Walter Parazaider's contrapuntal flute underlining his hopeful sentiments. As the years passed it became a 70s slow dance staple and Frank Sinatra even expressed an interest in recording it, on condition that it had an extra verse. "I thought about it, I called him back," revealed Pankow on talk show *The Chris Isaak Hour* in 2009, "and said 'I can't do

it'. It's like sewing another arm on your kid." Instead it became a B-side twice (backing 'Beginnings' the following year) on a run that made Chicago America's second most successful rock band ever after the Beach Boys, according to *Billboard* chart stats.

### 'The Coo Coo Bird'

Clarence Ashley
COLUMBIA 1929
A-Side: 'Dark Holler Blues'

**Yearning English folk given dark Appalachian twist.**

Before he lapped up the generous applause of the 60s folk revival, Clarence Ashley trod a lonelier path. The hell-raising Tennessee performer started playing banjo at eight, absorbing the Appalachian folk songs and ballads that would sprint him around the States in the 20s and 30s as part of travelling medicine shows. After an early foray into the hillbilly recording business as one third of Blue Ridge Mountain Entertainers (alongside mouth organist Garley Foster and fiddler Clarence Horton Greene), Columbia's Frank Walker (star-spotter of Hank Williams and Bessie Smith) persuaded him to sign solo terms in 1929. It yielded a two-track single defined by Ashley's driving, insistent clawhammer skills. While the A-side's pledge to become a runaway groom has faded since it was cut in Johnson City in late 1929, his take on traditional English folk song 'The Cuckoo' resonated across the globe. Key to its appeal were the additional lyrics Ashley brought to the table, transforming it from a simple tale of lost love into a lament about gambling's ills. His flowing yet rhythmically complex banjo was off the scale too, containing a subtle metrical shift — that swapped between 4/4 and 2/4 time in its 'bird call' section — that made it technically challenging to replicate. His B-side's popularity was assured when Harry Smith preserved it on 1952's *Anthology of American Folk Music*.

### ''Cos You Like To Love Me'

The Hollies
PARLOPHONE 1969
A-Side: 'He Ain't Heavy, He's My Brother'

**Guitarist's classy response to inter-band turbulence.**
As the Hollies matured as songwriters they developed a penchant for melodramatic numbers, without ever making the shift to a serious albums band. The moody Manchester outfit's singles rarely missed the mark though. And while Elton John dropped by to play keys on the sophisticated ballad A-side, helping it become a transatlantic smash (and a UK number 1, 19 years later, thanks to a Miller Lite TV ad featuring Jared Harris), it proved a relatively flimsy tourniquet around the gaping wound left by Graham Nash's defection (to Crosby, Stills & Nash). Fans who stayed true and flipped discovered one of the best in the Hollies' rather patchy B-side history, as guitarist Tony Hicks finally showed some writing mettle. Introduced by Bobby Elliott's snare shuffle and Allan Clarke's catchy harmonica riff, its swirling fairground organ and clipped verses all led up to a compulsive chorus, whose prominent three-way plea for harmony harked right back to Merseybeat's golden age. Add in Bernie Calvert's middle eight harmonium solo and it was an A-side worthy gem.

**'Crazyman Dance'**
George Michael
EPIC 1992
A-Side: 'Too Funky'

**Doomed pop star's last fling with the dancefloor.**
This single marked the end of an era for a defining 80s star. Written as George Michael started gathering material to follow-up 1987's *Faith* — a colossal US success that more than vindicated his decision to close the early Wham! chapter on his career — he put both songs aside as the perils of fame and his turbulent personal life became the focus of *Listen Without Prejudice Vol 1*, a heavy-handed set that drew much critical hawing about self-indulgence. Issued instead as a stand-alone single to raise money for Aids charities, 'Too Funky' flirted with the dominant new jack swing sound, while 'Crazyman Dance' transported Michael completely out of his comfort zone. A strange tale of an alien trying and failing to make his mark in New York, spun out over wheezing synthesised strings, it was one of the few solo tracks where Michael seemed to be having a ball. It was also his last release before he instigated legal action against Sony — a costly battle whose failure further impacted on his fragile state of mind.

## 'Crossing Over'

Van Halen
WARNER BROS 1995
A-Side: 'Can't Stop Lovin' You'

**Metal titans in unusually introspective mode.**

The suicide of a close friend inspired the only non-album B-side in Van Halen's 12-album career. Guitarist Eddie Van Halen first demoed his darkest, most emotionally raw song, 'David's Tune', in the early 80s, handling all its instruments and laying down some grief-stricken scratch lyrics. He had no plans to release it. Yet when arena rock veteran Sammy Hagar first heard the demo — days after he replaced David Lee Roth in 1985 — he was eager to flesh it out. Van Halen rejected the invitation, feeling it cut too close to the bone. He finally relented after their manager Ed Leffler died of cancer in 1993 and Hagar penned a thoughtful lyric that also touched on his father's passing. Despite being fully updated for their 10th studio LP *Balance* — the original demo version playing on the left channel, the reworked version on the right — the guitarist cut it from the final tracklisting (favouring 'Amsterdam' instead). When it surfaced as an uncredited bonus track on the album's Japanese edition, fan demand persuaded Van Halen to add it to the CD single of 'Can't Stop Lovin' You'.

## 'Crown Of Worms'

Megadeth
CAPITOL 1994
A-Side: 'Train Of Consequences'

**When two eras of metal collide...**

Midlands marauders Diamond Head had a seismic influence on US thrash metal. To many a lesser known part of the New Wave Of British Heavy Metal (NWOBHM) movement, the raw edges of 1980's seven-track debut *Lightning To The Nations* spread almost imperceptibly across the ocean. Its ability to bridge old school hard rock sounds with more gnarly punk influences would inspire no less than four cover versions from Los Angeles thrash leaders Metallica — 'Helpless', 'The Prince', 'It's Electric' and 'Am I Evil?' — the latter (B-side of 1984's 'Creeping Death') becoming a key staple of their live sets. Yet Megadeth singer and guitarist Dave Mustaine went one better than his old bandmates, co-writing the B-side to the urgent jackhammer riffing of 'Train Of Consequences' alongside their Robert Plant-inspired singer Sean Harris. Recorded with Megadeth's classic line-up — bassist Dave Ellefson, lead guitarist Marty Friedman, drummer Nick Menza — the stripped-back sound of 'Crown Of Worms' was curled around a crisp riff that could have been lifted straight from Diamond Head's debut, with Mustaine's dark vocals snarling through the signature murk. The pair have enjoyed a close friendship since, with Mustaine's management company Thrashville adding Diamond Head to their roster in 2017.

### 'Cry Myself To Sleep'

Steve Earle
EPIC 1984
A-Side: 'What'll You Do About Me?'

**Future country star tries to crack the chart code.**

Although he would prove one of the greatest country rock singer-songwriters of his generation, Steve Earle went down the covers route to try and score an early hit. The jobbing Nashville songwriter had placed material with Johnny Lee and Carl Perkins when he signed to Epic, recording a straight-up roots rockabilly LP that they put straight on ice when its first two singles flopped. In desperation he turned to producer Emory Gordy Jr, the pair rustling up a menacing cover of Dennis Linde's obsessive stalker tale 'What'll You Do About Me?' for his next A-side. Although its B-side was another cover, this time written by Paul Kennerly, 'Cry Myself To Sleep' chimed much closer with Earle's own tales of hardship, showing off the full gamut of his battle-scarred emotional range. And while it stalled at a lowly number 76 on the country charts, it was the first hint of how he would fare when he was co-opted into the 'new traditional' country movement. His version also brought it to the attention of Kentucky mother/daughter duo the Judds, who made it a country number 1 just two years later.

### 'Cuban Slide'

The Pretenders
REAL 1980
A-Side: 'Talk Of The Town'

**New wavers' show of group strength.**

On 'Mystery Achievement', the last track of the Pretenders' self-titled debut, singer Chrissie Hynde sang of wanting to "do the Cuban slide". But what was it? A dance? A drink? Some arcane sexual peccadillo? Fans had to wait for the centrepiece single from their second album to find out. They were rewarded with a firing testament to their first line-up's definitive dynamic: Martin Chambers powering out a reverb-laden Bo Diddley beat below Pete Farndon's driving staccato bass while James Honeyman-Scott showed off his full bag of FX-laden tricks and suspended chords, thrashing dear life from his electric guitar. Above it all sat Hynde's cool lyric about having two left feet as they carefully evoked a Cuban dance feel without quite descending into all-out pastiche. The song also concealed a brief but telling homage to the Who, Honeyman-Scott firing off power chords in its closing minute that replicated the opening bars of 'Pinball Wizard'. Its louche looseness ensured it became a Pretenders live favourite in the short touring season before Farndon and Honeyman-Scott's tragic deaths.

**'Cuckoo'**

Billy Connolly

POLYDOR 1975

A-Side: 'D.I.V.O.R.C.E.'

**Sleight of hand tale of a Glasgow goldfish.**

A highly risqué joke about a man who had murdered his wife and used her corpse as a bicycle stand was the unlikely making of Billy Connolly. The naturally comedic Glaswegian all-rounder, an ex-worker on Clyde's shipyards, first tried his hand as a folk singer, teaming up with Gerry Rafferty in mid-60s troupe the Humblebums. A decade later his ear for comedy and easy popular touch took him onto Michael Parkinson's Saturday night chat show, the place he shared *that* joke and became an institution. Connolly's stand-up skills didn't always translate into the recording studio, however, as the A-side's rewrite of Tammy Wynette's tale of marital break-up proved, even if it briefly topped the UK charts before Queen's 'Bohemian Rhapsody' took over. His cover of traditional English folk song 'The Cuckoo' [see also: Clarence Ashley's 'The Coo Coo Bird'] was another matter entirely, spotlighting the Big Yin's estimable banjo skills. After he played it straight on the first two verses, Connolly unexpectedly turned it into a tribute to

Glasgow's animal kingdom, as he took one simple comic device and exploited it to the maximum.

**'Cut Across Shorty'**
Eddie Cochran
LIBERTY 1960
A-Side: 'Three Steps To Heaven'

**Fatal car crash changes everything.**

The last song Eddie Cochran ever recorded, 'Cut Across Shorty' was easily on par with his biggest hits and destined to join them as his next single. The Minnesota maverick proved himself a gifted singer, guitarist, songwriter, producer and arranger, having knocked off three of the new style's most recognised singles ('Summertime Blues', 'Somethin' Else' and 'C'mon Everybody') by the time he was 21. And although it wasn't a Cochran original, this quickfire tale of two paramours battling to woo the mysterious Miss Lucy chimed with the times, its building verse topped by a snare-smashing chorus that seemed certain to bash its way into teenage hearts. Cochran had just finished a lengthy and triumphant UK tour when the taxi he and Gene Vincent were in spun out of control in Chippenham and hit a lamppost, the impact throwing Cochran onto the road. Unlike his fellow passengers, he never regained consciousness. Cochran was dying in intensive care when his tour manager Patrick Thompkins told reporters that his final single would be his doo-wop leaning tale of ascension to the pearly gates, 'Three Steps to Heaven', first earmarked as the flip of 'Cut Across Shorty'. It was a cynical final throw of the pop dice, perhaps, but also an inspired one, rewarded with a posthumous UK number 1.

# DUB B GOOD TO ME

*How a Jamaican revolution in sound changed the B-side game forever...*

The seven-inch single was always the main focus of the Jamaican music industry. A country that pressed far more 45s than any other territory — between 1962 and 1982, over 45,000 songs were released on Jamaican singles alone — the industry's hunger for material was seemingly insatiable. The emergence of dub helped assuage that need.

Pioneered by studio engineer King Tubby, after he was hired by Duke Reid to create instrumental versions of his rocksteady hits, by the early 70s the infamous dubplates at Tubby's Hometown Hi-Fi soundsystem were in hot demand as fans flocked to hear his one-off pressings. By using the mixing board in a whole new way, Tubby turned vocals into an instrument that was in complex interplay with the other musical parts, creating a deconstructed sonic puzzle — the dub version — that drew equal attention to the space between sounds as the sounds themselves. Soon Jamaica's greatest producers were all queuing up for Tubby to remix their masters.

Singles with a dub B-side (sometimes labelled 'Version') quickly became the norm. Not only did it please label bosses, obviating the need to come up with more than one original track per single, these dubs often became more popular than the A-sides, especially when played through towering speaker stacks at street parties, churches and dancehalls. As innovative producers such as Niney The Observer, Prince Jammy, Augustus Pablo and Lee 'Scratch' Perry built on Tubby's template — retooling their drum and bass-heavy creations with reverb, echo, flange and whatever effects were to hand — this B-side innovation not only begat a whole new genre, it invented the modern remix along the way.

Widely regarded as the very first dub B-side, the **Hippie Boys' 'Voo-Doo'** [Little Roy: 'Hard Fighter', BIG SHOT 1971] found mixer Lynford Anderson taking his sonic spanner to roots singer Little Roy's organ-dominated tale of perseverance, showing off his backing band's instrumental chops. Relatively tame by later dub standards, his versatile crew of core players (Alva 'Reggie' Lewis, Ronnie 'Ranny Bop' Williams Glen Adams, Aston Barrett and Carlton Barrett) would make further dub waves on productions with Bunny Lee, Joe Gibbs and Lee 'Scratch' Perry.

Augustus Pablo's inspired melodica melody on **Herman**'s **'River Nile Version'** ['East Of The River Nile', BIG SHOT 1971] helped both sides of the single become hits. A self-taught instrumentalist who also paid his dues as a session keyboardist, Pablo's intervention rode a bare bones rhythm rack knocked up by Lee 'Scratch' Perry's the Upsetters for producer Herman Chin-Loy. Not only did it make the plastic melodica (considered, by many, just a kid's toy) into a viable lead instrument with a haunting reach, it raised the dub instrumental to another level.

Widely known as 'the Originator' for being the first DJ to bring soundsystem toasting into the studio, **U-Roy** set the ground rules for all deejays to follow. His energetically bonkers vocal skills on **'Wet Version'** [Horace Andy: 'Where Is The Love', BIG SHOT 1972], a Bunny Lee-produced cover of Max Romeo's 'Wet Dream', boasted such playful energy that they all but obliterated the original's dark sexual undertones.

Raised in poverty in western Kingston, Yabby You was still known as Vivian Jackson when he experienced a visitation from angels singing "Be you, yabby yabby you". Compelled to get the melody on wax but lacking sufficient funds, the dreadlocked singer (named 'Jesus Dread' due to his Christianity) not only persuaded guitarist Earl 'Chinna' Smith, bassist Aston 'Family Man' Barrett and drummer Leroy 'Horsemouth' Wallace to be his backing band for free, but got King Tubby to remix the resulting **Vivian Jackson & the Ralph Brothers**' single ['Conquering Lion', NOW 1972]. Tubby's distinctive mitts are all over the superior **'Conquering Lion Version'** (and nearly every Yabby You single afterwards) accentuating its unusual rhythm (later repurposed again by Big Youth, Scotty, Augustus Pablo and Dicky Burton, among others).

Frequently overlooked next to King Tubby and Lee 'Scratch' Perry, **Keith**

**Hudson**'s talents as a producer were often obscured by his raspy vocal aspirations — he saw himself as a singer first and foremost. Off-the-map in the nicest possible way, **'No More Dogging (Version)'** ['No More Dogging', MAFIA 1972] gave just a crucial hint of his prowess on the boards (notably in its rhythmic click of guitars) prior to his maniacal mix-desk manipulation of Soul Syndicate to create 1974's beautifully austere long-form dub standard *Pick A Dub*.

Nicknamed 'Nine' after losing a thumb in a workshop accident, the largely unsung Niney the Observer had a gift for producing grassroots records that tapped into the harsh realities of Jamaica life. Issued under the alias **Niney All Stars**, **'Dub Stairs'** [Delroy Wilson & Niney All Stars: 'Half Way Up the Stairs', OBSERVER 1974] fully reimagined Delroy Wilson's soul-dipped cover of Sixto Rodriguez' original, Niney's merciless brass-tacks mix honing in on its propulsive bassline and slick guitar lick.

The stage name of Winston Rodney, **Burning Spear**'s stirring, plaintive voice became best known for extolling the teachings of black unity campaigner Marcus Garvey and his Pan-Africanism movement. Originally designed for soundsystem play only, **'Marcus Garvey (Version)'** ['Marcus Garvey', FOX 1974] became a word-of-mouth success that cut through to the masses thanks to its dub's spare orchestrations, marshalled by Rodney's producer Jack Ruby. Despite his UK label Island tampering with the mix to make it more palatable for white ears, it became a cornerstone of both the roots and dub movements.

For definitive proof that King Tubby played his four-track Dynamic mixing board like an instrument itself, look no further than his uncredited turn on **'Tubby's Vengeance'** [Vivian Jackson & The Sons of Jah: 'Jah Vengeance', MICRON MUSIC LIMITED 1975], his minimal mastery of its echoey horns and ethereal treatment of Yabby You's soulful vocal sounding heavier than a herd of rampaging elephants. Constantly evolving, there seemed no limit to where Tubby could have gone before he was assassinated outside his Kingston flat in 1989.

A name given to whichever session musicians cavalier Jamaican producer Bunny Lee was using at any given time, the **Aggrovators**' lack of a stable line-up didn't stop them establishing a depth-charged signature sound. And while the heavy tones of **'Politician Version'** [Barry Brown: 'Politician', JACKPOT 1975] kept some of Barry Brown's serious lyrics in place, it also gave a hint of what was to come via the superlative bass stylings of the young Robbie Shakespeare.

Shakespeare was in thunderous form again in one the heaviest dubs ever, the **Revolutionaries**' **'Kunte Kinte (Version 2)'** ['Kunte Kinte', CHANNEL 1 1976]. A song that established a style that has resonated throughout dub ever since, with its captivating synth line (later sampled for the Prodigy's 'Jericho') supported by Sly Dunbar's shifting hi-hats and textured percussion. It was memorably used as a masculine call to arms in *Lovers Rock*, the highlight of director Steve McQueen's 2020 *Small Axe* TV series for the BBC.

Lee 'Scratch' Perry wouldn't have become the mad visionary of legend had he not strayed far beyond genre boundaries imposed on him. Perry's talent for manipulating sound was perfectly demonstrated by the deep swampy feel of 'War In A Babylon (It Sipple Out Deh)' [UPSETTERS, 1976], a compelling roots reggae protest song as Max Romeo's powerful voice warned of a slippery society under siege. His band the **Upsetters** flipped it towards oblivion on **'Revelation Dub'**, chopping up the chorus to make it feel more ominous than ever.

Perry's often fractious relationship with his UK label Island started to hit serious rocks in the mid-70s. It all came to a head when Island summarily rejected the Congos' 1977 debut LP *Heart Of The Congos* — now widely regarded as a reggae masterpiece — simply due to his prolificacy. The visionary owner of Black Ark studios was so peeved he refused to even offer them the first single from the **Jolly Brothers** — a non-sibling vocal group from Saint Catherine — licencing it to a new United Artists subsidiary instead. **'Conscious Dub'** ['Conscious Man', BALLISTIC 1977]

retained the singers' sugar-sweet harmonies while drawing the instrumentation into sharper focus, revealing yet another side of Perry's idiosyncratic style.

Responsible for over 100 Jamaican number 1 hits, Joe Gibbs and Errol Thompson's formidable partnership as the **Mighty Two** witnessed them work with the island's biggest artists and a slew of its ever-changing labels. **'Two Sevens Clash (Version)'** [Culture: 'Two Sevens Clash', JOE GIBBS RECORD GLOBE 1977] proved their most influential dub outing, emphasising the spacey bassline of an unmistakable party-starter that found particular resonance with UK punks.

A critical link in the chain and one-time apprentice engineer at King Tubby's studio, Scientist took the art of dub to further creative heights when he was finally given the chance to do more than just repair amplifiers and televisions in Tubby's workshop. That was vividly evident on **Barrington Levy**'s **'Collie Weed (Version)'** ['Collie Weed', ROOTS FROM THE YARD 1979]. On his first ever dub mix Scientist accentuated the Roots Radics' harsh snare pattern and tinkling refrains, its huge success ensuring a regular berth at the mixing console.

Dancehall duo **Papa Michigan & General Smiley**'s fluid call-and-response style on 1980's first LP *Rub A Dub Style* revealed a particular prowess for over-dubbing Studio One classics. **'Dub-Down'** ['One Love Jam Down', 56 HOPE ROAD 1980] stripped the A-side's warm salutation to reggae's cross-cultural power right back to its deep throbbing pulse, creating a sonorous dub masterpiece along the way.

Ranked by many as the world's finest rhythm section, **Sly & Robbie** backed everyone from Grace Jones and Serge Gainsbourg to Bob Dylan, Black Uhuru and Gregory Isaacs, becoming one of dub's most visible success stories. The insistent, driving bass riff of **'Dub Boom'** [Ranking Dread: 'Fattie Boom Boom', GREENSLEEVES 1981] saw the duo essentially making a little go a very long way, showing just how addictive three notes and some cleverly patterned percussion can be in the correct hands.

One of Jamaica's most in-demand vocalists, **Johnny Osbourne**'s warm and

yearning tones helped make him a 70s reggae sensation. After exiling himself to work with Toronto's Ishan People, he made a successful return to home turf, racking up persuasive hit after persuasive hit. However, Osbourne was essentially absent from **'Back Off (Version)'** ['Back Off', THOMPSON SOUND 1981], allowing the Roots Radics' mighty riddim to take centre stage above the lightest of touches from producer Scientist. The uncredited King Tubby took a similar approach to **Jah Thomas' 'Walking Dub'** ['Walk And Skank', WITTY 1982], again instrumentalised by the Roots Radics, but this time majoring on a weaving flute solo.

**Prince Jammy** would make the transition to a king of dub. Another Tubby protégé, the one-time apprentice mixer from Montego Bay proved his perceptive grasp of the form with his chilling version of Junior Reid's 'Jailhouse' [JAMMY'S 1982] — a track detailing the unchecked police brutality rife on the island. **'Jailhouse (Version)'** swathed Reid's tones in deep echo, underlining its serious protest by maxing out its haunted organ refrain. Jammy would further reassert his musical importance three years later, thrusting Jamaica headlong into the new 'digital' age with Wayne Smith's 'Under Me Sleng Teng'.

Reggae's most widely known and revered performer, **Bob Marley** needs little introduction. Co-written with Lee 'Scratch' Perry in the 70s, 'Black Man Redemption' [TUFF GONG 1985] was a quality demo that was given a decent spit and polish (with added vocals from the I-Threes) when Island set about gathering material for 1983's posthumous album 'Confrontation'. Stripped of Marley's spiritual sustenance, its languid dub reading **'Black Man Redemption (Version)'** reasserted just how powerful his band the Wailers truly were.

**Cocoa Tea** married his smooth, easy-going vocal style to conscious lyrics that had a clear antecedent in Marley. As the 90s drew to a close he tapped right into the era's Rasta renaissance on 'Burn Satan' [XTERMINATOR 1998]. And although producer Philip 'Fatis' Burrell's musically complex yet blistering digital dub skills on **'Burn Satan**

**(Version)'** obliterated its heartfelt anti-New World Order sentiments, they helped revive a genre that, due to a paucity of new voices, had started to fall into serious decline.

While that was true in reggae, the dub pioneers' wholesale reinvention of how a recording studio worked was being applied almost willy-nilly in mainstream pop circles with everything from Ray Parker Jnr's 'Ghostbusters Theme' (1984) and Robin Gibb's 'Boys Do Fall In Love' (1984) to David Bowie's 'Absolute Beginners' (1986), Mick Jagger's 'Lucky in Love' (1986) and Fleetwood Mac's 'Little Lies' (1987) being refitted with a 'dub' B-side.

Dub's influence extended to booze-soused Scotland/Surrey folk singer **John Martyn**, forever treading a fine line between triumph and disaster after he started adding jazz and electronics to his music in the 70s. While Island boss Chris Blackwell's bright idea of pairing him with Lee 'Scratch' Perry for 1977's seventh studio LP *One World* was the source of his greatest dub moment — the phase-shifting, Echoplex-washed 'Smiling Stranger' — the combination of two wayward characters inevitably proved combustible ("In certain Jamaican recording studios the very mention of John Martyn's name would scare staff and locals," Blackwell later told *The Financial Times*). Martyn certainly applied Perry's teachings to **'Johnny Too Bad (Version)'** ['Johnny Too Bad', ISLAND 1980] fully inverting his cover of the Slickers' 1970 standard, his guitar histrionics at sea amid an echo-fest of backwards drums, ghostly horns and queasy backing vocals.

Dub even reverberated into the mix as the BBC spun-off a soft reggae single ['Reggae Rita', BBC 1984] from Children's TV show *Play Away*, starring its benevolent Trinidadian-British presenter Floella Benjamin. Credited to **Dr Dread Gosling** — in effect *Play Away* arranger and future Ed Sheeran collaborator Peter Gosling — **'Reggae Rita (Dub Version)'** was somewhat slight by the heavy-heavy standards most dub fans insisted on, but nonetheless excited a 2019 cover by UB51.

Having set out their stall and mined an all-time goth standard with 1979's first single 'Bela Lugosi's Dead' — whose echoing drums, bassline and effects betrayed an obvious debt to dub — **Bauhaus** made their affinity with the form explicit on their final 45. **'Here's The Dub (Special Effects By 'Loonatik &**

**Drinks')'** ['She's In Parties', BEGGARS BANQUET 1983] set about separating out its hit A-side's component elements before letting David J's weaving bassline, Daniel Ash's jagged guitar and haunting melodica figure (a nod to Augustus Pablo?) shine through.

If John Robie's mega-buffed, over-produced remix of *Low-Life* highlight 'Sub-Culture' [FACTORY 1985] was a divisive single to many **New Order** fans, it was particularly so for their designer Peter Saville, who hated it so much he refused to design its sleeve (possibly saving Factory money for the first time in his career). Its dub re-rereading **'Dub-Vulture'** undoubtedly improved on the A, separating out the bassline, beat and backing singers to accentuate its arpeggiated synth hook and overriding mood of gothic grandeur. New Order would make a feature of the dub remix afterwards as 'Bizarre Dub Triangle' ['Bizarre Love Triangle', 1986], 'True Dub' ['True Faith', 1987] and 'Touched By The Hand Of Dub' ['Touched By The Hand Of God', 1987] all attest.

Proof that many pop dub mixes were not really dub mixes at all, just lazily tinkered with filler instrumentals, was epitomised by **'Hot Girl (Dub Version)'** ['Hot Girl', CHIC 1988]. The latest failed attempt to sustain the early career of Italian disco siren **Sabrina**, she danced to it so enthusiastically on Spanish TV show *Nochevieja* that her breasts wriggled free, echoing the early controversy around her first hit 'Boys (Summertime Love)'.

Despite that crushing low, most modern techno, grime, house and dubstep tunes still customarily arrive with a dub version of some kind. And even if their creators haven't clocked the fact, they all owe Jamaica their dues.

## 'Daddy Cool'

The Rays
XYZ 1957
A-Side: 'Silhouettes'

**Deathless doo-wop ditty.**

Brooklyn vocal quartet the Rays were about to call it quits when they scored their all-defining hit. Formed by ex-Four Fellows singers Harold Miller and Walter Ford alongside Davey Jones and Harry James, they forged a working friendship with the songwriting/production partnership of Frank Slay and Bob Crewe, even though 1955's first single 'Tippity Top' vanished without trace. Two years later, down on their luck, they auditioned for Philadelphia's Cameo label. Rejected on the spot, they were seconds away from splitting when Clay — a Cameo employee by day — chased after them and begged them to sign to his and Crewe's new XYZ label instead. And while next single 'My Steady Girl' also flopped, heads turned to its sequel 'Silhouettes', a slow-paced doo-wop story-song with a clever twist, written by Crewe after he spied the shadow of two lovers in a passionate embrace from a train window. After being played by Dick Clark on his *American Bandstand*, XYZ was flooded with more orders than they could handle, so Cameo signed the group they had just rejected and watched them shadow-box into the US Top 3 (and inspire the Beatles' 'No Reply'). Unusually, the single's B-side also received heavy airplay. With its cool jive lyrics and call-and-response chorus, 'Daddy Cool' developed a cult unto itself, becoming an A-side hit for Australian novelty act Drummond in 1971 and UK rock 'n' roll revivalists Darts in 1977.

## 'Daddy Rollin' (In Your Arms)'

Dion
LAURIE 1968
A-Side: 'Abraham, Martin And John'

**Idiosyncratic New Yorker's haunted masterpiece.**

Dion rose to fame in the late 50s as the leader of the Belmonts, fronting both the sugar-coated doo-wop of 'A Teenager In Love' and strutting street anthem 'The Wanderer'. When the hits dried up in the early 60s, the New Yorker started gradually pushing his music towards blues and folk, all the while battling a debilitating heroin addiction. That was behind him when he staged a chart comeback with 'Abraham, Martin And John', a mellifluous celebration of the lives of presidents Lincoln, King and Kennedy that returned him to the US Top 10. Its off-the-cuff B-side was a different ball game altogether, showcasing a sound more reflective of the uncertain times. Recorded in the back of a bowling alley with percussion banged out on cardboard boxes, its churning blues riff and wiry lead guitars were more redolent of a Velvet Underground demo. While Dion ambiguously noted "it can be a love song or it can be about drugs" in the liner notes of 2000's career retrospective *King Of The New York Streets*, it represented a different, edgier side of the singer, wholly at odds with his clean-cut public image.

**'Dancin' Wild'**
Tom & Jerry
BIG 1957
A-Side: 'Hey, Schoolgirl'

**Simon & Garfunkel — the plucky teenage years.**
It wasn't long after Paul Simon and Artie Garfunkel bonded over their passion for rock 'n' roll that they started making their own. One afternoon, while trying to recall the words to the Everly Brothers' 'Hey Doll Baby', the Queens, New York high school seniors accidentally summoned their first single 'Hey Schoolgirl'. An instant party piece, they played it wherever they could and even tried to shop its Everly-esque harmonies and nonsense Little Richard nod ("Who-bop-a-loo-chi-bop!") to publishers on Tin Pan Alley. Their persistence paid off when they signed to Sid Prosen's Big imprint, adopting new stage names from MGM's cat and mouse cartoon when their own were deemed "too ethnic". After an alleged $200 bung to radio DJ Alan Freed and a payola slot on Dick Clark's TV show *American Bandstand*, the single jetted into the *Billboard* Top 50. And while B-side 'Dancin' Wild' was an equally infectious rug-cutter, its close harmonies hinted much more prophetically at what was to come. Despite the instant kudos of having a hit aged 16, Tom & Jerry's fortunes withered quickly, a series of follow-ups, solo efforts and pseudonymous recordings (Simon as True Taylor and Paul Kane; Garfunkel as Artie Garr) across several labels (Ember, King, Octavia, Tico, ABC-Paramount) failed to repeat the trick. Even when they hitched their wagon to the folk movement and recorded 1964's first album under their own name, *Wednesday Morning, 3AM*, the public initially proved indifferent.

**'Dante's Inferno'**
The Blues Magoos
MERCURY 1967
A-Side: 'One By One'

**One hit wonders drill into the fires below.**

By 1967 the Blues Magoos were doing things their fans were completely unprepared for. Long-term fixtures on the Greenwich Village club scene, with a residency at the Night Owl, the gritty New Yorkers tempered the roughness of their blues-inspired sound with natty suits that lit up onstage as they dodged between out-sized lava lamps. Marketed to rival the rise of San Francisco's flower power psychedelic scene, 1966's debut *Psychedelic Lollipop* barely lived up to its title, revealing a more than competent, bluesy garage band until they broke loose with a raucous take on John D. Loudermilk's 'Tobacco Road' featuring a full-on psych freak-out in the middle. It also concealed a Top 5 hit in '(We Ain't Got) Nothing Yet' that they were desperate to replicate on 'One By One' — a jaunty confection riddled with ringing guitars, Farfisa organs and sugary harmonies. Its B-side was off-the-scale and easily one of the most experimental offerings of the time. Stung by the chart fallout of radio DJs flipping their previous single 'Pipe Dream' for 'There's A Chance We Can Make It', they ensured there would be no repeat with 'Dante's Inferno'. A free-form, beat-less, avant-garde freak-out of heavy organ bursts and feedbacking guitars played through a broken Echoplex pedal, riven with unearthly groans, screams and whoops, it effectively summoned the hellish underworld of its title. Pink Floyd would attempt something very similar with 'Take Up Thy Stethoscope And Walk'.

### 'Date With The Blues'

Billy Williams
CORAL 1957
A-Side: 'I'm Gonna Sit Right Down And Write Myself A Letter'

**Smooth-tongued tale of terminal heartbreak.**

Billy Williams was much more than the "number 1 fool who loved and lost" portrayed on his most slinky B-side. The Texan-born pastor's son studied theology at Wilberforce University, but left mid-degree to lead the Charioteers and then the Billy Williams Quartet — a vocal foursome that enjoyed multiple turns on Sid Caesar's variety TV special *Your Show Of Shows*. Hits constantly eluded him until he worked with arranger Dick Jacobs on a gold-selling revival of Fats Waller's 30s smash 'I'm Gonna Sit Right Down And Write Myself A Letter', detailed with a stuttering trumpet refrain and crooning backing vocals. The same singers backed up its superlative, sad-eyed flip, its every quavering nuance conveying the deep hurt inside. Radio DJs also gravitated towards 'Date With The Blues', which charted on its own merits after featuring on Dick Clark's *American Bandstand* and became a staple of Elvis Presley's handpicked jukebox collection at Graceland. Williams tragically lost his singing career to diabetes in the early 60s and spent his final years helping alcoholics as a social worker.

**'Dear Father'**
Yes
ATLANTIC 1970
A-Side: 'Sweet Dreams'

**Nascent proggers caught between rock and a hard place.**
Yes survived where their progressive brethren faltered by continually pimping up their recipe. The London band that rose from the ashes of the British psychedelic scene not only had the serious intention of welding classical music with rock, they had the chops to do it. It took until second album *Time And A Word* for Yes to find the right balance between symphonic complexity and melodic ear candy, although not without much inter-band turmoil and, at times, all-out war with a producer (Tony Colton) not always considered up to snuff. The album's second single showed both sides of the divide, its A-side capturing them as close to live as possible, but shy of the adventurism they would soon be known for. By contrast 'Dear Father' was an urgent rocker that didn't hold back on pomp and circumstance. Centred around a searching Jon Anderson lyric about organised religion that seemed to flutter between acceptance and doubt before it concluded, with a hippy-ish shrug, "that's not where it's at." Its point was elaborately made over massed choirboy backing vocals and a full-on orchestral break that prompted a seemingly molten, maximum volume response from keyboardist Tony Kaye.

**'Dear God'**
XTC
VIRGIN 1986
A-Side: 'Grass'

**Existential B-side that became late controversial hit.**

Another tune aimed at the man upstairs, 'Dear God' was conceived at a time when XTC's chief songwriter Andy Partridge was wrestling "with the tail end of my belief". Recorded during troubled sessions for the Swindon band's 9th album, *Skylarking*, and inspired by a series of mawkish books filled with children's letters to a higher power, it started with a neat device — its opening verse voiced angelically by a child. It made Partridge's delivery even more resonant when he entered the folky refrain with a verse that queried the dichotomy between faith and self-delusion (ultimately concluding that God's words were created by man). Despite Todd Rundgren's rousing string arrangement and its easy melodic appeal, both band and label were hesitant about how its sceptical lyrics would play, and decided to excise it from the final album. Issued, without fanfare, on the back of Colin Mounding's hazy ode to alfresco love, 'Grass', US college radio stations soon made the atheist lament the main attraction. It proved so popular that Virgin were forced to retrofit it onto the LP, removing the charming yet lightweight 'Mermaid Smile'. While some stations received bomb threats from Christian evangelists for playing the song, the biggest headlines arrived when a Binghamton High School student forced a faculty member to play 'Dear God' over the school's PA at knife-point.

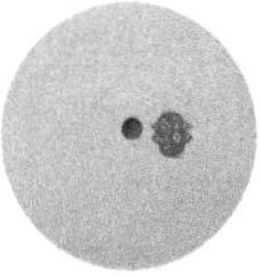

**'Debris Slide'**

Pavement

DRAG CITY 1990

'Perfect Sound Forever EP'

**Lo-fi Californians at primitive best.**

Not just one of the 90s most prolific B-Side acts, Pavement was one of the best. Before they embellished their gift for marrying memorable hooks with flurries of wild guitar punch on 1992's debut *Slanted & Enchanted*, songwriters Stephen Malkmus and Scott Kannberg's initially studio-based band was a much more primitive and ramshackle affair. One with a pronounced tendency for burying their most artful pop songs under a cavalcade of seething noise, sheeting distortion and wild shouting. 'Debris Slide' was a prime example. Part of a deliberately difficult and short seven-track EP recorded over two frantic days in late 1989, its sound bridged the Fall at their most wilfully obtuse with

Sonic Youth at their most snottily extreme. Yet somewhere amid its scatted repetitions of "wheeze hack cough" and "eyes in the socket", their melodic "ba-ba-bas" punched above the weight of its hissy production and rudimentary riffs. Awkwardly stupid Dada-esque fun, it drew the invaluable patronage of John Peel and more than held its own against their later material's more mannered flailing.

**'Deep Blue'**
George Harrison
APPLE 1971
A-Side: 'Bangla Desh'

**Deep down and personal with the 'Quiet Beatle'.**

Long before *Live Aid* was a glint in Bob Geldof's tear-stained eyes, ex-Beatle George answered his friend and mentor Ravi Shankar's plea to help raise awareness for the homeless Bengali refugees of the 1971 India-Pakistan war. His heartfelt stand-alone single 'Bangla Desh' was the starting-point for the same year's *Concert For Bangladesh* — a superstar charity event memorable for both the surprise appearance of Bob Dylan and the replaying of the A-side over documentary footage of the war. Recorded in Los Angeles, while pulling together arrangements for the show at New York's Madison Square Garden, the single's B-side was moving for a very different reason. It was written "one exhausted morning" the previous year, while Harrison was commuting between London and Liverpool to visit his mother, deteriorating in hospital with breast cancer. "It's filled with frustration and gloom," he told *Musician* magazine in 1987. "Not being able to do anything for suffering family or loved ones is an awful experience." Yet Harrison contrasted the undoubtedly devastating theme of 'Deep Blue' with upbeat chords and a stripped-down finger-picked melody that made its vocal all the more poignant. Among his warmest, most whimsical songs, it became a US jukebox favourite long after its A-side had fallen away and the benefit concert was forgotten. As with Paul McCartney, Harrison would sustain the Beatles' ethos for supplying quality B-sides throughout his solo career, whether it was his spontaneous ode to a friend's wife 'Miss Odell' ['Give Me Love...', 1973], emotive *Somewhere In America* offcut 'Lay His Head' ['Got My Mind Set On You', 1987] or the winding mystical instrumental 'Zig Zag' ['When We Was Fab', 1988].

## 'Deeper'

Orbital
OH'ZONE 1989
A-Side: 'Chime'

**"Listen to the sound of my voice and relax..."**

Best known as stadium-straddling techno giants, their shiny bald heads offset with torch-equipped spectacles, brothers Phil and Paul Hartnoll got their start making DIY music to beat the blues of their dead-end jobs. The brotherly duo, named after the M25 ring road that spun revellers to warehouse parties during the second summer of love, had a modest, minimal set-up — a four-track recorder, keyboards and drum machine clustered into a knocked-through stair cupboard in the family home. It was here, one balmy summer night, that they laid down 'Chime'. A 12-minute acid house anthem with a warm Detroit vibe, it cost its struggling creators just £3.75 to record (the price of a metal quality cassette tape) but would transport them to number 17 in the UK charts and straight onto *Top Of The Pops*, thanks to the intervention of pirate DJ Jazzy M and a licensing deal with FFRR's Pete Tong. If the A-side found them essentially making it up as they went along, to glorious effect, its hypnotising flipside 'Deeper' witnessed them rip a meditational guru's spoken words from one of their mum's relaxation CDs and have a trippy ball with it. Initially given AA status, the first pressing's original 15-minute version proved an acid sensation, the speaker's Bill Nighy-like invocations to relax balanced against the body moving exhortations of a squiggly Roland TB-303 bassline. Unlike the A-side it pointed to how Orbital's sound would develop in the very near future.

## 'The Delaney'

The Libertines
ROUGH TRADE 2002
A-Side: 'Up The Bracket'

**Music press darlings justify the hyperbole.**

The Libertines quickly created an enduring mythology. Celebrated as the 00s most important band by a weekly music press all but on its knees, the ever combustible pairing of songwriters Pete Doherty and Carl Barat made for plenty of brash, literate, arrogant, chaotic and funny column inches from joint frontmen who seemingly didn't care. The fact they could knock out great songs seemingly on a whim didn't hurt either, the tactical decision to employ ex-Clash man Mick Jones's ramshackle production creating an early volley of vibrant records mercifully free of corporate polish. Mysteriously issued only on the second CD single of 'Up The Bracket', 'The Delaney' was much better than most tracks on their debut album. Its opening salvo of riffs and joyful invitation to "Loop the loop on the old banjo" making it an early fan favourite that Doherty would retain for use with his next band Babyshambles. It also had the rare distinction of becoming a B-side twice. An explosive live version was tacked to the back of 2005's 'What Became Of The Likely Lads', a lament at the intra-band troubles that strained its creators' camaraderie.

## 'Diana'

Bryan Adams
A&M 1985
A-Side: 'Heaven'

**Canadian rocker lovestruck by 'People's Princes'.**

A lustful plea to Princess Diana, issued four years after she tied the knot to the Prince Of Wales, this B-side is an elephantine oddity in Bryan Adams' otherwise saccharine catalogue. Canada's pint-sized, pockmarked answer to Bruce Springsteen had been slogging it out supporting the likes of Loverboy, Journey and Foreigner before his third album *Cuts Like A Knife* made the critical incision. His crowning glory arrived with 1984's *Reckless*, a John Cougar Mellencamp-lite affair that defied critical pastings to sell over a million units in Canada and spawned no less than six hit singles. Among those was featherlight power ballad 'Heaven', a US number 1 written for widely panned rom-com *A Night In Heaven*. Chart buyers expecting more of the same were stunned by its rousing B-side paean to the "queen of all my dreams", Adams openly dissing Prince Charles and making his intentions explicit ("I just wanna lay ya!"). While the man that later took the Queen's portrait for a Canadian stamp maintained it was nothing more than a bit of light fun, his Bond girl partner Cecilie Thomsen demurred, and publicly claimed Adams did-the-do with the princess. Whatever the truth, the rollicking crowd-pleaser, issued as an A-side in Portugal, was retired from his repertoire forever after Diana's death in 1997.

## 'Did You No Wrong'

Sex Pistols

VIRGIN 1977

A-Side: 'God Save The Queen'

**Punk upsetters in rage-fuelled pomp.**

Amid the hype and hate, filth and fury, Sex Pistols cooked up some amazing songs. Effectively their Exhibit A, 'Did You No Wrong' harked back to their earliest incarnation as the Swankers in 1974, with music written by Wally Nightingale, who formed the band with his Christopher Wren schoolmates Steve Jones and Paul Cook in London's Shepherds Bush. Ousted shortly before they morphed into Sex Pistols, at manager Malcolm McLaren's insistence, Nightingale's legacy was a flat-out rock 'n' roll anthem whose bluesy riff cut through like an agitated take on David Bowie's 'Hang Onto Yourself'. Given a fresh lyrical coat of paint by incoming singer Johnny Rotten, it was as close to a love song as the group would manage, albeit one sustained by the controlled aggression of Jones' guitar. Its BBC-banned A-side, punk's national anthem, reputedly outsold any other single during the Queen's Silver Jubilee week, but was deliberately ousted from the top spot to avoid causing royal offence (Rod Stewart's 'I Don't Want To Talk About it' stood firm instead). As punk broke nationally Sex Pistols tossed off another trio of classic B-sides — a primal howl of individualism in 'I Wanna Be Me' ['Anarchy In The UK', 1976], a cover of the Stooges' 'No Fun' ['Pretty Vacant', 1977] and Rotten's parting rant about decaying suburbs, 'Satellite' ['Holidays In The Sun', 1977].

## 'Dinner With Drac'

John Zacherle

CAMEO 1957

A-Side: 'Igor'

**'The Cool Ghoul' fills the charts with gore.**

John Zacherle was an unlikely candidate for great ghouldom. A former World War II major, he was looking for a more relaxed profession when he started acting for TV stations in Philadelphia and New York, winding up as the linkman for WCAU's *Shock Theater* and introducing old Universal Studios horror films. Zacherle developed a spooky persona to amp up the drama, reciting horror-themed limericks from his crypt-like mad doctor's lab in a long black undertaker's coat, while interacting with freakish off-camera assistant Igor. His success prompted Cameo Records' head Bernie Lowe to entice him to record a single with house band Dave Appell and the Applejacks. Yet it was the B-side of his gruesome rockabilly tribute to 'Igor' that became Zacherle's signature tune. A comedic tale of a bloody vampire repast, 'Dinner With Drac' married Kal Mann's sick limericks about eating bat-wing confetti, pickled internal workings and mummy's veins above Appell's spindly guitar work. Christened 'The Cool Ghoul' by his TV colleague Dick Clark, the *American Bandstand* host considered Zacherle's B-side too scary for his teenage audience, prompting Cameo to re-record it, in two parts, for Zacherle's next single. Banned by the BBC, it devoured all competition in the States, eventually going Top 10. Despite strong stabs with 'Eighty-Two Tombstones', 'Dummy Doll' and 'I Was A Teen-Age Caveman', none of Zacherle's follow-ups had quite the same impact.

## 'Dirty Money'

Swing Out Sister
MERCURY 1986
A-Side: 'Breakout'

**The dark side of sophisticated pop.**

Swing Out Sister specialised in crafting credible chartbusters. Born from a chance meeting between A Certain Ratio keyboardist Andy Connell and Nottingham fashion designer/model Corinne Drewery at Manchester's Hacienda club, they added ex-Magazine drummer Martin Jackson and producer Paul Staveley O'Duffy to summon a blend of cinematic jazz pop distinguished by its use of real strings, horns and Drewery's distinctively throaty vocals. Those elements were in full communion on unashamedly commercial second single 'Breakout', whose infectious chorus helped it live up to its title on both sides of the pond. The soulful electro of its B-side 'Dirty Money' was more intriguing still. With its intertwined slap bass and dark electronic growls, it was much grittier than their usual stripe of sophisti-pop and matched the lyric's hesitant endorsement of doing whatever you needed in order to survive. It was Swing Out Sister at their complex best — as sharp as Drewery's precision fringe and much tighter than the retro-fixated loungy 60s fare they'd export to the Far East when western attentions dimmed.

## 'Disappointed'

Morrissey
HMV 1988
A-Side: 'Everyday Is Like Sunday'

**Ex-Smith pokes fun at fame.**

Morrissey moved fast to prove that he was a viable artist without Johnny Marr after the Smiths split in the summer of 1987. Having forged a new writing relationship with producer Stephen Street and musical foil in Durutti Column guitarist Vini Reilly, they hit the ground running with *Viva Hate*, a debut that discreetly blended synthesisers into Morrissey's traditionally jangly sound. A rousing tale of a rundown seaside town, 'Everyday Is Like Sunday' was one of its chief cheerleaders, yet a trio of robust 12-inch B-sides reaffirmed that there was still whole volumes of diaries for the singer to pillage. 'Disappointed' stood out from its fellow B-sides 'Sister I'm A Poet' and 'Will Never Marry' thanks to a juddering tremolo guitar figure that overtly nodded to the Smiths' best-known B-side 'How Soon Is Now'. Its pointed lyrics poked holes at Morrissey's rock star status, the singer sounding cheated that fame hadn't dramatically changed his life for the good as he had anticipated. It peaked with the dramatic announcement "This is the last song I will ever sing" to sampled sounds of wild celebration, before he denounced his retirement to a sea of groans. Morrissey reprised its fickleness of fame theme on another B-side, 'Get Off The Stage' ['Piccadilly Palare', 1990] — a biting denunciation of ageing rockers that he would naturally fail to heed.

## 'Disco Blisters And A Comedown'

Nicola Roberts
A&M 2011
A-Side: 'Beat Of My Drum'

**'Quiet' Girls Aloud member boasts the best tunes.**

The third member of Girls Aloud to launch a solo career, Nicola Roberts' extra-curricular activities marked her out as significantly flintier than her peers, as she tackled the perils of teenage tanning beds and launched a makeup range for girls with fair skin. The jerking synths and staccato beats of her Diplo-produced first single 'Beat Of My Drum' also drew a critical thumbs up, but proved arguably too leftfield for a swathe of Girls Aloud fans — it never made the Radio 1 playlist and stalled at number 27 in the UK charts. Anyone who failed to purchase its CD single also missed the pulsating electro-pop of its B-side 'Disco Blisters And A Comedown'. Every bit as enthralling as its title hinted, it saw the Cheshire chanteuse detail a very British weekend of drinking, clubbing, drinking and paying the price the morning after — its chorus capturing a sudden kebab shop realisation that her take-home quarry was not all he seemed (and more like hangdog MP John Prescott). As with much of Roberts' debut, *Cinderella's Eyes*, it was riven with knowing humour.

**'Do What You Gotta Do'**

Nina Simone

RCA VICTOR 1968

A-Side: 'Ain't Got No, I Got Life'

**Jazz singer's deepest, darkest blues.**

Nina Simone had a transformative effect on nearly every song she covered. Able to imbue a haunted quality that seemed to physically live through the song, the precocious North Carolina star was a 'freedom singer' in the truest sense, capable of bending any genre to her will. By the late 60s the civil rights activist was living in exile from America, disillusioned with its involvement in Vietnam and focussed on building up her European career. And while she scored a major UK chart hit with the A-side here — putting her indelible stamp on a protest medley from the musical *Hair* — it was the B-side's treatment of a Jimmy Webb number (first recorded by Johnny Rivers the previous year) that really hit the bullseye. While Simone retained its original arrangement, her delivery went several fathoms deeper, as she audibly bore the struggle of loving someone by letting them go. It was a stunning take that totally transformed Webb's paean to a free-spirited girl into a tragic hymn from a heartbroken woman, as she ushered her philandering partner out the door. It struck a deep chord with serial Simone sampler Kanye West, who got Rihanna to re-voice some parts for 2016's 'Famous' — a graphic treatise on celebrity idolisation.

## 'Doggin' Around'

Jackie Wilson

BRUNSWICK 1960

A-Side: 'Night'

**R&B showman at full tilt.**

Jackie Wilson had the vocal power of an operatic tenor. While the Detroit ex-welterweight boxer first showed his true talent in local churches, it was his rousing club performances alongside future Four Top Levi Stubbs that proved his destiny lay in the pop arena. Having more than impressed Elvis for his turns with Billy Ward and his Dominoes, by the late 50s he had several successes of his own including 'To Be Loved', 'Reet Petite' and the unstoppably sad 'Lonely Teardrops'. Maintaining that high watermark proved precarious and Wilson frequently risked falling into schmaltz with a string of singles overly reliant on female backing singers and fussy horn arrangements. He sounded as if he was desperately channelling Frankie Vaughan on 'Night', an operatic number adapted from a Samson and Delilah aria by Camille Saint-Saëns, yet long suffering fans found plenty of succour in its dramatically superior B-side. A dramatic piano-led blues about being the man left behind, 'Doggin' Around' reaffirmed Wilson's soul power as his great wailing lead pleaded with his straying partner to step back into line. It topped *Billboard*'s Hot R&B chart on its own merits.

## 'Don't Blame Me'

Ozzy Osbourne

EPIC ASSOCIATED 1991

A-Side: 'Mama, I'm Coming Home'

**Brummie bat-biter's biggest audible shrug.**

Ozzy Osbourne had every plan to retire, at the grand old age of 53, after touring 1991's 6th solo album *No More Tears*. The wild rocker's pension pot was boosted by the success of its second single 'Mama, I'm Coming Home', a melodic power ballad, co-written with Motörhead's Lemmy, that became his only Top 40 US hit. If that proved too sappy for some hardcore fans, its equally commercial yet hard-powered flip 'Don't Blame Me' was much more like it — thriving on the textured hard riffing of Zakk Wylde (on par with the late Randy Rhoads) and heavyweight percussion of Randy Castillo. As with the A-side's musings about escaping a toxic relationship, it found Osbourne in philosophical mode, contemplating his place in the universe and the next path to take. Osbourne clearly had a few cracks at it — another version, with different lyrics, appeared on the album's 2002 reissue — and used its title to frame 1991's career documentary. That attempt at a full stop floundered when reality TV ushered in new adventures.

**'Don't Look Back'**
The Temptations
GORDY 1965
A-Side: 'My Baby'

**Paul Williams shows his emotive force.**

The Temptations had become a well-oiled chart machine by the mid-60s. The Detroit quintet with the best shades, sharpest suits, finely tuned dance steps and most resonant vocal harmonies had forged a seemingly unbreakable partnership with songwriter Smokey Robinson that delivered smash after smash. Despite an outstanding lead from David Ruffin, 'My Baby' was one of the Temptations' weakest efforts, so it wasn't a total surprise when radio DJs started to flip the rare glitch in their hit matrix. They were rewarded with a high-stringed, emotive tour-de-force that more than made up for its A-side's failings. Written specifically for Paul William's gritty, gravelly baritone by Robinson, the band's original lead singer was already aware he faced diminishing opportunities to show off his chops. He called his doubters' bluff with a convincing turn that implored his hesitant, recently hurt would-be lover to let the past go, bolstered by the sound of his fellow Temptations in full harmonic flight. 'Don't Look Back' quickly became their regular show closer, Williams' bringing the house down as he strutted across stage to its "keep on walking" dictate. He put such an unmistakable stamp on it that the Temptations stopped playing it altogether after he left in 1971, ravaged by alcoholism. The only Temptations B-side to make the *Billboard* Hot 100, it was remade in reggae fashion by Peter Tosh and Mick Jagger in 1978.

## 'Don't You Pass Me By'

Cleo Laine
FONTANA 1965
A-Side: 'If We Live On Top Of A Mountain'

**British jazz's first lady in searing form.**

Cleo Laine quickly became the most recognisable UK jazz singer of her generation. Known for her formidable scat skills, the high cheek-boned stylist had tried her luck as a hairdresser, milliner, cobbler and bookseller before she unleashed her four-octave range in an audition for the Johnny Dankworth Seven in 1951. Seven years later she and Dankwork were married, the composer and saxophonist forever dreaming up fresh arrangements to match his wife's gilded lungs. After launching her solo career with 1964's *Shakespeare And All That Jazz* — a set that stitched the bard's verses to her husband's dashing arrangements — she began tackling more contemporary pop. Written by Doc Pomus with Mort Shuman, and first recorded by Patti Page in 1964, Laine's take on 'Don't You Pass Me By' was a sultry, genre-slippery one, with Dankworth's scintillating orchestration topped by a pained, longing delivery that resonated long after the needle had left the groove. Unlike its largely forgotten A-side, it enjoyed a lengthy second life on the northern soul scene.

## 'Don't Break This Rhythm'

Peter Gabriel
CHARISMA 1986
A-Side: 'Sledgehammer'

**Insight into ex-prog star's working methods.**

Having spent his prog-rock years dressing as a sunflower and pushing art-rock theatricality to the next level, Peter Gabriel spent the early stages of his solo career in a much darker place. Across a quartet of self-titled albums between 1977 and 1982 the ex-Genesis singer dropped the old bombast for shorter, more cryptic tunes that toyed with the possibilities afforded by sampling software. As critically lauded as they were, Gabriel hit on a whole new approach with 'Sledgehammer' — snaring his first US number 1 with an Otis Redding-inspired tribute to his penis. Built around a big beat, clever hook and a chain of not so subtle cock metaphors, the song owed much of its success to Stephen R.

Johnson's multi-*MTV* award winning video, as a stop-motion Gabriel consorted with plasticine dodgems, morphed into fruit and was serenaded by a pair of dancing headless chickens. The polyrhythmic rhythms and warped synth textures of its B-side 'Don't Break This Rhythm' made for an equally eccentric slab of user-friendly pop, albeit a less commercial one, that many fans favoured above the A-side. Effectively an early version of *So* album track 'Mercy Street' — its percussively dense instrumental slowed down and allied to a different melody — the link was initially far from obvious.

### 'Don't Make Promises'

The Union Gap featuring Gary Puckett
COLUMBIA 1967
A-Side: 'Woman, Woman'

**Transformative take on Tim Hardin folk tune.**

Gary Puckett had one of the most velveteen voices of late 60s pop. Yet the Minnesota singer that went to the same high school as Bob Dylan often wasted his gift on overly melodramatic ballads that alienated him from the in-crowd. While many of those tracks have aged as well as the Civil War togs his backing band wore during their late 60s heyday, the elaborately orchestrated power pop of A-side 'Woman, Woman' remains a million-selling exception. For its rarely heard B-side Puckett took a leaf from the Beau Brummels' book and covered the opening track from Tim Hardin's 1966 debut album, supplanting its simple folk sparseness with a brisk beat, horns, hypnotic bass and a typically rich, textured lead vocal. Neither ground-breaking nor particularly profound, it nonetheless transformed an introspective ode to decaying romance into a hip club toe-tapper that enjoyed its own brief chart run and a much longer life on the northern soul circuit.

### 'Don't Worry Baby'

The Beach Boys
CAPITOL 1964
A-Side: 'I Get Around'

**Ronettes' homage that surpassed the original.**

When he first heard the Ronettes' 'Be My Baby' on the radio, the Beach Boys' tortured songwriter Brian Wilson wondered aloud if he could match it. Wilson's ever supportive wife Marilyn reassured him that he could, with a gentle "Don't worry, baby". Wilson never forgot the exchange as he spent two days composing the music to lyrics KFWB-AM disc jockey Roger Christian had written with Phil Spector's elaborate production in mind. The similarities between the two were unmistakable. Written in the same key (E major) and effectively using the same rhythm, yet from its scene-setting first line ("Well it's been building up inside of me...") it was a much more unusual take on love — written from the perspective of an insecure and anxious man — with Wilson's vulnerable falsetto lead and buffering five-part harmonies easing the dislocation of its unexpected key change. Effectively a gift to the masses who bought into its A-side's celebration of pampered white Californian teenage life, Wilson rarely played one of his greatest creations live, ceding onstage performances to Al Jardine as he quit the road to try and save his mental health. It was not the last time the Beach Boys buried treasure on a B-side, they issued 'God Only Knows' — named by Paul McCartney as "the greatest song ever written" — on the back of 1966's 'Wouldn't It Be Nice'.

## 'Drowning In My Own Tears'

Simply Red
ELEKTRA 1985
A-Side: 'Holding Back The Years'

**Blue-eyed soul boys pay homage.**

Simply Red were often tarred as inauthentic soul music. As flame-haired flyers for the UK sophisti-pop movement (alongside ABC, Scritti Politti and Curiosity Killed The Cat) their sound was an *intended* hybrid — a buffed and polished, dancefloor-ready blend of jazz, R&B and pop. Nonetheless their most raw, authentic soulful work appeared on their B-sides — songs that didn't need the latest hi-tech fancy-dan production and let Mick Hucknall's unusually tender vocals do all the heavy lifting. This simple piano-led cover of Ray Charles' 1956 hit proved the point, Hucknall shifting through the emotional gears and sounding perversely happy to be so painfully wronged. It was a suitable contrast to an A-side that had arguably been rendered much better by Hucknall's first band Frantic Elevators three years earlier. Simply Red hit similarly sensitive soul cover highs when tackling Bill Withers' 'Grandma's Hands' ['Come To My Aid', 1985] and Cole Porter's 'Ev'ry Time We Say Goodbye' ['The Right Thing', 1986]. The latter even gained a rare promotion — from B-side to A-side — the following year.

### 'DWYCK'

Gang Starr
CHRYSALIS 1992
A-Side: 'Take It Personal'

**Golden age hip-hop party-starter.**

This single confirmed Gang Starr's status as one of the golden age's greatest acts. While the A-side portrayed the classic MC/DJ duo of Guru and DJ Premier as staunch defenders of the rap cause over robust skull-snapping beats and a spare Johnny Nash piano sample, its B-side duet with Bronx ballers Nice & Smooth really shook the foundations. Stripped back to just drums and bassline, 'DWYCK' (an acronym for 'Do What You Can Kid') allowed Greg Nice, Smooth B and Guru to show their off their contrasting lyrical skills unfettered, with Premier displaying his sparse turntable mastery between verses. Despite being heard from cars the breadth of New York City and the instrumental *du jour* for emerging ciphers, Gang Starr's attempt to retro-fit it to their *Daily Operation* LP was thwarted by their label. Its title was later resurrected for the ninth episode of Marvel TV series *Luke Cage* in 2016, which made its debt explicit by including Guru's enigmatic lyric "Lemonade was a popular drink and it still is" in its script.

### 'Early 1970'

Ringo Starr
APPLE 1971
A-Side: 'It Don't Come Easy'

**Nostalgic paean to ex-Beatle's very recent past.**

The Beatles wouldn't have been the Beatles without Ringo Starr. A vastly underrated drummer and peacemaker whose efforts to still the band's balmy internal relations at the turn of the 70s ultimately failed, Starr briefly became the most successful solo Beatle. It was not bad going considering the calibre of the competition. For his first post-split single he co-opted George Harrison to write 'It Don't Come Easy' — a lovingly crafted slab of post-Fab pop that seemed the best way forward for the man behind the most famous drum kit in the west. Its hopeful but heart-breaking B-side 'Early 1970' was a much rawer affair. An autobiographical look at his ex-bandmates — with each member getting a verse — Starr let his unreconstructed tones wonder aloud about what would happen next. Its charming depictions of Paul McCartney living on his farm, John Lennon in bed with Yoko Ono and guitar picker Harrison playing alongside him were topped by a self-deprecating final verse where Starr played up his alleged musical limitations against a backing track that gave the notion the lie — he had multi-tracked most of its instruments alone. A transatlantic Top 5 hit, the first in a small procession, Starr casually drifted out of the spotlight afterwards, often preferring the anonymity of session engagements.

## 'Easily'

Muse
WARNER BROS 2006
A-Side: 'Starlight'

**Devon space rockers at peak power.**

Even as stadium stardom beckoned, Devon's most illustrious trio continued their ingrained habit of sticking some of their best, most intriguing songs on B-sides (see also 'Nature 1' ['Plug In Baby', 2001], 'Futurism' ['Dead Star/In Your World', 2002] and 'Eternally Missed' ['Hysteria', 2003]). While radio-friendly A-side 'Starlight' was a cool exercise in the art of compromise without totally betraying your ethics, its razor-edged B-side 'Easily' traversed new plains. It also helped them emerge from Radiohead's long and suffocating shadow. A description of a near-perfect sexual experience, it was appropriately one of the band's more slinky and sensual offerings, allying yearning wordplay ("My mind refuses to let you go") to a harrying bassline and area-sized chorus. Recorded a little too late to make the cut for their bombastic 4th album *Black Holes And Revelations* and just a few aeons before they began slipping towards sci-fi self-parody, even Muse seemed shocked by how strong 'Easily' was when they played it live for the first time at a 'by request' charity show at London's Shepherds Bush Empire in 2017.

## 'Electric Music And The Summer People (Alternate Version)'

Beck

MCA 1999

A-Side: 'Cold Brains'

**Chameleonic songwriter realises a definitive take.**

Some songs can prove hard to shake. This B-side was a case in point — a track that followed its creator around since the mid-90s. First recorded as a much noisier and beat-laden affair during the session for 1996's second album *Odelay*, its breezy roll call of lyrical imagery ("Zigzag patients vibrating the ancients... villages burning... wandering children") wasn't far adrift from the loose free associations that helped Beck get branded the voice of the slacker generation when 'Loser' became a crossover success. Much later the Californian multi-tasker revealed its lyrics were intended as placeholders — nonsense words that he fully intended to replace (as did allusions to "mangling strangers" in 'The New Pollution' and talk of "discount orgies on the dropout buses" in 'Devils Haircut'). Re-recorded with a band during sessions for 1998's introspective *Mutations*, his second crack balanced 60s sounding acoustic guitars, tinkling pianos, swirling organs, sitars and handclaps with a wonderfully trippy synthesiser solo. It was an act of absolution as Beck finally found a fitting home for his teaming symbolism.

## 'Elvis Presley Boulevard'

Billy Joel

COLUMBIA 1982

A-Side: 'Allentown'

**Piano man's sideways salute to 'The King'.**

It took pint-sized New Yorker Billy Joel most of the 70s to finesse his blend of Beatles and Broadway for the masses, finally finding a sympathetic producer in Phil Ramone on 1977 blockbuster *The Stranger*. That relationship arguably peaked with their 4th consecutive collaboration *The Nylon Curtain* — a concept set about Reagan-era baby boomers that was his most Beatle-esque yet. Its chugging lead track 'Allentown' was the ideal taster, a sympathetic portrait of blue-collar workers amid the declining steel industry. Single buyers received a rare non-album Joel exclusive on its bitchier B-side. Above riffing guitars Joel chronicled a fictional visit to Graceland (a few years before Paul Simon made a similar trip) and lamented the hyper-commercialisation of the dead king, where visitors were proffered "plastic souvenirs of Elvis on the cross". It was a biting "goodbye to youth" from a pre-teen Elvis fan who, according to his website, first cottoned onto rock 'n' roll's power when he imitated Presley in elementary school. Joel used later B-sides to further hymn his heroes, hi-fiving Sam & Dave on a live 12-inch cover of 'You Got Me Hummin'' ['Tell Her About It', 1983] and cutting a passable John Lennon impression on 'I'll Cry Instead' ['An Innocent Man', 1983].

## 'EMF (Live At The Bilson)'

EMF
PARLOPHONE 1990
A-Side: 'Unbelievable'

**Hedonistic Epsom funkers' shouty signature tune.**
Captured live at the Forest Of Dean pub where they played their inaugural gigs, the B-side of EMF's first and biggest hit suggested they weren't as easily pliable as the next manufactured teenyboppers on the block. Ditto the ten sampled Black Panther profanities they snuck into A-side 'Unbelievable' — completely bypassing US radio programmers on its way to number 1. Built on a *Sound Of Music* sample, this self-titled indie/dance crossover B-side even let untamed keyboardist Derry Brownson loose on the mic before it broke down the Cinderford band's acronym: "E! Ecstasy/M! Motherfucker-motherfucker!/F! From us to you", in open defiance of the much tamer 'Epsom Mad Funkers' they had parroted at teen magazines. A founding moment and perennial encore, it was eventually tacked, uncredited, onto the end of 1991's debut *Schubert Dip*. As EMF gradually shed their younger fans, they used B-sides to knock off raw rock covers, putting Cream's 'Strange Brew' ['Children', 1991], Traffic's 'Low Spark Of The High Heeled Boys' ['They're Here', 1992] and the Stooges' 'Search And Destroy' ['Unexplained EP', 1992] through their highly danceable mangle.

## 'Endless Sleep'

The Poppy Family
LONDON 1969
A-Side: 'Which Way You Goin' Billy?'

**Definitive take on tragic teen standard.**

Masterminded by Canadian multi-instrumentalist and producer Terry Jacks, the Poppy Family progressed from a perfunctory barroom covers band to disenchanted soft rockers, as two singles of lightly poppy psychedelia slid by to mass indifference. Recorded on a shoestring, their third stab at pop stardom 'Which Way You Goin' Billy?' was a big-chorused Jacks original that made the most of their unconventional sitar/guitar/tabla set-up, with Jacks' wife Susan Pesklevits summoning a melancholic chorus that helped it turn gold. Jacks took the lead vocals on B-side 'Endless Sleep' — a cover of Jody Reynolds' echo-drenched drama about a drowning girl. An atmospheric doom scroll detailed with rubbery wah-wah and stomping drums, it was a potted demonstration of Jacks' growing confidence in the studio — skills he was keen to develop as money men forced his group out on the road. Although covered by Marc Bolan, Hank Williams Jr and Billy Idol, this B-side take caught the spirit of 'Endless Sleep' in *excelsis* and established a template for Jacks' 1972 solo outing 'Concrete Sea'.

**'Engine'**
Neutral Milk Hotel
BLUE ROSE 1998
A-Side: 'Holland, 1945'

**Underground band's truly underground B-side.**

Having released just one madly feted LP, Neutral Milk Hotel's other material has faced greater scrutiny than most. The 'fuzz-folk' brainchild of reclusive Louisiana songwriter Jeff Mangum, Neutral Milk Hotel started life playing a local laundromat in 1989 before morphing into a city-hopping solo project, with critical production input from childhood friend turned producer Robert Schneider. A series of bitty, short-run and often private releases preceded 1998's surprise indie hit LP *In the Aeroplane Over The Sea*, an oasis of cryptic pop that attempted to retell *The Diary Of Anne Frank* via woozy brass and lyrical freehand which became a key text for future indie-folksters. To back one of the album's strongest turns, Mangum took lo-fi to a new level, smuggling a tape recorder into the depths of London's Piccadilly Circus tube station, where he recorded the sparse and evocative 'Engine' — its obliqueness enhanced by the sound of an encroaching train and a lone person clapping at the end. Often introduced onstage as a children's song written during a brief happy period, it was audible proof that a simple approach could cut to the quick.

### 'Erotic City ("Make Love Not War Erotic City Come Alive")'

Prince

PAISLEY PARK 1984

A-Side: 'Let's Go Crazy'

**The Purple One's minimalist funk masterpiece.**

Few B-sides have enjoyed as much radio air time as Prince's 'Erotic City'. Recorded directly after seeing Parliament-Funkadelic in Los Angeles, DJs automatically locked into its moreish groove and all-pervading bassline. Loving detailed with squalling synths, spattered Syndrums and sly funk guitar figures, it found Minneapolis's foremost sonic manipulator playing with his own voice — speeding it up under his pseudonym Camille — as he joined Shelia E on the chorus (the first of her many telling contributions to his catalogue). While its maximalist A-side set the agenda for 1984s breakthrough *Purple Rain*, 'Erotic City' was a minimalist masterpiece that was as much about what was not happening than what was. And even though it was widely played by radio DJs (particularly the club-ready 12-inch single's seven-minute 'Dance Mix') debate still rages among Prince fans whether its key chorus lyric "We can funk until dawn" actually featured another four-letter word. Possible profanities aside, B-sides were a critical outlet for the hyper prolific and imaginative Prince. Whether it was the sparse funk of 'Irresistible Bitch' ['Let's Pretend We're Married', 1982], splintering guitars of 'All the Critics Love U In New York' ['Little Red Corvette', 1983], woozy heartbreak of 'Another Lonely Christmas' ['I Would Die 4 U', 1984], rain-drenched desire of '17 Days' ['When Doves Cry', 1984] or wicked double-entendres of 'Scarlet Pussy' ['I Wish U Heaven', 1988], he rarely left fans wanting.

### 'European Son'

Japan

HANSA 1981

A-Side: 'Life In Tokyo'

**London pretty boys revelatory change in direction.**
Signed to West Germany's Ariola-Hansa on the back of a talent contest, Japan's swift transition from New York Dolls-styled rockers into sophisticated synth poppers caught their label by surprise. Nothing showed the change more explicitly than 'European Son'. Written by singer David Sylvian after a 1978 US tour, it was intended as the centrepiece of their third album *Quiet Life*, with Giorgio Moroder pegged to produce it. Yet the Italian disco maestro rejected their demo and decided to sprinkle his magic dust over 'Life In Tokyo' instead. 'European Son' languished in the label's vaults until Roxy Music producer John Punter added a gush of airbrushed splendour to its Eurodisco synth arpeggios. Released as the B-side of 'I Second That Emotion' in Japan and on the Canadian 'Special Edition EP', it managed a hat-trick of B-side outings on the back of 1981's UK reissue of 'Life In Tokyo'. While a herd of incoming new romantics, Duran Duran in particular, would scale the charts with a very simpatico sound soon afterwards, this perennial bridesmaid finally became bride in 1982, issued as a A-side via a highly percussive Steve Nye remix.

**'Everybody Has Their Own Ideas'**
The Stone Poneys
SIDEWALK 1966
A-Side: 'So Fine'

**Linda Ronstadt's first studio date.**
Before she became one of the 70s biggest soft-rock music legends, Linda Ronstadt plied a very different trade. The one-time star attraction on the Tucson, Arizona coffeehouse circuit in family band the Three Ronstadts (alongside older siblings Peter and Suzi), she took a more concerted stab at fame with folk-rock trio the Stone Poneys (with guitarists Bobby Kimmel and Kenny Edwards). Scouted at Californian soul food restaurant Olivia's, budding west coast record executive Mike Curb asked them to record a cover of Johnny Otis's 'So Fine', previously a doo-wop hit for the Fiestas. While that was competent but routine, the Kimmel original on its B-side was anything but. Trading on the interplay between Ronstadt's clear vocals and Kimmel and Edwards' close harmonies, 'Everybody Has Their Own Ideas' landed somewhere between the unmasked innocence of Peter, Paul and Mary and gentle psychedelia of the Mojo Men. Issued in a tiny promotional run, it became a genuine rarity when the trio

escalated their barefooted popularity on the Los Angeles club circuit into being bona fide hitmakers with 1967's cover of Mike Nesmith's 'Different Drum'.

## 'Everybody Help The Boys Come Home'

William And Versey Smith
PARAMOUNT 1927
A-Side: 'When That Great Ship Went Down'

**Husband and wife duo's spiritual protest.**

While the first folk songs about the Titanic surfaced within weeks of the disaster, William and Versey Smith waited until the following decade to do theirs. The enigmatic husband and wife blues/gospel duo — variously reported to hail from Texas or the Carolinas — recorded just four songs in their lifetime, during a sole 1927 session in Chicago. The almost celebratory tone of William's growling lead vocal and acoustic guitar and his wife's high counterpoint and feisty tambourine on the A-side concealed a level of hubris — White Star Line blatantly refused to allow black people onboard its 'unsinkable' passenger liner. While that boasted an obvious commercial edge, 'Everybody Help The Boys Come Home' was a much better song — an early template for anti-folk rooted in the ecstatic music of the Holiness Church. As Versey's washboard clicked behind William's percussive strums, there was little ambiguity about the pair's heartfelt plea to return American soldiers to their home turf.

## 'Everybody Is A Star'

Sly & the Family Stone
EPIC 1969
A-Side: 'Thank You (Falettinme Be Mice Elf Agin)'

**Hard funk hits the mainstream.**

This single's contrasting sides bid a fitting farewell to the 60s, as a more uncertain decade began for its wild and brilliant creator. 'Thank You...' was a culmination of Sly Stone's funk craftmanship — its hard, James Brown-ish groove and harmonic complexity cementing his multi-racial band's 60s hit-making run with a fortnight's stop at the *Billboard* chart's pinnacle. Written for a planned but ultimately shelved studio album, B-side 'Everybody Is A Star' was among the psychedelically-edged fusionist's most gentle and reflective offerings, a breezy trumpet announcing its message of togetherness, respect and self-worth. Distinguished by a wordless breakdown where Texan cheerleader Sly, his brothers (Freddie and Rose) and Larry Graham traded lead vocals against a horn line with a strong hint of Otis Redding's 'Fa-Fa-Fa-Fa-Fa (Sad Song)', it showed how forcefully music could speak without words. The final classic-era Family Stone recording, Philadelphia hip-hoppers the Roots would turn its theme upside down on 2004's respectful inversion 'Star/Pointro'.

### 'Everyone I Meet Is From California'

America
WARNER BROS 1971
A-Side: 'A Horse With No Name'

**Chart rustlers show their pedigree.**
Dissed by Randy Newman as a poor man's Neil Young facsimile with a withering one liner "about a kid who thinks he's taken acid," America laughed all the way to the bank. Not only did the hallucinatory high-jinx of 'A Horse With No Name' become a huge hit worldwide, it knocked Young's 'Heart Of Gold' off the top of the US charts, proving ample vindication for the acoustic guitar-wielding close harmony trio of Dewy Bunnell, Berry Beckley and Dan Peak. Recorded during post-album sessions in London as Warner Bros debated how to break the band, its forthright B-side (released as part of a maxi-EP along with 'Sandman' in the UK), was a tumbling interplay of acoustic guitars, oblique words and folk-heavy vocal harmonies. "I'm probably as proud of that song as any song I've ever written," revealed Peek in the liner notes for 2000's *Highway* box set. "I had never even been to California, but... it seemed like virtually every person I ever met was from there." A label fudge ensured both songs were omitted from early US copies of America's self-titled debut. The A-side was tacked onto a frantic reissue while its B-side was re-recorded (as 'California Revisited') for follow-up *Homecoming*.

### 'Everything's Alright When You're Down'

The Jesus & Mary Chain
BLANCO Y NEGRO 1987
A-Side: 'Happy When It Rains'

**Reid brothers' best barbed wire kiss.**

"The early B-sides we didn't give a toss about," Jesus & Mary Chain frontman Jim Reid told thequietus.com in 2013. That was evident when they backed first major label single — feedback-lashed California surf anthem 'Never Understand' — with 'Jesus Fuck', a grinding exercise in noisy belligerence that the pressing plant refused to handle. Undaunted, they replaced it with a quickly improvised tune called 'Suck' that quickly descended into a list of howled profanities. Reid went on to recount how 1985's 'Just Like Honey' B-side 'Cracked' was simply a half-speed version of *Psychocandy* LP track 'The Living End' with a vocal quickly improvised on top. Yet the fractious, riot-starting band he formed in East Kilbride with brother William soon started to reassess the B-side's possibilities, using the platform to channel pent-up energies from the perfectionism at play in the album process. With its upbeat groove, fuzzy guitar attack and sheeting feedback, 'Everything's Alright When You're Down' was a partial return to their debut's dark mix of Phil Spector, Velvet Underground and surf-pop that, for many, trumped the A-side's more mannered commercialism. And while its lyrics shared the same downbeat optimism as 'Happy When It Rains', a couple of needless 'fucks' halted any chance of this extremely radio-friendly tune ever reaching the airwaves. Or it did until saxophonist Terry Edwards saluted its majesty on 1991's instrumental EP *Play The Music Of Jim & William Reid*.

## 'Fantastic Life'

The Fall

KAMERA 1981

A-Side: 'Lie Dream Of A Casino Soul'

**Peak Fall from their imperious early 80s phase.**

Few bandleaders led a more fantastic musical life than Mark E. Smith, burning through bandmates and creating his own lyrical landscape with the Fall — John Peel favourites that outlived and outwitted a whole wave of punk acts from the same era. Shortly after the Manchester upsetters had perfected their curious formula on 1981's high-octane mini-album *Slates* came 'Lie Dream Of A Casino Soul' — an exuberant slither of typically awkward Fall pop, with Smith drawling some of his most offkey verses over huge double drums and carnivalesque organ. As was so often the case with the Fall, its B-side was even better. The combination of Craig Scanlon's skeletal guitar and Marc Riley's swirling keys with

Steve Hanley's prowling bass and an incessant Krautrock-like rhythm supplied the ideal repetitious maelstrom for Smith's scalpel-sharp wordplay. Here partially obsessed with espionage, the voracious reader of "daft history books" referenced 1948's *Battle For Jerusalem*, a Siberian mushroom Santa, Rasputin, Whitechapel and Wakefield jail, providing ample food for thought for a growing legion obsessed fanboys and lyrical code-crackers. Or he did until the end when Smith concluded, possibly snickering to himself: "And I just thought I'd tell you some fantastic lies."

### 'Fat Girl'

Eazy-E
RUTHLESS 1987
A-Side: 'The Boyz-N-The Hood'

**Another side of the west coast lifestyle.**

To accompany the deadpan day-in-the-life diatribe of Eazy-E's first single — one of Dr. Dre's grittiest bass-driven productions — N.W.A's diminutive leader showed his less serious side. 'Fat Girl' found the charismatic if technically stilted rapper trying to cope with the unwanted affections on an overweight ex-lover (hammily played by close friend Ron De Vu) with "more chins than a Chinese phone book" (a zinger from the teenage pen of Ice Cube). As events took a turn for the worst in the second verse, the ex-drug dealer plotted his escape, swinging for his assailant with a harpoon gun and leaving every impression left that the blow connected (wordplay that bore an uncanny similarity to DJ Jazzy Jeff & the Fresh Prince's more radio-friendly chart hit 'Girls Ain't Nothing But Trouble'). With its rough, un-glossy production, Benny Hill-type humour and human beatboxing –the title was a nod to Brooklyn innovators the Fat Boys — it was an oddity that spoke strongly of the sensibilities of the time (anyone searching for cultural sensitivity in gangsta rap's first throes is probably missing the point).

### 'Fear Of Ghosts'

The Cure
FICTION 1989
A-Side: 'Lovesong'

**So wonderfully, wonderfully, wonderfully spooky...**

The Cure rank high among contenders for the best B-Side band crown. Ever since their inception in deepest darkest Crawley, the band fronted by the lipstick-smeared Robert Smith saved some of their crackerjack tracks for B-sides, be it the drip-drip drama of '10:15 Saturday Night' ['Killing an Arab', 1979), baggy dance steps of 'Harold And Joe' ['Never Enough', 1990] or dreamy melancholy of 'Twilight Garden' ['High', 2004]. When they brooked all odds by winning over America with their most depressing (and best) album *Disintegration* in 1989, its third single 'Lovesong' — a straightforward dedication to Smith's wife Mary — took them to the rarefied heights of number 2 in the *Billboard* chart, held off by Janet Jackson's 'Miss You Much'. Single buyers were rewarded with one of their grandest B-side curiosities — a spooky repurposing of keyboardist Roger O'Donnell's demo 'The Other Side', augmented with fresh parts. With its spectral sitars, muted choirs and curious percussive figures, 'Fear Of Ghosts' was a rapturous six-minute sprawl of gothic majesty topped by one of Smith's most poetic takes on depression, whispered conspiratorially and ethereally, its haunted mood lingering long after it wept to a finish. Unlike some of their more celebrated B-sides, the Cure deigned to play it live until 2019, when they celebrated the 30th anniversary of *Disintegration* at Sydney Opera House.

**'Feelin' Reelin' Squeelin''**

Soft Machine

POLYDOR 1967

A-Side: 'Love Makes Sweet Music'

**Canterbury scene leaders' deep first cut.**

One of the UK's most colourful underground bands, Soft Machine grew from humble origins in Canterbury pop/soul covers troupe Wilde Flowers to something far fiercer and untamed. Having changed their name when songwriters Kevin Ayers and Robert Wyatt started penning oblique originals that merged Dadaist tendencies with wild ensemble playing, Soft Machine became the 'other' house band at London's UFO Club alongside Pink Floyd. Both embodied the scene's blend of arch intellectualism and wilful hedonism, plying their trade in its darkened cellar below projections of films by Kenneth Anger and Jack Smith. Pipping their UFO rivals first single 'Arnold Layne' by a full month, 'Love Makes Sweet Music' was relatively straightforward psychedelic pop, clearly designed with radio play in mind. Its Wyatt-composed B-side had the opposite intention. A wacked-out cabaret abstract with Ayers' sonorous, Lurch-like creepy verses offset by Wyatt's elliptical pleas ("Are you happy? Are you happy?") before wild organ runs and screaming penny whistles joined the jostling throng, its sudden, disturbing fade-out only added to its mystery. It was also the sole Soft Machine recording to feature Australian guitarist Daevid Allen, forced back home when his visa expired.

**'Find The Cost Of Freedom'**
Crosby, Stills, Nash & Young
ATLANTIC 1970
A-Side: 'Ohio'

**The raw power of protest.**

Crosby, Stills, Nash & Young had just released their second album when the Kent State shootings took place on May 4, 1970. A day when members of the Ohio National Guard killed four and injured nine unarmed students, peacefully protesting the extension of the Vietnam War into Cambodia, it could have been much worse, with the soldiers firing 67 rounds in 13 brutal seconds. Inspired by John Filo's Pulitzer Prize-winning image of Mary Ann Vecchio kneeling over the dead body of Jeffrey Miller, its rush-released Neil Young written A-side was a scathing indictment of Richard Nixon's law-and-order approach to civil unrest — its bold calling out of the president by name making it impossible to ignore, unless you were a fearful AM radio programmer. As blunt and heavy-handed as the A-side was, Steven Stills' mournful B-side witnessed the military school graduate offering a more reflective response to the same tragedy. Recorded live, with the band sitting in a square and facing each other, it was a relatively simple but impactful song, whose subdued acoustic guitar picking preceded four spare lines — sung twice, the second time unaccompanied — in an intense union of harmony, melody and emotion. Two students who witnessed those shootings — Chrissie Hynde and Gerald Casale — would later enjoy rock careers in the Pretenders and Devo.

### 'First Taste Of Love'

Ben E. King
ATCO 1961
A-Side: 'Spanish Harlem'

**Urbane soul singer goes for self.**

Ben E. King's career with the Drifters was so fleeting he never got a chance to perform with the R&B vocal legends on tour. After locking horns with their nefarious manager George Treadwell over wages and royalties — King wrote the band's 1959's number 2 hit 'There Goes My Baby', but was persuaded to 'share' its writing credits — the Harlem-raised singer dropped his birth name Nelson for the more memorable stage name Ben E. King. It worked wonders as he wrapped his elegant baritone around the Latin-tinged, marimba detailed 'Spanish Harlem' — an instant pop classic and a hit straight off the bat. Many buyers were equally seduced by its romantic ballad B-side 'First Taste Of Love'. Flowing in a similar vein to the Drifters' 'Save the Last Dance for Me' (it shared a songwriter in Doc Pomus, here working with upcoming wunderkind Phil Spector), King's intimate delivery allowed listeners to follow every breath. And with its doo-wop backup vocals and Latin undertow it cemented the notion that R&B could weld catchy melodies to sophisticated arrangements accessible to the wider pop demographic — a point proved by King's next single 'Stand By Me'. While the A-side was arguably bettered by Aretha Franklin's blistering cover a decade later, Wayne Fontana and the Mindbenders played the B-side straight on the back of 1964's onomatopoeic chart creeper 'Um, Um, Um, Um, Um, Um'.

### 'Fish, Chips & Sweat'

Funkadelic
WESTBOUND 1970
A-Side: 'I Got A Thing, You Got A Thing, Everybody's Got A Thing'

**Groovy space-funkers get the munchies.**

Based on the 1966 song 'Baby, That's a Groove' that George Clinton penned as a Motown staff writer with Holland and Dozier, this B-side was not be the only time the colourful funk visionary took a small step backwards in order to power forwards. The heavily Sly Stone influenced recalibration was a seamless combo of doo-wop, psychedelic rock and funk that reflected his band's increasingly multi-dimensional vision after sharing festival stages with similar free spirits Jimi Hendrix, the MC5 and Iggy Pop, not to mention free-jazzers Ornette Coleman and Sun Ra. A stomping groove, enhanced by Bernie Worrell's swirling organ, Eddie Hazel's super hooky guitar line and Billy Bass's arch vocal jabs, it screamed of late nights and illicit behaviour. While Funkadelic gave every impression that they were trapped within an acid-induced nightmare of their own design on their second LP *Free Your Mind... And Your Ass Will Follow* later that year, 'Fish, Chips & Sweat' saw them shaking out of it and blinking into the daylight, possibly with a saveloy to go.

### 'Flim'

Aphex Twin
WARP 1997
A-Side: 'Come To Daddy'

**Electronic bad boy's fragile breakbeat lullaby.**

No one wrote melodies quite like Richard D. James. For all the myth and legend the Cornish lover of spectacle built around his Aphex Twin alias — deejaying on sandpaper, buying an armoured tank, living in a disused South London bank vault — the reason he was talked about as more than just an electronic innovator was his ability to conjure seductive and original drafts of delicate and cerebral electronica that pushed at the limits of what his home-wired equipment could achieve. If the disturbing A-side here was an in-joke that spiralled out of hand after Chris Cunningham's super creepy video scared the bejesus out of all who saw it, 'Flim' was its ideal counterpoint. Said to be EDM chief Skrillex's favourite song of all time, it was not hard to understand why. A sweet and gentle womb-like wonder, its nursery-rhyme feel and sweeping strings were a soothing balm that washed lingering worries away — perfect for peaceful reveries, catching the breeze or watching the sun go down.

### 'For Madmen Only'

Steppenwolf
DUNHILL 1972
A-Side: 'Ride With Me'

**Trippy landscape of feedback and drone.**

The Los Angeles band named after Herman Hesse's 1929 novel of transformation possessed a more open, experimental side than those who only knew the A-sides or heard them in the opening credits of *Easy Rider* could have guessed. Forever remembered for 1968's outlaw anthem 'Born to Be Wild' (whose barked invocation "heavy metal thunder" effectively named a genre), the black-clad long-hairs also wrote 'Monster/Suicide/America' — a three-part socio-political breakdown on the state of the union. One of the longest B-sides of its time, just shy of nine minutes, 'For Madmen Only' was cut from a similar cloth. Taking its title from a neon sign featured in Hesse's novel, the band used the studio to get darkly atmospheric: Jerry Edmonton's spooky backwards cymbals, George Biondo's cold bassline and Goldy McJohn's growling Lowrey organ drone providing a creeping dread canvas for Kent Henry and John Kay's scythed six-string murmurings. Included on early pressings before it was replaced with the less exacting instrumental 'Black Pit', the two different B-side gambit barely had any effect on the A-side's disappointing chart fortunes, as Steppenwolf's hard-rock hit machine started to sputter and fail.

**'Fortune Teller'**
Benny Spellman
MINIT 1962
A-Side: 'Lipstick Traces (On A Cigarette)'

**Future northern soul floor-filler.**

Benny Spellman was scouting for his first solo hit when he cut both sides of his best-known single. The New Orleans R&B singer had previously handled the honeyed bass parts on Ernie K-Doe's number 1 'Mother In Law' for Minit's in-house songwriter and producer Allen Toussaint, who gave him a decent shout on an A-side that detailed the tell-tale signs of infidelity in bluntly realistic fashion. Toussaint, writing under the pseudonym Naomi Neville, also supplied its B-side's tale of a fortune teller's romantic revelations over a jaunty three-chord guitar riff, barroom piano, choppy percussion and impactful horn injections. Instantly infectious, it out-classed the A-side by the sheer breadth of cover versions it inspired, with the Who, the Rolling Stones, the Hollies, Strawberry Alarm Clock and Robert Plant & Alison Krauss all trying it on for size. When Australian garage rockers the Throb made it a down-under hit in 1966, Spellman was starting to reassess his career options.

**'Frankie'**
Connie Francis
MGM 1959
A-Side: 'Lipstick On Your Collar'

**Tearful ballad from huge-selling pop goddess.**

'Lipstick On Your Collar' landed at a time when Connie Francis was regularly appearing on *The Jimmie Rogers Show* and battling Brenda Lee for the crown of rock 'n' roll's biggest female star. Still just twenty-one, , the New Jersey child performer and weekly TV regular had already experienced the fame game's contrasting fortunes — racking up ten flop singles for MGM before a final dice throw take on 'Who's Sorry Now', at her father's suggestion, broke her chart duck. Francis was well into her global hitmaking stride when this Brill Building A-side found her reading the riot act to some unidentified, shiftless paramour. Co-written by Howard Greenfield and Neil Sedaka about her very public crush on teen idol Frankie Avalon, Francis ad-libbed the spoken word intro to its sentimental B-side ("Frankie, wherever you are I love you"), to the initial disapproval of orchestra leader Ray Ellis. He nonetheless left it in and even repeated it at the close. He was wise to do so, Francis' plaintive tones gave a very real sense that she was hiding her heartbreak, as sweeping strings, tremolo guitars and male counter harmonies reinforced its tearful message.

**'Freedom Of Speak (We Got More Than Three)'**
De La Soul
TOMMY BOY 1988
A-Side: 'Plug Tunin''

**An unexpected blast of Dayglo sunshine.**

From the get-go De La Soul offered fans extra B-side flavour, far beyond hip-hop's standard servings of remixes and instrumentals. The sheer otherness of Long Island schoolfriends Posdnous, Maseo and Trugoy The Dove was immediately detectable on their first single — a hi-tech upgrade of a rough-cut demo that found producer and unofficial 4th member Prince Paul pulling out all the stops. While 'Plug Tunin'' evolved from a live routine based on a lift from the Invitations' 'Written on the Wall', with added snippets of Billy Joel and Liberace, the producer took a much simpler, more bugged-out approach on 'Freedom Of

Speak', looping and scratching a copy of James Brown's 'Superbad'. After being instructed to let loose on the mic, the trio's clever rhymes and carefree banter did the rest, culminating in Posdnous' bold statement: "The reason De La bad is 'cos we think." Paul cut them off abruptly at the three-minute mark, hinting at the skits that would land with full-force on the following year's *3 Feet High And Rising*, a kaleidoscopic debut that realigned the hip-hop axis.

## 'Fucker'

Eels
DREAMWORKS 1996
A-Side: 'Novocaine For The Soul'

**Raw heartbreak, simply expressed.**

"It's about being mad at yourself for falling in love... I was scared." So revealed Eels' awkward frontman Mark Everett at a 2001 Q&A session, answering a query about a B-side that stood in stark contrast to the A-side's quirky post-grunge pop. Short and undeniably bittersweet, 'Fucker' was riven with neurosis — a lovely afternoon spent with someone reminding its protagonist about his lonely life, a slow realisation that dawned over a gentle four-chord sequence, soft-padded drums and dreamy organ reverberations. Some of its dark mood would eventually leach directly into Eels' second LP *Electro Shock Blues* (sample song title: 'The Medication Is Wearing Off'), as the emerging master of the morose worked his way through the grief of losing his mother to cancer and sister to suicide in quick succession. As 2008's exhaustive *Useless Trinkets* compilation made plain, Eels rarely used B-sides as a dumping ground for substandard fare, even parcelling 1998's potential feel-good hit 'Everything's Gonna Be Cool This Christmas' onto the flip of 'Cancer For The Cure'.

## 'Funky New Year'

The Eagles
ASYLUM 1978
A-Side: 'Please Come Home For Christmas'

**Gilded fractious rockers get on down.**

While arenas resounded to the bombastic classic rock of the Eagles' huge-selling 5th album *Hotel California*, animosity was running high in their ranks. The Los Angeles band formed by ex-Linda Ronstadt backup singers Glenn Frey and Don Henley nonetheless took their good fortune seriously, with a slew of druggy, debauched antics that pushed rock 'n' roll hedonism beyond its clichéd limits. They were in a purging period when they fashioned this stop-gap holiday single, with Henley's soothing voice the ideal vehicle to communicate Charles Brown's festive A-side plea. Thinking ahead to the next public holiday, its Frey and Henley penned B-side 'Funky New Year' was a radically unexpected departure that tipped the wink to George Clinton's Parliament-Funkadelic with its slap bass, downlow groove and trippy keys. A simple song about a raging new year hangover, it surfaced two years before accelerating tensions between guitarist Don Felder and Frey tore the band apart. Having patched up their differences in 1994, the Eagles' revived this B-side to ring in the new millennium at Los Angeles' Staples Center... before promptly falling out again.

### 'Funnel Of Love'

Wanda Jackson
CAPITOL 1961
A-Side: 'Right Or Wrong'

**Queen of rockabilly in bewitching form.**

Encouraged by Elvis to pursue rockabilly when they toured together in the mid-50s, the one-time female singer with Hank Thompson's Brazos Valley Boys took the King at his word. And while Wanda Jackson managed a major Japanese hit with 1958's gimmicky 'Fujiyama Mama' and a minor one at home with 1960's 'Let's Have A Party', her paymasters started pointing her backs towards her country roots with 'Right or Wrong' — first written with Brenda Lee in mind. An A-side that's largely been forgotten since, its Charles McCoy and Kent Westbury penned flip has become an unforgettable part of Jackson's legacy. A meld of rockabilly and country lit up by Roy Clark's slinky guitar riff and Jackson's brilliantly sultry vocal take, 'Funnel Of Love' caught the bare madness of infatuation within 128 seconds. Covered by many (Demented Are Go!, Cyndi Lauper, SQÜRL), it finally found its way onto a Jackson album when she remade it with California creepers the Cramps for 2003's *Heart Trouble*. Hailed by Adele as the inspiration for 2010's bluesy hit 'Rolling In The Deep', the superstar singer covered 'Funnel Of Love' on New Year's Day 2011 in Manchester before inviting Jackson to open shows during the North American leg of her *21* tour.

# GOING BACKWARDS

*The decision to release backwards B-sides has often come with hair-raising and dubious results...*

Regarded by many as simply their best-ever B-side, the **Beatles' 'Rain'** ['Paperback Writer', PARLOPHONE 1966] found the Fab Four entering a brave new world, where the studio was another tool towards transcendence. An outtake from 1966's *Revolver* sessions, titivated to satisfy demands for a new single, the John Lennon-penned number about weather-moaning Brits was felt to be missing a groove until producer George Martin decided to manipulate the recording's speed — going much faster than usual, then playing it back at normal pace — to texturally change its sonic palette. Ringo Starr would later rate his thunderous hi-hat-led patterns as his best performance (although Paul McCartney's loud loping bass may just trump it), the song's deliberately 'trippy' soundscape accentuated further by Martin recording Lennon's lead vocal at a slightly slower speed.

Given a reel-to-reel tape copy to take home after the sessions, a judiciously stoned Lennon mistakenly threaded the tape the wrong way around, an act that inspired his backwards vocals at the song's coda (a repeat of first line "When the rain comes they run and hide their heads"). Although that version of events was later disputed by Martin, who claimed the idea as his own, 'Rain' was a fascinating delve into the psychedelic world. It marked a fork in the road in the Beatles' approach to studio work as they waved goodbye to the suits, moptops and deafening screams of Beatlemania and became a freeform, hirsute, experimental quartet whose numerous studio revolutions would gradually seep into the wider landscape. Reversing songs was just a part of that. As its engineer Geoff Emerick recalled in Kenneth Womack's 2018 book *Sound Pictures*: "They tried everything backwards, just to see what things sounded like."

Played backwards, most songs take on sinister overtones, provoking feelings

of unrest and disquiet. That was borne out by **Napoleon XIV**'s **'!aaaH-aH ,yawA eM ekaT oT gnimoC er'yehT'** ['They're Coming To Take Me Away, Ha-Haaa!', WARNER BROS 1966], issued just two months after 'Rain' and still the reigning don dada of backwards B-sides.

The brainchild of New York studio engineer Jerry Samuels, his sophisticated use of technology found him varying the speed of his vocal (and some creepy accompanying sirens) to echo his increasingly off-the-rails narrator's mood-shifting dissection of a failed romance, above a marching rhythm based on trad Scottish folk tune 'The Campbells Are Coming' that he created by looping a ten-second strip of tape. And although it was essentially just a straightforward reversal of the A-side's flirtation with public insanity, the B-side doubled down on its bad trip intensity, riling ex-*Creem* editor Dave Marsh so badly that he dubbed it "the most obnoxious song ever to appear in a jukebox" in 1981's *The Book Of Rock Lists*. Samuels' attention to detail no doubt irked him even more — he stipulated that the B-side's label was presented as a mirror image of the A-side (with everything printed backwards bar the catalogue number). For all its Marmite qualities, the single was madly marching to the top of the *Billboard* Hot 100 when it was swiftly banished from radio playlists — after complaints that the song made fun of the mentally ill — before the BMI withdrew its certification altogether.

The rogue's gallery of artists to go the backwards B-side route since Napoleon XIV have enjoyed mixed fortunes, with critics of the practice often complaining that, at its worst, the groove-filling exercise takes the notion of "Will this do?" to the next level. The **Yellow Balloon** — a band in name only, after Los Angeles' songwriter Gary Zekley deployed session musicians to cut a rival version of a song he'd penned for surf duo Jan & Dean — certainly had no time to come up with a flip. Indeed, by pressing reverse on **'Noollab Wolley'** ['The Yellow Balloon', CANTERBURY 1967], they accentuated the toothsome harmonies of their first US Top 30 hit. Its success necessitated a follow-up too, with ex-Mouseketeer Don Grady putting together a band whose self-titled debut LP, unloved at the time, is now considered a sunshine pop classic.

The backwards B-side was also a useful tool for the **Marquis Of**

**Kensington**, the brief incognito studio project of the Kinks' manager Robert Wace (alongside producer Mike Leander). A quick-thinking cash-in on the New Vaudeville Band's popularity, it found Wace doing his best Noël Coward impression over music hall harpsichord and jazzy guitars. Featured in Peter Whitehead's swinging London documentary *Tonite Let's All Make Love In London*, it even became a continental hit. That ensured many buyers were also privy to the genuinely ghostly and disturbing sound of **'Reverse Thrust'** (credited to the Marquis Of Kensington's Minstrels ['The Changing Of The Guard', CBS 1967]), a supremely sinister rewind of the jaunty A-side's instrumental.

The same simple chemistry ushered out all the ghosts in **Lloyd Green**'s **'Cinap (Pirt A)'** ['Panic (A Trip)', BIG A 1968]. A cool pedal steel cover of NYC Link Wray devotees' Palais Royals' early single that turned Green's great bendy notes, bathed in echo and reverb, into a flipped-out psychedelic instrumental far removed from the Nashville A-Team session guitarist's usual fare (bearing in mind his contribution to 100-plus US number 1 hits). As with Napoleon XIV's only smash, the B-side label was a mirror image of the A-side.

For New York's Buddah label, the notion of simply reversing an A-side solved two problems at once — it was cost effective and radio stations would never wantonly play the backwards version, effectively banishing the possibility of double-sided hits. Not only were in-house producers Jerry Kasenetz and Jeff Katz instrumental in perpetuating the brief backwards B-side boom, they were also wily enough to directly profit from it, elbowing their way into its songwriting credits.

Some of Buddah's backwards B-sides worked better than others. Take **Zal Yanovsky**. When the flamboyant lead guitarist and focal point of the Lovin' Spoonful became involved in a drug bust with wider repercussions (he was deported to his native Canada), they tried to reposition him as a solo star. Not only did **'Ereh Er'uoy Sa Gnol Sa'** ['As Long As You're Here', BUDDAH 1968] totally refresh the overly orchestrated pop of the A-side (rustled up by Turtles hitmakers Garry Bonner and Alan Gordon), it created something super-loopy that totally chimed with Yanovsky's fresh outlaw status.

Buddha would perpetuate the practice as they maxed-out cash registers during the bubblegum pop explosion. But it wasn't always a simple case of reversing the A-side — they had other crazy schemes to keep fans on their toes. Take the soothing tones of **Ohio Express**'s **'Zig Zag'** ['Yummy Yummy Yummy', BUDDAH 1969]. Rather than being just the lame novelty A-side played backwards it was a reverse of 1910 Fruitgum Company's '(Poor Old) Mr Jensen' (itself the flip of 1968's 'May I Take A Giant Step (Into Your Heart)'), from a fellow gang of anonymous studio musicians. Yet **'Pow Wow'**, the B-side of **1910 Fruitgum Company**'s final Top 5 US hit ['Indian Giver', BUDDAH 1969] was a seeming backwards anomaly — joke song 'Bring Back Howdy Doody' (about the children's TV puppet) written by sister label Super K Productions' staff writer/producer Steve Dworkin. Typically, Dworkin was left in the dark about the shenanigans and gravely peeved that he didn't even receive a writing credit (although, naturally, Kasenetz and Katz did). Vindication, of sorts, came when his song became an unreversed A-side via a cover by Flying Giraffe (another group of bubblegum session musicians, better known as Lt Garcia's Magic Music Box).

Regarded by some heads as one of the best psychedelic B-sides of all time, **Warm Sounds' 'Smeta Murgaty'** ['Nite Is A Comin'', DERAM 1968] witnessed the harmony duo of Denver Gerrard and Barry Younghusband pushing the envelope to the limit as they ladled additional overdubs and psychedelic effects over the backwards playing A-side, its unusual title coming from the sound reversal of A-side lyric: "It's big and black and strong".

Similarly mind-melting moves were afoot in Jamaica as Lee 'Scratch' Perry embarked on a production career that would see him hailed as dub reggae's resident mad genius. Perry discovered singer **Burt Walters** singing barefoot on the streets of East Kingston and quickly enlisted the

mentally unstable vocalist into a series of studio covers. **'Evol Yenoh'** ['Love Honey', UPSETTER1968] retained the same rhythm as its A-side's cover of the Drifters but played the vocals backwards, transforming a sweet pop song into an unhinged beast of speaking-in-tongues weirdness. Walters would drift back into obscurity after one more appearance with Perry — a lightly skanking cover of Bob Dylan's 'Blowin' In The Wind' (credited to Bob Dillon and on the B-side of Perry's breakout single 'People Funny Boy'), that matched the A-side's innovative sample of a baby crying with OTT wind effects.

Few will recall obscure Cincinnati baroque band **Jade**, Beatles fanatics who left behind a trio of singles and one album before vanishing into the mist. The warped merry-go-round of **'My Mary (More Than Ever)'** ['My Honey', GENERAL AMERICAN 1972] moved the backwards game further forwards, thanks to both the band's ambition and the studio skills of engineer Gene Lawson. Unlike most backwards B-sides, its lyrics were warped but clearly discernible, a mind-bending trick achieved by Jade singing the lyrics phonetically to emulate the sound of them being sung backward.

Looking for a thematic bond to their A-side's exposé of Queensland Premier Joh Bjelke-Petersen — a gerrymander who threw aboriginal people off their land and sold uranium mines on sacred sites — the **Stranglers** came up with **'Yellowcake UF6'** ['Nuclear Device (The Wizard Of Aus)', UNITED ARTISTS 1979], a reference to the chemical uranium hexafluoride. It was a vocal-free repurposing of 'Social Secs' (recorded in sessions for 1978's *Black & White*) and a joltingly powerful slice of backwards strangeness (whose central riff would resurface again, running forwards, on bassist J.J. Burnel's 'Do The European').

The band that really shared the forward-thinking Beatles' love of going backwards the most though, were Manchester baggy overlords the **Stone Roses**, who embarked on an unprecedented run of three consecutive reversed B-sides in the late 80s. Named after a Jackson Pollock painting (a self-referential nod to guitarist John Squires' distinctive splattered sleeve art), exhibit A, **'Full Fathom Five'** ['Elephant

Stone', SILVERTONE 1988] was the most straightforward of the lot, simply inversing an alternative mix of the A-side. They twisted the formula again on **'Guernica'** ['Made Of Stone', 1989], a reversal of the A-side's instrumental but with fresh and affecting lyrics that delt with the titular town's bombing during the Spanish Civil War. Were that not enough tomfoolery, **'Simone'** ['She Bangs The Drums', 1989] truly jumped the gun, with fans who preferred the cassette format receiving a backwards version of a demo of 'Where Angels Play', the B-side of their next single ['I Wanna Be Adored', 1989].

## 'Gambling Bar Room Blues'

Jimmie Rodgers
REGAL ZONOPHONE 1933
A-Side: 'Long Tall Mama Blues'

**Cautionary tale from 'the Singing Brakeman'.**

Jimmie Rodgers recorded some of country music's most moving early songs. The Mississippi-born singer ran away with a medicine show at 13 to become an entertainer, learning banjo and guitar before he perfected a blend of traditional country, work, blues, hobo and cowboy songs that frequently touched on hearth and home, kith and kin. After scoring big with 1928's first single 'Sleep, Baby, Sleep', Rodgers became a prolific studio figure, developing his trademark 'blue' yodelling country style while fighting a debilitating battle with tuberculosis. Although some of that weariness seeped into the A-side here, 'Gambling Bar Room Blues' was a more pungent entry in his catalogue of woe, set to the engaging refrain of Irving Mills' 'St. James' Infirmary Blues'. It found Rodgers largely ditching his yodel to sorrowfully recount how he murdered his friend for messing with his woman as Clayton McMichen's lonesome fiddle weaved around his slow-strummed chords. Issued months before his premature death at 33, John Mellencamp reprised it on 1996's all-star tribute album *The Songs Of Jimmie Rogers*.

### 'Genetic'
Sonic Youth
DGC 1992
A-Side: '100%'

**The B-side that caused an inter-band rift.**

When 'Genetic' failed to make the cut for Sonic Youth's seventh LP *Dirty* its writer — singer and guitarist Lee Ranaldo — had every right to feel aggrieved. Regularly restricted to a couple of songs on each album, while husband and wife team Thurston Moore and Kim Gordon bagged the lion's share, its exclusion flared up more than just professional beefs. This time it was personal. 'Genetic' addressed the difficult separation Ranaldo was going through and his feelings for his estranged son, his raw emotions bolstered by the studio dynamics of Nirvana's *Nevermind* production team Butch Vig and Andy Wallace. Moore was unmoved. He publicly objected to Sonic Youth "being set up for him to voice those issues in", while Ranaldo retorted that he was suffering from 'George Harrison syndrome' (a reference to the Beatle limited to two songs per album, regardless of their brilliance) and considering quitting. With its heart-wrenching theme and buzzsaw pop strengths, it was easy to see why 'Genetic' represented an unwanted B-side for Ranaldo, especially as the New York noiseniks were now seriously flirting with mainstream acceptance. Tellingly, he had zero credits on Sonic Youth's next album.

### 'Get Down, Make Love'
Nine Inch Nails
TVT 1990
A-Side: '5in'

**Double-horned industrial Queen refit.**

Trent Reznor, the Pittsburgh programmer and pint-sized one-man force behind Nine Inch Nails, always took great pleasure in peppering his live sets with soundtrack contributions and lesser-known B-sides. He treated both seriously. Nine Inch Nails were still in their infancy when he enlisted Ministry's Al Jourgensen to produce his take on Freddie Mercury's near-the-knuckle offering from Queen's 1973 *News Of The World* LP. Rather than ape Mercury's flaming desire he ramped up the sleaze, perforating its heavy beats and tense electro bass with pitch-shifted orgasmic groans (taken from a Japanese pornographic film) while chucking in a quick burst of Queen's 'We Will Rock You' at the death. If the chorus was a bit of a reach for Reznor's limited vocal range, his impassioned delivery compensated, his trademark snarl turning "Make love!" into a sinister-sounding dictate. Most bands are wary of tampering with Queen, so distinctive is their stamp, but this B-side not only paid irreverent homage, it hinted at the more metallic sound Reznor would pursue on second NIN album *Broken*.

## 'Get Rhythm'

Johnny Cash
SUN 1956
A-Side: 'I Walk The Line'

**Jaunty optimism, written with a King in mind.**

A country star who blossomed at the birth of rock 'n' roll, Johnny Cash embodied the best of both worlds, with a quick side of righteous gospel fury. The boy from the Mississippi delta, who would become known as 'The Man In Black', first wrote 'Get Rhythm' on an acoustic guitar for Elvis Presley, his fellow Sun Records outlier. A fast-paced rockabilly ditty about positivity — replacing sad thoughts with actions that lift the spirits — its narrator offered encouragement to a shoeshine boy struggling to cope with his job's tedious toils. When Presley moved to RCA, Sun boss Sam Phillips vetoed the potentially lucrative cover, so Cash recorded it instead with his regular partners the Tennessee Two (Luther Perkins and Marshall Grant). A razor-sharp mix of Perkins' jittery clipped guitar, Gant's thumping bass and Cash's weathered baritone, it complemented the boom-chicka-boom confessional of Cash's first number 1 hit 'I Walk the Line'. In 1969 new Sun owner Shelby Singleton tried to make the most of his investment by reissuing 'Get Rhythm' as an A-side, adding faux crowd noises to try and cash-in on the success of live LP *Johnny Cash At San Quentin*. Reinterpreted, rather differently, by Dr Feelgood and Ry Cooder in the late 80s, Cash also added guest vocals to Martin Delray's country hit in 1991.

## 'Getting Beaten Up'

The Piranhas
SIRE 1980
A-Side: 'Tom Hark'

**Coming of age tale rings horribly true.**

Written by guitarist Johnny Helmer about his teenage years in Southend-on-Sea, 'Getting Beaten Up' didn't pull its punches. A punky blast from the John Peel endorsed Brighton misfits, its tales of drinking at local pub the Esplanade ("where the lager tastes like lemonade") embedded the notion that fights were a natural rite of passage (or as Helmer succinctly put it "part of life"). The band's amped delivery benefited greatly from its lyrical specificity, singer 'Boring' Bob Grove bemoaning the sudden absence of his drinking pal Lorrie Henson while a skinhead gang danced a merry moonstomp on his face. Symptomatic of the Piranhas' hard-knock live sets, many fans were non-plussed when their Pete Waterman-produced remake of Elias & His Zig Zag Jive Flutes' 'Tom Hark' — a prominent showcase for saxophonist Zoot Alors — became a UK Top 10 success. That may have enjoyed an unusually long shelf life, thanks to its annoying adoption by England football fans, but the real treat was always on the other side.

## 'Gimme The Car'

Violent Femmes
SLASH/ROUGH TRADE 1983
A-Side: 'Ugly'

**Folk-punk pioneers' blast of teen angst.**

Few songs have had such direct consequences as this B-side. Asked to play an appropriate song for a National Honor Society induction at his Milwaukee high school, singer Gordon Gano and his bass playing friend Brian Ritchie launched into 'Gimme The Car' instead — a horny teenager's plea to borrow his father's four wheels so he could get intimate with a girl. Within minutes the hall erupted into mayhem, with the principal loudly calling a halt. While Gano's music teacher defended the pupil's right to self-expression, the principal and Gano's parents took a dimmer view and he was suspended. Curiously left off Violent Femmes' brimstone debut — as was its politically incorrect A-side

'Ugly' — both made for a great one-off single, Gano's unabashed snarl and slashing guitars matched by Ritchie's menacing acoustic bass and Victor DeLorenzo's skeletal drum menace. Uniquely cross-referenced on album track 'Kiss Off' (with the line "This will go down on your permanent record...") and a close cousin to 'Add It Up', 'Gimme The Car' has continued to resonate with fresh generations of angsty teens ever since.

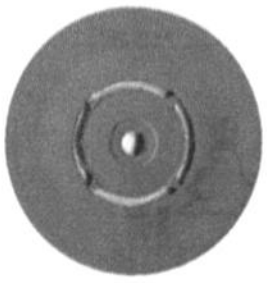

## 'Gismo My Way'

10cc
UK 1974
A-Side: 'The Wall Street Shuffle'

**Chilled instrumental showcases bespoke invention.**
Coming on like the mischievous kids next door, Stockport art poppers 10cc were hard and fast champions of the B-side art. Its four prolific writers used it as a place to stow unsinkable songs like '18 Carat Man Of Means' ['The Worst Band In The World', 1974], 'Channel Swimmer' ['I'm Not In Love' — US only, 1975] and 'I'm So Laid Back I'm Laid Out' ['People In Love', 1977] that their albums failed to accommodate. 'Gismo My Way' represented something of a departure. Written to showcase the Gizmotron device — a mechanical unit that straddled the bridge of an electric guitar and bowed the strings to simulate violin, viola, cello and contrabass — created by Kevin Godley and Lol Crème to counter the prohibitive costs of using orchestras in the studio, it was an appropriately meditative slab of spaced-out guitar exotica. Used to similar effect on *Sheet Music* album tracks 'Old Wild Men' and 'Baron Samedi', Godley and Crème became so obsessed by their creation they split the band to pursue the Gizmotron further. They spent a small fortune recording 1977's sprawling *Consequences* — possibly the only triple album to have started life as a B-side — to market the device, conjuring up elemental soundscapes amid a perverse narrative scripted and voiced by Peter Cook. While *Consequences* has since gained a cult following, the Gizmotron failed to catch on, despite marketing endorsements from Paul McCartney, Phil Manzanera and Jimmy Page. Or it did until an updated device (Gizmotron 2.0) surfaced in 2016. Incidentally, 'Gismo My Way' sounds even better at $33^{1/3}$.

## 'Give Him A Flower'

The Crazy World of Arthur Brown
TRACK 1967
A-Side: 'Devil's Grip'

**'God Of Hellfire' blasts hippy utopianism.**

Arthur Brown's outlandishly theatrical performances — a riot of extreme make-up and burning helmets — backed up his apocalyptic output and stentorian vocal delivery. A surprise hit on the 60s London underground scene, after a one-off show at the UFO Club spiralled into a residency, Pete Townshend was instrumental in signing his band to Track, joining a roster featuring Jimi Hendrix and the Who. While first single 'Devil's Grip' faithfully captured Brown's creepily psychedelic sound, its B-side was something else — a haughty Bonzo Dog Doo-Dah Band-like piss-take of the flower power fad. An exercise in shooting fish in a barrel that largely passed over their audience's heads, they would often crank Vincent Crane's knees-up piano vaudeville and lists of random flora beyond the 10-minute mark onstage, while crowds joined in on the chorus. And although the single flopped, Brown was still around as the age of the beautiful people came to an end, taking the incendiary 'Fire' to number 1 during 1968's summer of discontent.

## 'Gloria'

Them
DECCA 1964
A-Side: 'Baby, Please Don't Go'

**Timeless three-chord garage rocker.**

'Gloria' became short-lived Belfast band Them's most influential song. Dashed off by infatuated 18-year-old singer Van Morrison while touring Germany with his first outfit the Monarchs, record label machinations ensured it landed on the B-side of their Big Joe Williams' cover 'Baby, Please Don't Go' — a decision that undoubtedly hindered its popularity in the short-term. Barely wavering from its basic E-A-D riff, Morrison wailed and growled about his latest infatuation, feeling so taken that he was prepared to holler her name all night long. Short and sweet in B-side form (with guitar crunch courtesy of session player Jimmy Page), Morrison would later ad-lib entire sections during wild roaming gigs at Belfast's Maritime Hotel, stretching the song out farther and farther. Also popular on America's west coast, Them ended a residency at Los Angeles' Whiskey A-Go Go in 1966 with a version that caught Morrison and Jim Morrison (from support band the Doors) engaged in a lengthy call-and-response ('Gloria' became a Doors live staple thereafter). Covered almost endlessly since by everyone from AC/DC and David Bowie to Simple Minds, Patti Smith reworked it so completely that its familiar chorus chant took three full minutes to surface on 1975's 'Gloria: In Excelsis Deo'.

**'Go!'**
Tones on Tail
BEGGARS BANQUET 1984
A-Side: 'Lions'

**Maximum cowbell indie disco classic.**
Already an active side project when Northampton goth visionaries Bauhaus bade a pale farewell in 1983, Tones on Tail became a full-time gig for guitarist Daniel Ash and drummer Kevin Haskins, alongside former roadie turned bassist Glenn Campling. In welcome contrast to its fuzzily stoned smokers' delight A-side, 'Go!' was a chance to get the glad rags out, each member adding their distinctive stamp. Locked into a rhythm by Campling's pummelling disco bass riff and Haskins' cartoon-like way with five different cowbells, Ash's nonsense positivity and multiple "ya-yas" stuck in the mind long after it had ground to a close with a snatch of studio patter from engineer Derek Tomkins. Its extended 12-inch club version soon became a staple in alternative American dance clubs, prompting 'Go!' to be issued as an A-side in Canada and, anecdotally at least, "number 1 in Germany for about five weeks"– or so Ash told post-punk.com. Later sampled by Moby on his 1990 hit of the same name (sans exclamation mark), 'Go!' has featured extensively on big and small screen productions, from *Grosse Pointe Blank* and *Party Monster* to *Rick And Morty* and *Stranger Things*.

**'God Speed'**
Patti Smith
ARISTA 1978
A-Side: 'Because The Night'

**A poetic walk on the wild side.**

Those curious enough to flip over Patti Smith's one and only hit single would either be enraptured or repulsed at its wailing racket. Such is a divisive artist's life. Hustled into being by hit-seeking Bruce Springsteen producer Jimmy Iovine while working simultaneously on the Boss's *Darkness On The Edge Of Town* and Smith's *Easter* albums, 'Because The Night' burnished an almost complete Springsteen demo with a smattering of verse words and an anthemic chorus. If its directness was unusual for Smith, its six-minute-plus B-side gave hardcore fans her transgressive spirit *in excelsis*. A co-write with bassist Ivan Kral, 'God Speed' tapped into the vampiric energy and doomy mystery Smith had practically copyrighted during her often-improvised live turns at CBGB's on New York's Lower East Side, re-enacting her poems to blasts of feedback from guitarist husband Lenny Kaye. Named by Sonic Youth's Thurston Moore as one of his favourite songs in *Rolling Stone* magazine, it rivals early B-side 'Piss Factory' ['Hey Joe', 1974] — a harrowing spoken word account of working in a baby buggy factory at 16 — as Smith's most impassioned studio recording.

**'Good Riddance (Time Of Your Life)'**

Green Day

REPRISE 1996

A-Side: 'Brain Stew/Jaded'

**Strum-along demo that sparked a sales phenomenon.**

With its misty-eyed talk about forks in the road and lessons learnt in time, Green Day's best-known song has often been interpreted as a cosy reflection on past glories. However, 'Good Riddance (Time Of Your Life)' grew from a much more bitter seed. Written by Green Day frontman Billie Joe Armstrong about an ex-girlfriend who had just moved to Ecuador and inspired by students passing around an acoustic guitar at a house party in Berkeley, he told Guitar World that he prissily titled it 'Good Riddance' "just to express my anger... I didn't really think of it as being for an album or anything." That probably explains why it first surfaced on the B-side of a German single most hardcore Green Day fans have forgotten. Producer Rob Cavallo suggested they add strings when the Californian band re-recorded it for 1997's *Nimrod*, Armstrong replacing its hearty strum with delicate acoustic picking to emphasise its yearning tone. A testing experience for early adopters more used to bad-tempered guitars and morbid wordplay — many screaming "sell-out" — the rejigged version did just that, shifting over two million copies as an A-side in 1997, while being subsequently doomed to haunt high school graduations, weddings and funerals.

### 'Good Wizzard Meets Naughty Wizzard'

The Aquarian Age
PARLOPHONE 1968
A-Side: '10,000 Words In A Cardboard Box'

**Whimsical short-lived Tomorrow spin-off.**

The Aquarian Age was the result of the rancour that erupted when John Peel-endorsed freakbeat favourites Tomorrow split up. The studio project of drummer John 'Twink' Alder and bassist John 'Junior' Woo, they released just one single, its A-side's poppy psychedelia raging against singer Keith West (who quit Tomorrow to score a novelty hit with 'Excerpt from a Teenage Opera (Grocer Jack)'). With undoubted parallels to Jim Copp's children's ditty 'Frog Man', its far-out B-side transported listeners back to 1700, for a theatrical story of the two fumbling wizards over a cautious rumble of drums, dribbly bass and trippy keys. Apparently the template for a full-length play that even made it to the casting stages, that ground to a halt when Twink joined the Pretty Things and Wood took tentative steps to becoming a round-the-world yachtsman. A highly prized artefact among British psych collectors, 'Good Wizzard...''s exaggerated nature was also an influence on children's TV presenters Trevor & Simon.

### 'Green Onions'

Booker T. & the M.G.'s
VOLT 1962
A-Side: 'Behave Yourself'

**Stax house band's unplanned recording.**

As Stax Records' house band Booker T. & the M.G.'s played on a blizzard of hits for Sam And Dave, Wilson Pickett and Otis Redding during the Memphis label's 60s heyday. Proof that a racially integrated band could play funky music together, both sides of their most famous offering were a happy fluke. After waiting in vain for Sun Records' rockabilly singer Billie Lee Riley to show for a session, they cut A-side 'Behave Yourself', based around a groove their pianist and organist Booker T. had been playing in the clubs. Engineered by multi-tasking Stax supremo Jim Stewart, he was keen to release it but stressed the pressing need for an accompanying B-side. Booker T. came to the rescue again, transposing a minor key 12-bar blues he'd been messing with on piano to his Hammond organ as others improvised around him — Al Jackson cooking up a hypnotic beat, Lewis Steinberg a stalking bassline, Steve Cropper delivering a killer blow with his stabbing Telecaster guitar line. Recorded in a couple of takes, the first inkling that the song they dubbed 'Funky Onions' would take off came when WLOK DJ Rueben Washington cut off the A-side midway through to play 'Green Onions' back-to-back several times. The decision to make the B-side the A-side, just three months after release, was vindicated when it became a top US Top 3 hit, with successful covers by Henry Mancini, Count Basie and the Ventures, despite many young wannabes failing to master its deceptively difficult dynamic. It took until 1980 to have the same impact in the UK, going Top 10 after featuring in the Who's rock opera *Quadrophenia*.

## 'Grendel'

Marillion

EMI 1982

A-Side: 'Market Square Heroes'

**New wave prog act's epic 17-minute statement.**

Theatrical cheerleaders for the New Wave of British Progressive Rock movement, Marillion opened their recording account with a 12-inch single that showed off their commercial and atmospheric capabilities. While A-side 'Market Square Heroes' and seven-inch B-side 'Three Boats Down From The Candy' were catchy fantasy-tinged sing-alongs, jammed with Mark Kelly's Tony Banks-inspired keyboard runs, the Aylesbury band already pegged in the press as 80s throwbacks to early Genesis went the full Peter Gabriel on its ominous 12-inch B-side. Named after the monster at the heart of the Beowulf fable, 'Grendel' played to their early strengths — tightly written musical passages, soaring instrumental links and singer Fish's powerful narration skills (here borrowing from John Gardner's 1971 novel considering Beowulf from the monster's point of view). Heavily reminiscent of Genesis's 23-minute epic 'Supper's Ready' and boasting the same producer in David Hitchcock, Fish came clean about its origins to Loudersound.com in 2016: "We just thought, 'Let's write a big, long song, because that's what progressive rock bands do.' But yes, it was very, very Genesis-oriented." That also applied to its portrayal onstage, the singer sporting a tattered cloak and a replica of an Anglo-Saxon mask found at Sutton Hoo as he pulled out a crowd member and mimed his dismemberment at its climax. While many fans consider 'Grendel' a career pinnacle and regularly call for it at shows, Marillion have refused to play it live since 1983's Reading Festival.

## 'Grown Up Girls'

Eurythmics

RCA 1985

A-Side: 'There Must Be An Angel (Playing With My Heart)'

**Club-ready electro synth romp.**

Purveyors of bold, future-facing pop from the moment ex-lovers Annie Lennox and Dave Stewart pulled the plug on their retro-inclined incarnation as the Tourists, by the mid-80s Eurythmics were looking backwards again. In open defiance of the darker sounds demanded for their *1984* soundtrack, upbeat 4th LP *Be Yourself Tonight* delved back into classic soul and R&B for inspiration. It was epitomised by a duet with Aretha Franklin on 'Sisters Are Doin' It For Themselves' and the wafting Stevie Wonder harmonica solo on 'There Must Be An Angel', Lennox's hiccupping array of "de-da-das" and "oo-oo-oos" securing the duo their first UK number 1. Most early supporters plumped for the more robust charms of B-side 'Grown Up Girl' instead. A high-energy, electro dance epic that found the singer's electronically treated vocals flitting between French and English as she rebuffed a romantic rival with a slightly accusatory tone; the cold rush of Lennox booming "Dance! Dance! As if your heart would break!" was a reminder of how vital and experimental Eurythmics sounded when they broke the electro-pop mould with 1983's second LP *Sweet Dreams (Are Made Of This)*.

## 'H.A.A. (Here's Another Asshole)'

Black Sheep
MERCURY 1995
A-Side: 'North South East West'

**Superlative MC Hammer dis.**

In the early 90s every rapper worth their salt had a rhyme dissing MC Hammer. Widely perceived as a sell-out, who dumbed down his music in pursuit of lucre, the California rapper was taking hits from A Tribe Called Quest, Tim Dog and LL Cool J — even his white imperialist counterpart Vanilla Ice had a dig. Black Sheep, the latest addition to the Native Tongue collective, made a sideways snipe at Hammer when they guested on 'Skit 5' from De La Soul's overthought second LP *De La Soul Is Dead*. Hammer took note. And when he issued 1994's comeback LP *The Funky Headhunter* he let loose at the New York duo of Dres and Mista Lawnge, spitting "You're weak/You're meek/You're tryin' to grow feet" on its lead single 'It's All Good'. Black Sheep's response was unequivocal — 'H.A.A.' blasting him with both barrels over a suitably rough and ready sample of Biz Markie's laughing beatbox (lifted from Roxanne Shanté's 'Def Fresh Crew'). It's a moot point whether it was worth it — Hammer's fame had faded, bankruptcy was looming — but no self-respecting rapper would let a dis go unanswered.

## 'H-Eyes'

The Ruts
PEOPLE UNITE 1979
A-Side: 'In A Rut'

**Sadly prophetic anti-heroin tirade.**

Musically astute leaders of punk's second wave, west London's the Ruts balanced their focused attack with lashings of reggae and dub. Tied into the emerging Rock Against Racism movement from the off, they regularly supported the cause and forged a tight relationship with South London reggae band Misty In Roots, whose label put out 1979's first single. Anyone who listened to John Peel's BBC Radio 1 show would be familiar with the grinding power of 'In A Rut' and its chorus's double-edged growled exhortation to "Get out of it". Peel played its B-side 'H-Eyes' with equal enthusiasm, and it was hard not to be moved by its tightly-coiled warning about the perils of heroin use ("You're gonna wind up dead!"). With the DJ's endorsement it sold over 20,000 copies but, unknown to his bandmates, singer Malcolm Owen had a long-term problem with the drug. It flared up as early 80s chart success conflicted with issues in his personal life, Owen's habit leading to his temporary ejection from the Ruts. He completed rehab but succumbed again in 1980, this time fatally, ensuring that any play of 'H-Eyes' sends regretful shivers down the spine.

### 'Haliç'te Güneşin Batışı'

Moğollar
DISKOTÜR 1970
A-Side: 'Ternek'

**Enduring Anadolu psych classic.**

Moğollar borrowed their name from one of history's largest empires (the Mongols) as they set about freeing Turkish pop from western commodification. The progressive quartet had relocated to Paris and were writing towards their debut LP when they recorded 'Ternek' — a warped dance tune that witnessed guitarist Cahit Berkay showing off his baglama skills before Murat Ses's synths kicked into the groove. And while that sated early supporters, its B-side 'Haliç'te Güneşin Batışı' would go on to resonate around the world. A fevered blast of roughneck psychedelia built around Taner Öngür and Engin Yörükoğlu's trenchant bass and drum pulse, violinist Ersen Dinleten's ghostly interventions flattered to deceive before a sudden tempo change and Ses' spooky organ work made it feel like something cooked up on a mad LSD binge with Country Joe & the Fish. Late hip-hop visionary J Dilla transformed the source material when he dipped into the B-side's final breakdown to create the title track for 2001's landmark solo debut *Welcome 2 Detroit*.

### 'Happen To Die'

The Charlatans
SITUATION TWO 1991
A-Side: 'Over Rising'

**The late Rob Collins' finest hour.**

The Charlatans buried arguably their greatest B-side on a single that bridged the gap between their first two albums. 'Over Rising' marked the end of the band's tenure with original guitarist John Baker and transition from bowl-fringed Madchester scenesters into something more complicated and interesting, distinguished from their 'Madchester' peers by Rob Collins' swarming Hammond organ attack. If the A-side was a logical progression away from their *Some Friendly* debut's overly 60s retro-psych, the hyper-groovy 'Happen To Die' was a showcase of Collins' growing confidence. Often deployed to fill up the group's sound and bury its deficiencies, Collins effectively turned the Hammond into a lead instrument, rendering its strident bassline and Tim Burgess's allusive wordplay into ornamental features. Fate, however, would conspire further against the serially unlucky Collins as the 90s progressed. His unwitting role in a bungled armed robbery led to four months in prison before he tragically died in a car crash near Rockfield Studios in July 1996, where the band were wrapping up fifth album *Tellin' Stories*.

### 'Hard Like A Criminal'

Das-EFX
EAST WEST 1992
A-Side: 'Straight Out The Sewer'

**Straight-up storytelling from 'iggedy' rap duo.**

Das-EFX were different to their golden age hip-hop peers. Spotted at a talent show by EPMD's Erick Sermon and Parrish Smith, the Brooklyn duo of Skoob and Dray were quickly co-opted into their Hit Squad crew (alongside Redman, K-Solo and Knucklehedz). For much of 1992's primitively produced debut *Dead Serious*, Dray and Skoob were anything but, peppering their pop-culture-riffing rhymes with a tongue-twisting 'iggedy' vocal tick that added multiple syllables and became an instant trademark. Kept aside to keep B-side hard-rocks content, 'Hard Like A Criminal' was noticeably lighter on the 'iggety's and higher on the pair's narrative skills, as they role-played attending the same house party from two rival viewpoints (one even shooting the other) over superbly muddy breakbeats that celebrated their self-created 'sewer' style. When Das-EFX's trademark was unapologetically teethed by the likes of Ice Cube, Common and Kool G Rap it left the pair at a career crossroads. Their decision to stick with more of the same on 1993's second LP *Straight Up Sewaside* proved pivotal.

**'Harder'**
PJ Harvey
ISLAND 1995
A-Side: 'Send His Love To Me'

**West Country singer at her most viscerally direct.**

It's hard to contain a grin at the lascivious fun of 'Harder'. After the frazzled nerves and frayed neuroses of PJ Harvey's first two albums, the bluntly honest Yeovil singer-songwriter began applying more glitter to her creations, ditching the trio format and taking her writing into unexpected waters on 1995's orchestrally lush and theatrical third LP *To Bring You My Love*. That was more or less forgotten on the flipside of its final single. Over a twisted, distorted guitar riff as primal and irresistible as Howlin' Wolf or Robert Johnson, 'Harder' found Harvey making an exaggerated paean to her man's appendage (apparently "made out of cold steel"), the singer getting hot and bothered about her lover's bedroom prowess in a leer of desire that nodded right back to the vicious blues-punk delivery of her debut *Dry*, albeit from a more liberated position. Harvey's B-sides, often railing against the prevailing wind, have remained a source of rich pickings throughout her career.

**'Harlem Congo'**
Chick Webb
DECCA 1938
A-Side: 'I Got A Guy'

**Diminutive swing giant pulls out all the stops.**

The first great jazz drummer, Chick Webb set a high bar for swing-era percussionists. Having taken up drums as a remedy for stiff joints in his teens, the Baltimore teen defied his spinal tuberculosis diagnosis and moved to New York at 17, playing with Johnny Hodges, Benny Carter and Duke Ellington using a kit augmented with custom-made pedals. After forming his own band, on Ellington's advice, his late 30s residency at Harlem's Savoy with singer Ella Fitzgerald saw him ranked among the era's greatest bandleaders. The pair recorded together prodigiously until Webb's death in 1939, their chemistry abundant in the svelte celebration of 'I Got A Guy'. Webb's instrumental B-side 'Harlem Congo' easily eclipsed it. A fast-paced ode to his NYC neighbourhood, lit up by Chauncey Haughton's plummeting clarinet solo and Taft Jordan's punchy trumpet, it was finessed by Webb's madly swinging 20-second drum solo, just before the band delivered its triumphant coda. Used to soundtrack the torture of Albert Basserman's character Van Meer in Alfred Hitchcock's spy film *Foreign Correspondent*, Webb's tour-de-force has lost none of its enduring power.

### 'Have Yourself A Merry Little Christmas'

Tori Amos
EAST WEST 1998
A-Side: 'Spark'

**Stripped, melancholic take on festive favourite.**

There has been a long tradition of sappy Christmas B-sides. An easy way to potter with sleighbells and send a slightly cheesy greeting to fans, the festive cover version also comes cheap. Flame-haired Maryland singer-songwriter Tori Amos took a more singular approach when she tackled the festive standard Hugh Martin and Ralph Blane wrote for 1944's Judy Garland film musical *Meet Me In St. Louis*. Released just after Easter on the back of the intense and complex 'Spark' — a traumatic song recalling a recent miscarriage — Amos stripped 'Have Yourself A Merry Little Christmas' back to the piano and voice template that dominated her breakthrough work. Her ethereal tones suited its madrigal-like stature and kept fidelity to the original's melancholy air — a song so sad that Garland rejected its first draft and the film's producers lobbied for a rewrite. There is little doubt that Amos's take fulfilled the original's brief to make the character Esther "smile through the tears".

### 'He's All I Got'

The Supremes
MOTOWN 1966
A-Side: 'Love Is Like An Itching In My Heart'

**Schizoid northern soul floor-filler.**

The Supremes were at peak power in the mid-60s, second only to the Beatles in terms of chart invincibility. They diverted from their pop roots on the unquestionably broody Holland-Dozier-Holland-penned A-side — a far more soulful-leaning outing than usual, lit up by Diana Ross's carnal first take vocal brilliance and a robust floor-filling performance from Motown house band the Funk Brothers. All parties were in equally fleet form on 'He's All I Got', a keeper in its own right that kept faith with the typical Supremes sound. The song's sophisticated plot — a vindictive woman is out to sabotage the singer's relationship, who begs her to consider her feelings and repair the damage done — its gloomy verses paved the way for an indelible chorus that soared like the sun. A relative chart failure by Supremes standards (next single 'You Can't Hurry Love' started a run of four consecutive number 1s), that was largely immaterial to UK northern soul devotees, who clutched both sides to their hearts.

### 'Heartbreakers Beach Party'

Tom Petty & the Heartbreakers
BACKSTREET 1983
A-Side: 'Change Of Heart'

**Short and goofy ode to the good life.**

B-sides could be fun too. Sharing a title with a short MTV film that was Cameron Crowe's first directing gig (but quickly pulled for using bootleg footage), 'Heartbreakers Beach Party' showed Florida songwriter Tom Petty and his band in ultra-relaxed mode. With Petty's vocal channelling David Bowie and his band Elvis Presley's 'Crawfish', its louche groove and lyrical celebration of the joy of eating wieners and potato salad made it a shoe-in for the soundtrack of a teen beach movie. Petty almost sounded like Jonathan Richman when he commanded "Alright jones, let's dig some clams" before its bongo solo, later declaring "Okay another modern classic" with a giggle. The B-side of a hit that never quite was from a time the Heartbreakers' pursuit of streamlined arena rock was bringing in diminishing returns, Petty's commitment to fun was also evident on the mashed potato rockabilly jive of 'Gator On The Lawn' ['A Woman In Love', 1981] and sweet country ramble of 'Girl On LSD' ['You Don't Know How It Feels', 1994].

### 'Heaven And Hell'

The Who
TRACK 1970
A-Side: 'Summertime Blues'

**'The Ox' gets existential on rambling rocker.**

To back up a weighty live take of Eddie Cochran's teen rebellion anthem from their stop-gap *Live At Leeds* LP, the Who delivered a slice of rock theatre written and sung by their tall, thundering bassist John Entwistle. Flailing around a devilishly simple riff and wailing vocal pleading for eternal life, Entwistle's lead-style melodic bass somehow brought order to the chaos, knitting together the virtuosic extremities of Pete Townshend's guitar and Keith Moon's drums. Unveiled at a time when Townshend was stumped about where to go next, their chief songwriter later rued that 'Heaven And Hell' should have been an A-side (and probably would have been, had Track not requested a B-side at short notice). That was backed up by their decision to use it as the opener for their *Tommy* shows circa 1969/1970 and at Woodstock, 'Heaven And Hell' allowing Townshend and Moon to limber up while the man nicknamed 'The Ox' (and with his own signature B-side on the flip of 1966's 'The Kids Are Alright') stood stock still between them. Entwistle recorded a much slower take for 1971's first solo LP *Smash Your Head Against The Wall* and contributed further powerful B-side fare with his Hammer-styled tribute to Moon 'Dr Jekyll & Mr Hyde' ['Call Me Lightning', 1968] and a failed attempt to buck his own stereotype with 'The Quiet One' ['You Better You Bet', 1981].

## 'Heavy Hitters'

Kanye West

ROC-A-FELLA 2004

A-Side: 'All Falls Down'

**The playful side of the college dropout.**

On the back of the insightful 'All Falls Down', one of Kanye West's most self-aware singles, the Chicago producer-turned-rapper showed a more playful side at odds with his public image. West took a gentle piano loop and old school beatbox to the party on 'Heavy Hitters' and made them sing, weaving sleek violins inside its rhythm and securing a pleasing second verse from long-term friend GLC. Even his sometimes-contested rhyme skills sounded vintage on relatively humble, down-home brags about changing the game and getting paid, before he called for everyone to throw up their Roc-A-Fella hands (in reference to Jay-Z's record label). If its sentiments were unremarkable in a hip-hop era dominated by 50 Cent's glossy gangsta rap, they showed a more carefree side that would be overtaken with self-absorption and narcissism when fame truly bit in hard. Originally intended for West's solo debut *The College Dropout*, 'Heavy Hitters' became a B-side twice instead, also backing up the holy bridge building of 'Jesus Walks'.

### 'Hello It's Me'

The Nazz

SGC 1968

A-Side: 'Open My Eyes'

**Todd Rundgren's first song is far from puppy love.**

Named after an obscure Yardbirds song, the Nazz made no secret of their love of British rock. The Philadelphia quartet fronted by singer Stewkey and guitarist Todd Rundgren gained momentum after a 1967 show supporting the Doors, but were forever battling the populist tendencies of their manager Michael Friedman. The dichotomy was clear on their first single, which backed the pacey Who-like psychedelic pop of 'Open My Eyes' with 'Hello It's Me', a startlingly mature ballad from 19-year-old Rundgren. Based around the intro chords jazz organist Jimmy Smith used to tackle Civil War standard 'When Johnny Comes Marching Home', Rundgren's funereal outing took listeners through the telephone call when he broke-up with his high school sweetheart (albeit with dramatic licence — he later admitted her hippy-hating father put the kibosh on the relationship). Picked up in preference to the A-side by Boston radio station WMEX, it became a local sensation but barely bothered the *Billboard chart*. While Rundgren revisited it on 1972's solo LP *Something/Anything?* — upping the tempo to claim his biggest-selling solo hit — for many the solemn heartbreak of the Nazz original remains its definitive take.

### 'Hey Gyp (Dig The Slowness)'

Soul Survivors

CRIMSON 1967

A-Side: 'Expressway To Your Heart'

**Donovan gets prime-time garage rock treatment.**

When radio programmers first heard Soul Survivors they assumed they were black. It was an impression their label encouraged, aware of the momentum an R&B chart placing could have on their first single — a horn-packed, effects enhanced slab of soul that blew off the *Billboard chart* doors for its writers and producers, Kenny Gamble and Leon Huff. When their manager secured them a spot on ABC's *Joey Bishop Show*, the cat came out of the bag, the all-white Philadelphia trio of Kenny Jeremiah with brothers Richie and Charlie Ingui possibly blowing their chances of a first US number 1. Its B-side's cover of relatively obscure Donovan 1966 single 'Hey Gyp' (itself loosely structured on Kansas City Joe & Memphis Minnie's 1930 blues lament 'Can I Do It For You') was equally forceful, veering far off-road from the original's casual acoustic strum. While Jeremiah made unreliable promises to buy a Chevrolet, a Ford Mustang and a Cadillac in a trade-off for love, Gamble & Huff punched up the wah-wah guitars, adding a freaked-out mid-section that made the most of Paul Venturini's organ psychedelics.

## 'Hey Hey What Can I Do'

Led Zeppelin
ATLANTIC 1970
A-Side: 'Immigrant Song'

**Folk oddity.**

Having toured their first two albums relentlessly, Led Zeppelin finally had the chance to slow down when it came to writing their third. To get things started guitarist Jimmy Page and singer Robert Plant retreated to a cottage in Snowdonia, determined to broaden their horizons and keep pushing the boundaries, developing an acoustic foundation that added greater depth to their music. It was where they conceived 'Hey Hey What Can I Do', the only Led Zeppelin song never to appear on an album. Led by Page's 12-string acoustic guitar and typically intricate drum and bass interplay between John Bonham and John Paul Jones, it made the most of Plant's ability to seemingly blend soul, blues and rock within the space of a song. While there were certain oddities at play — its massed backing vocals, Jones's mandolin filigree — it was possibly the most outwardly commercial song they had recorded, one that made their third album's folk influences explicit. It certainly defied its B-side status, becoming a classic rock radio station staple. Never played live by Led Zeppelin's original line-up, Page and Plant dusted it off when they embarked on 1995's acoustic tour, Page even duck walking across the stage when they played at Washington's US Air Arena.

### 'Hip Hop Vs Rap'

KRS-One

JIVE 1993

A-Side: 'Sound Of Da Police'

**Hip-hop eats itself on back-in-the-day standard.**

Hip-hop's self-styled 'Teacha' has never been short of an opinion or 12. To back the rap founding father's tale of police brutality (a standout on 1993's first solo album), KRS-One delivered a lesson to new jacks, drawing a distinction between the music ("rap is something you do") and the culture ("hip-hop is something you live"). To underline his point, the second half of 'Hip Hop Vs Rap' was entirely made up of borrowed lines from rap joints — lyrical sampling, if you will — with the well-known and obvious (Run-DMC, Public Enemy, Eric B & Rakim, Cypress Hill) intersected with the more arcane (Eastside Connection, Jimmy Spicer, Joeski Love, Boogie Boys) as he flaunted his old school credentials. KRS-One being KRS-One, he referenced himself several times too, going right back to Boogie Down Productions' 'The Bridge Is Over' — his infamous response to MC Shan B-side 'The Bridge'. While KRS-One would reprise the same trick, to less success, on 1997's 'Bring It Back', DJ Sinbad's intricate bootleg megamix was even better, dropping in instrumentals of all the name-checked songs.

### 'Hit 'Em Up'

2Pac

DEATH ROW 1996

A-Side: 'How Do U Want It'

**Beefing B-side that changed the face of hip-hop.**

'Hit 'Em Up' was irreversible. A turning point in the very real feud between 2Pac and The Notorious B.I.G. — the two biggest rap stars of their generation, close friends before either was famous — it had a seismic impact on all parties involved, altering the course of hip-hop history. The rancour between the pair stemmed back to 1994, when 2Pac was shot and robbed at New York's Quad Studios while attempting to visit B.I.G. there, his suspicion that the rapper was involved compounded by the release of BIG's unrelated single 'Who Shot Ya'. Incendiary from the start for its musical reworking of 'Get Money' by Junior M.A.F.I.A. (B.I.G.'s proteges), the B-side's early declaration "I fucked your bitch/ You fat motherfucker" didn't so much thrown down the gauntlet as smash it into B.I.G.'s face, as a machine-gun-speedy 2Pac insulted his rival's physique, accused him of biting his style and somehow kept its chorus on a pop tip. Yet it went way beyond ruthless dis verses at its finale, as a freestyling 2Pac picked fights with rappers Mobb Deep and Chino XL, threatened to kill all and sundry, before he turned on the entire east coast and screamed "Bring it!" While riveting, the song had very real consequences. It spiralled into an ugly, pitched battle between the artists' respective labels, Death Row and Bad Boy, before both rappers were murdered within six months of each other — in murky circumstances that remain unsolved to this day. Few can recall its K-Ci & JoJo-assisted A-side, but everyone knows 'Hit 'Em Up' — a reminder that when rap beef becomes real beef the consequences are dire.

### 'Home Of The Whale'

Massive Attack

CIRCA 1992

'Massive Attack EP'

**Trip-hoppers' unlikely folk dabble.**

'Home Of The Whale' saw Massive Attack try something different as they tried to figure out where to head next after the befuddling success of 1991's debut LP *Blue Lines*. The Bristol band that slimmed down from DJ soundsystem Wild Bunch into carriers of the trip-hop torch swerved left by hooking up with relatively unknown songwriter and cellist Caroline Lavelle, who suggested covering an old Irish folk number. Massive Attack stripped it right back to some curious dub textures, whale song and echoed percussion, allowing Lavelle's transcendent vocals to weave the sorrowful tale of a husband who "ne'er returns from hunting the sperm" garlanded with her sad yearning cello at its outro. The sole new track on a stop-gap EP of remixes, Lavelle would later rework the song with

Marius De Vries for 1999's big screen thriller *Eye Of The Beholder*, while Massive Attack added looming bass textures to an all-new 'Mayday Mix', issued to raise awareness of environmental issues on 2018's World Oceans Day.

**'Honey, Don't!'**

Carl Perkins

SUN 1956

A-Side: 'Blue Suede Shoes'

**Double-sided gold from forgotten rock 'n' roll original.**

After Elvis Presley left Sun Records for RCA, label owner Sam Phillips set his sights on promoting Carl Perkins. "You're my rockabilly cat now," he told the slick-haired Tennessee songwriter with just a few regional hits to his name. Perkins responded in kind, writing two of his most definitive songs. Based on an observation of real-life male vanity, A-side 'Blue Suede Shoes' was solid proof of Perkins' genius as a rock songwriter. It swiftly rose to number 1 after its TV debut on *Ozark Jubilee* and became Sun's first million-seller (and a hit again for Presley within a year, albeit 19 places lower). Perkins and his band — his brothers Jay and Clayton, drummer W.S. Holland — also played its B-side 'Honey, Don't!' on the show, an unconventional number whose non-linear chord changes shook up the whole rockabilly scene as much as its lyrical flip on a 'honeydew' list. Adored by the Beatles and part of their live set from 1962 onwards, they not only covered it on 1964's *Beatles For Sale* (with Ringo Starr taking lead), all four performed it individually after they split — Paul McCartney playing it live, John Lennon on the soundtrack of 1971's homemade film *Clock*, Starr alongside Perkins on a 1986 TV special and George Harrison at 1987's Taj Mahal concerts. Ultimately overshadowed by Presley's success, Perkins never gave up the ghost, writing for Johnny Cash and Patsy Cline and penning another timeless B-side in 'Matchbox' ['Your True Love', 1957] that the Beatles turned into a US A-side in 1964.

**'Hound Dog'**

Elvis Presley

RCA VICTOR 1956

A-Side: 'Don't Be Cruel'

**The King's trademark song.**

'Don't Be Cruel' was a serious departure for Elvis, a move away from the rockabilly that made him, buffeted by the smooth vocal harmonies of the Jordanaires. But it was its B-side, 'Hound Dog', that would eventually become the biggest hit of Presley's career and, in many respects, his defining moment. Written by Jerry Leiber and Mike Stoller and first recorded in a blues style by Big Mama Thornton in 1953, Presley heard it when he saw Freddie Bell and the Bell Boys play the Sahara on the Las Vegas strip (at the same time his own Vegas revue at the New Frontier Hotel was bombing badly). He based his stab on the Texan band's parody version, keeping truck with its slightly altered lyrics (seemingly sung towards a dog rather than Thornton's gigolo), reputedly powering through thirty-one takes to get what he wanted on acetate. Yet it was his pelvis-shaking television performance of 'Hound Dog' on *The Milton Berle Show*, before the single was released, that launched Presley simultaneously into superstardom and infamy — upsetting conservative white America and being slammed for its vulgarity (the ensuing controversy prompted Presley to sing the song to a Bassett hound on his next TV appearance). Ironically kept off the US number 1 spot by its A-side, the single became a rare first in recording history — both sides topped the charts — with 'Hound Dog' holding its own for ten weeks before becoming the bring-down-the-house finale at Presley's live reviews. A definitive singles artist, Presley regularly slipped out B-side gold to his committed fans, be it the high static cut and thrust of '(Marie's The Name) His Latest Flame' ['Little Sister', 1961], groovy Romeo antics of 'Rubberneckin'' ['Don't Cry Daddy', 1969] or heartbroken balladry of 'It's A Matter Of Time' ['Burning Love', 1972].

**'Housepower'**
MC Lyte
FIRST PRIORITY 1989
A-Side: 'Cha Cha Cha'

**Rap originator embraces house.**

MC Lyte was a queen of hip-hop firsts. The hard-knock Brooklyn MC was the first female rapper to receive a gold single, the first to play Carnegie Hall and first to receive a Grammy nomination. She was also an early adopter of underground house music. To accompany a lean A-side that made fresh hay from Fearless Four's 'Rockin' It' and Cerrone's 'Rocket In The Pocket' came a bolt from the blue from a rapper who previously deployed B-sides for stone cold dis songs (cf. her definitive Antoinette destruction 'Shut the Eff Up! (Hoe)' ['Lyte As A Rock', 1988]). Key to it all was labelmate and producer King Of Chill. He paired a club-friendly Chicago bassline with slow, low interweaving synths, mixing short melodic phrases with funky beats as Lyte posed the simple question "What we need?" to a repeat of the title. If the seven-inch flip felt like a routine dabble, the just shy of twelve-minutes twelve-inch mix was a loose-limbed rave revelation, several worlds apart from the hip-house fusions of Fast Eddie, Tyree Cooper or Kool Rock Steady. Knowingly or not, it presaged Lyte's transition to a more smoothed-out sound in the early 90s.

# I WANNA B LIKE YOU

*Oddities and one-offs — B-sides in a previous age — wandering lost in the digital era...*

The death of the B-side is the biggest casualty of streaming culture. While some B-sides did little more than mop-up substandard surplus material from an album campaign, its better brethren safely housed misfits that simply didn't fit anywhere else — just like the digital orphans rounded up here.

Several worlds away from the conveyor-belt stars that infected the planet as TV talent shows began to dictate the face of pop, Latin America's biggest superstar, **Shakira** boasted the natural sass, charisma and, well, X-Factor her mirror-hogging wannabes lacked. The Colombian multi-instrumentalist was at her singular finest on 'Objection', an anthemic mix of pop, rock and tango whose leftfield lyrics (sample quote: "Next to her cheap silicon/I look minimal") further accentuated her *sui generis* status. Bizarrely omitted from the various remix options on the single's B-side, the percussively dense and intense **'Objection (Afro Punk Version)'** (2002) was a rare glimpse into its snake-hipped siren's intensity when she performed it live. Curiously left to dangle in no man's land, it finally surfaced as a bonus track on the limited edition *Washed And Dried* version of 2001's *Laundry Service*. Should have been a B-side though.

That equally applied to **Beyoncé**'s **'A Woman Like Me'** (2006). A superior slab of sultry, slow-burn R&B that multi-tracked Queen Bey's vocals over the horn arrangement from Simon Haseley's 'Hammerhead' (a Bond theme that never was), it found her repeatedly pushing a moot point: could a would-be suitor could possibly keep up with her? Written for her character Xania — the glamorous girlfriend of a murdered French football coach — in Shawn Levy's big screen reinvention of *The Pink Panther*, unlike her other offering for the soundtrack ('Check On It'), it was never officially released, with fans forced to bundle through the DVD's extras to locate its 'full performance' video.

Arguably hip-hop's most prolific content provider, **Lil Wayne** made his name in the early 00s by spinning freestyles over existing instrumentals on a succession of free, downloadable mixtapes. And while he wasn't the format's breakout star — step forward 50 Cent — he legitimised the form, forgoing traditional LP releases to craft efforts whose strongest peaks might previously have been titivated into powerful, street-oriented B-sides. First featured on his 15th official mixtape (there are many more unofficial ones) *Dedication 2*, **'Where Da Cash At'** (2006) used his own 'Fireman' beat to serve up a high-rolling prostitution fantasy three-way with the laidback Currency (the first act signed to Wayne's Young Money label) and no-nonsense Big Pun prodigy Remy Ma. While Wayne stole the show with the nonchalant quip "I make more than I can fit in this quote", its street heat helped embed the self-styled 'best rapper alive' into the hip-hop mainstream.

Treated with suspicion by dyed-in-wool hip-hoppers, wary of their so-called skills, California rap-rockers **Linkin Park** had started to mess with their own modus operandi in 2007, bringing in veteran Def Jam producer Rick Rubin as a fresh pair of ears. Sung in a deep register by their in-house rapper Mike Shinoda (rather than 'singer' Chester Bennington), **'No Roads Left'** (2007) was a shift from nu-metal's core values and a change of pace — orchestral elements and huge guitars meshing to create a dark, dirgy lighters-in-the-air rock ballad. Although never played live, it became a fan favourite after it appeared on the iTunes edition of third LP *Minutes To Midnight*.

Self-made Italian-American pop diva **Lady Gaga** outran the 'new Madonna' headlines as soon as she had a bigger canvas to paint with. **'Dirty Ice Cream'** (2007) saw her making the most of what she could afford. Recorded the previous year with producer Rob Fusari, it found the New Yorker conjuring a bubbling cauldron of dirty electro disco pop as its creator trilled the value of trusting your instincts when unnerved by an outsider's attentions. Stylish and seemingly effortless, it briefly appeared on Gaga's MySpace page, but not on 2007's debut LP *The Fame* (or its many expanded iterations thereafter), despite prominently featuring in her Lollapalooza set that year.

One-time R&B-styled Pennsylvanian party-starter and pug-nosed pop bruiser **P!nk** was in combative form as 2008 rolled around, using her sparks-flying fifth album *Funhouse* as open heart therapy after splitting with her husband, motocross racer Carey Hart. One of several outings culled from its final track list, **'Could Have Had Everything'** (2008) was a surprisingly bouncy, contrarily jaunty affair, its music openly defying its lyrical laments of "screwing myself over" as P!nk refused to cede to the depths of despair that, say, Linda Thompson, Marvin Gaye or even Phil Collins embraced during their 'divorce' periods. Briefly available as B-side to 'So What' on some CD formats in Europe (and a US deluxe edition bonus track), P!nk's very public purging didn't preclude a happy ending — she reconciled with Hart in 2009.

In-house issues threatened to derail **Paramore**'s swift rise from obscurity after the platinum success of 2007's second album *Rise* — with the perpetually troubled Tennessee band's engine room huffily jealous of the media focus centred on their powerhouse singer Hayley Williams. It is possibly one reason that the tumultuous fan favourite **'Adore'** (2008) got lost in the shuffle. Tailored to their balladic strengths and a hint at more commercial form to come, its bruised tale of young love was a non-corny slow dance at the close of the emo prom, elevated by an arena-friendly hook. Rarely played live and not even used as a bonus track, it reached wider ears via fan-made bootleg CD *The B Sides*.

**Kesha**'s rise to the top was as swift as it was total. Within eight short months, the California singer went from supplying the vocal hook on rapper Flo Rida's US number 1 'Right Round' to becoming a solo superstar after her first single 'TiK ToK' set a digital sales record (over 600,000 downloads in a week — slim pickings in today's money). Written for her debut LP *Animal* but dropped from the final cut, strutting club banger **'Fuck Him He's A DJ'** (2010) would have been an ideal B-side, letting lose the singer's more risqué side. Instead it was left floating in limbo until it was belatedly commandeered onto 2011's remix album *I Am The Dance Commander + I Command You To Dance*.

Introspective Canadian rap stylist **Drake** also struggled to find a suitable home for **'Girls Love Beyoncé'** (2013). Performed in tandem with silk-voiced Cocaine 80s singer James Fauntleroy, the pair indulged in a bout of collective soul-searching about twisted relationships and their concurrent insecurities above a repeated flip from Destiny's Child's 1999 hit 'Say My Name'. First issued on Drake's OVO Soundcloud blog in April, the buzzwordy banger was ultimately deemed surplus to his next full-length *Nothing Was The Same*. Nonetheless, it may have helped smooth Drake's way into Beyoncé's affections, with the pair combining on marital duet 'Mine' (from Beyoncé's self-titled fifth studio album) later that year.

**Justin Timberlake** defied all the odds. When he left NSYNC in 2002, it was still rare for a millennium boy-band member to forge a successful solo career. The Tennessee singer managed it by going against type — his solo debut

*Justified* embracing the Neptunes' glitchy electronics and funky production as he repurposed material first penned with Michael Jackson in mind. Timberlake's edginess was a given when he conjured up **'Body Count'** (2013) — a playful melange of Spanish guitar, saxophone blurts, frantic hip-hop beats and producer Timbaland's breathy adlibs — during sessions for third LP *The 20/20 Experience*. Given its heavily sexualised lyrics ("I had a shy little quite girl/But now she sings opera... loud!"), it would have made perfect B-side sense for the recently hitched Timberlake, but appeared as a bonus track on the album's deluxe edition instead.

Beyond being a potential B-side, many fans ranked **Taylor Swift**'s **'New Romantics'** (2014) as her greatest hit that never was. Written alongside Swedish chart-botherers Shellback and Max Martin, its galloping tenacity was a far cry from the country stylings that made the Wyomissing-raised singer-songwriter a teenage pop phenomena and generational voice. With its greedily appropriated 80s synthpop stylings, it was among Swift's most direct pop missiles as she essayed a more carefree approach to matters of the heart than usual. Danceable, upbeat and hook-loaded, it was somehow omitted from fifth studio LP *1989* by Swift and her handlers (with *Rolling Stone* over-egging its absence as "one of pop's greatest crimes") and eventually appeared as a bonus song on its deluxe edition.

**Rihanna**'s unapologetic trap anthem **'Bitch Better Have My Money'** (2015) was purposely designed to reassert the Caribbean Queen's cross-cultural appeal. Titled after a Fly Guy monologue in Keenen Ivory Wayans' 1988 blaxploitation spoof *I'm Gonna Git You Sucka*, it showed her ability to swag as hard as any rapper out there. It also generated oven-ready headlines for its vividly violent self-directed video, as Rihanna took out her beef with a male accountant (Mads Mikkelsen) by kidnapping, torturing and killing his girlfriend (Rachel Roberts)... as you do. And while one of its songwriters, Bibi Bourelly, boldly stated he came up with its chassis while 'vibing' with producer pal Deputy in Los Angeles, that claim bore virtually no water to anyone who'd heard Texan rapper Just Brittany's grimy doppelgänger 'Better Have My Money', issued nine months earlier. The song's extensive writing/production credits underlined its importance in laying the sonic groundwork towards Rihanna's simmering 8th LP *Anti*.

Compton rapper **Kendrick Lamar**'s kinship with jazz was made explicit when he issued surprise LP *Untitled Unmastered*. It gathered together the remaining demos — songs that would, in a previous age, have probably have become B-sides — recorded in the sessions for his experimental modern masterpiece

*To Pimp A Butterfly*. Its opening track **'untitled 01 08.19.2014'** (2016) set the twitching tone as it morphed from a burst of sonorous if slightly unhinged pillow talk into a concentrated blast of apocalyptic imagery that cited *The Book Of Revelation*. Lamar listed global warming, 9/11 and Flight 370 as portents for end times, his bracing if condemnatory spiel leavened by free-jazzing pianos, blaring trumpets, loose double bass and reverb-drenched drums.

Initially a vehicle for the solo psychedelic expeditions of Australian songwriter and producer Kevin Parker, **Tame Impala** began transitioning into a ruthlessly melodic pop hothouse in the late 00s. **'List Of People (To Try And Forget About)'** (2017) helped Parker set the evolutionary tone as he brooded about getting over an ex-lover so he could safely add them to his forgotten list. Among the first tracks written for third album *Currents*, it was first considered as a potential A-side before familiarity eventually bred contempt ("I was so over it by the time I was finishing the album," Parker told Beats 1's Zane Lowe). And although it was a little light on the laser focus that made its candid confessionals feel like such a creative rebirth, it proved a keeper among fans when eventually issued as a bonus track on the *Collector's Edition*.

Designed as an exclusive online B-side for his Tame Impala collaboration 'Call My Phone Thinking I'm Doing Nothing Better', **'Where The Fuck Did April Go'** (2020) witnessed the **Streets** return to a much-changed British rap landscape, where massive success using native subject matter and your own accent was no longer a novelty. A wry, Pinteresque ode to lockdown life that mocked the empty platitudes of big corporations ("We're all in this together") and his fellow Brits' newfound aspirations ("My next-door neighbour thinks he's a DJ — shut up!"), Mike Skinner's lament to the summer that never was had the sly impact of a great lost B-side confessional. He certainly saw it that way, telling fans: "I just wrote a tune the same way other people might talk to a therapist!"

## 'I Am A Cliché'

X-Ray Spex

VIRGIN 1977

A-Side: 'Oh Bondage Up Yours!'

**Punk maverick explodes into being.**

X-Ray Spex's first single was as exhilarating as anything to come out of punk. Seconds after its butter-wouldn't-melt spoken word intro, Poly Styrene's great feminist rallying cry rang loud and true above Jak Airport's fuzzed-out guitars and Lora Logic's squalling saxophone. Its typically self-deprecating B-side was every bit its rival — confirmation that the Londoners hadn't just toppled off some wonky punk production line. Riven with spiky energy, it witnessed Styrene using repetition to her advantage, screamed refrains of "Huri yama yama" and "boring boredom" battling Logic's careening sax and their band's buzzsaw energy, a unique dynamic that proved short-lived (within weeks, a clash of egos forced Logic to quit). That Styrene was anything but a cliché is a given. A pioneer who used her unorthodox voice to rail about consumerism, postmodernism and identity, her actions helped wedge open the door for female-led punks such as the Slits, the Raincoats and the Banshees to follow. While her vast cultural footprint is explored in daughter Celeste Bell's 2021 documentary *I Am A Cliché*, this B-side sets out her stall in under two minutes.

### 'I Believe To My Soul'

Ray Charles and His Orchestra
ATLANTIC 1959
A-Side: 'I'm Movin' On'

**Soul visionary in hurting mode.**

A piano-playing marvel, completely blind from age seven, Ray Charles was instrumental in bringing the new sound of R&B into the mainstream. The talented Florida singer, writer and arranger started to find his voice in the mid-50s, running off a stream of sophisticated yet gritty soul hits that made critical inroads into the white pop market, while showing his versatility on albums that traced blues, jazz and country. Cut in his final session for Atlantic, the A-side's cover of Hank Snow's 50s standard was Charles' first full country release and an unexpected shift of gears that added congas and maracas to the porch song brew. Covering similar emotional terrain, original B-side 'I Believe To My Soul' was even better — slow jazzy piano chords underpinning his soulful warning to the lover who had just yelped "Oh, Johnny!" in her sleep. Charles didn't stint on decorative detail either, adding John Hunt's you-lookin'-for-trouble trumpets and his own multi-tracked backing vocals (as he impersonated his missing-in-action backing singers the Raelettes). It was another pop crossover that assisted Charles as he lobbied for racial equality in the southern states.

## 'I Can Feel The Ice Melting'

The Parliaments
REVILOT 1967
A-Side: '(I Wanna) Testify'

**Silky smooth doo-wop points to a funky future.**

Before he got supersonically funky, George Clinton went through a decade of growing pains with first band the Parliaments. While the colourful North Caroline visionary — a hairdresser turned Motown songwriter/producer — put the band together in the back of his barbershop, logistics ensured only Clinton made it to Detroit to record this single, its other parts fleshed-out by local session singers and musicians. Although the deep commercial groove of '(I Wanna) Testify' tapped deep into the summer of love zeitgeist with its easy exhortation "Be free!", its more conventional flip was its more affecting side. A heart-tugging psych-soul serenade, 'I Can Feel The Ice Melting' found Clinton using his easy charisma to charm a reluctant paramour, its highly distinctive vocal stylings hinting at the funky road ahead (his band's transition into Funkadelic-Parliament was expedited by a contractual dispute over the Parliaments' name). Clinton later produced a 1989 cover of the B-side for Otis Day and the Knights (fictional band in *National Lampoon's Animal House*), while indie renegades Yo La Tengo chanced an off-the-cuff pop in 2015.

## 'I Can't Take It'

Carla Thomas
ATLANTIC 1962
A-Side: 'I'll Bring It Home To You'

**Queen of Memphis soul's early stirrings.**

Carla Thomas kept her powder dry until she was 17. Her first mark proved indelible, however. A duet with her father Rufus Thomas, one of the first acts on Sun Records, 'Cause I Love You' might only have been a regional hit but it paved the ground for Jim Stewart's Stax — a Memphis label wholly devoted to black music. With both Stewart and Atlantic producer Jerry Wexler in her corner, Thomas trained her sights on the national charts, scoring big with 'Gee Whiz' and this answer record to Sam Cooke's 'Bring It On Home To Me'. Thomas was at her intimate best on its begging B-side. A midtempo plea for her lover to quit messing with her heart that took in vamping strings and tremolo guitars before settling into an almost jaunty skank, qualities that ensured a second life as a northern soul standard. When Thomas's success was eclipsed by Aretha Franklin at the 60s tail, she effectively swerved the studio for good, making rare and impromptu live turns in the kind of unreconstructed Memphis clubs her father used to frequent.

### 'I Can't Turn You Loose'

Otis Redding
VOLT 1965
A-Side: 'Just One More Day'

**King of Soul at his upbeat best.**

Otis Redding's passion spilled through his short, expressive catalogue. The preternaturally gifted Macon singer and songwriter spent the early part of the 60s honing his skills with upcoming Memphis label Stax, finally breaking cover in the pop charts in 1965. While his hooky, moving ballad 'Just One More Day' seemed tailored with that in mind, his pop fans proved to have wilder tastes than expected. They favoured its pounding head-of-the-class B-side instead — an exercise in controlled dynamics as Redding toiled with the trauma of letting a loved one go. The singer built one of his greatest songs out of very little late one night in the studio, taking a riff from guitarist Steve Cropper before adding horns and some quickly-written verses. That said nothing of the sheer heart and soul he packed into his primed-to-explode performance, sung in an almost-preaching, semi-strangulated style over imperious backing from Booker T. and the M.G.'s. A regal showstopper at Redding's live performances, that fact was capitalised on by everyone, from Janis Joplin, Aretha Franklin, Ike and Tina Turner and Mick Jagger (who sang it at the White House for Barack Obama in 2012). No cover could quite match up to the original though, a standard from a soul colossus whose career was cut short by a fatal air crash in Wisconsin two years later.

### 'I Don't Think I'm Ever Gonna Figure It Out'

Elliott Smith
KILL ROCK STARS 1996
A-Side: 'Speed Trials'

**Light but dark jaunt from troubled songwriter.**

By 1997's third solo album Elliott Smith was at the peak of his powers. The troubled Portland songwriter had carved his reputation in indie-poppers Heatmiser prior to letting loose his inner demons on 1994's brittle lo-fi debut *Roman Candle*. His most deeply affecting songs arrived three years later, seemingly in droves, with Elliott saving two non-album affairs for the B-side of 'Speed Trials'. The two-minute sprint of 'I Don't Think I'm Ever Gonna Figure It Out' just won out over the heavier-going 'Angeles'. A delicate balancing act between its downbeat lyrics — bemoaning his inability to decipher people's emotions — and the foot-tapping bounciness of his acoustic guitar, Smith used his speedy, intricate and nuanced fingerpicking to underline his existential distress. While Smith's career would vault from playing tiny clubs to the Oscars soon afterwards (after 'Miss Misery' featured in Gus Van Sant's *Good Will Hunting*), his very real struggles to figure it out only intensified; battles with heroin, alcohol and depression ending when he violently stabbed himself to death in 2003.

**'I Feel Love'**

Donna Summer

CASABLANCA 1977

A-Side: 'Can't We Just Sit Down And Talk It Over'

**Unstoppable futuristic disco standard.**

A meeting of minds between its Boston-born singer and heavily moustachioed Italian-born producer Giorgio Moroder, 'I Feel Love' changed pop forever. A session singer who went to Germany to sing in hippie musical *Hair*, Summer was doing backing vocals on a Three Dog Night album when she caught the attention of Moroder's writing partner Pete Belotte. Together the trio turned out 1975's softcore epic 'Love To Love You Baby', whose orgiastic gasps and groans earned a BBC ban, and Summer the unwanted nickname "the Linda Lovelace of pop". The tight team were already working on their fifth album together, *I Remember Yesterday*, when they forged its fierce mesh of electronics and soul at Moroder's Musicland studio. Precision tooled on Moogs, its synthesised rhythms and real-life kick drum were augmented by an arpeggiated bassline whose subtle delay created a heady strobing and flickering effect. Topping it all was Summer's one-take ethereal vocal — a rhapsodic tribute to her new lover (and subsequent life partner Bruce Sudano) that felt like it was coming from another dimension entirely. Which was the point — it was designed as music of the future, from an album that took a tour through dance history. First issued as B-side to a more obviously chart-friendly ballad, it took off in UK clubs, where it was quickly switched to the A-side and whirred its way to number 1, with a profound impact on disco culture. As David Buckley recounted in *Kraftwerk: Publication*, it prompted Brian Eno to breathlessly inform his Berlin studio partner David Bowie: "This single is going to change the sound of club music for the next 15 years." Given its impact on Hi-NRG, house, techno, trance, EDM and every other form of dance music since, that now seems ridiculously conservative.

### 'I Go Crazy'

Queen
EMI 1984
A-Side: 'Radio Ga Ga'

**Stadium giants return to rock roots.**

Too raw to fit with the stylistic pick 'n' mix of their 11th studio album *The Works*, Queen reclaimed their rock roots with 'I Go Crazy', to the relief of many diehard fans. If the A-side's confused commentary on television's popularity heavily relied on singer Freddie's Mercury's charisma and a big budget video restaging of Fritz Lang's *Metropolis* to pull off its infantile chorus, its B-side channelled far more primal thrills. Written by Brian May about taking his girlfriend to see a band and then, improbably, losing her to its lead singer, this self-confessed 'heavy indulgence' received a lukewarm reception when first presented to May's bandmates. "The other three hated it so much they were ashamed to play it," he told *Faces* magazine in 1984. Queen evidently had a change of heart, turning in a rocket-fuelled performance that maxed out their massed vocals and May's heavily overdriven guitars. While Queen rarely served fresh meat on B-sides, there were odd exceptions: a reading of early live favourite 'See What a Fool I've Been' ['Seven Seas Of Rhye', 1974], Roger Taylor's almost solo 'A Human Body' ['Play The Game', 1980] and Mercury's self-spoofing falsetto lighting up 'Soul Brother' ['Under Pressure', 1981].

## 'I Heard It Through The Grapevine'

The Slits
ISLAND 1979
A-Side: 'Typical Girls'

**Sassy punk-reggae cover joy.**

The Slits always intended their take on Barratt Strong and Norman Whitfield's soul standard as a B-side. In contrast to Gladys Knight or Marvin Gaye's tremulous tale of rumoured infidelity, the all-female amalgam of punk bands the Castrators and the Flowers of Romance stripped it back to something far more primal and dubby, without the help of producer Denis Bovell (whose dub mastery defined their debut LP *Cut*). Riding on top of Tessa Pollitt's fathom-deep bass, Max Edwards' intuitive drumming and Viv Albertine's scratchy guitars was singer Ari Up in the form of her life, dementedly switching between whooping, pained yelps and almost spoken phrases that rendered its mind-losing lyrics entirely believable. She even subverted the words, the second chorus declaring "I heard it through the bassline" as the band sung out its horn parts (they couldn't afford a brass section). Highlighted by Island as the Slits' first single, the band successfully swerved that intervention (and the fateful novelty status that might have followed), for an anachronistic B-side that remains something else.

## 'I Love Rock 'n' roll'

The Arrows
RAK 1975
A-side: 'Broken Down Heart'

**Anthemic sing-along that nearly missed hit status.**

British glam rock trio the Arrows were convinced they'd nailed a hit when they recorded 'I Love Rock 'n' roll'. Written as an impassioned response to the Rolling Stones' 'It's Only Rock 'n Roll (But I Like It)' by singer Alan Merrill (although guitarist Jake Hooker got a co-writing credit to settle a longstanding debt), he was gutted when producer Mickie Most opted for ballad 'Broken Down Heart' as an A-side instead. Although Most was later persuaded to flip sides by his wife Christina Hayes, Merrill's rallying cry was further hindered by an English newspaper strike and might have been lost forever had television producer Muriel Young not caught the Arrows performing it on *Pop 45* and offered the band their own series. Joan Jett was touring Britain with The Runaways in 1976 when she caught the Arrows' TV show, revealing to Twitter that she "was blown away by the song that screamed hit to me". The Runaways disagreed, however, and Jett didn't get to record it until 1979, when she put down a rough take with ex-Sex Pistols Paul Cook and Steve Jones for the B-side of 1979's first solo single 'You Don't Own Me'. Jett returned to it again with new band the Blackhearts two years later, essentially aping the Arrows' original (and their fashion sense) in Chris Applebaum's poised barroom video, whose regular MTV rotation finally made it a worldwide hit.

**'I Love You'**
The Zombies
DECCA 1965
A-Side: 'Whenever You're Ready'

**B-side belter from luckless British invaders.**

The Zombies' failure to achieve more widespread success is mystifying. The slightly geeky looking Hertfordshire band hit the ground running, scoring a big transatlantic hit with 1964's first single 'She's Not There' that made them instant US stars, far bigger than they were at home. Despite the chemistry of Rod Argent's jazz-inspired keys with singer Colin Blunstone's soulful tenor and a gift for trenchant melodies, the hits quickly faded, with 'Whenever You're Ready' proving their third successive flop. Those who took the purchase plunge got plenty of extra bang from its harmonic B-side. Written by guitarist Chris White, 'I Love You' inverted the standard verse/chorus formula to emphasise its protagonist's buttoned-up misery — rendered mute every time he tried to make his love plain. Covered by San Jose's People! in 1971, its still commercially fizzing originators looked on in envy as it became a Top 20 US hit and number 1 in Japan, Australia and Italy. So persuasive were People!'s subtle alterations, the Zombies incorporated them wholesale when they hit the reunion trail in the mid-00s. For many, the crisp original still wins out.

### 'I Started Loving You Again'

Merle Haggard and the Strangers
CAPITOL 1968
A-Side: 'The Legend Of Bonnie & Clyde'

**Outlaw country legend's lonesome pledge.**

When Johnny Cash played San Quentin prison in 1958, Merle Haggard was in the audience, serving a prison bid for burglary. Keeping-it-real helped the singer dubbed 'the Hag' become a country phenomenon, finding public redemption through song as he haunted the bars of his native California. An originator of the Bakersfield sound — a rougher and readier take on Nashville country that let rock and blues in through the back door — Haggard's best songs were his most tender. Haggard had just played a show in Dallas with his band the Strangers when he asked his singer-songwriter wife Bonnie Owens to get him a hamburger. When she returned, minutes later, he had the pained, perpetually heartbroken lyrics of 'Today I Started Loving You Again' down in full. The shadow to his relatively upbeat distillation of Bonnie Parker and Clyde Barrow's murderous reign, it became a belated country hit when covered by fellow outlaw singer Sammi Smith in 1975. And whether voiced by Kenny Rogers, Dolly Parton or Emmylou Harris since, it's become staple on the jukeboxes behind most country bars' swinging doors.

### 'I Packed My Suitcase, Started To The Train'

Memphis Jug Band
VICTOR 1928
A-Side: 'Bob Lee Junior Blues'

**Scratchy sound of the 20s Memphis underground.**

The jug band was the quintessential expression of Memphis music. A no-frills set-up that used household instruments as its base: old jugs, washboards, a bass made from washtub and a broom handle, augmented by pie-plate banjos, fiddles and mandolins, with makeshift kazoos made by placing wax paper over combs. Such instruments were at the beating heart of Memphis Jug Band, the shape-shifting outfit first assembled by guitarist and singer Will Shade in 1925. Spotted by travelling talent scout Ralph Peer (whose scalps included Mamie Smith and Fiddlin' John Carson), he secured a deal with Victor that found them recording prodigiously up until 1930, when the tide of fashion began to turn. While not as well-known as 'Stealin', Stealin'' (included on Harry Smith's *Anthology Of American Folk* compilation), 'I Packed My Suitcase...' showed off Shade's understated compositional prowess, its bluesy escape narrative soulfully rendered by Jennie Mae Clayton, before Shade added some leaving threats of his own. The bitter truth was Shade could never leave Memphis or give up on his band — keeping the faith through its many changing line-ups until his death in 1966.

### 'I Say A Little Prayer'

Aretha Franklin

ATLANTIC 1968

A-Side: 'The House That Jack Built'

**Queen Of Soul's transformative gem.**

Burt Bacharach and Hal David's scored a US Top 10 hit twice within 12 months with 'I Say A Little Prayer'. While regular muse Dionne Warwick's 1967 version came first and hit the Top 5, despite requiring multiple takes, just under a year later the daughter of a real-life reverend proved her ability to powerfully remake songs as her own. Aretha Franklin had no intention of covering it when she entered New York's Atlantic Studios to record *Aretha Now* at the turn of 1968. Franklin sang it for the heck of it as her backing singers the Sweet Inspirations worked through songs they had planned. But they developed such a groove, producer Jerry Wexler decided to capture it. By cleverly shifting its arrangement from G to A-major, it transformed into a moving plea to the lord, freeing Franklin to further demonstrate her devastating emotional range. Bacharach recognised its power. "It's a better record than the record we made," he told NPR in 2010. "Aretha just makes it seamless, the transition going from one change to another change. You never notice it." That was proved when Franklin's B-side started to generate its own independent airplay, eventually becoming her ninth consecutive Top 10 *Billboard* hit. The Detroit soul queen already had a long history of brilliant B-sides. Whether it was her first swing at Otis Redding's signature song 'Try A Little Tenderness' ['Just For a Thrill', 1962], barmy Muscle Shoals session fruit 'Do Right Woman — Do Right Man' ['I Never Loved A Man (The Way I Love You)', 1967] or her sumptuous collaboration with Curtis Mayfield, 'Loving You Baby' ['Something He Can Feel', 1976], they always counted.

## 'I Shall Not Be Moved'

Charley Patton

PARAMOUNT 1930

A-Side: 'Jesus Is A Dying Bedmaker'

**Definitive take on gospel blues standard.**

If not the first Delta bluesman to make a record, Charley Patton became one of its biggest early recording stars. The diminutive, sharp-dressed Mississippi native packed them in the aisles at plantation dances, spiriting between blues, ragtime and gospel with his guitar showmanship and powerful barrelhouse vocals. While the man dubbed 'father of the Delta blues' was also a classy songwriter — as his driving early Paramount singles 'Pony Blues', 'Shake It And Break It' and 'Tom Rushen Blues' attested — this single spoke of his interpretative nous. While the A-side's singular take on a traditional gospel song saw Patton plays his guitar with increasing vigour and pace, its B-side utterly surpassed it. An African-American spiritual that dated back to slavery, 'I Shall Not Be Moved' rang with defiant emotion in Patton's dignified brogue. As with the A-side he started it slowly, gradually hitting a groove before putting the pedal down, his voice straining every time he asserted his unwavering faith. A key song during the 50s/60s civil rights movement, it has been reworked by everyone from Lonnie Donegan and Joan Baez to Johnny Cash and Public Enemy since, but never with quite the same bulletproof conviction.

## 'I Want To Live In A Wigwam'

Cat Stevens

ISLAND 1971

A-Side: 'Morning Has Broken'

**Long-haired Londoner at play.**

An unlikely update of an olde-worlde secular hymn mashed up with a keyboard sketch of Catherine Howard — a song for a concept album about the six wives of Henry VIII — gave Cat Stevens his biggest hit. While the A-side's prettified melody, played with panache by Rick Wakeman, became a transatlantic smash that sent tremors around the globe, single buyers were equally seduced by the charms of its wistful B-side. A combination of the lyrical idealism of John Lennon's 'Imagine' combined with flowing, nursery rhyme-like repetitions, 'I

Want To Live In A Wigwam' was not as simplistic as it first sounded, its subtle choral effects underlining Stevens' talent for ornamentation (first demonstrated on 1970's multi-layered *Tea For The Tillerman*). As the equally gentle insurrection of 'Granny' ['Matthew And Son', 1966] and astral instrumental 'Crab Dance' ['Sitting', 1972] proved, Stevens deployed B-sides to show off his more playful asides — or he did before he abandoned music altogether in 1977, only to return in 2006.

### 'I Will Be'

Christina Aguilera
RCA 2002
A-Side: 'Dirrty'

**Teen star stripped and vulnerable.**

Change hung in the air as Christina Aguilera geared up to her second album *Stripped*. Determined to break free from her teenybopper past, she launched a brash, bikini-heavy new image with the sweaty hip-hop club banger 'Dirrty', a partial duet with rapper Redman. Aguilera was at pains to claim it represented her real persona, with perceptions of the former *Mickey Mouse Club* TV regular seemingly skewed by the success of her co-star Britney Spears. It was a divisive move. The singer predictably caught critical heat for being overtly sexual in America and registered a relative flop, while bum-rushing the UK's number 1 spot. Aguilera showed more familiar colours on its powerful piano ballad B-side, 'I Will Be'. An inspirational song about taking your destiny in your own hands, it reflected her difficulties growing up in a house riven with domestic violence (a subject later addressed publicly on LP track 'I'm Okay'). Having pulled back from the vocal histrionics that marred 1999's self-titled debut, this flawless vocal take was very much on par with 'Beautiful', the world conquering hit that came next.

### 'I Will Survive'

Gloria Gaynor
POLYDOR 1978
A-Side: 'Substitute'

**Unfadeable disco anthem.**

Gloria Gaynor was having a difficult 1978. In the three years since the 30-year-old New Jersey singer had scaled the charts with her belting cover of the Jackson 5's 'Never Can Say Goodbye' her recording contract with Polydor was nearly up, her mother had died and she had just come out of hospital for spinal surgery (after suffering a bad fall onstage). There was one glimmer of hope. Polydor's new president wanted her to cover the Righteous Brothers' 1975 single 'Substitute'. When Gaynor requested a meaningful song for its B-side, producers Freddie Perren and Dino Fekaris offered something they'd written two years previously. Built on an insidious guitar and trumpet groove, interwoven with strings, Gaynor gave 'I Will Survive' everything — delivering disco's most assertive female vocal despite being in a back brace during the session. Part of its genius was the way it kept building and building, layering and layering, Gaynor's acute timing negotiating a clever false ending before its defiant chorus kicked in again. A classic marriage of soulful expression and disco danceability, it could have been lost forever had Gaynor not taken multiple copies to her DJ friends at New York's Studio 54 and watched its notoriously sniffy clientele gradually fall under its spell — its club success effectively forcing Polydor into reversing its A and B-sides. Widely perceived as an end-of-relationship fable, it was inspired by Fekaris' experiences as a songwriter — specifically his joy after landing the movie theme for 1969's George Schaefer comedy *Generation* after being fired as a Motown staff writer. The ultimate karaoke tune, it became a transatlantic number 1, its empowerment theme resonating within the gay community at the beginning of the AIDS crisis.

### 'I Will Take You Home'

Ed Sheeran
ATLANTIC 2014
A-Side: 'Bloodstream'

**Driving effort from 2010s pop phenomenon.**

Ed Sheeran was the 2010s most divisive pop figure. To his millions of fans, the Suffolk-raised ex-busker and Nizlopi guitar tech was a chameleonic pop marvel, able to turn his hand to any genre, capable of slaying Glastonbury with just six strings and a loop pedal. To his detractors he was a hideously wholesome manchild with inappropriate tattoos, epitomising all that was wrong with music while hogging streaming revenue with far-from-original songs (cf. his legal battles with Marvin Gaye's estate). To back a tensely-paced single tracing Sheeran's first experience of rave drug ecstasy, he let slip 'I Will Take You Home' — a road song that began with the unlikely image: "I stole a car last night." Stripped right back to acoustic basics, lightly detailed with harmonica, organ and Sheeran's own double-tracked harmonies, the almost Simon & Garfunkel-sounding fable was charming enough to turn floating voters to his side. Later featured in Courteney Cox's TV show *Cougar Town*, its opening line made more sense when it emerged Sheeran could not legally drive at the time — he passed his test the following year.

## 'I Wish You Wouldn't Say That'

Talking Heads
SIRE 1977
A-Side: 'Uh-Oh, Love Comes To Town'

**Art-punks' skewed pop manifesto.**

Years before 'Once In A Lifetime' made them early MTV stars, Talking Heads were the misfits at the ball — appearing strangely fully-formed towards in the year that punk broke with a thinly produced debut full of hyper-trebly guitars, overly intellectual lyrics and jerky rhythms that tapped into singer David Byrne's nervous stage energy. While that album 77 became a key post-punk text, it was not a peerless one, thanks to the band's eagerness to try everything at once. The spin-off A-side was a case in point, its exuberant pop crowded out with steel drums. While the marimbas and bells of 'I Wish You Wouldn't Say That' were similarly over-egged, it won the battle thanks to Jerry Harrison's trippy organ figure and Chris Frantz and Tina Weymouth's propulsive drum and bass work — an early taste of the muscular pulse that would define their highest peaks. Its sinister admission — "I've told lies without a hint or regret" — seemed a better fit with the stabbing guitars and bilingual chorus of 'Psycho Killer', which it also became B-side to before the year was out.

## 'I Won't Be Home For Christmas'

Blink-182
MCA 1997
A-Side: 'Josie'

**Cali punks' subversive seasonal sentiments.**

Alongside near neighbours Green Day, Blink-182's pioneering brand of emo-punk-pop set a blueprint for populist chart-hustlers from Boxcar Racer and Biffy Clyro to Busted. Tucked away on the back of 'Josie' — a single that fantasised drummer Scott Raynor's ideal girlfriend — was a patched-up Xmas ditty that would have a much more enduring impact for its intractably juvenile creators. A titular inversion of Bing Crosby's Christmas standard honouring overseas soldiers during World War II, Blink-182's yuletide yarn found their snotty singing-bassist Mark Hoppus offering up resistance to the notion of being "nice to the people you can't stand all year" as he spent a not-so-silent Christmas Eve in jail after taking a baseball bat to Christmas carollers. To double the fun, it blended the San Diego band's chirpy trademarks — fast-tempos, choked guitars and massed sing-along choruses — with a 'Deck the Halls' choral intro, chiming church bells and stark closing plea: "Please post my bail!" It was already an established alt-rock Xmas mainstay when it became a chart-topping Canadian A-side during Christmas 2001.

**'I'll Be Around'**

The Spinners

ATLANTIC 1972

A-Side: 'How Could I Let You Get Away'

**Super seductive essence of Philly soul.**

The Spinners' sustained 70s success showed Motown's grand folly in letting them go. Having spent much of the 60s trying to second-guess the charts in search of a breakthrough, the former Detroit doo-woppers finally scored with the Stevie Wonder-penned 'It's A Shame' in 1970, but were still shown the door. Enter Aretha Franklin. The Queen of Soul's word was powerful enough for Atlantic president Henry Allen to take the contractual plunge, with almost instant rewards. Despite a slightly tin-eared choice of the A-side — an achingly sad song of self-pity that didn't quite hit the mark with radio DJs — its chivalrous, heart-breaking B-side 'I'll Be Around' instantly stole the waves. It found producer Thom Bell ladling on Philly soul adornments — female background singers, horns, strings (and here, bongos) with Sigma Studio house band MFSB — against the expressive harmonising lead vocals of Bobbie Smith and Phillipé Wynne, masters of the subtle details. Despite tracing the plight of a man caught in stasis, unable to move on from a relationship, it still sounded upbeat and hopeful as it topped the R&B charts and shuffled seductively into the *Billboard* Top 3.

## 'I'll Feel A Whole Lot Better'

The Byrds
COLUMBIA 1965
A-Side: 'All I Really Want To Do'

**Beat combo's hesitant power-pop.**

The Byrds' jangling marriage of folk and rock was an instant treat. Having scored a number 1, at the first time of asking, with their cover of Bob Dylan's 'Mr Tambourine Man', they retained the formula for its follow-up — rush-released to try and bury Cher's take on the same song. However, its B-side, written and sung by guitarist Gene Clark, was easily the better half. A bittersweet tale about breaking off a relationship, written about the unwanted attentions of female fan and built around a riff based on the Searchers' 1964 hit 'Needles and Pins', it was a seamless synthesis of the Californian band's key influences — Bob Dylan and the Beatles. The latter was particularly prominent in Roger McGuinn's chiming Rickenbacker sound, inspired by George Harrison's outro to 'A Hard Day's Night' and the cue for a generation of 80s indie guitar stylists. Despite its B-side status, Columbia put their might behind it and it reached number 103 in its own right on the *Billboard chart*. Later covered by Flamin' Groovies and Tom Petty, it would prove Clark's closest brush with a self-penned hit. He went solo soon afterwards as McGuinn and rhythm guitarist David Crosby stepped up to The Byrds' songwriting plate.

## 'I'm Gonna Leave You'

Dusty Springfield
PHILIPS 1966
A-Side: 'Goin' Back'

**UK soul diva's most heart-wrenching ballad.**

Dusty Springfield seized the day after the Beatles kicked open the early 60s US market. The London soul-singer already had British hits under her belt with folky trio the Springfields (alongside brother Tom), but blew the transatlantic doors off in 1963 with Johnny Franz's Spector-inspired production 'I Only Want To Be With You'. Within a few short years she had established herself as the UK's finest soul singer, capable of holding her own with Aretha Franklin, Gladys Knight and Dionne Warwick. The hits were still in plentiful supply when Springfield added her uncommonly soulful voice to Goffin and King's loss of innocence tale 'Goin' Back' (covered by the Byrds the following year), backing it with a stirring ballad of vintage quality. A heavily orchestrated walkout tale repositioned as a necessary triumph, Springfield's haunted intimacy made the sentiments of 'I'm Gonna Leave You' all ring true. Written alongside backing singer Madeline Bell and regular compositional foil Lesley Duncan, Bell's uptempo, horn-drenched version also became a B-side (when it should have been an A) to 1968's 'I'm Gonna Make You Love Me'.

## 'I'm So Lonesome I Could Cry'

Hank Williams
MGM 1949
A-Side: 'My Bucket's Got A Hole In It'

**The greatest country song ever written?**

Hank Williams weaved heartbreak into his greatest work. The lovelorn Alabama songwriter was in peak hitmaking form as the 40s drew to a close, the raw emotions of his best songs tapping into his rocky relationship with his wife and manager, Audrey Sheppard. Originally intended a spoken-word piece for his alter-ego Luke the Drifter, 'I'm So Lonesome I Could Cry' was a pitch-perfect piece of songwriting craft that even spooked its own creator — so much so his fellow musicians had to persuade him to get it down on tape. Its strengths lay in its simplicity, Williams taking the starting image of a whippoorwill and building on it, showing how everything else — the midnight train, a robin, the moon, a falling star — became lonely through the prism of his own conflicted gloom. Yet the real cause of his distress was held back until its devastating final line. His desperation was matched by Jerry Byrd's plaintive pedal steel and Tommy Jackson's lonesome fiddle, the lack of drums only amplifying the funereal appeal of its carefully couched lyric — he could cry… but he doesn't. Fearing it might be far too genteel and arty for his rural fans, Williams stuck it on the B-side of an old blues ditty that did all the necessary chart business. Sadly, his too-short life sputtered out ignominiously before it became an all-time country standard. Endlessly covered since, Williams' desperate original remains one of the saddest songs ever recorded.

### 'I'm Thinking To-Night Of My Blue Eyes'

The Carter Family
VICTOR 1929
A-Side: 'Engine One-Forty-Three'

**Country music's first stars.**

The Carter Family's touching tales of ordinary lives made them the first rural mountain group to find chart success. Based in remote southwestern Virginia, the trio of husband and wife A.P. and Sara Carter alongside sister-in-law Maybelle were wildly ahead of their time, their two lead female singers developing the 'Carter picking' style of acoustic guitar, its bass notes played by thumb, that would dominate and define early country music. Once signed by Victor talent scout Ralph Peer, the fame-hungry A.P. was industrious in scouting fresh material for the trio to record, the travelling tree salesman readily repurposing haunted old hymns, blues, ballads and parlour songs for Sara's melancholy contralto voice. 'I'm Thinking To-Night Of My Blue Eyes' was a classic example, far more resonant than its train wreck ballad A-side. An old traditional hillbilly song about a man that got away, with possible English folk roots, Sara's crying voice was couched by A.P.'s restrained harmony and Maybelle's steady strum. The Carter Family were much more dysfunctional than they first appeared — the ties fraying between the manipulative A.P. and fame-hating Sara as soon as they made it big. They divorced in 1936 after she had an affair with one of A.P.'s cousins, Coy Bayes. Three years later Sara summoned the estranged Bayes to the altar — boldly issuing a come-get-me plea with this B-side via a border radio broadcast from Mexico.

### 'I'm A Man'

Bo Diddley
CHECKER 1955
A-Side: 'Bo Diddley'

**Double-sided monster debut.**
Bo Diddley was a unique figure among rock 'n' roll's first generation. The black Stetson sporting singer and guitarist born Ellas Bates in Mississippi, moved to Chicago when he was eight. The classical violin student changed tack after hearing John Lee Hooker and gained his street name playing local clubs and bars in the hope of landing a deal, until a demo did the trick with Chess subsidiary Checker. Diddley didn't-diddle around when it came to recording his first single, capturing the raw power of his two strongest songs. For the A-side he picked his theme tune, a simple blues ditty whose thick tremolo guitars laced what would quickly become known as the Bo Diddley beat — a booming chunka chunka rhythm swiftly appropriated by Buddy Holly and the Rolling Stones (who dropped all Diddley songs from their set as a mark of respect when they toured the UK together in 1963). For its sizzling, highly sexualised B-Side, he summoned fresh flavour from a bluesy harmonica and a devastating riff on his homemade square guitar, his vocals spelling out the word "M-A-N" at the end of each chorus to emphasise his swagger. It purposefully echoed the phraseology of Muddy Waters' 1954 hit 'Hoochie Coochie Man', Diddley's reinvention prompting Waters' to pen an answer song in 'Mannish Boy'. 'I'm A Man' would become a bona fide rock 'n' roll standard in its own right, and hit the US Top 20 via a Yardbirds cover a decade later.

**'I'm Fly'**
Kool G Rap & DJ Polo
COLD CHILLIN' 1986
A-Side: 'It's A Demo'

**The arrival of hip-hop's 'mobfather'.**
Kool G Rap locked straight into the groove when he visited Marley Marl at the DJ and producer's Queensbridge flat for an exploratory demo session. Marley captured his fast-paced delivery, confident lispy flow and street-corner storytelling style in an instant, their demo quickly turning into the fledgling Cold Chillin' label's second single. The A-side's pimp-ish proclamations were given an extra boastful boost on B-side 'I'm Fly', G Rap spitting technically tricky rapid-fire rhymes over Marl's bare-bones beats and hooks (what DJ Polo added is a moot point). And if rhymes about driving a Caddy Seville, dining on lobsters and bathing in a jacuzzi of champagne would soon sound hackneyed, they were fresh

at the time. They hinted at the finesse that would see him crowned hip-hop's 'mobfather' on 1990's *Wanted: Dead Or Alive* — the tipping point for the early 90s mafioso subgenre. Automatically inducted into Marley's all-star Juice Crew afterwards, G-Rap doubled down on his instant rep, sweeping the floor with his charged verse on 1991 posse cut 'The Symphony'.

### 'I'm In Love Again'

Fats Domino
IMPERIAL 1956
A-Side: 'My Blue Heaven'

**Post-war pop giant's breakthrough text.**

Having wedged open the chart door with 1955's rugged take on 'Ain't That A Shame' and chased Pat Boone's white bread cover up the charts, Fats Domino cemented his stardom with this 45. The shy yet cheerfully chubby New Orleans singer and pianist — whose barrelling 1949 single 'The Fat Man' has been widely cited as the first rock 'n' roll record — finally started to woo white audiences with show-stopping boogie-woogie turns at DJ Alan Freed's 1953 Cleveland Arena show and 1955's New York Rock 'n' Roll Jubilee Ball. The other side of his smooth serenade through pop standard 'My Blue Heaven' was a buttery demonstration of the distinctive Fats groove, its two-minute declaration of love eclipsing the A-side and becoming his first big-time chart hit. Written with long-time collaborator Dave Bartholomew, the upbeat melody, head-over-heels lyrics and distinctively twangy delivery mashed with Domino's bluesy piano playing and a lightly jazzing saxophone. While the Beatles' George Harrison claimed 'I'm In Love Again' was the first record to turn him onto rock 'n' roll, his bandmate Paul McCartney covered it in 1991 (as B-side of 'The One'), joining a long line of interpretations from Bill Haley, Little Richard and Ricky Nelson.

### '(I'm Not Your) Steppin' Stone'

The Monkees
COLGEMS 1966
A-Side: 'I'm A Believer'

**Pre-Fab Four's accidental proto-punk classic.**

The Monkees' popularity was exploding when their second single emerged in late 1966, just two months after their primetime Saturday morning TV show went to air. To back their bubblegum take on the Neil Diamond-written A-side, the made-for-television group gave Paul Revere And The Raiders' 'Steppin' Stone' much more gutsy insouciance than its original take, as drummer Micky Dolenz (the only Monkee to perform) issued a powerful warning against those who wanted to use him to climb the social ladder — a B-side that became a hit in its own right (reaching number 20 on the *Billboard* chart). Despite debates about the group's authenticity, they quickly grew into their roles, influencing many others to form a band (including the Sex Pistols, who covered it during their dying throes, and even PJ & Duncan). They did much more than just monkey around on equally essential B-sides such as adventurous Carole King cover 'Take A Giant Step' ['Last Train To Clarkesville', 1966] or the atmospheric folk rock of 'As We Go Along' ['The Porpoise Song', 1968].

### 'I'm Sorry'

Brenda Lee
DECCA 1960
A-Side: 'That's All You Gotta Do'

**Atlanta teenager tracks US country staple.**
A child star since she was six, when her reward for winning a school talent show was to perform on local radio show *Starmakers Revue*, Brenda Lee was also a seasoned TV regular by the time she reached double figures. Raised in a poor family in Georgia's red-clay belt and dubbed 'Little Miss Dynamite' for her powerful voice, Lee was just 15 when she recorded 'I'm Sorry' with Patsy Cline's band and producer Owen Bradley. The diminutive Lee's performance, racked with lovesick yearning and a cool spoken word section (added at Lee's insistence), became one of the first examples of the Nashville Sound — a dreamy fusion of country, pop and strings. Despite its B-side status, Decca held back its release for several months — concerned about the perception of a teenager singing about affairs of the heart with such passion. That worry proved unfounded when American DJs flipped the single and took it to number 1, knocking the Hollywood Argyles' novelty hit 'Alley Oop' for six.

## 'Ice Ice Baby'

Vanilla Ice
ULTRA 1990
A-Side: 'Play That Funky Music'

**Novelty rapper breaks *Billboard* chart.**

Vanilla Ice helped bring rap from the streets to the suburbs. The photogenic Miami-raised white rapper had graduated from breakdancing to performing at Dallas's City Lights nightspot, where he forged a strong working relationship with Earthquake, the club's DJ. Earthquake came up with the ideas for both sides of his first single: the A-side's rather obvious sampling of Wild Cherry's 1976 hit and the B-side's more innovative jacking of Queen and David Bowie's 1981 number 1 'Under Pressure' (a lift Ice would ludicrously later try to deny). Ice allied it to tales of cruising down Miami's A1A Beachfront Avenue in his 5.0 Mustang before he rocked the stage (and cooked his rivals "like a pound of bacon"), not all the words his own. As poppy as the A-side was, radio rejected it, with the dominos finally falling Ice's way when Georgia DJ Darrell Jaye played 'Ice Ice Baby' instead. Others soon followed suit. Heavy rotation of its $8,000 video by MTV satellite network *The Box* spread the word even faster until it became the first hip-hop song to top the *Billboard* Hot 100. Success brought its creator both instant wealth and instant problems, with Bowie and Queen petitioning for their piece of the pie. As did Death Row rapper Mario 'Chocolate' Johnson, with man mountain label boss Suge Knight allegedly persuading Ice to cough up by hanging him over a 15th-floor hotel balcony from his ankles.

## 'Ice Machine'

Depeche Mode
MUTE 1981
A-Side: 'Dreaming Of Me'

**Minimalist synthpop masterpiece.**

Depeche Mode had yet to refine their hit formula when they stepped out of the Essex shadows with their first single 'Dreaming Of Me'. A blippy slice of synthpop-by-numbers, its second-hand sounds and wistful chorus merely hinted at songwriter Vince Clarke's way with a hook, grazing the UK charts at 57. Its far superior B-side harked back to the Basildon band's roots as Composition

Of Sound — a minimalist trio, fronted by Clarke, clearly under the influence of Orchestral Manoeuvres in the Dark. Their fortunes changed with the arrival of singer Dave Gahan and a new name swiped from a French fashion magazine — totally apt for its stark, dark, downbeat B-side, as the edgy menace of Gahan's unvarnished vocal enhanced its pushy bassline and haunting arpeggio. A hidden gem that outstripped most of their first album *Speak & Spell*, it proved to be highly influential, with covers arriving from downtempo Norwegian duo Röyksopp and Swedish synth-poppers SPOCK. Depeche Mode would continue their love affair with the B-side even as US stadiums beckoned, but their best remains their very first.

### 'If The Papes Come'

A Tribe Called Quest
JIVE 1990
A-Side: 'Can I Kick It?'

**East Coast boom-bap built on dusty jazz.**

A Tribe Called Quest made the critical link between old jazz grooves and hip-hop's future. The Queens, New York trio — the next members of the Native Tongues stable out of the blocks after De La Soul — hinted at their jazzy fascinations on 1989's debut LP *People's Instinctive Travels And The Paths of Rhythm* and made them explicit on this B-side. Built around a drum sample from Lou Donaldson's 'Pot Belly', detailed with snatches of Spoonie Gee, Slick Rick and some spaced-out Jimi Hendrix dialogue, it allowed 19-year-old rapper Q-Tip to turn on his lyrical charms — his super relaxed, soulfully stoned sing-song wordplay as intimate as if he was whispering into your ear. A relatively well-known flipside whose sound design became a template for Digable Planets' 'Rebirth Of Slick (Cool Like Dat)', it has since appeared on various mixes and compilations, but in shortened, remixed form. The full original B-side trumps all though, thanks to a closing verse by Afrika Baby Bam, their early mentor from Jungle Brothers.

**'In Time'**
Jungle Brothers
WARLOCK 1989
A-Side: 'Black Is Black'

**Peaceful protest from Native Tongues progenitors.**
Mike G's opening verse on 'In Time' predicted that a black man would soon claim the US presidency. While the trio of New York schoolfriends completed by Afrika Baby Bam and DJ Sammy B didn't possess a crystal ball into Barack Obama's 2009 inauguration, they did openly support Jesse Jackson's democratic candidacy at the time. The song worked for its hopeful prophesy of more peaceful times over a spartanly produced, manually flipped loop of Average White Band's 'Would You Say'. The first of the Native Tongues posse to make an album, Jungle Brothers sowed its seeds with their open embrace of Afrocentrism, jazz samples and forward-thinking fusions with the incoming house sound. 'In Time' was also the first studio outing for A Tribe Called Quest rapper Q-Tip, who took the 3rd verse and joined in on the 4th as they kicked props to Boogie Down Productions, Public Enemy and Afrika Bambaataa. Jungle Brothers used the exact same beat for 'Promo' — a radio advert for Red Alert's radio Kiss-FM show that was extended into the B-side of their next single, 'Straight Out The Jungle'.

**'Incense And Peppermints'**
Thee Sixpence
ALL AMERICAN 1967
A-Side: 'Birdman Of Alkatrash'

**Rare first pressing of Strawberry Alarm Clock.**
If ever a song evoked the 60s it was Strawberry Alarm Clock's flower power anthem. An unlikely hit, it had a far from easy birth. 'Incense And Peppermints' started life as an untitled instrumental, written by keyboardist Mark Weitz and guitarist Ed King (later of Lynyrd Skynyrd) as a B-side for Brit-aping garage band Thee Sixpence. Things got murkier when producer Frank Slay asked John Carter and Tim Gilbert to write trippy, nonsensical words for it and enlisted 16-year-old Shapes of Sound singer Greg Munford to take lead vocals. The result was an intense pop/psych fusion, whose fuzzy guitars, swirling organs and fussy hand percussion was topped with discordant vocal harmonies in faux English accents.

Adopted by Los Angeles radio stations over the A-side's quirky garage-punk, MCA subsidiary Uni sensed a hit — flipping sides as they licensed the single. By its second pressing it was credited to Strawberry Alarm Clock (as another group was using Thee Sixpence's name) and made a slow climb to the US top spot. A cameo in Richard Rush's *Psych Out* and its inclusion in Mike Meyers' *Austin Powers: International Man Of Mystery* would confirm its longevity in the psychedelic cannon. Controversially, Weitz and King failed to receive a writer's credit or a single sixpence for its creation. "We were told that was the price we had to pay to get started in the business," revealed King on their website.

### 'Insane Asylum'

Koko Taylor & Willie Dixon
CHECKER 1967
A-Side: 'Fire'

**Badass blues duet.**

Koko Taylor's belting embrace of the blues took no prisoners. Raised on cotton plantations in Tennessee, she was talent-spotted by prolific composer Willie Dixon, who took her under his wing and primed her to exploit the new electrified blues era. After signing her to Chess subsidiary Checker, Dixon produced 1965's first hit 'Wang Dang Doodle', but the pair's various attempts to follow it up floundered, however much Dixon titivated her intrinsic soul power with firing horns and jaunty beats. It meant this wild card B-side duet was slow to get its dues. 'Insane Asylum' lived up to its title as Dixon described falling in love with a girl driven crazy by bad romance over a wild descending sax break and foreboding Hammond organ, before Taylor begged to be taken as a slave in tones that could raise the dead. While covered by Long John Baldry, Diamanda Galas and Oxbow (beside Marianne Faithful, with gender roles reversed), Dixon's low baritone and Taylor's unhinged passion have reigned imperious, not least when featured in Noah Hawley's 00s TV crime drama *Fargo*.

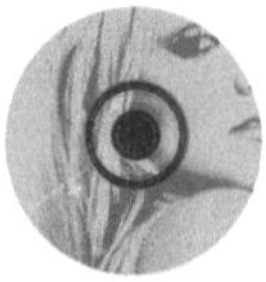

## 'Intimidated'

Britney Spears

JIVE 2001

A-Side: 'I'm A Slave 4 U'

**Girl next door's edgy reinvention.**

By her third album, 19-year-old Britney Spears was fully invested in trying to shed the doe-eyed Catholic schoolgirl image fostered by her indelible 'Baby One More Time' video for something much more brassy and overt. The A-Side's woozy bump-and-grind beats and unambiguous title made it explicit that the one-time star of Disney's *New Mickey Mouse Club* franchise was abandoning her coquettish past and tapping hard into the dirty funk aesthetic producers the Neptunes had perfected on hip-hop hits for Jay-Z and Mystikal. While it later emerged 'I'm A Slave 4 U' was originally intended for Janet Jackson, the singer's influence was much more overt in Spear's cultured vocal stylings on 'Intimidated'. A hard-hitting serving of R&B-pop sass courtesy of super-producer Rodney Jerkins (under his Darkchild guise), replete with chanted breakdown "B-R-I-T-N-E-Y", it shuffled Spears beyond the teen pop sphere and prefigured the darker roads ahead. An underrated B-side within a surprisingly progressive canon, 'Intimidated' gained wider exposure in John A. Davis's animated sci-fi flick *Jimmy Neutron: Boy Genius*.

## 'Is You Is Or Is You Ain't (Ma' Baby)'

Bing Crosby and the Andrews Sisters

DECCA 1944

A-Side: '(There'll Be A) Hot Time In The Town Of Berlin (When The Yanks Go Marching In)'

**Effective pop reading of Louis Jordan standard.**

Bing Crosby was part of the bloodstream of American showbusiness. An influential 30s radio star whose intimate bedside manner and cosy conservatism hit home with a wide demographic, Crosby seemed able to turn his cultured baritone to all manner of pop styles, peaking with 1941's evergreen take on Irving Berlin's 'White Christmas'. By the time he was topping the charts with the A-side's orchestral ode to US troops in World War II, Crosby had added film idol to his resume, thanks to his easy freewheeling banter with Bob Hope as they vied for the affections of Dorothy

Lamour in *The Road* series. Although it was a B-side, Crosby's swinging take on Louis Jordan's standard (recorded for the film *Follow The Boys*) proved equally popular with his huge fan base, as his distinctive croon (recorded first thing in the morning, when his voice was huskier) arrived on the back of an evocative trumpet intro, before nippily trading doubts about a lover's fidelity with the Andrew Sisters. As with Jordan's original — the B-side of 'GI Jive' — Crosby's version made it number 2 on the *Billboard* chart and kept his star lustrously alive. His image took a hit long after his death, as tales of gambling, philandering and drinking emerged.

**'It's Not A Game'**
Pete Rock & CL Smooth
ELEKTRA 1993
A-Side: 'Lots Of Lovin''

**Golden age duo in majestic harmony.**
A spirit of friendly creative rivalry was at the heart of the two far-from-slim albums Pete Rock & CL Smooth produced during their brief but brilliant early 90s reign. A-Side 'Lots Of Lovin'' was another soulful, dreamy evocation of New York street life that Kanye West would cite as his favourite beat by his favourite producer. Rock's signature crate digging enthused B-side 'It's Not A Game' too, as the producer mixed up elements of the Isley Brothers' 'Take Inventory' and Compost's 'Buzzard Feathers' with waves of vocal samples. Rock's plentiful adlibs weaved around Smooth's cultured wordplay as his fast-tripping multi-phonic 'Mecca Don' flow detailed the seriousness of their joint enterprise, while also appealing to more spiritual concerns. It was indicative of their rich form that they kept it off their debut LP *Mecca And The Soul Brothers* — a conspicuously filler-free 75-minute boom-bap banquet. Unusually, they not only made a video for the B-side, they used a coveted slot on BET television show *Teen Summit* to perform it live.

**'It's Your Dynamite'**
Girls Aloud
FASCINATION 2009
A-Side: 'Untouchable'

**Indubitably infectious pop.**

Girls Aloud exceeded all expectations, including their own. Brought together by public phone voters on TV talent show *Popstars: The Rivals* in late 2002, few anticipated the contrasting quintet of Cheryl Tweedy, Nadine Coyle, Sarah Harding, Nicola Roberts and Kimberly Walsh would do anything but fizzle to dust once their supply of TV oxygen expired. Those expectations were dashed when they forged an indefatigable partnership with Brian Higgins and his Xenomania production team on 'Sound Of The Underground' — the first of a string of 20 consecutive Top 10 hits packed with state of the art, 21st-century pop. It's a moot point whether the electro-thumping 'It's Your Dynamite' would have enjoyed the same rarefied chart air had it been anointed A-side status. Dancy, edgy and effortlessly attitudinal, it boasted a much more trenchant chorus hook than the tranced-out 'Untouchable' — a blatant stab at the clubs that proved their first UK chart misfire, entering at 11. In their prime Girls Aloud proved themselves redoubtable B-side queens, regularly giving fans maximum VFM whether banging out the flighty future funk of 'Androgynous Girls' ['Love Machine', 2004], taking lyrical pot-shots at supposedly more credible rivals on 'Hoxton Heroes' ['Can't Speak French', 2008] or showing off their balladic growth on 'Memory Of You' ['The Loving Kind', 2009].

**'It'll Be Me'**

Jerry Lee Lewis

SUN 1957

A-Side: 'Whole Lot Of Shakin' Going On'

**The Killer, raw and wild.**

One of early rock 'n' roll's true greats, Jerry Lee Lewis embodied the music's wild, hedonistic spirit. The Louisiana singer was a childhood piano prodigy whose aptitude for his instrument was matched by his wild streak of showmanship and entrenched fear of God — a dichotomy that was ever-present when he washed up at Memphis's Sun Studios after being chucked out of bible college. He quickly discovered his true calling. 'It'll Be Me' was intended as the follow-up to his first single, a revved-up run through of Ralph Mooney's 'Crazy Arms' that quietly disappeared without trace. Determined not to flop again, its writer and producer Jack Clement put Lewis and his band through more than half a dozen different takes to try and capture its full potential. When he was confident he had the goods, Clement asked: "Now what do you want to do for the flip?" It prompted Lewis to whip out his salacious rockabilly take on 'Whole Lot Of Shakin' Going On' — a life-changing moment for all present, that necessitated an instant swap of sides. Lewis did not totally neglect 'It'll Be Me', however, re-recording another slower take to close 1958's first self-titled album. The song gained further lives in covers by Tom Jones, Deep Purple, the Move and Cliff Richard, with Britain's answer to Elvis narrowly missing the UK top spot when he made it an A-side in 1962.

### 'Jack The Ripper'

LL Cool J
DEF JAM 1988
A-Side: 'Going Back To Cali'

**A rapper scorned.**

The cover of Kool Moe Dee's 1987 LP *How Ya Like Me Now* depicted its grinning creator standing in front of a Jeep Wrangler, its front tyre crushing a red Kangol hat. For LL Cool J, the Queens, New York rapper whose calling card was a red Kangol, it amounted to pure provocation. As if that wasn't bad enough the ex-Treacherous Three man's album was littered with snide disses that accused Cool J of stealing his style. Cool J jumped straight to his defence after Rick Rubin looped up a stark lift of the Soul Searchers' 70s funk anthem 'Ashley's Roachclip' that played perfectly to his bragging smarts. With ripper-like ferocity he declared himself "Jason with an axe/But I put it on wax" as he sliced away at Moe Dee's rep and labelled him a desperate copycat. The animosity didn't end there. A further flurry of disses flew back and forth — Moe Dee with 'Let's Go' and 'Death Blow', Cool J with 'To The Break Of Dawn' — as both MCs proclaimed themselves victorious.

### 'Jeane'

The Smiths
ROUGH TRADE 1983
A-Side: 'This Charming Man'

**Unfairly neglected slice of life.**

B-Sides mattered to the Smiths. The fact that the preeminent Manchester indie band's best-known song 'How Soon Is Now?' (and the possibly superior 'Please Please Please Let Me Get What I Want') first appeared on the 12-inch flip of 'William, it Was Really Nothing' spoke volumes. With so many great B-sides littering their singular career — 'Back To The Old House' ['What Difference Does It Make?', 1984], 'Asleep' ['The Boy With The Thorn In His Side', 1985], 'Unloveable' ['Bigmouth Strikes Again', 1986] — homing in on one is a tricky ask. Nonetheless 'Jeane', the other side of their breakthrough hit, stands apart. First recorded with producer Troy Tate during abandoned sessions for their debut LP, its stripped-down state accentuated its punchy stop-start riff, capturing their brawnier leanings as Morrissey evoked images of the Woodfall films he was so fond of with his sad-eyed tale of failure. Rarely mentioned by the band, who quickly dropped it live and failed to include it on compilations — further entrenching its cult appeal — 'Jeane' enjoyed two further B-side lives via Sandie Shaw's acoustic cover ['Hand In Glove', 1984] and Billy Bragg's slow solo reading ['Greetings To The New Brunette', 1986]. B-sides would become The Smiths' ultimate undoing, when their fastidious attention to detail was compromised by the pressures of keeping the show on the road. The tipping point was relatively benign — Morrissey's insistence they cover Cilla Black's 'Work Is A Four Letter Word' as a B-side for 'Girlfriend In A Coma'. "I didn't form a group to cover Cilla Black songs," protested exhausted guitarist Johnny Marr, who made his excuses and left.

**'Jilted John'**
Jilted John
RABID 1978
A-Side: 'Going Steady'

**The 'Gordon is a moron' song.**

'Jilted John' swept the school playground. Many could relate to the titular character's melancholic tale of getting dumped by his girlfriend Julie for the better-looking "cool and trendy" Gordon, played out over a simple but resonant two-chord riff. It found its sad protagonist firing out every insult he could think of — Julie was a tart, a bitch, a slut; Gordon a creep, a puff and, most memorably of all, a moron — before he cried to the chip shop, weeping vinegary tears at the injustice of all. The first song ever written by 18-year old Manchester Polytechnic drama student Graham Fellows, he put it on the B-side of 'Going Steady' — an equally catchy tale of snogging, bus shelters and more chips as he proclaimed love to a girl called Sharon. Thanks to airplay from Manchester's Piccadilly Radio and then BBC Radio 1's John Peel, the B-side gained greater currency, transitioning into a Top 5 hit that shifted nearly half a million copies. For three months its creator was everywhere — in teen magazines, on *Top Of The Pops*, chatting up Gail Tilsley on *Coronation Street* — but his follow-up singles and sole LP *True Love Stories* stiffed. Fellows' story could have ended there too, had he not transformed into aspiring singer-songwriter John Shuttleworth in the 80s, a brilliantly storied comedic role that subsumed all else.

## 'John Henry'

Lonnie Donegan's Skiffle Group
DECCA 1955
A-Side: 'Rock Island Line'

**Start of the UK skiffle craze.**

Lonnie Donegan was the first global superstar of British pop, inventor of a style of music that turned pop culture on its axis. That music was skiffle, a bluesy, hot-tempo take on American folk that simultaneously made it accessible — all you needed was a guitar or banjo, a homemade tea chest bass, a thimble and a washboard. Originally the banjoist in Chris Barber's Dixieland-styled jazz band, at first Donegan played his skiffle sets during the interval. Noting that they were becoming as popular as the main event, some were included on Barber's 1954 album *New Orleans Joys*. When Decca spun off this single, it was clear that his frantic, Lead Belly-inspired take on Clarence Wilson's 1929 folk anthem was the main attraction. Its B-side 'John Henry' — another spirited take on an American classic — was no idle slouch though. And while Donegan's plaintive reading of the semi-mythical steel-driving African-American folk hero set off at a clip, it was his emotive, hollering vocal that resonated, earnestly transmitting the heavy toil of digging out a railroad track. The single hit the UK and US Top 10, far eclipsing the album it came from, and set off a nationwide skiffle boom. And although Donegan only got paid his performance fee, he gained something far more valuable — stardom. Hit after hit quickly followed for the Glasgow-born 'King of Skiffle' before his place in pop hearts was usurped by the Beatles and the Rolling Stones.

## 'Jolene'

The White Stripes
SYMPATHY FOR THE RECORD INDUSTRY 2000
A-Side: 'Hello Operator'

**Yowling makeover of Dolly Parton's country standard.**

It's hard to underestimate the importance of this single for the White Stripes. A-side 'Hello Operator' was the first song Radio 1 DJ John Peel ever played by the band, but far from the last, his sage endorsement helping the Detroit garage duo of Jack White and Meg White capture a generation with their jaw-chattering back-to-basics meld of primitive blues guitar and unremitting tribal drums. Its equally popular B-side showcased their cover of Dolly Parton's merciful plea, 'Jolene'. And while Jack White was faithful to the original's minimalist guitar/vocal tension, he took it somewhere else too, sounding wracked and raw as he let forth his buzzsaw anguish at losing his man — jilted sentiments that proved highly divisive among some of the more conservative elements of Parton's fanbase. It was his bloodied emoting that made it a highlight of the White Stripes shows as they gradually refined its dynamics further, slaying Glastonbury festival's 50th-anniversary with it in 2002. A similarly emotive reading from Blackpool's Empress Ballroom became an A-side in 2004.

## 'Julie Don't Live Here'

The Electric Light Orchestra
JET 1981
A-Side: 'Twilight'

**Lost showstopper from ELO's late synth phase.**

Designed to "pick up where the Beatles left off", the Electric Light Orchestra combined pop with classical instrumentation. The early 70s brainchild of the Move songwriters Roy Wood and Jeff Lynn, they struggled to get the balance right until the mid-70s, with Wood long gone and Lynne goaded by his father to write a 'proper tune'. That sparked his competitive spirit. A string of majestically orchestrated, chorus-heavy singles descended like spaceships into the UK Top 10 after 'Evil Woman', a quick filler tune for 5th LP *Face The Music*, set the pace. By 1981 Lynn had ditched their trademark strings for electronics and summoned up *Time* –a concept album about a man transported into the year 2095, epitomised by 'Twilight''s warped propulsion and sci-fi synths. A relative flop that just scraped the Top 30 in the UK, its B-side boasted a rare treat in 'Julie Don't Live Here' — a driving tale of a man searching a familiar town for someone long-gone, it closely echoed the sentiments of LP track 'The Way Life's Meant To Be'. Lynn's fidelity to his conceptual urges doubtless explains its marooned B-side status.

### 'Jump'

Aztec Camera
WEA 1984
A-Side: 'All I Need Is Everything'

**Rock anthem alchemised into folk ballad.**

Aztec Camera had a wayward streak. The jangly Scottish band led by precocious teenage singer-songwriter and guitarist Roddy Frame weren't shy of dashing expectations, effectively waving goodbye to their youthful naiveté when they brought Mark Knopfler in to produce 1984's second LP *Knife*. Issued on the B-side of its flagship single, a cover of Van Halen's 'Jump' — recorded just six months after the original — underlined the point. Gone was its creators' bombastic reliance on a six-note Oberheim OB-Xa synth riff, as Frame stripped it right back to chords not a million miles removed from the Velvet Underground's 'Sweet Jane'. The 12-inch's 'Loaded Version' extended the conceit further, Frame letting fly with a wigged-out guitar solo that doubtless charmed its creators (who gave their approval to Frame's cheeky take). In its wake Aztec Camera regularly used B-sides for transformative cover versions, putting trad socialist anthem 'The Red Flag' ['How Men Are', 1988], Bob Dylan's 'I Threw It All Away' ['Working in a Goldmine', 1988] and Cyndi Lauper's 'True Colors' ['The Crying Scene', 1990] through the mangle.

### 'Just A Memory'

Elvis Costello and the Attractions
F-BEAT 1980
'New Amsterdam EP'

**Man of song at his most intimate.**

Declan MacManus had spent so much time in the trenches, getting his act down pat at Putney's Half Moon pub, he was convinced he would not fail when he transformed into Elvis Costello the same year his namesake died. The wiry Costello's upstart determination won-out, assisted by the acquisition of crack backing band the Attractions. The Liverpool raised-songsmith was also a helplessly prolific writer — his 4th album in as many years, *Get Happy!!*, blasted through 20 tracks in just 48 minutes. He showcased three more on the EP accompanying 'New Amsterdam'. 'Just A Memory' was its peak — a heart-wrenching break-up song about endings and loss. Written for Dusty Springfield to add her crackling vocal firepower to, its spartan, demo-like treatment found Costello spouting plain truths over Steve Nieve's restrained piano figure and trademark swirling organs, the singer double-tracking his own yearning harmonies. Springfield eventually deigned to record it — on the condition that Costello wrote an extra verse — for 1982's *White Heat*, but ruined it with offkey production. Nonetheless this desperate ballad was adored by fans already regularly nourished with quality B-sides.

## 'Just Like Tom Thumb's Blues (Live Version)'

Bob Dylan
COLUMBIA 1966
A-Side: 'I Want You'

**Electric live fire alongside the Band.**

A sunshine highlight from 1966's sprawling double album *Blonde On Blonde*, the A-side proved that Bob Dylan boasted the conventional pop chops he possibly saw himself as being above. Its B-side was a rare case of a live recording eclipsing its studio counterpart. Dylan penned narrative ballad 'Just Like Tom Thumb's Blues' for his first real rock album, 1965's *Highway 61 Revisited*. Its extensive lyrical evocation of a man in wild pursuit of wine, women and song in the border town of Juarez — before events took a nasty turn for the worse — played to the roaming Minnesota songwriter's known strengths and came littered with literary allusions to Jack Kerouac, Edgar Allen Poe and its titular mythical folk figure. Captured towards the end of his 1966 UK tour in Liverpool, it was fulsome proof of his live prowess as a newly electrified performer, and his intimate connection with backing group the Hawks (later the Band) — a much tighter reading than the *Albert Hall* bootleg tracked three days later in Manchester. Although widely perceived as an albums artist, Dylan often slipped jewels onto his B-sides, from the intricate painted lady of 'She Belongs To Me' ['Subterranean Homesick Blues', 1965], performative one-night stand of 'Spanish Is the Loving Tongue' ['Watching The River Flow', 1971] to the playful phonetics of 'Rita May' ['Stuck Inside Of Mobile With The Memphis Blues Again', 1977].

## 'Just Passing'

The Small Faces
DECCA 1967
A-Side: 'I Can't Make It'

**Sharp-dressed pop vignette.**

It wasn't just their merry consumption of amphetamines that helped Small Faces move at lightning speed. The modish-looking cockney outfit impressed with their high-energy, tough-take on R&B, bolstered by singer Steve Marriott's all-or-nothing delivery and kitchen sink lyrics. Not all was harmonious in the camp when their last single for Decca emerged, issued purely to fulfil contractual obligations and saddled with a chart-haltering double whammy — the BBC had banned it and the band refused to promote it. That meant very little exposure for its wonderfully bucolic B-side 'Just Passing' — a co-write with bassist Ronnie Lane that told the tale of Marriott's police harassment over a false drug accusation. "Wise men they wrangle," emoted the artfully dodging singer over playful acoustic guitar and impressionistic keys, but the real beauty lay in its tiny details — the music hall count-in, the honking bike horns, the band's barely suppressed laughter throughout. Performed live on the *Morecombe & Wise* TV show later that year, it was an instant signpost to the LSD-inspired psychedelia soon to come, all done and dusted in seventy-five wonderfully atmospheric seconds.

# KARAOKE AND B-YOND

*From instrumental flips that veer wildly off-piste to the straight karaoke B-side...*

To a notorious control freak like Phil Spector, the B-side was more a pain in the jacksy than a necessary evil. The producer's hatred of letting radio DJs decide which side became the hit found him taking extreme action — pairing his painstakingly crafted pop gems with absolute no-hopers jocks wouldn't touch with a bargepole. Credited to the **Ronettes** without featuring a whisper from the New York trio, incongruous instrumental **'Tedesco And Pitman'** ['Be My Baby', PHILLES 1963] namechecked studio Wrecking Crew guitarists Tommy Tedesco and Bill Pitman, letting them stretch out their six-string skills across a jazzy chaise longue. Elsewhere, Spector used B-sides as a forum to experiment — trialling out the huge reverbs, echoes and overloaded pre-amps that he would incorporate into his ever-building wall-of-sound.

**'Waltz For A Pig'** ['Substitute', REACTION 1966] has always been a curio in the Who catalogue. An oddly arresting Hammond-driven, sax-heavy instrumental, the Ginger Baker-written tune (jokily credited to Harry Butcher) was in fact the upcoming Graham Bond Organisation (Bond and Baker with Dick Heckstall-Smith and Mike Falone) responding to a plea from the Who's manager Kit Lambert, who needed an instant B-side to get around a judicial ban imposed by their former producer Shel Talmy (which had thwarted its original B-side 'Circles'). Far from a masterpiece, the song credited to the **Who Orchestra** served its purpose — getting *Substitute* back on the shelves and helping to extricate the band's business affairs from the past. It also bought Baker his first car.

That probably wasn't a Bel Air Sport Coupe 409, the Turbo-Fire Chevy that **Brian Wilson** paid homage to on the B-side of 1962's 'Surfin' Safari'. Nonetheless

its smooth propulsion could be felt in the breezy groove of **'Summer Means New Love'** ['Caroline, No', CAPITOL 1966], a melody clearly patterned on old style 50s pop ballads. Originally recorded for the ninth Beach Boys album *Summer Days (And Summer Nights!!)* by the studio-locked songwriter, it was widely seen as forerunner to Wilson's advanced arrangements for *Pet Sounds*. Used as the exit song on Beach Boys' fiftieth Anniversary Reunion Tour in 2012, its melody was eventually transformed into 'Somewhere Quiet' — a bonus track on the deluxe edition of Wilson's 2015 LP *No Pier Pressure* — with lyrics by keyboardist and backing singer Scott Bennett.

The percussively acute free jazz ramble of **'Groon'** ['Cat Food', ISLAND 1970] proved that **King Crimson**'s sole foray into the singles market would not be forgotten, despite *Top Of The Pops* not giving the A-side the leg-up their label probably hoped for. Far from a throwaway B-side, 'Groon' became a key part of their exploratory live sets with its ever-changing mix of individual solos and dissonance. A fifteen-minute take from Delaware's Wilmington Armoury witnessed guitarist Robert Fripp let rip on an EMS VC3 synthesiser, processing Ian Wallace's solo drum solo to create something sonically discrete (as hissily preserved on 1972's off-the-rails live outing *Earthbound*).

When they first met in the early 60s, John Lennon was so impressed with session player **Billy Preston**'s keyboard wizardry he wanted him to join the band. Paul McCartney vetoed, of course, but Preston continued to stack up the credits with the Fab Four, earning him the nickname 'the fifth Beatle' while spreading the love in studio stints with Sam Cooke, Little Richard and the Rolling Stones. He cemented his cultural icon status on the flip of his first solo single **'Outa-Space'** ['I Wrote A Simple Song', A&M 1972], a rug-cutter that captured Preston playing a clavinet through a wah-wah pedal in-the-moment, before he overdubbed extra organ parts and handclaps. When the A-side stalled at number 77, radio DJs did the magic flip and Preston's innovative creation narrowly missed the top spot (and won a Grammy for Best Pop Instrumental Performance). It also enjoyed star billing when Preston joined George Harrison's band for his only ever solo tour in 1974.

Long before he twigged the seductive power of his how-low-can-he-go voice and became the 'Walrus of love', Barry White was quite the auteur, writing and producing female trio Love Unlimited and showing off his orchestral chops with the **Love Unlimited Orchestra**. In contrast to its lush, violin-led A-side, **'Sweet Moments'** ['Love's Theme', 20TH CENTURY 1973] was a rhapsodic slow jam with plenty of potential for a seduction and long lingering shades of Lalo Schifrin. A bad-ass keeper from the don dada of bedroom soul, its groove has lived on since, underscoring the rap moves of Three 6 Mafia, Spice 1 and MC Eiht.

London songwriter, producer and arranger Charles Blackwell cut his industry teeth working with forward-thinking but troubled sonic auteur Joe Meek in the early 60s. Sadly, Meek's Triumph label folded before he could issue the **Charles Blackwell Orchestra**'s long-in-development debut *Those Plucking Strings*. He did manage to rescue his take on folk standard 'Freight Train' [COLUMBIA 1962], however, coupling it with a rattling western-themed take on great British orchestra leader Norrie Paramor's **'Death Valley'**. Blackwell later turned that B into an A-side, penning a lyric over its arrangement for Gene Vincent's 1963 single 'Held For Questioning'.

An accomplished studio guitarist, before and after he broke through with 1967's 'By The Time I Get to Phoenix', **Glenn Campbell**'s virtuosic sprint through '**William Tell Overture'** ['Southern Nights', CAPITOL 1977] even knocked its bold orchestral arrangements firmly into the shade. Issued on the B-side of his second and final chart-topper, his reins-off *Bonanza*-styled electric guitar rush through Rossini's parting opera (then best known as the theme music for TV's *The Lone Ranger*) finally got down on wax what had been a show-stopping part of his live act for years — Campbell stealing the show by shredding above his head.

Never one to hold back in the live arena — once chucking a drink over his Deep Purple bandmate Ian Gillan — Ritchie Blackmore was in a more sedate frame of mind when he recorded **Rainbow**'s **'Wiess Heim'** ['All Night Long', POLYDOR 1979]. Knocked up over a few spare studio hours, his hymn to his

Long Island domicile was a trillion miles apart from the A-side's dated and overtly sexist radio-friendly sing-along. With the eyes-wide-shut thrust of Blackmore's sustained Fender Stratocaster harmonics, multi-tracked many times over, brushing up against Don Airey's meditative keys, it was a rare triumph of style and sensitivity.

First released as an A-side for the Japanese market, **'Crystal Japan'** ['Up The Hill Backwards', RCA, 1981] was a hidden treasure instrumental that **David Bowie** tacked onto a B-side to stop his fans paying extortionate import fees. Written for a slightly terrifying Japanese TV ad for shochu manufacturer Crystal Jun Rock, it boasted one of Bowie's most gorgeous, rising and falling resolutions, with subtle nods to 'Warszawa' and 'Art Decade' (from the instrumental Side 2 of 1977's *Low*). Originally pencilled in as the closing track on *Scary Monsters (And Super Creeps)*, Nine Inch Nails' Trent Reznor later confessed that he subconsciously stole its melody for 1994 LP cut 'A Warm Place'.

Similarly polished production and state of art drums helped rouse **'The Passion'** ['Flaming Desire', MERCURY 1982] above the madding throng as Yorkshire guitar hero **Bill Nelson** started to extricate himself from his proggy past in Be Bop Deluxe. A solo endeavour in a very literal sense — Nelson played all instruments himself — its groove-heavy chassis seemed to bridge the new romantic era with free-flowing jazz and a guitar motif that harked back to Duane Eddy.

**INXS** were another act mixing it up on **'The Sax Thing'** ['To Look At You', ATCO 1983]. An old-fashioned jazz instrumental, it was almost entirely out of keeping with where the Sydney band were headed in the early 80s, disavowing their pub rock roots to pursue a sleek modern funk sound that chimed with MTV. Their B-sides worked as a little light relief, honing in on individual members' compositions. A frisky affair from the pen of guitarist and saxophonist Kirk Pengilly, it made the most of his jazz pedigree and the underplayed percussive talents of Jon Farriss.

If that had its roots firmly in the past, **'Moments In Love'** ['Into Battle EP',

ZTT 1983] helped establish how samplers would be used over the next decade. A studio-based alliance between Trevor Horn, Anne Dudley, Gary Langan and J. J. Jeczalik all centred on the sampling possibilities of the Fairlight CMI, **Art of Noise** were completed by journalist Paul Morley (who created an eight-page manifesto of their guiding principles) and launched Horn's ZTT imprint. An early chillout blueprint, its ten-minute surrender to sensuality was recycled as an A-side two years later, sampled by everyone from LL Cool J, Nas and Charli XCX, and played as Madonna and Sean Penn made their wedding vows.

Written by banjo player Jem Finer as a tribute to Ennio Morricone's spaghetti westerns, **'A Pistol For Paddy Garcia'** ['Dirty Old Town', STIFF 1985] showed an unknown side of the **Pogues**, without losing any of the A-side's Celtic-punk propulsion — Ewan MacColl's ode to a dying hometown delivered as a snarled warning. With its whistles, trumpets, banjos, reverbed guitars and inevitable tin whistles, it hinted at the more cosmopolitan musical palette of later Pogues releases, if not the subsequent disaffection of their saw-toothed wordsmith Shane MacGowan.

**Duran Duran**'s pitch to become James Bond theme composers was as audacious as it was off the cuff. Their Bond superfan bassist John Taylor was at a post-Wimbledon party with his girlfriend Janine Andrews (a Bond girl in 1983's *Octopussy*) who introduced him to producer Albert 'Cubby' Broccoli. Taylor's drunken gambit about getting someone 'decent' to do a theme song paid off when Broccoli set up a meeting with Bond composer John Barry for Roger Moore's final film as 007 (although the notoriously prickly Barry took some winning over). The resulting Fairlight-dominated 'A View To A Kill' [PARLOPHONE 1985] may not have been the classic Taylor hoped (even though it became the only Bond theme to top the *Billboard* Hot 100), but slowed down B-side **'A View To A Kill (That Fatal Kiss)'** came up trumps, Barry using a 60-piece orchestra to display its sturdy bone structure.

Rated by some as **Prince**'s best B-side — although it has some hefty competition — the super-swirly **'Alexa De Paris'** ['Mountains', PAISLEY PARK

1986] witnessed the Purple One do what he often did onstage: let his guitar do the talking, here playing off against Sheila E.'s unhinged percussion and Clare Fischer widescreen orchestral arrangements. One of the few flips excised from 1993's *Hits* box set, it was later reimagined as a solo piano piece for his romantic film comedy *Under The Cherry Moon*.

Almost as studio-slick as Dire Straits, **'Money Changes Everything'** ['Bigmouth Strikes Again', ROUGH TRADE 1986] was one of three Johnny Marr instrumentals to find a first home on one of the **Smiths**' B-sides — in this case because singer Morrissey simply refused to write words for it. Often played live so Morrissey could take a breather before the encore, its multi-layered swagger and swoon certainly captivated Bryan Ferry, who penned some lyrics, ladled on a vat of additional studio gloss and retitled it as 'The Right Stuff' the following year. And while Marr willingly replayed his parts for Ferry, he later confessed the Top 40 single felt a little 'blow-waved'.

It was easy to miss **'Batabid'** altogether. Shuffled onto the second CD of 'Pagan Poetry' [ONE LITTLE INDIAN, 2001], it found **Björk** immersing herself in beatific-sounding harps and minimally muffled new-age electronics (almost like an outtake from Aphex Twin's *Selected Ambient Works*). Her co-producer Arca later flagged it as a touchstone for 2017's 9th outing *Utopia*, after he invited the Icelander to reconsider some past directions in order to move forwards. Its influence was explicitly felt amid its serene closer 'Future Forever'.

The art of reinvention was perhaps too subtly played on **Little Richard**'s **'Funk Proof'** ['Try To Help Your Brother', MAINSTREAM 1975] — a blazing funk instrumental whose squiggling brass turns and insidious guitar groove drove deep into mid-70s funk revolution (just as its A-side tapped into the slow groove soul of Curtis Mayfield). And if there was little audible evidence that Little Richard even appeared on that B-side — no piano, no piercing holler — it was topped by Cliff Nobles, who definitely didn't play a note on his career-defining hit.

After three flop singles for Atlanta, the searing Alabama soul singer thought

he had finally cracked it with 'Love Is All Right' [PHIL-LA OF SOUL 1968] as he made the most of the nucleus of the Philly horn section soon known as MFSB. Those dreams were dashed when its instrumental version — dubbed **'The Horse'** after a dance step — took off in its own right after a DJ in Tampa, Florida accidentally played the wrong side. Within a week, 10,000 copies of 'The Horse' had been sold in Tampa alone. Within a month it was galloping up the *Billboard* Hot 100, where it was narrowly held off by Hugh Masekela's 'Grazin' In The Grass', another instrumental. With a hit single on his hands, Nobles had little choice but to support it on tour, suppressing his usually assertive onstage exclamations and simply demonstrating its dance steps. To compound matters further, his label continued to release singles under the name **Cliff Nobles & Co** (including 1968's 'Horse Fever' and 1969's 'Switch It On') on which he didn't sing a note. Even when Nobles gave up the ghost and abandoned the music industry for construction, 'The Horse' refused to die, becoming a marching band anthem played by high school bands up and down the States.

**'Keep Your Lamp Trimmed And Burning'**
Blind Willie Johnson
COLUMBIA 1929
A-Side: 'Lord I Just Can't Keep From Crying'

**Imperious early blues.**

Blinded aged seven by his enraged stepmother, who threw lye in his face, Johnson's work was deeply spiritual, intense and moving. A gospel blues performer who busked his way through the small towns and cities of his native Texas, there was a palpable tension to the A-side's plea for the Lord to relieve his burdens and cares, sung alongside Willie B. Harris — the female singer he married a day after meeting in 1927. Johnson added more than a hint of New Testament apocalypse to the traditional 'Keep Your Lamp Trimmed And Burning' on its superior B-side. An allegory for the day of judgement, gifted a haunting edge by the soulful bends of Johnson's slide guitar, there was much heartstring twanging between his impassioned 'chest singing' and his wife's bell-clear comebacks. Johnson had done more than his fair share of hard living when he died from malaria in 1947, leaving less than three dozen songs behind him but all with a significant impact. This B-side alone was covered by Skip James, Andrew Bird, Hot Tuna and Jorma Kaukonen, who, try as they might, failed to capture its complicated soul.

### 'Kelly Watch The Stars (Moog Cookbook Version)'

Air
SOURCE 1998
A-Side: 'All I Need'

**More than just a remix.**

Britpop was dying on its knees when Air's patented take on loungecore took off. Along with their near neighbours Daft Punk, the Paris duo of Nicolas Godin and Jean-Benoît Dunckel's stylish brand of electronica hit all the right notes, with 1998's debut LP *Moon Safari* turning platinum. They were at the end of its promotional campaign, readying final single 'All I Need', when sometime Beck sidemen Moog Cookbook tackled their admiring ode to *Charlie's Angels'* TV starlet Kelly Garrett. While the duo of Roger Manning Jr and Brian Kehew came with form — having already imparted dancefloor glee to covers of Nirvana's 'Smells Like Teen Spirit', Soundgarden's 'Black Hole Sun' and the Eagles' 'Hotel California' — their wilful combination of 70s analogue instrumentation with Air's futuristic sheen made for sumptuous high-end disco cheesiness. With its fortunes boosted by sweetcatatoniauk's homemade YouTube splice through Tommy Seebach's 'Apache', it gained an instant club kudos that its chilled-out A-side failed to match.

### 'Ken'

Kate Bush
EMI 1990
A-Side: 'Love And Anger'

**Sexy ode to then GLC leader.**

Almost hidden on the back of the last single culled from Kate Bush's *Ulysses*-inspired *The Sensual World* album came a spot-on parody of late 80s film theme tunes. It was a grand rebuff for those who painted her as an overly serious and/or batty performer. Belying her tortured recluse image, the Kent singer-songwriter was happy to let her hair down on a theme tune for Comic Strip's TV film *GLC: The Carnage Continues* — an action-styled retelling of Margaret Thatcher's takeover of Ken Livingston's Greater London Council that she also soundtracked. 'Ken' was an instantly infectious, tech-savvy slab of power pop, Bush signifying her game face with an opening primal scream as hard-edged LinnDrum beats and crashing Fairlight stabs (all with a whiff of Peter Gabriel's 'Sledgehammer') built to a chorus refrain hailing Livingston as "a funky sex machine". For an artist often perceived as overly precious and precocious, Bush regularly used B-sides as a forum for extended play. Be it the prettified secret liaison of 'Under The Ivy' ['Running Up That Hill', 1985], unrestrained animal impressions of 'Walk Straight Down The Middle' ['The Sensual World', 1989] or a husky take on Marvin Gaye's 'Sexual Healing' ['King Of The Mountain', 2005] that interweaved uilleann pipes into the mix.

**'Kill All Your Friends'**
My Chemical Romance
REPRISE 2007
A-Side: 'Famous Last Words'

**Sassy ode to the funeral wake.**

Divisive New Jersey emo kings My Chemical Romance could hardly be described as press darlings. Roundly disdained for their uniform image — ironed-on black jeans, jet black hair, piercings, tattoos — matters came an unsavoury head as bottles and glasses, some possibly containing lager, rained down at 2006's Reading Festival. It did nothing to dent their easy talent for summoning roof-raising, radio-friendly B-sides, every bit equal to the main event. Riding a wave of feedback before launching into a riff heavily reminiscent of Pixies' 'Where Is My Mind?', 'Kill All Your Friends' was a fist-pumping platform for singer Gerald Way's wry existential reflections ("I was killing before killing was cool"). The chorus was the thing though, a succession of poppy "ba-bas" leading to the big reveal for the singer's death spree: "We all wanna party when the funeral ends." Way later tweeted his regret that he left this cheery death ode off parent LP *The Black Parade* — a florid OTT rock opera about cancer that variously aped Queen, the Beatles and the Doors and featured a bizarre guest spot by Liza Minnelli.

### 'King Tubby Meets Rockers Uptown'

Augustus Pablo
YARD MUSIC 1974
A-Side: Jacob Miller: 'Baby I Love You'

**Dub takes over the world.**

Dub was already a thriving staple of soundsystem parties in Jamaica and the UK when this single emerged. Its B-side lit a sonic revolution far beyond its insider demographic. While the emotive lovers rock of the A-Side was lit up by Jacob Miller's seamless vocal take — the future Inner Circle singer pleading for his lover to stay true — it was the spare melodica refrains of Augustus Pablo that gave it a unique edge. A seasoned studio figure who had played keys for Lee 'Scratch' Perry and Keith Hudson, Pablo was coming into his own, his instrumental prowess raised to warp level nine at the hands of engineer and dub pioneer King Tubby. 'King Tubby Meets Rockers Uptown' took the shakedowns on their album *Ital Dub* one step further, the engineer using a battery of custom-made effects to alter Pablo's already evocative melodica lines, now seemingly drifting off into infinity, while Carlton Barrett's drums were re-looped to create an otherworldly pattering effect (which, in turn, became an instant staple of the new 'rockers' style). A pinnacle in the nascent art of dub, it turned King Tubby into its producer *du jour*, in heightened demand for his trickery on a bewildering array of dub B-sides thereafter. This B-side's appeal exploded further when Sex Pistols singer Johnny Rotten played it on Tommy Vance's late-night Capital Radio show on July 16, 1977 — arguably day one of the great punk/reggae love-in. Dub's subterranean basslines would subsequently penetrate punk and its immediate followers, evident in the low-end fretwork of Bauhaus' David J, Siouxsie & the Banshees' Steve Severin and Public Image Limited's Jah Wobble.

### 'La Bamba'

Ritchie Valens
DEL-FI 1958
A-Side: 'Donna'

**Infectious Tex-Mex magic from ill-fated star.**

At just 17 Ritchie Valens was on the cusp of a great career. The self-taught Los Angeles singer and guitarist, born Richard Valenzuela to Mexican parents, was primed to dent impressionable teenage hearts with his second single 'Donna', a plaintive tribute to his girlfriend. For its B-side he adapted an 18th century Mexican folk song from Veracruz, often used at wedding dances, and transformed it into a rock 'n' roll anthem alongside stellar Los Angeles studio musicians Carol Kaye and Earl Palmer. Despite not actively speaking Spanish, Valens summoned its vocal hook by learning the words phonetically. "Because it was all in Spanish... I figured 'Nobody's gonna play that'," his Del-Fi records President Bob Keane later told NPR. "We didn't want any mixed airplay." At first Keane was proved correct, as 'Donna' sauntered to number 2 in the *Billboard chart*. Then tragedy struck... Booked onto Buddy Holly's Winter Dance Party tour in early 1959, Valens caught a chartered plane from Clear Lake (alongside Holly and The Big Bopper) that crashed a few minutes after take-off, killing all onboard (and inspiring Don McLean's 'American Pie'). Shortly after Valens' death, DJs flipped 'Donna' for 'La Bamba'. And while it only peaked at 22 it helped open doors for other Latino artists. Fuller recognition arrived with the 1987's Luis Valdez's film biopic *La Bamba*, as Los Lobos' accompanying cover became the first all-Spanish song to top the US charts.

### 'La-Di-Da-De'

Doug E. Fresh & the Get Fresh Crew
REALITY 1985
A-Side: 'The Show'

**Heavily sampled rap storytelling standard.**

Doug E. Fresh & the Get Fresh Crew were unique. The Harlem-based quartet boasted an innovative set-up that combined Fresh's 'Human Beat Box' with British-born MC Ricky D's storytelling prowess and DJs Barry B and Chill Will's turntable mastery. They made the giant leap from live to chart success look easy too, with the A-side's easy mix of comedy (including a brief send-up of the Beatles' 'Michelle'), vocal and deck skills (with heavy use of theme from *Inspector Gadget*) becoming a strong fixture on *Billboard*'s Hot R&B/Hip-Hop charts and a Top 10 UK hit. Yet its flip has become the more influential side since. A one-take showcase for MC Ricky D's lyrical skills, 'La-Di-Da-De' was a deft description of its creator's day — from waking up in the morning to bumping into ex-lovers (and their mothers) later on — replete with its own mirror scene, a sung portion of A Taste of Honey's 1981 hit 'Sukiyaki' and full description of his Oil of Olay beauty regime. After Ricky D changed his name to Slick Rick, 'La Di Da De' took on a life of its own, becoming one of hip-hop's most sampled songs with The Notorious B.I.G., Beastie Boys, Beyoncé and Miley Cyrus all borrowing heavily from its lyrical template. The ultimate tribute came in 1993 when Dr. Dre's new prodigy Snoop Doggy Dogg broke an unwritten rap rule and covered it in full (retitled 'Lodi Dodi') on his five-million selling debut *Doggystyle*.

## 'Ladies Of Cambridge'

Vampire Weekend
XL 2007
A-Side: 'Mansard Roof'

**New Yorkers' peppy afro-pop has instant impact.**

Vampire Weekend's joyful first single put African music at the epicentre of indie rock. The cerebral New York quartet, graduates of Columbia University, mastered their tricky dynamics with shows at literary societies and parties that combined bright indie pop melodies with highlife guitars, piping organs and undercutting rhythms to create a sound they called 'Upper West Side Soweto'. If the fidgety A-side seemed at pains to stress its cleverness — its title referenced a 17th-century French architect — within its two-minute span, 'Ladies Of Cambridge' did much better within its added 30 seconds. Above a quick-fire guitars-drum-organ tapestry, singer Ezra Koenig warned his partner not to take leave, his dark mutterings about a familial 'morbid streak' made hyperreal by Jessica Pavone's meandering violins and a gradual slowing of pace. It was a neat distillation of the youthful energy that pulsed through the following year's self-titled debut, who's equally short and sharp songs explored atypical ideas about Manhattan bus routes, grammar and class.

## 'Lady With The Spinning Head'

U2
ISLAND 1992
A-Side: 'One'

**B-side that spawned three *Achtung Baby* tracks.**

'Lady With The Spinning Head' was a perfectly meta treat for U2 fans, gifting them a piece of the bigger puzzle to figure out for themselves. One of the first songs the Irish rockers wrote during early sessions for 7th LP *Achtung Baby*, it found them struggling to develop a new direction. With co-producer Brian Eno briefed to erase anything that sounded "too traditionally U2", they had nearly ground to a halt and were unsure whether to continue when the ever-hopeful 'One' emerged from the ether. And while the uptempo dance thrust of 'Lady With The Spinning Head' sat on the reject pile, they soon started to pillage it for parts. Elements of the track informed no less than three songs on the final album, from its close cousin 'Utraviolet' and the industrially made-over 'Zoo Station' to the Edge's riff on 'The Fly' (at its three-minute mark). They realised it was much better than they thought when scouting for supporting B-sides and remixed it — creating a fan favourite. Not best known for their B-side generosity, U2 also served up 'Sweetest Thing' ['Where The Streets Have No Name', 1987], a Top 5 UK hit when it was re-recorded 11 years later.

**'Lamplight'**
Bee Gees
POLYDOR 1969
A-Side: 'First Of May'

**The song that split the band.**

Ongoing tensions in the Bee Gees camp came to a head when choosing the only single from sixth studio LP *Odessa*. Considered by many as their most complex and challenging outing, the elaborately packaged double album started life as ambitious concept set *Masterpiece* before the idea was nixed amid musical differences between songwriting brothers Barry and Robin Gibb. Those exploded when choosing its sole single. It quickly became a pitched battle between Robin's hymnal 'Lamplight' — its writer was convinced its big three-part harmony chorus made it a chart-topper — and Barry's stately solo '1st Of May', an orchestral number dedicated to the birthday of Barnaby, his Pyrenean mountain dog. Ultimately presided over by manager Robert Stigwood, who had already stoked tensions by demanding a double LP, it caused Robin to fire an angry warning shot via the pages of *Melody Maker*, as he promised to "...take my songs off the album if Mr Stigwood doesn't want to see eye-to-eye". And although '1st

Of May' made it into the UK Top 10, it faded just as quickly, while Robin made good on his threat. He would keep his distance for 15 months, showcasing his strengths on 1970's *Robin's Reign* before returning to the fold.

### 'Later On'

Brian Eno
ISLAND 1974
A-Side: 'Seven Deadly Finns'

**Ambient pioneer warps and mangles Robert Fripp.**

Keyboard wizard and Roxy Music renegade Brian Eno was between his first two solo albums when he made this compelling one-off single. Backing 'Seven Deadly Finns' fast and furious art-punk turn — full of jolting lyrics about Finnish men, French prostitutes and strange Japanese sex acts — was something that hinted at the ambient worlds to come. But only just. More unnerving and meditative than the woozy melange of each long side of Eno's 1973 *No Pussyfooting* LP with Robert Fripp, it remixed together portions of 'The Heavenly Music Corporation' and 'Swastika Girls'. A pure showcase of the King Crimson man's otherworldly treated guitar (before it became codified as Frippertronics) and Eno's primitively layered Revox tape loops, it retained the spontaneity of their union. And while it had none of the clarity or sophistication of Eno's later ambient work, its oblique strategies and intuitive clutter compelled the listener towards a deep sleep or, if they'd had a few, a rolling nightmare.

### 'Leftovers'

No Doubt
INTERSCOPE 2000
A-Side: 'Ex-Girlfriend'

**Stately paced break-up anthem.**

The one band to make genuine commercial hay during the 90s American ska revival (a re-tread of British 2-Tone rather than a genuine third wave) rested harder on the photogenic qualities of No Doubt's lead singer than her band's capacity to skank. A femme fatale of the old school — heavy Kohl eyes, creamy complexion, bright red lipstick — Gwen Stefani's ability to throw the right shapes while looking above it all was effortlessly compressed into the A-side's adrenaline-fueled self-fulfilling prophecy (a shot across the bows to future husband Gavin Rossdale, singer in faux-grungers Bush). Its B-side 'Leftovers' had been in the band's collective pocket for several years. Another take on Stefani's pained break-up with bassist Tony Kanal (that also bequeathed 1997's breakthrough hit 'Don't Speak'), it came packed with allusions to life on the road and the dubious signifiers of its backstage wristbands. Played at a much pacier tempo when it was aired during 1997's *Tragic Kingdom* world tour, No Doubt re-worked it as slow-paced reggae track, whose lovers rock feel chimed with its deep sense of disappointment.

## 'Leroy'

Jack Scott
CARLTON 1958
A-Side: 'My True Love'

**Prison fable from Detroit's real slim shady.**

Detroit's first white rock 'n' roll star was also the first balladeer to really cut through. Raised within country and hillbilly music, the fulsomely quiffed and darkly handsome Scott was a prolific songwriter with a powerful voice — all the better to deliver his sharp turns of phrase. After recording two local hits for ABC-Paramount ('Baby She's Gone', 'Two Timin' Woman') in 1957, he switched to Carlton for the minimalist slow-dance of 'My True Love' — the sound of his sonorous moans above the Chantones' cooing backing hitting the *Billboard* Top 3. B-side 'Leroy' was better — a blast of high-energy fun, as Scott detailed the plight of a perpetual jailbird who "just can't go straight" over hard rocking beats. Originally titled 'Greaseball' but changed at the last minute at label boss Joe Carlton's insistence, it featured striking solos from Scott's long-term guitarist Dave Rohiller and saxophonist George Kazakas. With an appealing rawness the Elvis-indebted A-side lacked, 'Leroy' later enjoyed a solo run up the charts.

## 'Let Down Your Guard (Rough Mix Edit)'

Madonna
MAVERICK 1994
A-Side: 'Secret'

**Queen of Pop stripped to bare essentials.**

To promote 'Secret', lead single from 6th LP *Bedtime Stories*, Madonna made her first attempt at reaching fans via the world wide web. "Hello all you cyberheads," she joshed on a playful audio teaser, "welcome to the 90s version of intimacy… You can hear me, you can even see me, but you can't touch me!" Conscious that the A-side's heady whiff of R&B might not translate in all territories, European followers were given an added incentive beyond her internet enticements with the inclusion of a second, exclusive Dallas Austin collaboration. Boasting more than just a tip-of-the-hat to early Prince and the raging new jack swing scene, 'Let Down Your Guard' found Madonna pleading for a little uninhibited between-the-sheets action over an all-consuming bassline, cackling adlibs and the kind of glitchy minimalist synths Austin would perfect on TLC's *FanMail*. Its '(Rough Mix Edit)' disclaimer was superfluous though — a more polished version never emerged. And while non-album flipsides are a rare occurrence in Madonna's vast catalogue, special mention must go to 'Into The Groove', the *Desperately Seeking Susan* anthem initially tossed away on the US B-side to 'Angel'.

### 'Lift Him Up That's All'

Washington Phillips
COLUMBIA 1928
A-Side: 'Take Your Burden To The Lord And Leave It There'

**Gospel singer's genre-defying hymn of peace.**

The details of this founding father of American gospel's life are as scant as they are telling. Born in Freestone County, Texas, Washington Phillips farmed near Teague but made a bigger impression as 'jack-leg preacher' — attending churches with the hope of speaking — and as a preternaturally soothing singer. While the hypnotic hymnal A-side of 1927's first single made an instant impression, its jauntier B-side came up trumps, proving the most transcendent work in Phillips's small but affecting catalogue (18 songs recorded between 1927-29) as he recalled the tale of Jesus and a Samaritan at the well. Equally striking was the lengthy outro on its otherworldly music box-sounding instrument. Listed by his label, unhelpfully, as 'novelty accompaniment' and initially attributed to a dolceola, eyewitnesses claim he played a bespoke instrument that Frankensteined together several others (possibly a box zither, phonoharp and gizmo-less celestaphone). Never seen or used since, it added a calming nuance and emotional depth to 'Lift Him Up That's All' — a sound as divine as its source of inspiration.

### 'Like Me'

Dizzee Rascal
XL 2007
A-Side: 'Sirens'

**Fame's pressures inspire introspective grime heater.**

Dizzee Rascal set the early grime pace. Not only did the teenager from Bow make its most creative music, he defined the new rhyme standard with 2003's debut LP *Boy In Da Corner* that has remained since. Four years on his abrasive sound had been smoothed away for more catchy, danceable efforts that leant heavily on his knack for snaggle-toothed pop hooks. If sampling metallers Korn on A-side 'Siren's was all a bit meh, Dizzee saved the day with its foxhunting video conceit — an inspired riff on the British class system — and by putting 'Like Me' on its seven-inch B-side. The equivalent of a movie mirror scene, it found him reflecting on everything — his place in the game, the price of fame, the seismic changes in his life — over a wafting flute and heavily percussive backdrop (more reminiscent of second LP *Showtime*). And although his sharking voice and quickfire intellect did the heavy lifting, its repeated conclusion — "Nobody got my back like me" — underlined the singularity of his quest.

### 'Like The Seasons'

The Turtles
WHITE WHALE 1967
A-Side: 'Happy Together'

**Warren Zevon ballad soothes troubled souls.**

The Turtles' bespoke sonic optimism was a distinct balm against the harsh realities of the day. The far from innovative west coast quintet rested on the resplendent harmony vocals of Mark Volman and Howard Kaylan — tight friends who first bonded in Westchester High's a cappella choir. Despite the Top 10 success of 1965's first single (a cover of Bob Dylan's 'It Ain't Me Babe'), the wheels were starting to fall off their chart charabanc when they took a punt on Gary Bonner and Alan Gordon's 'Happy Together'. Honed and developed over months on the road, the pure economy of its hippy-dippy sunshine pop saw it replace the Beatles' 'Penny Lane' at the *Billboard* summit. Flippers were greeted with something equally enticing. A tender and bittersweet ballad about love's changing face, 'Like The Seasons' was the ying to the A-side's yang, and a preview of bigger, better things to come from the pen of teenage labelmate Warren Zevon (then trading as Stephen Lyme). It wasn't the first time the Turtles tried to give Chicago's 'Excitable Boy' a leg-up — Zevon co-wrote 'Outside Chance' with Glenn Crocker for the flip of 1966's 'We'll Meet Again' and had already seen 'Like The Seasons' first surface on 'Can I Get to Know You Better?' to a tide of indifference. His third-time luck proved a boon for all.

### 'The Little White Cloud That Cried'

Johnnie Ray
OKEH 1951
A-Side: 'Cry'

**Heart-wrenching vocals light path for rock 'n' roll.**

Johnny Ray's two biggest hits surfaced on one single. The baby-faced Dallas-born singer was getting by as pianist in Detroit's Flame Showbar when disc jockey Robin Seymour persuaded Columbia's Danhy Kessler to cut a test record with him. The only white artist signed to Okeh (its black R&B subsidiary), the clock was already ticking when Ray's first singles 'Whiskey And Gin' and 'Tell The Lady I Said Goodbye' failed to sell beyond the Midwest. His searing take on Churchill Kohlman's 'Cry' was as much the gamechanger as its self-penned, sentimental B-side 'The Little White Cloud That Cried' — an autobiographical tune that touched on his teenage loneliness after suddenly losing his hearing (unlike Morrissey, Ray's hearing aid was for real). Given added heft by the Four Lads' cooing backing harmonies, Ray claimed it let people reveal "the emotion they're afraid to show". Its A and B-sides would simultaneously become America's number 1 and 2 chart hits, turning the shy, partially deaf Ray into a teen idol. Soon known as 'the Prince of Wails', the intensity of Ray's early vocals helped open the door for Elvis, while his signature B-side was covered by the Bachelors, Marc Almond and Peggy Lee.

## 'Livery Stable Blues'

Original Dixieland Jass Band
VICTOR 1917
A-Side: 'Dixieland Jass Band One-Step'

**The first jazz recording ever.**

The earliest B-side in this book also codifies a genre. Jazz first emerged as a distinct style in the Original Dixieland Jass Band's home town of New Orleans at the turn of the 20th century, the all-white quintet gaining a reputation for their "jassed up" instrumental sets that took them all the way to a prestigious show at New York's Reisenweber's Café. Declared "the first sensational, musical novelty of 1917" in *The New York Times*, Columbia were first label to declare an interest, but passed on a deal after reputedly finding the material "too hot" (and perhaps too close to its roots in bordellos, where pianists covered up the squelching noises). Their loss was Victor's gain. Cut live in one take, its whimsical A-side, defined by Larry Shield's wild tremolo clarinet, failed to take off as a dance as all parties hoped. Yet the novelty of its happily chaotic B-side more than compensated. A raucous affair that gave equal space to Shields' squealing clarinet, Eddie Edwards' trombone, Nick LaRocca's cornet, Henry Ragas' piano and Tony Sbarbaro's pounding bass drum, it found the band using their instruments to imitate various barnyard animals. When the B-side's popularity catapulted them onto the lucrative vaudeville circuit (and even UK shows) they changed the spelling of 'Jass' to 'Jazz' to stop kids painting over the 'J' on their promotional posters. 'Livery Stable Blues'' popularity would also lead to a major copyright dispute between its members, with the courts eventually disallowing ownership after ruling it was based on a melody already in the public domain. And while the resulting sourness probably did for ODJB's longevity, their place in musical history was assured.

## 'The Loneliness Of A Middle Distance Runner'

Belle and Sebastian
JEEPSTER 2001
A-Side: 'Jonathan David'

**Scottish indie bastions' graceful chamber pop.**

Belle and Sebastian took pride in delivering quality B-sides. The gangly Glasgow group, who met on a college course for unemployed musicians, chose to back their purest pop moment to date with a long-time live favourite. A song that first gained notoriety as a 1998 BBC John Peel session and was tipped to succeed the self-effacing 'This Is Just a Modern Rock Song' as an A-side, it made more sense as a substantial B. Its imagery of rainy fields and railway stations put the listener in the locus of kitchen sink drama *The Loneliness Of A Long Distance Runner*, Alan Sillitoe's 1959 short story of bleak prospects and escape, with B&S imagining a future that's the "colour of blood, chaos and corruption" for its once happy narrator. Such poetical ambiguity should not ghost over the fact that its author Stuart Murdoch was a runner of some repute, completing 1986's Glasgow Marathon in under three hours — a show of stamina from someone portrayed as a shrinking violet, and at odds with his band's bed-wetting, bookish image. And with its vintage Hammond groove, scratchy guitars, wavering but impassioned lead vocal and whistling coda, 'The Loneliness Of A Middle Distance Runner' was possibly *the* archetypal Belle and Sebastian song.

**'Lonesome For A Letter'**

Sanford Clark

MCI 1956

A-Side: 'The Fool'

**One hit wonder's rockabilly wonder.**

Future 60s pop legend Lee Hazelwood was DJing at KRUX in Phoenix, Arizona when he penned Sanford Clark's breakthrough single. Despite boasting a soothing baritone of his own, Hazelwood rather fancied his chances as an impresario and enlisted guitarist Al Casey to find him a singer. Casey suggested old school pal Clark, a US Air Force man just back from Johnston Island in the Pacific. It was a natural fit. Far from flush at the time, Hazelwood cut a deal with local label MCI (Music Counselors Inc) that allowed him abundant studio time to nail the A-side. There was one proviso: he had to use a song published by MCI for its B-side (guaranteeing the label an equal royalties split should the single take off). Written by Tom and Jerry Ollier, 'Lonesome For A Letter' was its ideal counterpart — a nervy tale of long-distance love that majored on Clark's quavering sincerity over Casey's rockabilly jiggery pokery. Thanks to the support of Cleveland DJ Bill Randle, 'The Fool' made waves, with Dot Records taking over manufacture when MCI struggled to meet demand.

### 'Lord Of Karma'

Tears for Fears
FONTANA 1991
A-Side: 'Laid So Low'

**Blustering big budget rock anthem.**

By the early 90s Tears For Fears had transformed from sulky council house kids mixing cod psychology with synthesised melancholy into stadium rockers keen to deploy every bang and whistle at their disposable. That reached its apex on 1989's *The Seeds of Love* as Roland Orzabal and Curt Smith spaffed over a million pounds paying retro homage to psychedelic-era Beatles. Orzabal's pricey perfectionism continued on its follow-up, and Smith had bailed when he decided to tart-up old B-side 'Tears Roll Down' ['Sowing The Seeds Of Love', 1989] into 'Laid So Low' to start his solo odyssey. Many fans favoured its flip 'Lord Of Karma' — a busy, driving meld of expensive synth bounce and overridden guitars that chimed with Orzabal's almost Hendrix-mannered declamations about super-egos, reaping what you sow and whatever a "mystic pain-o-rama" is when it's at home. A sure-fire stadium slayer, it was a stark contrast to earlier B-sides that revelled in experimentalism, from the expressionistic proto-ambiance of *Songs From The Big Chair* ['Shout', 1985] to the looped backing of the BBC shipping forecast on 'Pharaohs' ['Everybody Wants To Rule The World', 1985].

### 'Love Hurts'

Roy Orbison
MONUMENT 1961
A-Side: 'Running Scared'

**Pain-monger's wrenched triumph.**

Roy Orbison had much to thank the Everly Brothers for. Seemingly fated to be a one-hit wonder after his band the Teen Kings failed to build on the momentum of 1956's rockabilly turn 'Ooby Dooby', the slick-haired Texan filled a desperately needed hole on the B-side of the Brothers' next single 'All I Have To Do Is Dream', offering up an ode to his first wife 'Claudette' (and even writing its lyrics down for them on the nearest shoebox). After it went to number 1, 'Claudette' had its own sweet chart run, reaching number 30 on the *Billboard* Hot 100. Vindicated, Orbison signed a deal with Acuff-Rose Music, the Everlys' publisher. Working at his pain-wracked, operatic best on 'Running Scared', he returned the favour by covering 'Love Hurts' on its flipside (a song by husband-and-wife team Felice and Boudleaux Bryant from 1960's *A Date With The Everly Brothers*). Its almost genteel orchestral arrangement chimed with the Big O's doomed gravitas as he gave grave warning that love was a hurting thing that scarred, wounded, marred and may even be an illusion ("made to make you blue") — sentiments that felt more painful given the later tragedies in his life (losing his wife to a motorcycle accident, his eldest sons in a housefire). Later a standalone 70s hit for former Traffic drummer Jim Capaldi and Dunfermline hard-rockers Nazareth (and an Emmylou Harris live staple, following her 1973 duet with Gram Parsons), the doom-struck Orbison rarely let quality control slip, also chucking out sinister country rocker 'Candy Man' on the back of balladry masterclass 'Crying'.

## 'Love In Vain Blues'

Robert Johnson
VOCALION 1939
A-Side: 'Preachin' Blues (Up Jumped The Devil)'

**King of delta blues' masterpiece.**

No one looms larger in blues history than Robert Johnson. Legend has it that the little-photographed Mississippi singer and guitarist got the devil to retune his guitar when he took it to the crossroads of Highways 49 and 61 in Clarksdale — in exchange for his soul. And while he returned with a formidable technique that gave him instant top billing, his tenure proved desperately brief, Johnson dying in circumstances so murky that they've sustained his legend since. Released six months after Johnson's death, the A-side of his final single paid tribute to his major influence Son House and let him show off his complex guitar artistry (when Keith Richards first heard it, he thought two people were playing together). Yet it was utterly despondent B-side 'Love In Vain Blues' that became his most celebrated recording. Using Leroy Carr's 'When The Sun Goes Down' as its melodic base, it found Johnson weeping at a railroad station as he watched the object of his unrequited love pull away. And while his pain felt palpable, it was the intricate detail — the two lights on the back of the train — and his matter-of-fact delivery that left no doubt she was gone for good, as a sparse guitar strums underlined his emptiness. Johnson saved its most touching detail to the end, letting out two heartbroken moans of "Oh, Willie Mae". First introduced to rock audiences on the Rolling Stones' 1969 LP *Let It Bleed*, Eric Clapton also covered it on 2004's full-length homage *Me And Mr Johnson*.

### 'Love Me Or Leave Me'

Sammy Davis Jr
DECCA 1956
A-Side: 'Something's Gotta Give'

**All-round entertainer at his snazziest.**

Sammy Davis Jr beat the odds to become one of the world's most popular entertainers. The Harlem born son of a showgirl and a dancer made his big screen debut aged five (in *Rufus Jones For President*), the same year he joined the family trade in the Will Mastin Trio — his formative education a heavy schedule of singing, dancing and impressions in hotels and nightclubs. A friendship with Frank Sinatra changed his fortunes forever, but he feared his Rat Pack dalliances were over when he lost an eye in a car accident. The chart-topping success of 1954's first solo LP *Starring Sammy Davis Jr* proved him wrong and a string of hits followed, with Davis Jr's seriously scatting take on Johnny Mercer's 'Something's Gotta Give' proving irresistible. There was greater orchestral swing to its other side, 'Love Me Or Leave Me', that better showed off the nuances of his voice, as he pledged undying allegiance before unveiling a scat masterclass in its second verse. Teaming with energy and verve, the B-side enjoyed its own chart run and became an integral part of Davis Jr's all-singing, all-dancing live repertoire.

### 'Love On (Shine On)'

Cliff Richard
ROCKET 1976
A-Side: 'Devil Woman'

**Pop's Peter Pan shows his songwriting chops.**

The pop idol that ushered in the late 50s British rock 'n' roll boom built himself a reputation that even withstood his mid-60s public declaration of Christianity. Cliff Richard's way with a hit and very public profile — he had his own Saturday night TV show (*It's Cliff Richard*) — gave him a 70s ubiquity few could compete with. That changed in 1975, when his unbroken 16-year chart streak abruptly ended, as if he had been jinxed. The Halloween-spiced 'Devil Woman' — the soft rocking tale of a man asking a fortune teller to break a spell — double-bluffed his way back to the top, chiming with the popularity of supernatural horror films such as *Carrie* and *The Omen*. First premiered on ITV's *Russell Harty Show* in late 1975, B-side 'Love On (Shine On)' was a carefully orchestrated pledge of devotion that showed a more ethereal edge and revealed Richard's largely hidden side as a songwriter. And while the A-side was eventually put through the satanic grinder by Cradle of Filth, with predictable results, its intimate B-side showed Richard's devotees had every right to back their man when affecting originals such as 'Nothing Left For Me To Say' ['My Kinda Life', 1977] or 'Lindsay Jane' ['The Best Of Me', 1989] stacked up proudly against his better-known A-sides.

### 'Love You Blind'

Celine Dion
COLUMBIA 1992
A-Side: 'If You Asked Me To'

**Rare fan treat from stingy Québécois balladeer.**

Celine Dion's transformation from Quebec pop anomaly to international superstar grew wings when the Disney corporation paired her with Peabo Bryson for the title theme of 1991's animated blockbuster *Beauty And The Beast*. The following year's self-titled English-language album was a full-pelt transformation, her insipid French pop dance past superseded by slickly-produced R&B fodder with five songs from the mighty pen of Dianne Warren (including the A-side here) and even a tender ballad from Prince. Sheryl Crow co-wrote rare non-album B-side 'Love You Blind', a spectral slow-funker whose earnest pleas for a better world showed Dion's power as an interpreter and worked the angles of her powerhouse voice much better than the by-rote ballads and Titanic vocal showboating that prevailed. Many of Dion's fans stopped physically buying her singles as the 90s wore on, feeling jaded by the constant re-use of existing tracks, their forums bursting with jealous carps about Madonna or Alanis Morrisette giving back so much more.

**'The Love You Gave'**
Dolly Parton
MERCURY 1962
A-Side: 'It's Sure Gonna Hurt'

**Country superstar in pure pop mode.**

The distinctive twang of country music's most honoured woman is noticeable by its absence on her second single. The 4th of 12 children living in a one-room cabin in Tennessee's Smoky Mountains, Dolly Parton started writing and singing her way out of poverty aged ten, becoming a regular on Cas Walker's *Farm And Home Hour* radio and TV shows and making local waves with first single 'Puppy Love' at 13. Three years and high school had passed when Parton and writing partner uncle Bill Owens signed a publishing deal with Buddy Killen. Killen, a critical early ally, arranged for her to record a demo that became her second single. And while the nervously anticipated heartbreak of its 50s styled A-side made much of the Merry Melody Singers' backing power, B-side 'The Love You Gave' was far more incisive, a lunge at the bubblegum jugular as a wronged Parton wept lonely tears after her lover's departure. Parton was so proud to hear her single on Knoxville radio station WIVK she said she "walked around for days with my chest all stuck out. Somehow, nobody noticed." And although the single bombed, Parton refused to be vanquished, pitching her talents through Nashville before 1967's 'Dumb Blonde' bore irrefutable country chart fruit.

**'Lyrical Rundown'**
Twin Hype
PROFILE 1989
A-Side: 'For Those Who Like To Groove'

**The harder side of hip-house.**

Twin Hype's open embrace of hip-house was a dangerous gamble. The real-life New Jersey twins — Glennis (The Sly) and Lennis Brown (Slick) — were quick to jump on its fusion of fast beats and electric piano lines, married with old soul and funk samples, when it took off in clubland. As its title hinted, A-Side 'For Those Who Like To Groove' was more concerned with the art of getting down than deep political analysis, becoming a transatlantic club favourite especially popular at Manchester's Hacienda (where house heads favoured its 'Club Groove

Mix'). B-boys blitzed the darker delights of 'Lyrical Rundown' instead. Its heavy bass, hard-nosed horns, squealing sax and swirling pianos all bore the driving production stamp of Hollywood Impact (best known for his work with King Sun) as the twins responded with a menacing call to arms. When it resurfaced on 1991's valedictory 'Double Barrel' EP, Twin Hype were effectively over, victims of hip-house's fleeting popularity, while the likes of Jungle Brothers, Queen Latifah and Doug Lazy all successfully changed lanes.

# MIND YOUR LANGUAGE

*You don't have to understand the lingo to appreciate the foreign language flip...*

Before English was widely accepted as pop's *lingua franca*, artists were often asked to re-record their singles in another language. Whether to deeply ingratiate themselves with fans in foreign markets or to quash rival non-English cover versions, the results were rarely considered pivotal moments and regularly became an easy B-side go-to when the song cupboard was otherwise bare. It threw up some pleasing anomalies along the way.

There are few more classic examples of the dashed-off B-side becoming a chart behemoth than **Lolita**'s **'Seemann (Deine Heimat Ist Das Meer)'**. The chart career of the racily named Viennese singer Edith Zuser had started to flounder when her label suggested covering Corrado Lojacono's recent Italian hit 'Quando La Luna' to reverse the slide. Asked to summon a B-side on the fly, conductor Werner Scharfenberger and lyricist Fini Busch rustled up a pleading melody to match a lover's benign acceptance of a seafarer's wanderlust. It proved a godsend. When 'La Luna (Quando La Luna)' [POLYDOR 1960] failed to ignite, Polydor threw their weight behind the B-side instead, the surprise German number 2 even crossing over to America. It peaked at number 5 on the *Billboard chart* — one of only a handful German language songs to do so — although it's hard to escape the feeling that there was a lot of nudge-nudge wink-winking behind the enduring schlager anthem's success. Later a UK number 1 for Petula Clark (as 'Sailor'), it would take 24 years before its status as the US's biggest German-language hit was seriously challenged — by another B-side.

Conceived by guitarist Carlo Karges after watching balloons being released at a Rolling Stones concert in West Berlin, **Nena**'s **'99 Luftballons'** ['99 Red Balloons',

EPIC 1984] was a game-changer that resonated in both its English and German versions. A pre-emptive strike against an impending world war — started, in the song, by a war-hungry general mistaking harmless balloons for UFOs — its popularity prompted Nena to produce an English A-side for the UK. And while its powerful verses, keen synth hook and anthemic chorus took it to number 1, Nena weren't shy in expressing their disapproval. "I think the song loses something in translation and even sounds silly," keyboardist and co-writer Uwe Fahrenkrog-Petersen complained to *No 1* magazine (although it could be argued the translation's naïveté accounted for its charm).

Oddly, their blushes were largely spared internationally, with the German original's juxtaposition of a harmless party decoration with war's monstrous machinations triumphing over the English A-side in America, where it was only held off the top of the *Billboard* Hot 100 by Van Halen's 'Jump'. Nena's titular singer also became a media sensation in the UK for her unshaven armpits, briefly glimpsed in the song's video and seized upon by xenophobic tabloid hacks. Fans even raised banners reading 'Nena we love your armpits' when they toured Britain.

Always keen to reach the widest possible audience, Motown chief Berry Gordy often got his artists to record in French, Spanish, Italian and German. Nonetheless **Marvin Gaye**'s transcendent German translation of 'How Sweet It Is', **'Wie Schön Das Ist'** ['Sympatica', CBS 1964] remains a genuine rarity in the soul superstar's deep catalogue, not least for the bruising ballad A-side — a song Gaye recorded only once and in German.

Languages also seemed to figure high on the **Pet Shop Boys**' minds in the early 10s. In contrast to the droll and erudite A-side's tales of "speaking English as a foreign language", **'Entschuldigung!'** ['Love Is A Bourgeois Construct', X2 2013] was written as an apology (its title translates, roughly, as 'excuse me') for pop's eldest statesmen's inability to speak much German, despite spending so much of their time in the music industry's second biggest market. And while its throbbing electronics were deliberately reminiscent of Kraftwerk, the robotically spoken words "Ich nicht sprechen Deutsch" relied on poor grammar and bad pronunciation to underline its wider point.

A synth-pop retelling of David Bowie's breakthrough hit 'Space Oddity', **Peter Schilling**'s 'Major Tom (Völlig Losgelöst)' [ELEKTRA 1983] enjoyed number 1 success in Germany and Austria. When issued in America, Elektra hedged their bets by getting the Stuttgart singer to record English B-side **'Major Tom (Coming Home)'**, with Schilling picking up on Bowie's original train of thought to pronounce "Give my wife my love" before transmitting live from some glowingly-lit afterlife. Fully embraced by MTV, its charms have sustained the intermittent hitmaker since, thanks to cult TV franchises *The Americans*, *Deutschland 83* and *Breaking Bad*.

Reanimated after Bowie covered 'Amsterdam' on the B-side of 1973's 'Sorrow', complex, toothy Belgian singer **Jacques Brel**'s songs of love, death and desperation resonated worldwide after he fled the family's Brussels cardboard factory to make his name in Paris. A man who never sang a song he hadn't written himself, **'Laat Me Niet Alleen'** ['Marieke', PHILIPS 1961] is often considered his best — a pleading, desperate, bleeding confessional full of fear and desertion, written after his pregnant mistress Zizou chucked him out. First recorded for 1959's 4th LP *La Valse à Mille Temps*, Brel re-recorded Ernst van Altena's translation to back his other stab at the Dutch market 'Marieke' (a move that would later prove the making of native singer Liesbeth List). Famously debased into Terry Jacks' 'Seasons In The Sun' by lyricist Rod McKuen (and given the full histrionics by Dusty Springfield, Shirley Bassey and Barbra Streisand), Brel acolyte Marc Almond had it re-translated when he covered it for 1982's *Untitled*. But the take that stacks up strongest against Brel's Dutch B-side is Momus's 'Don't Leave', issued on the B-side of 1999's 'Nicky' (itself a cover of Brel's 'Jacky').

While Momus would gain notoriety for covering Bowie's comeback single 'Where Are We Now' within 24-hours of the original surfacing, blonde-bobbed Italian singer and actress **Caterina Caselli**'s was similarly quick off the mark. She left a deep impression on the Rolling Stones' 6th number 1 with **'Tutto Nero (Paint it, Black)'** ['Cento Giorni', CGD 1966] as her harmonic-minor coo subverted Jagger's sneering bark. As with the A-side, it was recorded for her starring role in Ettore Maria Fizzarotti's film musical *Perdono*. Caselli would go to eclipse her character's quest for fame by becoming one of the most influential producers and managers (behind Andrea Bocelli, Piccola Orchestra, Avion Travel and Negramaro) in Italian pop.

Bilboa folk-poppers **Mocedades** took a more standard route to stardom — competing in the Eurovision Song Contest. Although they came second in 1973's competition, pipped to the post by Anne-Marie David's 'Tu Te Reconnaîtras' (Luxembourg), many regarded 'Eres Tu' [PHILIPS 1973] as the hit of the evening. Even the small scandal about whether its writer Juan Carlos Calderon had copied Berta Ambrož's 1966 Yugoslav entry 'Brez Besed' couldn't stop it becoming the first Spanish language song to reach the US Top 10. The English version on the B-side, **'Touch The Wind'**, would enjoy far greater resonance down the years. A somewhat loose translation — as were its equivalents in German ('Das Bist Du' — 'You Are That'), French ('C'est Pour Oi' — 'It Is for You') and Italian ('Viva Noi' — 'Long Live Us') — with everyone from Eydie Gormé and Percy Faith to the Shirelles and Johnny Mathis embracing its complex harmonies.

Whether with **Miami Sound Machine** or solo, Gloria Estefan managed to confidently straddle success in two languages. The former had notched up seven albums, mostly in Spanish, when 'Dr Beat' became a European hit, prompting their label Epic to get them to re-record their 1984 LP *A Toda Maquina* in English (as *Eyes Of Innocence*). They crowned their crossover credentials the following year with **'No Me Vuelvo A Enamorar'** ['Words Get In The Way', CBS 1986], a Spanish version of the A-side that helped usher in the rich heartfelt pop ballads that dominated Estefan's solo work. Estefan has enjoyed a bilingual recording career since, putting Spanish B-sides on the back of 'Anything For You' (1988), 'Don't Wanna Lose You' (1989) and 'Coming Out Of The Dark' (1991), while also scoring a huge *Billboard* Hot Latin Song hit with 1993's explicit ode to her Cuban homeland 'Mi Tierra'.

Originally the theme song of the soap opera *Reina de Corazones*, **Enrique Iglesias' 'Bailando (Spanish Version)'** ['Bailando (English Version)', REPUBLIC 2014] was a straightforward tale of a man who falls in love with a woman after watching her dance. A co-write with long-time collaborator Descemer Bueno, Iglesias had all but forgotten it when he was energised by Cuban reggaeton duo Gente De Zona's cover version. Re-recorded in a similar fashion, it spent 41 weeks at the summit of *Billboard*'s Hot Latin Song chart and, aided by a Spanglish remix (featuring a typically quirky rap by Sean Paul) became the highest charting Spanish-language single of all time. Issued in multiple versions globally, only the UK seemed immune to Iglesias' chart monster — its English-sung A-side managing just one fleeting week in 75th position.

Before their robotic counterparts were let loose on the global festival circuit, **Kraftwerk** toyed with vocal takes in various languages. A spooked tale of shop window mannequins coming to life and going clubbing, the melody line for 'Showroom Dummies' was developed during mid-70s live improvisations. Among the more whimsical thrills of their 6th LP *Trans-Europe Express* — arguably the big hit that never quite arrived — their first multi-language song arrived pre-packed in German, English and French takes. Sounding stranger and otherworldly outside their clipped mother tongue, **'Les Mannequins'** ['Showroom Dummies', CAPITOL 1977] became a collectible when it surfaced outside France as an American B-side.

Julian Cope's talents ran deep. The 22-year-old singer with **Teardrop Explodes** showed just a glimpse of his involved inner life with his seamless French delivery on **'Traison (C'Est Juste Une Histoire)'** ['Treason (It's Just A Story)', MERCURY 1981], a re-release of their third single blessed with all-new B-sides. Seemingly recorded for the hell of it — it wasn't issued as an A-side in France — it demonstrated just why early 80s big-hitters Duran Duran and U2 feared what his band might do next.

You have to wait until its second half, but then it happens — the **Beach Boys** are singing in Japanese. First written for Mike Love's abandoned solo LP *First Love*, the gloopy, Erhu-enhanced **'Sumahama'** ['It's A Beautiful Day', CARIBOU 1979] was a relaxing change of pace, despite a simpering vocal take and faux-oriental string arrangements. Indeed, the B-side was the only place fans could wallow in its full mellow glory — the closing Japanese verse was faded out on that year's buffed to the maximum *L.A. (Light Album)*, regarded by many as a triumph of style over substance.

Although it's strictly an instrumental, Japanese surf-rock quartet **Jackie and the Cedrics' 'Sukiyaki Stomp'** ['Scalping Party', NORTON 1995] had an abundantly good time thrashing through the melody of late actor and singer Kyu Sakamoto's original misfit hit, 'Sukiyaki'. A heart-rending 1961 Japanese success as 'Ue O Muite Aruko', its tale of loss and isolation was first chanced upon by UK music exec Louis Benjamin, who got his charges Kenny Ball & His Jazzmen to record an instrumental that he retitled after his favourite Japanese food. Benjamin's cultural sleight of hand might have been the end of the story had a Washington-state DJ not started playing the original, with Capitol cashing in to make 'Sukiyaki' the only Japanese-language song to top the US charts.

Long before they were famous, ABBA's **Bjorn & Benny Agnetha & Frida** recorded in their mother tongue. Even then, they had their sights set on a European market that didn't necessarily speak English. That was the logic behind the onomatopoeic title of 'Ring Ring (Bara Du Slog En Signal)' [POLAR 1973] — a track that came third in the Swedish Eurovision selection and became the group's first UK single (backed by album track 'Rock'n Roll Band'). The 100,000 or so Swedish fans who snapped up a copy also copped rare Swedish-language B-side **'Äh Vilka Tilder'** — a jaunty bit of fluff that remains the sole ABBA song without an English equivalent. And while the maritally-troubled pop sensation's big breakthrough 'Waterloo' was first recorded in their native tongue — adapted into English for 1974's *Eurovision Song Contest* — ABBA soon stopped recording in Swedish altogether, allowing other native artists to pick up the slack.

### 'Made Of Glass'

Kylie Minogue
PARLOPHONE 2005
A-Side: 'Giving You Up'

**Pint-sized popstress in ecstatic form.**

Issued just before her larger than life Showgirl Greatest Hits Tour was halted due to breast cancer diagnosis, both sides of this single showed the slings and arrows of the diminutive Australian actress/singer's fortune. One of two new tracks intended to boost sales of yet-another-compilation (*Ultimate Kylie*), 'Giving You Up' was just about up to par, but perfunctory by the flab-free standards set by her producers, Xenomania. All parties redeemed themselves with its glittering B-side. 'Made Of Glass' was everything the A-side wasn't — edgy, fresh and original — as a sultry Minogue took a restrained, almost covert stance as the song turned on a whispered half-rap about "bohemian boys and Brazilian girls". For once Minogue's almost robotic disconnect worked in her favour, burrowed between the winding synths and cymbal rushes of its trancey electronic backing. A song apparently first demoed by ex-S Club 7 shortie Rachel Stevens, it was promoted as a double A-side in Australia, where it received the lion's share of radio play.

## 'Maggie May'

Rod Stewart
MERCURY 1971
A-Side: 'Reason To Believe'

**Rites-of-passage romp launches Stewart solo.**

Although well established by 1971, Rod Stewart's solo efforts had fared poorly in comparison with his work with the Jeff Beck Group and the Faces. That pattern seemed certain to repeat when 'Reason to Believe' — a cover of US folk singer Tim Hardin more than suited to Stewart's aching rasp of a voice — was chosen as lead single from *Every Picture Tells A Story* and stalled at number 19 in the UK charts. Then something untoward happened — DJs started playing its unconventional, mandolin-led B-side instead. An ornate ode to an older seductress that mingled quiet triumph with rueful regret, its no-chorus structure was reliant on the chops of guitarists Ronnie Wood and Martin Quittenton (Stewart's co-writer). In 2007 Stewart told *Q* magazine that 'Maggie May' was a true story about losing his virginity at the Beaulieu Jazz Festival when he was 16, but nearly abandoned because "the label said it didn't have a melody". While Stewart's conflicted vocal did much to seduce the listener, the mandolin riff played by Lindisfarne's Ray Jackson was equally unforgettable. It later prompted a threat of legal action over royalties, with Jackson still smarting over Stewart's liner note credit to "the mandolin player in Lindisfarne. The name slips my mind" and the sight of Radio 1 DJ John Peel miming his part on *Top Of The Pops*.

### 'Magic Roundabout'

Jasper Carrott
DJM 1975
A-Side: 'Funky Moped'

**Booinngg! Toytown rudeness from Birmingham comic.**

Designed to break Jasper Carrott into the mainstream firmament via the medium of a comedy single, 'Funky Moped' aced the brief, albeit in a way nobody anticipated. An autobiographical tale of two-wheel love that featured Carrott's old Moseley schoolmate Bev Bevan and production by ELO's Jeff Lynne, it defied label DJM's expectations by hitting the UK Top 5. And while the BBC insisted on playing its A-side, its popularity was all to do with its B-side — a music-free snatch of risqué stand-up that satirised Serge Danot's popular children's television show of the time. An excerpt from a self-pressed acetate called *Carrott In The Club*, what was purported to be a stolen script quickly became a coarse playground essential. Its central debate about whether Florence was a virgin — her increasingly indignant denials about being a 'brazen hussy' only supported by a stoned rabbit with ulterior motives — was soon learnt verbatim beyond the confines of the Magic Garden. It helped Carrott court a much wider audience and move into TV.

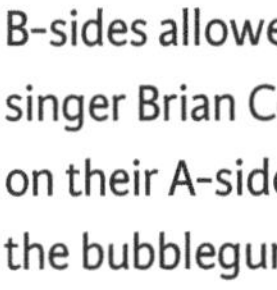


### 'Man From Mecca'

The Sweet
RCA VICTOR 1973
A-Side: 'Little Willy'

**Manufactured glamsters' potent hard rock nugget.**

B-sides allowed the Sweet to show their true colours. With the exception of singer Brian Connelly, the heavily glam-styled Londoners never got to feature on their A-sides, producer Phil Wainman enlisting session musicians to replicate the bubblegum pop that gushed from the pens of their managers Nicky Chinn and Mike Chapman (steady suppliers of similar radio-friendly glam for Mud, Suzi Quatro and Arrows). The Sweet did, however, control their B-sides, backing their biggest US hit 'Little Willy' with a ferocious metallic beast predicated on guitarist Andy Scott's killer riffs and psychedelic lyrics about wildcats, white mice and groupie clothes. Further detailed with a backwards guitar break, it unmasked the hell-raising act that had somehow been subsumed beneath their teenybopper image (a schism that witnessed younger sisters playing their As and older brothers digging the untamed Bs). If you flip over just about any of the Sweet's classic singles, self-penned rockers such as 'Restless' ['Ballroom Blitz', 1973], 'Burn On The Flame' ['The Six Teens', 1974] and 'Medusa' ['Action', 1975] showed the true grit lurking beneath the glitter costumes and tottering heels. Wounded by their public image — "Like four dissipated old whores, mincing about on *Top Of The Pops*," carped drummer Mick Turner in 1974 — the Sweet eventually unchained themselves from Chinn and Chapman. And although 1975's resulting *Sweet Fanny Adams* stiffed commercially, it became a cult classic, not least for its title track's punkish portrait of teenage delinquency.

**'The Man With The Horn'**
Phil Collins
VIRGIN 1985
A-Side: 'Sussudio'

**Funky aside from 80s pop's unlikely king.**

While Patrick Bateman declared 'Sussudio' "a great, great song, a personal favorite" in one of his excruciating discourses in *American Psycho* — Brett Easton Ellis' ornery novelistic portrait of 80s capitalist dysfunction — he clearly wasn't the only one. Genesis' pint-sized drummer's nonsensical musings and cheesy synth horns didn't so much muscle in on Prince's funk-pop territory as forcefully violate it, shooting Collins to the top of the *Billboard* Hot 100 despite many Genesis fans actively hating it. It mattered little to its creator. By 1985 the former child actor was far bigger than the prog rock band that nurtured him, playing both legs of *Live Aid* and churning out lachrymose hits at will. Long suffering fans took solace in UK B-side 'The Man With The Horn' (flip of 'One More Night' in the US), a driving, upbeat, brass enhanced leftover from sessions for 1982's *Hello, I Must Be Going!* LP that far outranked several of its filler tracks and was closer in spirit to 'Paperlate', Genesis's funk-laced collaboration with Earth Wind & Fire.

## 'Mars Bars'

The Undertones
SIRE 1979
A-Side: 'Jimmy Jimmy'

**Short and sweet fan favourite.**

The Undertones had impeccable credentials. The Derry punk quartet, formed in the backdrop of The Troubles, married three-chord, two-minute pop anthems with genuine council house chic, and gained an instant supporter in Radio 1 DJ John Peel, who widely trumpeted 1978's first single 'Teenage Kicks' as his all-time favourite song (his gravestone later bore its opening line "Teenage dreams so hard to beat"). Backing 'Jimmy Jimmy', their first UK Top 20 entry, came another tale of mild teenage mischief, its tongue-in-cheek lyrics married to an equally memorable tune. Damian O'Neill and Michael Bradley's ode to the restorative "work, rest and play" ethos of Mars of Slough's signature chocolate bar included an invocation to "go raid the Spa" for further supplies as singer Feargal Sharkey outlined its health properties ("Glucose for energy/Caramel for strength") in his tremulous vibrato, dissing poorer rivals Twix and Buttons along the way. A blast of raw sugar energy that became a chant-along live favourite, it was difficult to listen to 'Mars Bars' without experiencing a sudden craving.

## 'Me, Myself And My Microphone'

Nine
PROFILE 1995
A-Side: 'Whutcha Want?'

**Rugged Bronx rhymer's bragging rights.**

Nine boasted a great grits-and-gravy voice. The New York rapper first showed his vocal artillery on Funkmaster Flex and the Ghetto Celebs' 1993 single 'Six Million Ways To Die', ruffling enough industry feathers to land a solo deal. Deep on every level, his string-saturated first single 'Whutcha Want?' was years ahead of the competition and should have made him a star. Its 12-inch bonus B-side 'Me, Myself And My Microphone' was equally on-point .With its braggadocious threats to "smack you with a ball full of skills" and "stick your neck in the news if you try to get loose" over a heady lift from Ahmad Jamal Trio's 'Perfidia', it showcased the raw and gravel-throated schtick long before DMX and Ja Rule made whole careers from it. And while Nine added a further layer of homage by sampling Run-DMC's greatest B-side 'Sucker MCs' for the chorus, he would later dis the Hollis trio on 'Lyin' King', his wide-angled takedown of fake emcees.

### 'Memory Gospel'

Moby
MUTE 1998
A-Side: 'Honey'

**Superstar DJ's stab at glacial minimalism.**

B-sides may be a vinyl anachronism to some, but that didn't stop the future-proofed Moby embracing them hard. That trend was particularly pronounced around the *Play* era — the New York dance behemoth shuffling out a succession of meditative tone poems that contrasted with his A-side's clubbier mash-ups of dark electronics and soulful roots vocals (often sampled from the archives of US folk anthologist Alan Lomax). While *Play* was shamelessly monetised at the time, with every track licensed for commercial use, it seems Moby was ahead of the curve in terms of figuring out a survival strategy after the collapse of physical product. 'Memory Gospel' was one of his more deceptive creations — an intimate five-note sprawl that, like 'Porcelain', burrowed its way firmly below the skin, a female voice repeating "Yeah" before a second wave of strings and one-fingered piano ornamentation doubled-up its meditative pull. Effortlessly cinematic and full of zen rapture, it was later leased to the soundtracks of *40 Days And 40 Nights* and *Southland Tales*.

### 'Mentally Mad'

Ultramagnetic MCs
NEXT PLATEAU 1987
A-Side: 'Funky'

**Rap innovation from the Boogie Down Bronx.**

Ultramagnetic MCs seemed to speak a different language to their rivals. One of the first groups to take a more complex approach to the art of rhyming, the Bronx quartet's mind-boggling lyrical skills left their rivals for dust. 'Mentally Mad', arguably the first horrorcore song on wax, was the epitome. A back-and-forth between Ced-Gee and former psychiatric patient Kool Keith, both deployed complicated rhyme schemes to boast of being revolutionists "with skills of Malcolm X" as they bragged about how crazy they were. Beyond the verbal invention, it was a bruising showcase of Ced-Gee's radically forward-looking production skills. Among the first groups to explore the sampler's potential as an instrument, their snaffling of the fuzzing bass from James Brown's 'Blues And Pants' might have been par for the course, but the addition of all sorts of other sonic strangeness on top (not least DJ Moe Love's turntable wiki-wiki) certainly wasn't. Its intense collage of sounds undoubtedly influenced fellow golden age production giants Bomb Squad and the nascent UK hardcore scene.

### 'Middle Of The Night'

The Clovers
ATLANTIC 1952
A-Side: 'One Mint Julep'

**Doo-wop doozy introduces an edgier brand of R&B.**

The Clovers made their own luck. The Washington D.C. vocal group evolved from Armstrong High School before they were joined by the smooth vocal lead of John 'Buddy' Bailey. When Baltimore entrepreneur Lou Krefetz made them the stars of his tiny Rainbow imprint, Ahmet Ertegun took an interest, selling them his dream of his newly-established Atlantic imprint as a hot rhythm and blues label. Not only did Ertegun encourage the Clovers to adopt a more rhythmic approach, he took a hands-on approach, penning many of their hits (the first song he wrote, 'Don't You Know I Love You', topped the US R&B charts). To back the novelty of 'One Mint Julep' (a sure shot from Rudy Toombs, grandmaster of drinking anthems), Ertegun summoned 'Middle Of The Night', a desperate fable of yearning and desire that caught Bailey in tremulous form over a bluesy piano figure. Both sides went Top 3 on the *Billboard* R&B chart as the Clovers racked up more hits in their six-year tenure than any act in Atlantic's history.

## 'The Model'

Kraftwerk

EMI 1981

A-Side: 'Computer Love'

**Robots intersect the new romantic era.**

Time almost caught up with Kraftwerk with this single. An electronic band that anticipated the future, the cosmopolitan Düsseldorf outliers sculpted a hypnotic brand of 'machinemusik' that set the sonic template for everything from hip-hop to rave. And while the A-side's tale of spending hours in front of a home computer looking for love was insanely prescient, few thought so at the time, the single stalling at a lowly number 36 on the UK charts. When EMI noticed DJs were playing 'The Model' instead — a track from 1978's *The Man Machine* that *still* sounded like the future — they took a punt on reversing sides, apparently against Kraftwerk's wishes. With BBC Radio 1's surprise endorsement, Ralf Hütter's deadpan vocal about high-fashion models strutting their stuff in Cologne nightclub the Bagel cut through the mundane chart fodder of the day, his bandmates' twinkling Micromoogs, Polymoogs and Minimoogs becoming the last word in cool in a new romantic era blitzed with fame-hungry androgynes. The first UK number 1 for a German group (although Goombay Dance Band were hot on their heels), 'The Model' has been covered by everyone from the Members to the Balanescu Quartet and Rammstein, but never bettered.

## 'Modern Girls & Old Fashion Men'

The Strokes

ROUGH TRADE 2003

A-Side: 'Reptilia'

**Regina Spektor duet puts cat among the pigeons.**

By their second album *Room On Fire*, the Strokes had two years of unimaginable success under their belts. Not bad going for a bunch of snotty, apparently well-heeled New York alt-rockers with more than a handful of Velvet Underground, Television and Modern Lovers albums in their collections. If the panicked warning of 'Reptilia' suggested there had been very little progression from their lean and mean debut *Is This It*, its rare exclusive B-side — a duet with Russian-born songwriter Regina Spektor — showed they had at least dredged a few more songs from the locker second time around. 'Modern Girls & Old Fashion Men' was anything but throwaway, a rawer, defiantly indie guitar chug undercutting its lyrical contrast between the sexes, both parties locked into the mantra "Oh yes, we're falling down" as their relationship collapsed around them. The pile up of Spektor's strident wails with Julian Casablancas' Iggy Pop-ish whine reminded a little of Nancy Sinatra and Lee Hazlewood's high watermark sing-speak pop.

**'Moment Of Truth'**
Whitney Houston
ARISTA 1987
A-Side: 'I Wanna Dance With Somebody (Who Loves Me)'

**Doomed chanteuse's ballad from simpler times.**

By her second album, Whitney Houston had mastered a dynamic that alternated between bouncy dance tunes and quiet storm ballads that rested on the New Jersey powerhouse's vocal prowess. To back its Grammy winning A-side — the song that made Houston an international star — she repeated that marketable formula, favouring a spare synth-dominated ballad that was omitted from the LP in favour of 'You're Still My Man'. A song from the pens of Jan Buckingham and David Paul Bryant, 'Moment Of Truth' cast the 23-year-old superstar questioning the veracity of her love affair and seeking absolution, all too aware it could fall apart. And while its production was state of the art, in line with Yamaha DX7 dominated sound of Madonna's 'Live To Tell', Houston stamped her fragile personality all over it, her final plea of "Let out your feelings tonight" seemingly coming from the heart. The title of 1987's high-grossing stage review, it became a B-side twice, also making up the numbers on 1995's 'Exhale (Shoop Shoop)'.

**'Mona Lisa'**
Nat King Cole
CAPITOL 1950
A-Side: 'The Greatest Inventor Of Them All'

**The 20th century's greatest love song?**

A prominent black entertainer in an era of profound change, Nat King Cole often found himself at the centre of a storm beyond his own making. A celebrated jazz pianist and pioneer for racial equality, the Alabama-born Cole was a reluctant vocalist badgered into singing by a big-spending client at Los Angeles nightclub the Sewanee Inn in 1937, where his trio held a residency. Afterwards his silky-smooth baritone became a crucial part of his armoury, obscuring even his formidable piano skills as he crossed over into the 40s pop charts. Written by Ray Evans and Jay Livingston for the Paramount film *Captain Carey, U.S.A.*, original adverts for the single focused solely on its vocal-heavy A-side with no mention of 'Mona Lisa' whatsoever. Yet Cole's suave and sophisticated paean to "the lady with the mystic smile" in Leonardo da Vinci's famous painting would not be denied. The B-side finally took off when its writers and Cole embarked on a Paramount press junket and radio DJs began playing it instead, seduced by Cole's silky piano vamps and the gentle guitar flourishes in Nelson Riddle's subtle arrangement. A personal Cole favourite, it became his third number 1 and biggest hit, with everyone from Elvis Presley, Willie Nelson, Conway Twitty and his daughter Natalie adding it to their repertoires. It was famously used in Alfred Hitchcock's tense 1954 thriller *Rear Window*, just two years before Cole became the first African-American entertainer to host his own TV show.

**'Monk's Mood'**
The Thelonious Monk Quintet
BLUE NOTE 1949
A-Side: 'Who Knows'

**Modern jazz standard takes on a life of its own.**

The 40s witnessed a significant changing of the jazz guard. Out went the metronomic pulse of pre-war big band/swing music, in came the complicated improvisations and raw excitement of bebop. New York-raised pianist Thelonious Monk was among the most vibrant figures of the new guard. His percussive technique and compositional playfulness — drawing on classical technique and the Harlem stride piano tradition, augmented with his own ideas about silence and dissonance — made him a natural ally of Blue Note, the label that defined jazz's changing times. The slowly unfurling sprawl of 'Monk's Mood' was a perfect illustration of his craft, Monk allowing the almost lazy, wayward horns of George Taitt and Sahib Shihab to set the tone before letting loose a winding, wistful solo over Bob Paige and Art Blakey's textured rhythmic backing. A staple of his live sets thereafter — and a song that has influenced succeeding jazz generations since — he reprised 'Monk's Mood' with John Coltrane in 1957, as the saxophonist battled heroin addiction over a six-month residency at Greenwich Village's Five Spot club. Their unhesitating chemistry was caught at full tilt on 2005's belatedly released *Thelonious Monk Quartet With John Coltrane At Carnegie Hall*, Monk's cascading arpeggios and Coltrane's assured soloing throughout its eight-minute reading knocking even this pivotal B-side into a cocked hat.

## 'Monkey Talk'

Little Stevie Wonder
TAMLA 1962
A-Side: 'Workout Stevie, Workout'

**Boy Wonder's jiving harmonica frenzy.**

Long before he became the enemy of the B-side, routinely using it as a dumping ground for instrumental versions of the A-side, Stevie Wonder issued a series of jewels that spoke volumes about his prodigious gifts (see also: 'Tears In Vain' ['Pretty Little Angel'] and 'This Little Girl' ['Hey Harmonica Man'], both 1964). 'Monkey Talk' was among his most inspired. Like its happy-clapping pseudo gospel A-side, it was audibly designed to show off the 12-year-old Michigan-born multi-instrumentalist's prowess on keyboards, harmonica and percussion — here letting loose a bongo frenzy. Beyond a short spoken word section, this practically instrumental jam (written by early mentor/producer Clarence Paul) allowed plenty of space for Motown house band the Funk Brothers to show off their bluesy roots. It was Wonder's ripe harmonica blasts that shone through though, drowning out their squealing horns before he whooped "Yeah, yeah, yeah" in-between breaths. At once silly, carefree and joyous, it was an oddity packed with charm, whose fade-out arrived far too soon.

## 'Moonlight Serenade'

Glenn Miller and His Orchestra
BLUEBIRD 1939
A-Side: 'Sunrise Serenade'

**Song that summoned Word War II newsreels.**

Glenn Miller's sophisticated sound became synonymous with World War II. The former trombonist and arranger for the Dorsey Brothers had struck out with his own orchestra and was enjoying a residency at New Rochelle's Glen Island Casino when his take on Frank Carle's 'Sunrise Serenade' became a Top 10 US hit. Yet it was his signature dreamy foxtrot on the other side, already used as theme music for his radio broadcasts on NBC, that moved listeners to tears. 'Moonlight Serenade' played hard on Miller's distinctive sound — using a high-pitched clarinet (played here by Wilbur Schwartz) for the melody, doubled up by a saxophone section an octave lower — that offered a reassuring sense of calm in turbulent times, standing in stark contrast to the uptempo tunes dominating the US pop charts. Miller would rule those charts in its wake — scoring 31 Top 10 hits in 1940 alone — before forgoing civilian life and joining the army, where he played for troops and was regarded as one of the war's greatest morale boosters. And while conspiracy theorists have speculated wildly about his unexplained disappearance in 1944 — his aircraft vanished over the English Channel — the longevity of his greatest B-side (made famous again by Frank Sinatra in 1966) cemented his status as a swing great.

**'Move'**
Miles Davis
CAPITOL 1949
A-Side: 'Budo'

**'Cool' B-side that took bebop in a new direction.**

His dexterous trumpet solos with Charlie Parker's quintet helped make Miles Davis a central figure in jazz's bold new era. The restless Juilliard dropout, who had the unenviable task of replacing Dizzy Gillespie in Parker's intense band, found a cooler, mid-register voice to match his improvisational style. That continued into his solo work with Gil Evans, baritone saxophonist Gerry Mulligan, pianist John Lewis and a cast of players that would meet informally at Evans' Manhattan apartment (eventually tagged as the Miles Davis Nonet). Together they forged a relaxed yet intricate sound that retained the elasticity of bebop's sonic heat. Recorded in early 1949 alongside its harmonically surprising A-side 'Budo', 'Move' didn't waste any of its short airspace, pairing the melody between Davis' trumpet and Lee Konitz' alto sax with Mulligan's baritone and Bill

Barber's tuba counterpoint, while harmonies from trombonist J.J. Johnson and French hornist Sandy Siegelstein intersected its shuffling beat. A commercial misfire along with Davis's other early Capitol singles, it was only when the sessions were united on 1957's compilation *Birth Of The Cool* that they started to seriously impact on jazz's harmonic language.

**'Move Over Ms. L'**

John Lennon

APPLE 1975

A-Side: 'Stand By Me'

**Only non-album B-Side of ex-Beatle's solo career.**

Most of the music that emerged during John Lennon's mid-70s year-and-a-half long 'lost weekend' was little to write home about. Estranged from wife Yoko Ono and partying harder than usual with celebrity friends in Los Angeles, the US number 1 success of his Elton John duet 'Whatever Gets You Thru The Night' patched over the uneven, over-produced frailties of its parent album *Walls And Bridges*. 'Move Over Ms. L' was supposed to appear there, but was cut from the running order (in-between 'Surprise Surprise' and 'What You Got') just three weeks before its release, due to Lennon's lingering dissatisfaction with its country and western-styled take. He revived it again during the chaotic sessions for 1975's covers album *Rock 'N' Roll*, imbuing it with the same off-the-cuff spirit in which he blasted through its oldies selection. A horn-enhanced throwback whose mostly nonsense lyrics poked gentle fun at Ono (offering up the peace treaty: "I'll forgive your trespasses if you forgive me mine"), it was almost equal to the A-side's fervent take on Ben E. King's soul standard. Covered at amphetamine tempo by one of Lennon's regular drinking buddies Keith Moon for the ill-fated Who man's only solo LP *Two Sides Of The Moon* (issued the same month as this single), Moon also made it the B-Side for 'Solid Gold'.

**'Mr. Record Man'**

Willie Nelson

LIBERTY 1961

A-Side: 'The Part Where I Cry'

**King of outlaw country at vulnerable best.**

Willie Nelson was a starving musician when he wrote 'Mr. Record Man'. The Waco born singer-songwriter pinballed around the States in the 50s, going from one itinerant job to another in Texas, Oregon and Washington, all the while trying to catch a break as a songwriter and performer. His short-lived early 60s tenure in Houston proved pivotal. When he tried to shop songs, including future standard 'Crazy', to country producer Larry Butler for just $10 apiece, Butler refused to look a gift horse in the mouth. Instead he offered Nelson a job in his band Sunset Playboys and helped him make contacts in Nashville. It was where Nelson would ultimately place 'Crazy' with Patsy Cline, 'Hello Walls' with Faron Young and 'Funny How Time Slips Away' with Billy Walker. Those successes helped Nelson land a solo deal with Liberty and finally get 'Mr. Record Man' recorded to his satisfaction. And while its lonesome sentiments seemed to encapsulate his early struggles and strife, neither it or its tear-ravaged A-side 'The Part Where I Cry' took off as hoped, in part due to his unique vocal phrasing. The Red Headed Stranger didn't leave it at that though, including 'Mr. Record Man' on 1962's debut LP *...And Then I Wrote*, 1965's *Country Willie: His Own Songs* and 1989's *A Horse Called Music*, reflecting its enduring importance in his canon.

**'Murder By Numbers'**
The Police
A&M 1983
A-Side: 'Every Breath You Take'

**Bottle blondes' off-the-cuff creation.**

The Police were at their steamrollering chart peak when 'Every Breath You Take' became a transatlantic number 1. A Sting cash cow later sullied by its clueless appropriation in Puff Daddy's Notorious B.I.G. tribute 'I'll Be Missing You', its B-side was even darker than A-side's stalker sentiments. Written and recorded in one-take at Montserrat's AIR Studios during sessions for 1983's final album *Synchronicity*, 'Murder By Numbers' saw Sting repurpose some unused lyrics to the jazzy chords that guitarist Andy Sumner was strumming, while drummer Stuart Copeland played live in the dining room (in a separate building altogether) and roadies Danny Quatrochi, Jeff Seitz and Tam Fairgriev added live handclaps. With lyrics honing in on the evil deeds of politicians and their murderous power, the B-side drew a furious response from TV evangelist Jimmy Swaggart, who publicly denounced the band as "sons of Satan". Sting avenged the disgraced preacher five years later when performing it onstage with Frank Zappa (captured on his *Broadway The Hard Way* live album). A fan favourite revived on the Police's 00s comeback tour, its title was appropriated for an iffy 2002 psychological thriller starring Sandra Bullock.

**'Muskrat Ramble'**
Louis Armstrong and His Hot Five
OKEH 1926
A-Side: 'Heebie Jeebies'

**Impeccably rendered New Orleans-style jazz.**
Louis Armstrong dominated the 1920s American music scene. The charismatic Louisiana trumpeter and singer personified the optimistic spirit of the times, creating a series of landmark singles that have rarely been matched. While A-side 'Heebie Jeebies' became famous for Armstrong's impromptu scat — he quickly improvised when his lyric sheet fell off its stand halfway through recording — 'Muskrat Ramble' outclassed it, becoming the group's most frequently covered number. A lively stab at trombonist Kid Ory's 1921 instrumental, it found Armstrong and Ory locked into a state of friendly rivalry, vying for the limelight as Ory's trombone matched Armstrong note for note before adding a slow slide for good measure. A US Top 10 hit independent of the A-side, it was later transposed to big band arrangements by Lionel Hampton, Woody Herman and Roy Eldridge, (with Ray Gilbert adding lyrics in 1950), epitomising the enduring appeal of Armstrong's music (despite its authorship being disputed by both pianist Lil Hardin and trumpeter Sidney Bechet). Many have tried to update 'Muskrat Ramble' since, but few have recaptured the original's good-time ambiance.

**'My Adolescent Dreams'**
The Cribs
WICHITA 2007
A-Side: 'Don't You Wanna Be Relevant?'

**Wakefield wonders' pile-driving punk angst.**

The Cribs applied the same ramshackle shut-up-and-play-the-hits approach to their B-sides as their As, maintaining that they took as much thought and care over them. The band of Jarman brothers (guitarist Ryan, bassist twin Gary, younger drummer Ross) made their impact with a divisive, home-styled brand of kitchen-sink indie, often recklessly out of tune, their early amateurism bringing comparisons to the equally shambolic Libertines. In contrast to this double-single's organ-drenched other flip 'Kind Words From The Broken Hearted', 'My Adolescent Dreams' didn't skimp on the noise. After an opening squeal of feedback its raw tranche of *laissez-faire* punk thrash and Gary's football chant "oh-oohs" backed Rayan's poetically ambiguous lines about belief and flattery, before he let loose a solo that sounded like a livid Robert Fripp being squidged into a straightjacket. Short but beautifully barbed, it captured the spirit of the band's early live shows, forever teetering on the verge of collapse, with one twin or other invariably swinging from the rigging.

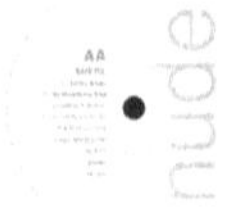


**'My Insatiable One'**
Suede
NUDE 1992
A-Side: 'The Drowners'

**Britpop B-side that thinks it's an A.**
Suede's first single launched the Britpop movement. A band deliberately out of step with the diminishing grunge movement and desperate dance stylings of the baggy generation, Suede arrived swathed in mystique and self-belief, bagging 'Best New Band in Britain' front covers before they'd recorded a note. If the darkly chugging 'The Drowners' was a foundational moment — singer Brett Anderson's strung-out Bowie-isms matched by Bernard Butler's glam rifferama — its slivering, carnal B-side only heightened the erotic charge. Written at the peak of their early creativity in under an hour and widely perceived as a homoerotic anthem (long before Anderson claimed to be "a bisexual man who never had a homosexual experience"), Anderson later said it was written about himself through the eyes of old flame Justine Frischman (later of Elastica). And although the single just sneaked inside the UK Top 50, its impact soon snowballed, winning Single of the Year in both *NME* and *Melody Maker*. Morrissey immediately covered 'My Insatiable One' on that year's *Maladjusted*

world tour (albeit with the profanities omitted), his endorsement a dream come true for singer Anderson, who revealed Suede's B-side manifesto to author Dave Thompson thus: "Everything had to be brilliant... When the Smiths put out a single, all their B-sides would be amazing, a world you could live in for months. I always thought that was a brilliant idea, something that Suede should do." Suede lived up to their promise, racking up enough for a double B-sides album *Sci-Fi Lullabies* by 1997. Many of those tracks featured guitarist Richard Oakes, the 17-year-old superfan who covered this B-side, with a note saying "take me or leave me", after Butler's abrupt departure in 1994.

### 'My Love Is Like A Spaceship'

Big Boy Pete
CAMP 1968
A-Side: 'Cold Turkey'

**Bonkers flip of British psychedelic crown jewel.**
Pete Miller never looked back after seeing Chuck Berry at Norwich's Regent Theatre in 1957. He sold his electric Hornby train set, bought a second-hand guitar and set his sights on the charts with local band the Offbeats. A subsequent 60s stint in Peter Jay and the Jaywalkers found him recording with Joe Meek and touring with the Beatles, the Rolling Stones and Cream, without realising anything near their success. Weary from touring, Miller turned solo in 1966 and set up his own lava lamp littered home studio, recording hundreds of demos that he tried to place with publishers with mixed success. Polydor subsidiary Camp took a punt on way-out A-side 'Cold Turkey', conceived and played while tripping on acid, but changed Miller's name to Big Boy Pete. Miller responded by doubling down on the weirdness for its flip, exploring the sci-fi fascinations aroused by Stanley Kubrick's *2001: A Space Odyssey* movie. A spectral stomp built around a metronomic fuzz-guitar riff, the literal vocal 'beeps' of 'My Love Is Like A Spaceship' were as much as an unchained oddity as the echoed electronic sounds and backwards guitars that ghosted through its mix. And while it flopped, Miller's decision to send a doppelganger out on tour only deepened his mystique.

## 'My Standard Break From Life'

Alkaline Trio
VAGRANT 2001
A-Side: 'Hell Yes'

**Chicago punks' dark redemption song.**

Alkaline Trio plugged into a collective need for noisy guitar thrash. The Chicago power band boasting two strong songwriters in guitarist Matt Skiba and bassist Dan Andriano, spent five years toiling in the wilderness, working other jobs to make ends meet. By the early 00s their marriage of uplifting punk melodies with societally dark lyrics started to cut through, aided by a label shift to indie giant Vagrant and a more melodic mainstream sound. 'Hell Yes' was a prime example — an upbeat punk hymn to self-styled High Priest of the Church of Satan, Anton LaVey, with its tongue firmly in cheek. The Adriano written B-side apparently came to him in less than 20 minutes, during a louche period when he was down on his luck, living near a north Chicago crack house. Its heavy allusions to alcoholism ("My obsession's in a pint glass") and all-round lack of zest were cleverly offset by no-frills punchy band dynamics and sincere vocals. Its personal sentiments were reflected in the live setting too, where Adriano usually played it solo.

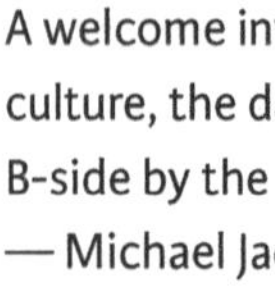

## 'Never Gonna Let You Go (Kelly G Bump-N-Go Mix)'

Tina Moore
SCOTTI BROS 1995
A-Side: 'Never Gonna Let You Go (Silk's King Of Clubs Mix)'

**Birth of an old school UK garage anthem.**

A welcome inversion of sound, with roots in 60s Jamaican soundsystem culture, the dance remix had largely eradicated the need to record a discrete B-side by the early 90s. Much abused by major labels with B-side averse stars — Michael Jackson, Celine Dion, Mariah Carey — it gave Tina Moore instant club credibility and a hit she could never have anticipated. The Wisconsin R&B singer failed to shake the applecart with 'Never Gonna Let You Go', its subdued mix aimed at US house fans by Chicago DJ Steve 'Silk' Hurley. Yet her ardent lyric about holding on for that special man resonated far deeper in the interfering hands of Silk acolyte Kelly G, whose B-side mix added a jumbo bassline and the sort of skipping beat that would come to typify two-step. An early warning of UK garage's appeal, the wider world caught up when the B-side became an A-side two years later, reaching the UK Top 10 where it was appended with a fresh set of remixes of the remix.

### 'The New Rap Language'

Spoonie G & the Treacherous Three
ENJOY 1980
A-Side: 'Love Rap'

**'Love rapper' turns on the accelerator.**

Nephew of veteran R&B producer and Enjoy label founder Bobby Robinson, Harlem's Spoonie G gained a rep as the 'love rapper' for the A-side here — an intimate, romantic outing that also introduced his erstwhile rhyme partners in the Treacherous Three. G had just amicably ceded his place in the group to Special K before he let them shine on its incredible B-side. Rappers Kool Moe Dee and LA Sunshine responded with fire, proving their lyrical chops over eight turbo-primed minutes. Delivered in a much fleeter style — cramming as many syllables into each line as possible — than hip-hop fans had heard before, the impact of 'The New Rap Language' is incalculable, not least since speed and flow quickly became crucial constituents of a battle rapper's armoury (making this the ultimate precursor to Eminem's supersonic speed 'Rap God'). In-house Enjoy producer Errol 'Pumpkin' Bedward's live beats were off-the-scale too, with added percussive ballast coming from G's conga-playing brother Pooche Costello. It put all parties on the expanding rap map and, unlike so many of hip-hop's foundational tracks, hasn't been over-played or lost its freshness since.

### 'New Warm Skin'

Simple Minds
ARISTA 1980
A-Side: 'I Travel'

**Mystery and menace of the pre-stadia years.**

Long before they were lost to windswept stadium rock, Simple Minds were a make-up wearing oddity whose avant-gardist tendencies spooked their paymasters. The band's lightning quick journey from Glaswegian punks Johnny & the Self Abusers to electronic rockers was epitomised by 'I Travel'. Just how the A-side's resonant fusion of Roxy Music and Moroder, cold war and disco, missed the charts is a mystery that Arista's marketeers have never accounted for. Boasting a similar sense of European gothic drama as Ultravox's 'Vienna', B-side 'New Warm Skin' found the slightly robotic sounding Jim Kerr taking a sideways swipe at the growing trend for cosmetic surgery over creepy synths and jagged guitar fills. A heavy lurch towards the Sparks, Kraftwerk and Berlin-era Bowie inspired Euro-disco sound they'd perfect on 1981's *Sons Of Fascination/ Sister Feelings Call* double LP, it was a million miles away from the stadium-sized fist-pumpers that later won them fame. Simple Minds B-sides would become negatively proportional to their success, the subsequent dribble of overblown live tracks and poxy instrumentals signifying laziness more than contempt.

**'New York State Police'**
UK Subs
GEM 1980
A-Side: 'Teenage'

**Punk's hardy perennials' searing stage anthem.**

Despite being in the frame in 1976 and making their name at London stronghold the Roxy, UK Subs missed the first wave of punk to sweep the British isles. Being lumped in with cartoon second-wavers like the Exploited did them a grave disservice — UK Subs were better than many realised, been-around-the-block singer Charlie Harper (an anachronistic 32 when they started) supplying growly cockney vocals above Nicky Garratt's super-literate guitar thrash. The punchy 'Teenage', their most-radio friendly tune, did enough to get them on *Top Of The Pops*, prompting closer scrutiny of their wares. Those who bought the single got more than they bargained for with 'New York State Police' — a powerful chant-along to the 82nd precinct boys and their brand of enforcement (although the line "Keep your mouth shut or we'll break your nose" seems incredibly quaint in the post-George Floyd landscape). A staple in the relentless punk-stagers' sets, it has been played by innumerable drummers and bassists since but sung by only one man — the indefatigable Harper, the last punk standing.

### 'No Ordinary Love'

Deftones

MAVERICK 2000

A-Side: 'Change (In The House Of Flies)'

**Sade as you've never heard them before.**

Deftones didn't just shovel any old crap onto their B-sides. As the Sacramento alt-metallers graduated from cult act to stadium-troubling mainstream force, B-sides became a vital proving ground — a safe space to experiment with atmospheres and effects, to push at the limits of their writing. They also proved partial to tipping baseball caps to their heroes, hymning more obvious influences such as Helmet's 'Sinatra' ['Minerva', 2003] and Drive Like Jehu's 'Caress' ['Diamond Eyes', 2010], even using their first B-side to cover Smiths' B-side 'Please Please Please Let Me Get What I Want' ['7 Words', 1995]. While those efforts were often shrouded in ripping distortion, brutal screams and clattering beats, Sade's sultry 1992 hit 'No Ordinary Love' was given a more reverent treatment. The looping thrum of Chi Cheng's dubby bass gave a green card to singer Chino Moreno to add an air of suppressed sexuality and sinister obsession to its previously chaste tale of devotion — a neat counterpoint to the shiver-down-the-spine creep-out of 'Change'.

### 'No. Fourteen'

Love

ELEKTRA 1966

A-Side: '7 And 7 Is'

**Cult west coast folk rockers do the math.**

One of America's first racially-mixed rock groups, Love were the counterattack to the British Invasion. The band that lived communally in a Los Angeles mansion even gave the Byrds a run for their money with their merge of moody folk ballads, psychedelia and jazzy tempo twists. An answer to the question posed by the atomic explosion of wild and exhilarating proto-punk '7 And 7 Is' — as fierce as Love ever got — came in its brief but enervating flip, 'No. Fourteen'. A previously unused outtake, it gave further insight into the enigmatic talent of songwriter and leader-in-chief Arthur Lee. With lyrics that spoke clearly of depression, insomnia and paranoia (possibly caused by the ingestion of colourful stimulants) it was a jaunty jig about going to Virginia to level out, aided by magic capsules of the red and blue variety. When the original Love line-up petered out after 1967's lush-string laden *Forever Changes* — their popularity still largely centred in Los Angeles due to a reluctance to tour — this single proved their sole dent on the *Billboard chart*.

**'Nobody's Dirty Business'**
Mississippi John Hurt
OKEH 1928
A-Side: 'Frankie'

**Pitch-dark folk menace from under-radar bluesman.**
Mississippi John Hurt proved a major influence on the early 60s folk explosion. The self-taught blues singer and guitarist spent most of his life doing farm work around the tiny country town of Avalon, often playing square dances accompanied by white fiddler Willie Narmour. When Narmour triumphed in a 1928 fiddle contest, he recommended Hurt to Okeh producer Tommy Rockwell, who took him to Memphis to cut this debut single. While Hurt's gentle, tranquil singing and fluid fingerpicked guitar are in place on the A-side — a variant of the 'Frankie and Johnny' fable, with a woman shooting her two-timing lover down — its companionable B-side was more disquieting and affecting. Hurt's agreeable, almost conversational touch just about disguised dark and vengeful threats that plugged right into the cycle of domestic violence, along with empty promises to behave when his woman took him back. Unlike the character he portrayed in song, Hurt was a humble man. When his five follow-up singles for Okeh also flopped, he returned to farm work as if nothing had happened. Eventually tracked down by blues fanatic Tom Hoskins, he made an unexpected return at 1963's Newport Folk Festival, where the frail, stooped 72-year-old finally found a mass audience for his beautiful and chilling songs.

**'Nocturne'**
Ash
INFECTIOUS 2001
A-Side: 'Candy'

**Triumph snatched from the jaws of adversity.**
"In the 90s we had to record four B-sides for each single and sometimes that was a nightmare," Tim Wheeler told Loudersound.com, giving an insight into the label demands of the time, with vinyl and multi-CD formats all needing to be filled. There was an upside though: "It also gave us a chance to have fun and experiment a lot." The wide-eyed romance of 'Nocturne' was among the sweeter yields of the B-side treadmill, the County Down pop-punkers making productive use of the orchestra that also weaved its majestic way through A-side 'Candy' (the 4th of six singles from third album *Free All Angels*, a veritable B-side bonanza). Better still, its wistful lamentation — "Sometimes I dream that we die young" — was delivered almost matter of fact, several worlds away from the youthful singalongs that brought Ash indie notoriety. A big inter-band favourite, Wheeler later rued not including it on an album, a charge that could equally apply to the heightened punk sensibilities of 'Day Of The Triffids' ['Kung Fu', 1994], jerky juxtapositions of 'I Need Somebody' ['Goldfinger', 1996] or carefree clatter of 'Where Is Our Love Going' ['A Life Less Ordinary', 1997].

**'Not Fade Away'**
The Crickets
BRUNSWICK 1957
A-Side: 'Oh, Boy!'

**The irreplaceable genius of Buddy Holly.**
One of the first rock stars to fight for creative control of his music, contractual limbo with Decca forced Buddy Holly to record nearly interchangeable songs as a solo performer and with his backing band the Crickets. The geeky, clean-cut Texan singer and guitarist, who practically set the template for Merseybeat, was in a creative purple patch as 1957 drew to a close, chasing the Top 10 success of 'That'll Be The Day' and 'Peggy Sue' by putting two of his greatest songs on a single 45. While 'Oh, Boy!' rightly established itself as a needy pop standard, 'Not Fade Away' was more iconic. It caught its horn-rimmed spectacle-wearing creator riding the 'hambone' rhythm (with its stress on the second beat) popularised by Bo Diddley, the Crickets supplying vocal "bops" as Holly's hiccupping vocals pledged his undying devotion before he demonstrated some of the six-string invention that would inspire Eric Clapton to pick up a guitar. Issued just two years before

Holly's tragic plane crash death, 'Not Fade Away' was revived by the Rolling Stones for their first UK hit in 1964. Birmingham bassist Geezer Butler made a more veiled tribute, cribbing its lyrics for Black Sabbath's 'NIB' five years later.

### 'Now That You're Gone'

Delta 5
ROUGH TRADE 1979
A-Side: 'Mind Your Own Business'

**Cheesed-off mutant disco from Leeds.**

The world wasn't quite ready for Delta 5. The Leeds quintet founded by singer/guitarist Julz Sale with ex-Mekon Ros Allen, quickly became part of the city's thriving post-punk community, their mixed line up (three women, two men) in open defiance of the male-dominated times. Delta 5's sound was equally radical — disco and punk mutating together over jagged chords, strident drums and the forceful low end of Allen's double bass and Bethan Peter's electric counterpoint. Their first single was a fully-formed conceptual statement. A-side 'Mind Your Own Business' honed in on petty arguments within a relationship over an insistent bass and drum pattern, cut through with funky guitar chords straight from the school of Gang Of Four. Flip 'Now That You've Gone' moved matters several months on, with the relationship at an end and recriminations in full swing. A hollowed-out inversion of the same intractable groove, they undercut its disorienting cocktail of punk and funk with a neat line in sarcasm.

### 'Nowhere At All'

Lou Reed
RCA 1976
A-Side: 'Charley's Girl'

**Punk godfather shows his credentials.**

By the late 70s Lou Reed's solo output was more miss than hit. 1975's double album *Metal Machine Music* drew a line in the sand — four sides of almost unlistenable white noise that was either perceived as an expensive fuck-you to his label or active career suicide. To compound matters, New York's most disruptive son was being sued by his ex-manager. Almost penniless yet living in the Gramercy

Park Hotel alongside his trans muse Rachel Humphreys, his bills footed by a sympathetic RCA paymaster, Reed reciprocated by making the most traditional rock album of his career. There were sentimental hints throughout the Velvet Underground's career, but *Coney Island Baby* was where Reed finally laid his battered and bruised heart on the line. And while the breezy stomp of 'Charley's Girl' was the sort of three-chord formulaic fare an ex-Pickwick in-house songwriter could probably turn out in his lunch break, its blustering bluesy B-side was another matter entirely. Above Bruce Yaw's great driving bassline and unapologetic glam stomp, Reed pleaded for divine intervention in his confusing love life, any slight vocal gap filled by ex-Kiss guitarist Bob Kulick wilding in and out of the mix. A rare exclusive B-side from the pop-obsessed but album-centred Reed, it was a cute sonic pointer to the rawer adventures of 1978's self-lacerating *Street Hassle*.

### 'Oh I Apologize'

Barrett Strong
TAMLA 1959
A-Side: 'Money (That's What I Want)'

**Robust flip of first ever Motown hit.**

Everyone from the Beatles, Rolling Stones, Led Zeppelin and Flying Lizards had a good shot at 'Money (That's What I Want)' without ever bettering the raw energy of Barrett Strong's original. Among label boss Berry Gordy's earliest signings, reluctant lead singer Strong gave it his all — his material neediness matched by a superlatively buoyant melody. Its B-side stuck to the formula established with Marv Johnson's first official Motown single 'Come To Me' — a formula that had previously failed — of using a slow tune to compliment an upbeat A-side but with an upgrade in quality control, yet the gospel-tinged 'Oh I Apologize' was every bit as powerful as the A-side. Written by Gordy with a young Smokey Robinson, it caught the stage-shy Strong at his most nuanced, keening with regret over sweeping backing vocals and the Funk Brothers' embryonic instrumentation. By the time its lyrics, middle eight and melody had been comprehensively appropriated by John Lennon for 1970's 'Isolation', Strong and songwriting partner Norman Whitfield were one of Motown's most successful in-house teams, responsible for hits by the Temptations, Marvin Gaye, Edwin Starr and Gladys Knight.

### 'Oh Little Boy (What Did You Do To Me)'

Mary Wells
MOTOWN 1964
A-Side: 'My Guy'

**Soul stunner from Motown's first female star.**

Mary Wells occupies a special place in Motown fans' hearts. In the early 60s the Detroit singer helped establish the label's sound, lending her husky and dramatic voice to songs such as 'Two Lovers' and 'You Beat Me To The Punch', written and produced by Smokey Robinson. In contrast to the wholesome pop crossover of 'My Guy' — more down-to-earth sweetness from Robinson's pen — 'Oh Little Boy' witnessed Wells go right off the emotional rails. Built upon a slightly offbeat chant of "Sh-bop sh-bop" by session singers the Andantes, the jilted Wells lamented her unwanted single status by pouring out her anguish in a charged, edge-of-sanity performance. It packed an extra surprise at the two-minute mark, as labelmate Liz Lands unleashed a powerful mini-aria that seemed to encapsulate all of Wells' explicit pain. An unmistakable gem backing a *Billboard* number 1, it proved to be Wells' last single for Motown. The 21-year-old took up the Beatles offer to open up their UK tour before she signed to 20th Century Fox, with greatly diminished returns.

### 'Oh Woman, Oh Why'

Paul McCartney
APPLE 1971
A-Side: 'Another Day'

**The beleaguered ex-Beatle's greatest vocal?**

Paul McCartney's announcement that the Beatles were splitting up broke a pact of silence with the other members. His decision to release his first solo album *McCartney* just two weeks before the band's valedictory *Let It Be* prompted further ill will among critics, who slammed it mercilessly, casting him as the villain of the piece. Some of the furore had died down when he issued his first post-Beatles 45 gambit, 'Another Day'. And if the A-side was a slightly cautious, rather twee, highly 'Eleanor Rigby'-styled affair (later disparaged by John Lennon in extended McCartney put-down 'How Do You Sleep?'), its B-side was a completely different animal. McCartney's raspiest and fiercest vocal track,

'Oh Woman, Oh Why' found him in a difficult place, hands tied at the bottom of a well, a gun-toting woman standing over him. Yet it was his part-buried screams, as if *inside* that well, that eclipsed the lyric's allegorical possibilities. It was a heady match for the song's gnarly blues guitar, gospelly backing vocals and minimal but pulsating bass, the whole embellished, a little hammily, with gunshots at the end. The first in a long line of non-album McCartney B-sides that held true to the Beatles' fascination with quality flips, other B-side highs include the piano boogie of 'Little Woman Love' ['Mary Had A Little Lamb', 1972], pro-animal sentiments of 'Long Leather Coat' ['Hope Of Deliverance', 1992] and ten-minute plus 'Secret Friend' ['Temporary Secretary', 1980], a song that foreshadowed 1993's the Fireman project with Youth and gave further proof that McCartney really was the weirdest Beatle.

## 'Old Gangsters Never Die'

The Sinister Ducks
SITUATION TWO 1983
A-Side: 'March Of The Sinister Ducks'

**Mischief makers' pitch-black cabaret.**

The Sinister Ducks were a happy accident. Formed spontaneously in 1979 at Northampton club the Deadly Fun Hippodrome, their first show drew scorn and bewilderment from its bemused punters. When they released their sole single four years later, the trio of Capt. José da Silva (moonlighting Bauhaus bassist David J), Max Acropolis (ska band saxophonist Alex Green) and Translucia Baboon (comic book superhero pioneer Alan Moore) were better known. And while the kazoo-laced A-side's quacking, slightly Bonzo Dog Doo-Dah Band-like tale of "web-footed fascists" was doubtless every bit as silly and throwaway as that first show, its B-side was something else entirely. An adaptation of a soliloquy from Moore's 1976 surrealist play *Another Suburban Romance*, 'Old Gangsters Never Die' mixed Silva's two jazzy chords and Acropolis's smoky sax with a light night diatribe about Hollywood, sex, murder and betrayal that showcased Moore's storytelling vim and dramatic range. It came immaculately packaged too, the A-side's spiky Savage Pencil graphic folding out into a B-side comic strip by regular Moore collaborator Garry Leach.

**'Omega'**

The Enid

EMI 1977

A-Side: 'Golden Earrings'

**Creeping strangeness from cult British proggers.**

The Enid were a band out of time. The elaborate brainchild of ex-Barclay James Harvest orchestral arranger Robert John Godfrey and an ever-rolling cast of bit-part players, their long and often drawn-out, classical music-inspired overtures won a resilient fan base as they plied their arcane trade amid the growling immediacy of punk. Despite their preference for lengthy expositions, the Enid were contractually obliged to issue shorter and sharper singles too. So, they followed 1977's big-sounding but aptly christened second LP *Aerie Faerie Nonsense* with a hammed-up cover of old obscure 30s song, augmented by Godfrey's first vocal performance (a questionable tactic — he came on like an overbearing headmaster). Its B-side was something unique, however, utterly divorced from the Enid's previous output before or since. Two minutes of highly experimental, almost ambient music, whose shifting carpet of deep bass synth and spacy electronics was offset by the errant plucking of a mandolin. It remains the biggest curveball in this wilfully wayward band's slight, bewildering catalogue.

**'Omnibus'**

The Move

REGAL ZONOPHONE 1968

A-Side: 'Wild Tiger Woman'

**Brummie chart-brothers break their spell.**

The Move were among the late 60s most accomplished pop forces. The first band ever played on BBC Radio 1 (with 1967's 'Flowers In The Rain'), the Birmingham troupe had four Beatlesque Top 5 hits under their belt when they went decidedly primal with 'Wild Tiger Woman'. A stab at channelling the heavier sounds of touring partner Jimi Hendrix, it not only jarred with fans craving the power pop of its predecessor 'Fire Brigade', Radio 1 banned it, objecting to the lyric: "Tied to the bed/She's waiting to be fed". 'Omnibus', on the other hand, was embraced with open ears. Its distinctly English offer to take a ride on a horse-drawn carriage retained the melodic sensibilities of previous singles, its sparkling pop hook augmented by a great psychedelic guitar turn from its painfully shy writer Roy Wood. After it flopped the band agreed with fans that 'Omnibus' should have been the A-side. They even vowed to quit if their next single wasn't a hit — luckily 'Blackberry Way' went right to the top.

**'One More Big Time Rock And Roll Star'**
Stevie Nicks
MODERN 1985
A-Side: 'Talk To Me'

**Faltering rock goddess' big hair ballad.**

On the face of it Fleetwood Mac's Stevie Nicks was at the top of her game in the mid-80s. The reality was a little more sinister. The ever-mystical Nicks was suffering from a debilitating cocaine addiction that had impacted negatively on both her live and studio output — reflected in her diminished writing contribution to 3rd solo album *Rock A Little* (just three tracks) and the gruff hoarseness of her voice — more pained than sexy. And while Jimmy Iovine's thick high-gloss 80s production on 'Talk To Me' certainly fit the times (it would prove Nicks' last US Top 10 hit), the single concealed a rare bonus on its B-side. 'One More Big Time Rock And Roll Star' found the high priestess of American bohemia exploring a heavier sound as she recalled a card sent by an ex-paramour and reflected on stardom. It was Nicks at her tender, balladic best, stacking up woes and parading heartbreak like a badge over a writhing squall of rocking guitars. And while she declined to name the "undercover music lover" at its core, fans have speculated that it was Eagles' guitarist Joe Walsh.

**'Ooh The Dew Doo Man'**
Resident Alien
DEWDOO MAN 1991
A-Side: 'Mr Boops'

**One-off folly by rap production giant.**

In 1990 Prince Paul was riding the crest of a wave. After producing De La Soul's debut *3 Feet High And Rising*, the in-demand 20-year-old Stetsasonic DJ was offered his own label by Def Jam boss Russell Simmons. Initially reluctant, the arrival of an advance prompted him to round up some neighbourhood friends — including Resident Alien and Mic Tee Lux — to record a typically high-concept set. The first single to emerge had plenty of bang, its A-side falling in line with the overall Native Tongues vibe riding high at the time. Its short but super sweet B-side 'Ooh The Dew Doo Man' was way more innovative though — a production masterclass that merged hard raps with the endless funk of Tony Avlon & the Belairs' 'Sexy Coffee Pot', dreamy pianos with snatches of dialogue from children's TV show *Bigfoot and Wildboy*. Neither married with Simmons' poppy expectations and he promptly pulled the plug. It made Resident Alien's *It Takes A Nation Of Suckas To Let Us In* album one of the decade's great lost releases... until the internet brought it back.

## 'The Otherside'

The Apple
PAGE ONE 1968
A-Side: 'Doctor Rock'

**Psychedelic diamond in the rough.**

The late 60s British underground was a hotbed of blues rock that took easily to psychedelia's window dressings. Case in point: mostly unremarkable Cardiff time travellers The Apple. Despite having a name that shamelessly aped a well-known Beatles organisation, they laboured in vain for success, making bad singles choices that hindered their progress — exemplified by mawkish A-side 'Doctor Rock'. Trippy tale of the heart 'The Otherside' aced it. A fatalistic look at a failed relationship penned by bassist Jeff Harrod, it saw Dennis Regan mourning the "cell of misery" he was stuck in above the lush fanfare of Charlie Barber's piano and Robbo Ingram's wah-wah guitar. Interest in The Apple had all but been composted when this B-side featured on 1980's *Chocolate Soup For Diabetics* compilation, with the original Page One edition of 1969's debut *An Apple A Day* becoming a sought-after rarity. The Apple's other prized psych moment, the rough and ready 'Buffalo Billycan', was also a B-side ['Let's Take A Trip Down The Rhine', 1968].

**'Over And Over'**
Bobby Day
CLASS 1958
A-Side: 'Rockin' Robin'

**Doo-wop stalwart's party anthem.**

It took the best part of a decade for success to come Bobby Day's way. The well-travelled Texan singer, a long-standing figure in Los Angeles' doo-wop community, suddenly had two self-written hits at once — sweet honeybee fable 'Buzz-Buzz-Buzz' with the Hollywood Flames and the harder rocking 'Little Bitty Pretty One' with his band the Satellites (although an instant cover by Thurston Harris fared even better). The Leon Rene-penned 'Rockin' Robin' made it a swift hat-trick, with Day using its B-side to showcase a self-written paean to romantic persistence, A swinging number, heavy on the small details — intricate guitar fretwork, twittering sax play, seamless harmonies — it let Day's sincere vocal work its charms. Although 'Over And Over' briefly followed the A-side onto the *Billboard chart*, it fared much better after a wailing, drum-heavy makeover by the Dave Clark Five in 1965. Along with Michael Jackson's full-throated take on the A-side, it remains Day's best-known song.

**'Over The Rainbow'**
Erasure
MUTE 1991
A-Side: 'Chorus'

**Synth pop masters at full throttle.**

Erasure was in rude health as the 90s kicked in. The duo of ex-Depeche Mode, Yazoo and Assembly synth wizard Vince Clarke and untried, super-camp singer Andy Bell were in the midst of an unbroken run of fizzing chart success, with a battalion of high-paced hits at their disposal. They proved a double boon for fans. Erasure knew the value of a good B-side and blessed single buyers with gems such as 'Don't Suppose' ['Chains Of Love', 1988], 'Paradise' ['Drama', 1989] and 'Dreamlike State' ['Star', 1989] that could easily have been flipped into A-sides. 'Over The Rainbow' was not, as might be expected, sequin-encrusted Bell's pop at Judy Garland's signature song from *The Wizard Of Oz*, but an original that saw Clark tip his hat to the formative influence of Orchestral Manoeuvres in the Dark. Previously a guitarist, Clarke started using synths after hearing their 1979 single 'Electricity', whose melody he appropriated in full, adding the speaking clock samples they used on 1983's *Dazzle Ships* for good measure. To make it more meta still, Bell's lyrics namechecked ABBA and Thin Lizzy's 'The Boys Are Back In Town'. It made for a jaunty slice of lovelorn drama, right up there with Erasure's best.

# PARTY TIME

*When the seven-inch single's time constraints entailed getting busy with the scissors.*

When the ten-inch 78 rpm record became the norm in the late 1910s, they came with limitations — any song above three minutes would noticeably degrade in sound quality. Combined with fast demands of radio programmers, the three-minute convention continued when 45 rpm singles were introduced. As technology improved it became possible to cut the grooves closer — Bob Dylan broke the mould with 1965's six-minute-plus 'Like a Rolling Stone' — but that was a rare exception, with many labels circumventing the problem of longer songs by splicing them into two parts (often crudely, to many deejays' dismay). There was a fiscal advantage to the practice too — the hey presto! instant Part 2 B-side. The rise of the 12-inch single, in deep disco demand by the late 70s, effectively consigned the practice to dust.

There was a whiff of wild fortune to the way **Ray Charles and His Orchestra** accidentally broke into the US pop charts with 'What'd I Say'. The blind Georgia born singer and pianist had made his name as an emotionally gritty R&B performer until a number he freestyled onstage at a club in Brownsville, Pennsylvania — backing singers the Raeletts repeating back his every lyric — made up the slack during a contractually stipulated four-hour show. The crowd's ecstatic response prompted its studio reading, an equally wild-roaming affair that engineer Tom Dowd pared down to six-and-a-half minutes before it was lopped in two for release. While its hit 'Pt. 1' majored on the seductive repetitions of Charles' Wurlitzer electric piano's relatively unheard charms, **'What'd I Say Part II'** [ATLANTIC 1959] accentuated the verbal back-and-forth, capturing the fervour of a preacher and congregation in rapturous union. An R&B standard later covered by Gene Vincent, Elvis and Jerry Lee Lewis, Charles regarded it as his signature song, closing out all his subsequent concerts with its call-and-response.

The effortlessly cool sound of '**Smokie — Part 2**' [HI 1959] witnessed **Bill Black's Combo** truly hitting their stride. The happy-slapping Memphis musician — upright bassist in Elvis Presley's early trio — was adjusting to straightened circumstances after Presley's manager/fixer Colonel Tom Parker forced him out the frame. Session dates at the all-new local Hi imprint saw him forge a close bond with guitarist Reggie Young, the pair linking into a group alongside Joe Lewis Hall (piano), Martin Willis (saxophone) and Jerry Arnold (drums). While its upbeat 'Part 1' was essentially the same tune, the laid back flip — recorded using down-tuned guitars and accentuating Hall's upfront piano vamps — was the keeper, eclipsing the A-side to become a US R&B number 1 and Top 20 pop hit.

In its first reading **Little Stevie Wonder** played bongos on 'Fingertips', an instrumental on the 12-year-old's first LP *The Jazz Soul Of Little Stevie*. By the time he was wowing crowds on the Motortown Revue package tour it had transformed into a showcase of the blind Michigan talent's advanced harmonica skills. Having worked the crowd at Chicago's Regal Theater into a froth with his performance, Wonder had a sudden change of heart when it came time to take his bow. '**Fingertips — Pt 2**' [TAMLA 1963] captured his unplanned encore, building on its first part's youthful exuberance with an electric call-and-response crowd segment, befuddled bassist Joe Swift calling out "What key?" as intense young drummer Marvin Gaye and a Cuban-flavoured brass section went loco. Radio wholeheartedly embraced the B-side, Wonder scoring Motown's second US number 1 with it. It would take him nearly a decade to reach the top again.

The sole single **Little Richard** recorded with Jimi Hendrix (then plying his trade as Maurice James) showed the latter's talents in their infancy, his intricate intro echoing Curtis Mayfield's graceful stye as they combined on a slow-burning soul ballad by Richards' ex-chauffeur, Don Covay. A rare glimpse of Richard's under-played balladeer skills, so often obscured by screams and shouts, '**I Don't Know What You've Got But It's Got Me — Part II**' [VEE JAY 1965] captured him in wide-eyed preacher mode, chastising his unfaithful, money-grabbing lover for pulling the wool over his eyes. The Richard-Hendrix partnership would quickly lapse — doomed from the moment Richard caught fans screaming for Hendrix to play the guitar with his teeth.

The two-part single was something of a godsend to soul brother number 1 **James Brown**. His pivotal late 60s/early 70s 45s invariably arrived in stores chopped in two (see also: 'Papa's Got A Brand New Bag', 'Cold Sweat', 'Get Up (I Feel Like Being A) Sex Machine', 'Hot Pants' et al). Widely known as 'the hardest working man in showbusiness', Brown was a highly pragmatic bandleader who, despite several wooing approaches, kept the civil rights movement at arm's length from his music. The murder of Martin Luther King in April 1968 was a tipping point, with Brown writing the most politically-charged song of his career as riots raged in the streets. Its B-side, **'Say it Loud — I'm Black And I'm Proud (Part 2)'** [KING 1968] majored on his call-and-response chorus with a group of Los Angeles children and helped his defiant anthem stay top of the US R&B chart for six straight weeks. Brown's political awakening lasted barely a year — in early 1969 he performed at Richard Nixon's inaugural presidential ball.

**Fleetwood Mac** showed two very different sides of their psyche on their 7th single. While the A-side's self-deprecating lyrics and stop-start electric blues blurred the lines between blues and heavy metal (and helped inspire Led Zeppelin's 'Black Dog'), there was a hint of the spaghetti-western to Peter Green's bleakly brooding Spanish guitar instrumental **'Oh Well — Part 2'** [REPRISE 1969]. It caught the troubled six-string god multi-tasking — also playing bass, cello, timpani and cymbals — while girlfriend Sandra Elsdon added recorder and Jeremy Spencer piano. Considering the A-side throwaway, Green lobbied in vain for 'Part 2' to become top dog, his disaffection growing when 'Part 1' became a number 2 UK hit (and the first Mac single to penetrate the US Hot 100 charts). Effectively Green's last stand, he quit the following year.

By any measure a strange choice for a single, it's arguable that **David Bowie**'s label missed a simple trick by putting **'Memory Of A Free Festival Part 2'** [MERCURY

1970] on the B-side. Reworked from his second self-titled LP at his label's bequest, 'Part 1' found Bowie waxing nostalgically about the rainbows, clouds and grass at a Beckenham gathering over a child's Rosedale Electric Chord Organ. Producer Tony Visconti's decision to start the mantric 'Part 2' with its massed chant about a 'sun machine' coming down meant if effectively functioned as a song in its own right, tapping into a communal love-up while introducing Bowie's new henchmen Mick Ronson and Woody Woodmansey on a rare flop.

Uncharacteristically heavy and aggressive by their previously pastoral standards, **Genesis**'s second single was a belligerent denouncement of military mythology that caught ex-Charterhouse public schoolboy Peter Gabriel rebelling against his privileged past. With most of Gabriel's pro-Gandhi, anti-dictatorial chest-beating on the A-side, **'The Knife (Part 2)'** [CHARISMA 1971] let the flutes loose, simmering massed chants of "We are only wanting freedom" prevailing until the spoken word instruction "Okay men, fire over their heads!" gave the cue to wig-out. Heavily inspired by the Nice, Genesis' most stirring and theatrical early number would stay in their set, often as their curtain call, into the late 70s.

An eight-and-a-half-minute epic about the souring of the 60s dream after President Kennedy's assassination, **'American Pie — Part II'** [UNITED ARTISTS 1971] was the lesser heard half of **Don McLean**'s definitive folk-pop strike. While 'Part I' exorcised his long-running grief at the 1959 plane crash death of Buddy Holly — styled as "the day the music died" — its second half detailed the travails of a "generation lost in space", its pining for the good old days packed with allusions to Apollo 11, the Rolling Stones and Janis Joplin. While McLean repeatedly refused to decode his lyrics — once quipping that they meant "I never have to work again" — the single struck a chord that has continued to resonate since. It also cast a larger shadow over the New Yorker's career, many mistaking McLean as a one-hit wonder.

Presidential matters were also uppermost in **Marvin Gaye**'s mind on his first single of 1972. An extension of the socially conscious mode of the previous year's concept album *What's Going On*, it found him detailing the "misery in the land" over a rhythmic bedrock highly indebted to Curtis Mayfield. Majoring

on his multi-tracked vocals rather than its frail melody, **'You're The Man (Part 2)**' [TAMLA 1972] cut to the chase on the upcoming presidential election, Gaye mellifluously intoning "Politics and hypocrites is turning us all into lunatics" before unleashing a series of frustrated screams at those in his sights. Effectively torpedoed by Motown — label head Berry Gordy actively pressured radio stations to drop it (DJs were hardly punching the air in any case) — it forced him to shelve its intended parent LP too.

The first single by perpetual trier/future public enemy **Gary Glitter** was the result of a 15-minute jam session initiated by TV show *Ready, Steady*, Go's house bandleader Mike Leander, after David Essex failed to show up for a rehearsal. Leander got the show's warm-up act Paul Gadd — a man with a decade's worth of flops under an army of pseudonyms — to join in an improvisation over his song 'Shag Rag, That's My Bag' with plentiful big guitar riffs, handclaps and the spacious syncopated pulse of two drummers (a formative influence on Adam and the Ants). Edited down and retitled for Glitter's first single, the distinctive "Hey!" chants of the mostly instrumental '**Rock And Roll Part 2'** [BELL 1972] impacted on the airwaves rather than 'Part 1''s reminisces about blue suede shoes and Little Queenie. After six months it was a transatlantic smash, the stadium sports staple setting glam's puffed-up new ace-face up for a stint of tottering around in silver platform boots and Bacofoil capes in public, while committing unspeakable crimes in private.

**The Isley Brothers'** singer Ronald was equally mesmeric whether purveying sultry lovelorn heartache or the angry frustration of '**Fight The Power Part 2'** [T-NECK 1975], cut in one emotive take over his sibling Marvin's lugubrious bassline. The Ohio fire-starters had perfected their soul/rock fusion sound when they laid down this storming and intense two-part funker — written on the same day as 'Harvest For The World' — picking up the baton of social unrest thrown down by Stevie Wonder, Curtis Mayfield and the O'Jays as trust in the government grew perilously low. While the A-side's angry lyric about the powers that be and the "bullshit going down" — bleeped out on air — brooked no argument, 'Part

2"s infectious chant of "Fight it!" topped a forceful reminder of the brothers' instrumental smarts. A formative influence on Public Enemy's Chuck D, he rewired its sentiments to provide a hip-hop anthem for Spike Lee's *Do The Right Thing* movie in 1989.

The plight of imprisoned boxer Reuben 'Hurricane' Carter — wrongly convicted of a triple murder by corrupt cops — and his prison-penned autobiography *The Sixteenth Round* inspired **Bob Dylan** to return to the protest songs arena (with a word count that put his biggest rivals in the shade). While its most concise moments took up the 3:45-minute A-side, the one-time 'voice of a generation' was in revived, snarling form on the five-minute **'Hurricane (Part II)'** [COLUMBIA 1975] as he weaved around Scarlet River's searching violin figure. More than just paying scathing lip service to a trial he termed a 'pig circus', Dylan visited Carter in Rahway State Prison at that year's end and raised over $100,000 for his defence at a Madison Square Garden concert. It still took another decade before Carter's convictions were overturned.

Not content with helping to define the style and sound of Gamble & Huff on early 70s productions for the O'Jays, Three Degrees and Billy Paul, Philadelphia singer and songwriter **Bunny Sigler** became a hitmaker with the swinging falsetto of **'Let Me Party With You (Part 2) (Party Party Party)'** [GOLD MIND 1978]. A song that channelled Marvin Gaye's 'Got to Give it Up' over the swirling horns of Instant Funk, his unimpeachably tight nine-piece backing band, the humble seven-inch single was not quite enough to contain the 12-minute plus exuberance of its full album freak-out. Nonetheless its B-side offered a tempting taste of their pumping instrumental prowess.

Its funky rumblings were superseded on **Funkadelic**'s definitive single. Titled after a fan's comment about a show in Washington DC, **'One Nation Under A Groove — Part II'** [WARNERS BROS 1978] maxed out on the spaced-out New Jersey band's beautifully jumbled instrumental chops, giving particular airtime to their incoming new guitarist Michael 'Kid Funkadelic' Hampton, a teenager still trying to get to grips with his first guitar synthesiser above displaced chants of "Feet don't fail me now!" An all-summer-long R&B chart-topper, its conjoined parts all coalesced onstage, Funkadelic often extending it way beyond the half-hour mark until both band and audience were exhausted. Its deep-grooves would be heavily mined by Dr. Dre to create G-Funk.

While Funkadelic's leader George Clinton and bassist Bootsy Collins were instrumental in mentoring Roger Troutman's band **Zapp**, **'More Bounce To The Ounce Part II'** [WARNER BROS 1980] showed they already had their groovy Talkbox-laden funk down pat. Troutman created a robotic voice for his slightly voyeuristic concerns (titled after a 50s Pepsi ad slogan) by routing a Vocoder through a synthesizer, adding an otherworldly air to the looped drum refrain, handclaps and gut-punching bassline that would be sampled half-to-death by the incoming hip-hop generation. Also issued on a club DJ-friendly 12-inch single, the decision to split this epic jam into two parts for the seven-inch was a reverential nod to the two-part doozies summoned by Zapp's funk forefathers.

**'The P Is Free'**
Boogie Down Productions
B-BOY 1986
A-Side: 'South Bronx'

**Bare bones hip-hop with attitude.**

The first Boogie Down Productions single to gain traction, 'South Bronx' was a livid response to MC Shan B-side 'The Bridge', as rapper KRS-One forcefully contended Queensbridge was the real birthplace of hip-hop. The ensuing 'Bridge Wars' effectively launched the duo onto a bigger stage, a perfect platform for their voluble frontman to impart more unified visions, as he revelled in his self-styled role as 'The Teacha'. 'The P Is Free' hinted at what was to come. A beatbox and slackness jam, it adopted a similar template to Doug E. Fresh & the Get Fresh Crew B-side 'La Di Da Di', with affiliate D-Nice handling the vocal bass kicks and splattery cymbals while KRS kicked props to his DJ Scott La Rock, boasted he was "ruling hip-hop" and related a brash frontline fable about girls trading sex for crack-cocaine. Uncut, low-budget hip-hop with minimal production input — recorded in one take for $25 — its historical importance (it's time-dated with the signature line "Fresh for 86, suckas!") just about trumped its sonic deficiencies. A more sanitised reggae-styled remix later surfaced on 1997 debut LP *Criminal Minded* that added samples of Yellowman's 'Zungguzungguguzungguzeng' and the Natural Ites' 'Picture On The Wall' but replaced the word 'pussy' (the 'P' of the title) with 'girlies'.

**'Painting Pictures'**
Adele
XL 2008
A-Side: 'Make You Feel My Love'

**Rare rock-out from brassy soul siren.**

The hype behind Adele became inescapable after she won BBC's *Sound Of 2008*. The teenage London singer who, like Amy Winehouse, polished her skills at the Brit School, had the billowingly powerful voice to back it up, augmenting her confessional songs with a smattering of vintage soul sass and sprinkle of modern pop polish. She ended the campaign for debut album *19* with a cover of Bob Dylan's 'Make You Feel My Love'. Much better than Garth Brooks and Kelly Clarkson's murderous stabs, it was a relative flop — until it became a go-to showcase tune for *X-Factor* contestants — while its B-side 'Painting Pictures' slipped under the radar. Built around Ben Thomas's moody blues guitar riff, it started seriously rocking in its second verse as Adele scratched a lyrical itch with rich brushstrokes and effortless pizzazz. It showed another side to her songwriting — the looser, live-band approach suiting her elastic timbre much better than the bruised, self-conscious ballads that made her fortune.

**'Paradise'**
The Shangri-Las
RED BIRD 1966
A-Side: 'Past, Present And Future'

**Wall-of-sound girl group perfection.**

The Shangri-Las embodied the bad girl ethos. The broody no-nonsense Cambria Heights quartet revelled in their rivalry with the Ronettes — looking the part in tight leather outfits and slick go-go boots while their tales of tragic teen romance resonated with been-there authenticity. They also had a producer, George 'Shadow' Morton, every bit as eccentric and talented as Phil Spector, culminating in the revving motorcycle sound effects of 1964's definitive death disc 'Leader of the Pack'. The final Shangri-Las pop hit was a two-sider that captured them at their most tragic and brilliant. There was undeniable pathos to 'Past, Present and Future' as Mary Weiss' bleak spoken words spilled out over the gloomy waltz of Beethoven's 'Moonlight Sonata', but it was a leftfield choice that backfired in chart terms — reaching a lowly number 59. The real *tour-de-force* was its B-side take on Harry Nilsson's 'Paradise' (previously attempted by the Ronettes in 1965). It played to the Shangri-Las' collective strengths, Weiss's wailing, melodramatic lead soaring above thunderous background harmonies and a typically grandiose Morton backing track that pumped the volume way beyond the realms of clarity. It just trumped the hushed, ashen 'Dressed In Black' ['He Cried', 1966] — another death disc — as their greatest B-side.

### 'Parker's Mood'

Charlie Parker All Stars
SAVOY 1948
A-Side: 'Barbados'

**The Bird's moody blues breaks the mould.**

Charlie Parker broke all the rules. A singular figure in post-war jazz, the man nicknamed Bird was unreliable in virtually all aspects of life — except when he was onstage. After his fiery mid-40s collaborations with Dizzy Gillespie, the Kansas city saxophonist pushed the envelope to the hilt with his approach to melody, rhythm and harmony. It helped codify bebop — the revolutionary new movement that ripped up old conventions and opened new possibilities. Parker was at the peak of his powers when he recorded this single in New York. And while functional A-side 'Barbados' is rarely remarked upon, its nocturnal-sounding B-side is a bona fide jazz standard. A sideways take on the blues, 'Parker's Mood' unveiled an unusually soulful side of his style and brought out the best in his dream team of trumpeter Miles Davis, pianist John Lewis, bassist Curly Russell and drummer Max Roach. Bookended by Parker's harmonically advanced alto-sax solos, improvised in-the-moment, it redefined jazz at a stroke, taking it to a new level of abstraction and artistry.

### 'Pictures Of Bernadette'

Talk Talk
PARLOPHONE 1986
A-Side: 'Give It Up'

**Grand lashings of stadium-sized regret.**

Talk Talk had a more unusual career trajectory than most. The London-based outfit started life as a manicured *Smash Hits* poster band but quickly exceeded their flash-in-the-pan expectations, escaping their new romantic stylings to embrace a more organic sound. The addition of producer, multi-instrumentalist and unofficial 4th member Tim Friese-Green was critical, adding texture, atmosphere and know-how to their grand ambitions. An outtake from sessions for 1986's 3rd LP *The Colour Of Spring*, this B-side was a showcase of a more strident Talk Talk sound that seemed to defy genres. Driven by Paul 'Rustin Man' Webb's up-down bassline, it married pure pop skills (a massive chorus) with textual trickery and musical surprises — a heavy metal guitar solo, wild ramping organs — as Hollis's vocals dripped Proustian regret. Unusually, the 12-inch single majored in on 'Pictures Of Bernadette', adding an eight-minute dance mix that further exposed the complex circuitry beneath its bonnet. Talk Talk moved away from such wanton grandiosity afterwards with the blurry pastoral ambience of *Spirit Of Eden* and *Laughing Stock*, before gradually disappearing into the horizon.

### 'The Plague'

Scott Walker
PHILIPS 1967
A-Side: 'Jackie'

**Ex-Walker Brother's prescient cinematic original.**

As a 60s teen pop idol, Scott Walker laid down the breadcrumbs for what would follow — not so much peering into the void as diving straight in on their greatest hit 'The Sun Ain't Gonna Shine Anymore'. After splitting from the Los Angeles trio, Walker's first solo single — a Mort Shuman translation of Jacques Brel's 'Jackie' — garnered instant controversy when it was prissily banned by the BBC for its 'stupid-ass' references to drinks, drugs, queers and virgins. It's just as well that they ignored its none-more-black B-side too. Walker's first composition to make vinyl, 'The Plague' was a million miles adrift from the smooth crooner image he had previously cultivated. It found him loosely assuming the role of a Bible Belt preacher, his baritone boom letting rip with blackly repulsed, Camus-inspired lyrics that reeked of doom and despair over gloomy chimes, swerving strings and an apocalyptic wall of howling guitars before it dropped out, in its harrowing finale, to just his anguished "la la las" over a rumble of voodoo drums. While Walker's work would get increasingly outré and experimental as he aged, an adventurer to the last, 'The Plague' planted the demon seed for what would follow. Walker acolyte Marc Almond covered both sides of this single — this B-side on 1986's 'A Woman's Story EP', 'Jackie' five years later.

### 'Plumskinzz'

KMD

ELEKTRA 1991

A-Side: 'Nitty Gritty'

**A tragic tale of two brothers.**

KMD had a rough industry ride. An acronym for Kausing Much Damage, the Long Island-trio first peeped above the parapet when rapper Zev Love X took the closing verse on 3rd Bass's dis anthem 'The Gas Face'. It led to a mutually supportive relationship, with 3rd Bass executively producing KMD's witty and whimsical debut *Mr. Hood*. The B-side of its second single 'Nitty Gritty' underlined the symbiosis between X, his brother DJ Subroc and Onyx The Birthstone Kid as all three took turns to drop fidgety, elaborate verses over a rousing loop of Bobbi Humphrey's 'Blacks And Blues'. A lusty sequel to LP track 'Peachfuzz', the filthy-minded, barely allegorical 'Plumskinzz' was so good it was chopped into two parts (with the now departed Onyx's verse omitted) for 1993's follow-up *Black Bastards*. Or it would have been had Elektra not shelved the LP due to its provocative artwork (a cartoon of a 'Sambo' being hanged). It was a double blow for X, the last man standing after Subroc was killed in a road accident. Cast into the wilderness, he clawed his way back from the brink as incognito masked rap saviour MF DOOM at the 90s end.

### 'Police Truck'

Dead Kennedys
CHERRY RED 1980
A-Side: 'Holiday In Cambodia'

**One-fingered salute to corrupt cops.**

Dead Kennedys changed the punk game. The Californians ran affairs on their own terms after setting up a label, Alternative Tentacles, that brought the likes of Butthole Surfers, Alice Donut and No Means No to wider ears. They had barely ventured outside the Bay Area when their second single compressed the essence of punk into the shortest space possible. With its rattling bassline and killer guitar riff, 'Holiday In Cambodia' sent shivers down the spine even before singer Jello Biafra's animated vocal skewered phony leftism with unerring precision. Satirical B-side 'Police Truck' had equal bite. Written from the perspective of corrupt police officers "playing cops for real", its attack on endemic corruption and entrenched values also packed in a sing-along chorus and some super-speedy Dick Dale-like guitar work above its surf rock beat. And while it later showed up in computer game *Tony Hawks Pro Skater* to some fan consternation (Biafra lost control of their back catalogue in a royalty dispute), the wider Dead Kennedys' B-side game was unimpeachable — from dark jazzy mugging fable 'The Prey' ['Too Drunk To Fuck', 1981] to the graphic cabaret of 'Saturday Night Holocaust' ['Halloween', 1982].

### 'Popeye The Hitchhiker'

Chubby Checker
PARKWAY 1962
A-Side: 'Limbo Rock'

**Dance craze king in prime form.**

One of many artists to emerge from Philadelphia's burgeoning rock 'n' roll scene, Chubby Checker found his niche as the dance craze king. Best known for his 1958's enthusiastic take on Hank Ballard and the Midnighters' B-side 'The Twist', Checker undertook non-stop rounds of shows and interviews until a performance on Dick Clark's *American Bandstand* proved the tipping point. Novelty dance hit after novelty dance hit followed, with pacey A-side 'Limbo Rock' tapping into a mini-craze for calypso music. It was followed into the

*Billboard* Top 10 by its B-side 'Popeye The Hitchhiker' — a typically forthright invitation from Checker to do the 'Popeye' dance over boogie-flavoured piano and bluesy sax. Checker notched over 30 formulaically styled hits before the bubble burst in 1966. Seemingly consigned to haunt the oldies circuit, hip-hop reversed his fortunes — first when he duetted with the Fat Boys on 1988's update of 'The Twist', second when DJ Muggs sampled 'Popeye The Hitchhiker' for House of Pain's breakthrough hit 'Jump Around' in 1992.

**'Pork'**
The Pharcyde
DELICIOUS VINYL 1993
A-Side: 'Passin' Me By'

**Whimsical west coast rappers show inner steel.**

Issued just six months after the Los Angeles riots, the Pharcyde's debut album stood in stark contrast to the gangsta rap that politicised the city's disaffected music fans. Closer in spirit to De La Soul's *3 Feet High And Rising*, *Bizarre Ride II The Pharcyde* was among the most whimsical hip-hop sets to emerge: a note-perfect trade-off between the comedic smarts of its four interchangeable rappers (Imani, Fat Lip, Slim Kid Tre and Bootie Brown) and J-Swift's keen-eared production prowess. A-side 'Passin' Me By' was its perfect miniature, an update of the demo that persuaded Delicious Vinyl's Mike Ross to allow them full creative control. By the time it became a single J-Swift had bailed, forcing a group rethink. 'Pork' was the first evidence the Pharcyde had a harder side. New producer LA Jay married tougher beats with samples from Miles Davis Quintet's 'Freedom Jazz Dance' as its four rappers went for broke. And while it couldn't upstage the A-side, it offered plenty of fresh food for thought.

**'Pow'**
The Lovin' Spoonful
KAMA SUTRA 1966
A-Side: 'Rain On The Roof'

**Good-time hitmakers at spritely best.**

The Lovin' Spoonful's 'electric good-time music' rolled the best of rock, jug-band, folk and blues into an accessible package. Centred around the writing talents of New York frontman John Sebastian and his melodic interplay with Canadian guitarist Zal Yanovsky, they enjoyed a gilded run of hits (including 'Do You Believe In Magic?', 'You Didn't Have To Be So Nice' and 'Summer In The City') where the B-sides were invariably on par with the As. To back the gentle romanticism of 'Rain on the Roof' came the turbo-powered 'Pow', a harmonica and slide guitar enhanced tale of comedic mishaps with the sort of cutting chorus hook Sebastian excelled in. Woody Allen liked it so much he used it as the opening theme of his first feature film, *What's Up, Tiger Lily*, which he also got Sebastian to score. Working in healthy competition to the Byrds, they continued to reinvent themselves single-by-single until Yanovsky was ousted in 1967, after being busted for marijuana possession in California.

**'Powerhouse'**
The Raymond Scott Quintet
MASTER 1937
A-Side: 'The Toy Trumpet'

**Long-time cartoon assembly line staple.**

A musical prodigy who spent much of the 30s as staff pianist with CBS Radio's house band, Raymond Scott jumped at the chance to form his own group in 1936. The first song the New Yorker's Quintet (actually a sextet) played on *The Saturday Night Swing Session*, 'The Toy Trumpet' became his first single. Yet it was another Scott original, its squirming B-side 'Powerhouse', that resonated down the decades. A showcase of Scott's advanced compositional skills and his band's dexterity, it witnessed the horns of Pete Pumiglio, Dave Wade and Dave Harris tackle two seemingly disparate themes at different tempos. A composition so involved it could be seen as a precursor for the breathless sounds of bebop (anticipating the complex work of Charlie Parker and Dizzy Gillespie), it enjoyed a second life in numerous cartoon action sequences (for *Bugs Bunny*, *Sylvester*, *The Simpsons*), often used to signify repetitive, machine-like activity. And while its ubiquity belies how ahead of the curve 'Powerhouse' was, the single's A-side also endured after lyrics were added for Shirley Temple musical *Rebecca Of Sunnybrook Farm*.

**'Pressure Drop'**
The Clash
CBS 1979
A-Side: 'English Civil War'

**Punky reggae party.**

The Clash never pretended to be great at reggae. Their evident love of the music pulled them through. The London punks married intense political commitment with a willingness not to be restricted by musical boundaries, turning their fans onto rockabilly, ska, funk, hip-hop and electro as they blistered their way through four albums (including a double and a triple) in their first three years, while still managing to give single buyers a little extra to chew on. They had two stabs at covering the Toots & the Maytals song popularised in Jimmy Cliff's 1972 film *The Harder They Come* for a B-side. Dissatisfied with their first attempt with Lee 'Scratch' Perry (intended to back third single 'Complete Control') they managed to deliver the goods the following year. Blessed with more snarl than the happy-go-lucky original, there was undeniable force to its groovy bass skank as Joe Strummer's perpetual sore throat supplied the crucial conviction Toots Hibbert's words demanded. While the Clash absolutely mauled Junior Murvin's 'Police & Thieves' on their debut (prompting Murvin to dramatically demure: "They have destroyed Jah work!"), their more cultured, slow-burn version of Willie Williams' 'Armagideon Time' ['London Calling', 1979] ranks equal to this as their greatest B-side turn.

**'Pretty Baby'**
Roy Harper
STRIKE 1966
A-Side: 'Take Me Into Your Eyes'

**Idiosyncratic tribute to Bert Jansch.**

By the time Roy Harper established himself at London's Les Cousins folk club in the mid-60s he already had a colourful back story. A would-be skiffle musician who faked insanity to get out of the Royal Air Force, Harper had survived ECT treatment and stints in asylums and jail before busking his way through Europe. That wealth of experience poured into sessions for 1967's first solo LP *Sophisticated Beggar* — a set that touched on his past problems (the still poignant 'Committed') and set in stone his outsider status. While there was a band-oriented focus to the on-point psychedelia of 'Take Me Into Your Eyes', non-album B-side 'Pretty Baby' was an unabashed tribute to his Scottish folk contemporary Bert Jansch. The beatnik simplicity of its delicate guitar fingerplay and lingering vocal cadences tapped deep into Jansch's vulnerable humanity as Harper joined the dots to his vinyl debut — playing guitar on 'My Lover' (from Jansch's 1965 LP *It Don't Bother Me*).

### 'The Pride And The Pain'

Roxy Music
ISLAND 1973
A-Side: 'Pyjamarara'

**Art-rockers at their most avant-garde.**

It's testament to the flood of original ideas that besieged early Roxy Music that they declined to include either 'Pyjamarara' or first single 'Virginia Plain' on 1972's self-titled debut. Flamboyantly androgynous in their look (dinner jackets and feather boas), with a predilection for putting scantily-clad models on their covers, Roxy Music brought colour and adventure into the charts. In opposition to the A-side's pulsing postmodern glam, 'The Pride And The Pain' launched listeners into a strange beat-less universe, as writer Andy Mackay played a mellifluous oboe above Brian Eno's synthesised wind howls and a curious piano refrain. Phil Manzanera's trademark guitars had barely chimed when three sudden whipcracks struck, distorting the idyl out of shape. The odd incomprehensible vocal rasp that followed only deepened the intrigue as baroque choral yowls sounded. For sheer mystery and otherworldliness, it just won out over Bryan Ferry's dreamy instrumental 'Sultanesque' ['Love Is The Drug', 1975], the softer R&B inversion of 'Trash 2' ['Trash', 1979] and Manzanera's transcendental atmospherics on 'Always Unknowing' ['Avalon', 1982].

### 'Prologue To History'

Manic Street Preachers
EPIC 1998
A-Side: 'If You Tolerate This Your Children Will Be Next'

**Newly slimmed trio at peak power.**

As with loose contemporaries the Smiths and Suede, Manic Street Preachers made a point of packing their early B-sides with left-of-centre bounty, be it the louche acoustic desperation of 'Bored Out Of My Mind' ['Motorcycle Emptiness', 1992], shock tactics of 'Patrick Bateman' ['La Tristesse Durera (Scream To A Sigh)', 1993] or rouge lipstick lies of 'Donkeys' ['Roses in the Hospital', 1993]. The band that slashed its way from the valleys of South Wales to the forefront of UK pop were emerging from a dark place in 1998 — having decided to continue after the disappearance of founder Richey Edwards (his car abandoned near the Severn Bridge, a notorious suicide spot). While soul-searching and self-doubt coursed through 1998's *This Is My Truth Tell Me Yours* it was noticeably absent on both the Spanish Civil War themed A-side (a track originally earmarked for a B-side) and the propulsive piano-driven punk of 'Prologue To History'. While its references to rugby fly-half Phil Bennett, runner Steve Ovett and Happy Mondays' singer Shaun William Ryder betrayed bassist Nicky Wire's familiar obsessions, it was James Dean Bradfield's anguished howl and Sean Moore's powerplay drumming that firmly established it as a fan favourite. Bradfield later told *The Japan Times* that it should have replaced mawkish Edwards' tribute 'Nobody Loved You' on the album: "We were very uneasy with it."

## 'Puffin' On Blunts And Drankin Tanqueray'

Dr. Dre

DEATH ROW 1992

A-Side: 'Dre Day'

**Producer extends beef on freestyle frenzy.**

The second single from Dr. Dre's breakthrough solo set *The Chronic* put the boot into Eazy-E. Formerly his accomplice in N.W.A, Dre made a very public exit after voicing concerns about the alleged fiscal malfeasance of manager Jerry Heller — the subsequent beef providing great entertainment for hip-hop fans. A classic posse cut, this 12-minute B-side roped in fellow Death Row signings Lady of Rage and the Dogg Pound's Daz and Kurupt to sustain Dre's grievances, the rapping producer topping and tailing the mellow melee by taking casual pot-shots at Eazy-E, Tim Dog and Luther Campbell. While Lady of Rage showed some restraint (she was a new artist with plenty to lose), Kurupt was less discreet, his disses of Above the Law rapper Cold 187um and Kokane (both signed to Eazy's Ruthless label) delivered in a smoky flow at one with the hi-end synths Dre fashioned above the sturdy chassis of James Brown's 'Funky President'. It inevitably prompted a flurry of return dis tracks, but none that made their way quite so high up the US hit parade.

### 'Push It'

Salt-N-Pepa
NEXT PLATEAU 1987
A-Side: 'Tramp'

**Frisky rap hit, popular in maternity wards.**

Salt-N-Pepa opened the door for female rappers. The New York duo were working as part-time telephone operators at Sears department store when Salt's boyfriend Hurby 'Luv Bug' Azor asked the duo (then called Super Nature) to help on a song he was producing for his audio college course. Although the resulting single 'The Show Stoppa (Is Stupid Fresh)' was only a moderate success, it earned them a deal with upcoming independent Next Plateau. Convinced that their rap remake of Otis Redding and Carla Thomas's soul blues standard 'Tramp' had real street potential, they threw together 'Push It' in double-quick time for the flip, the duo adding their sparse suggestive raps to Fresh Gordon's off-the-cuff synthesiser riff in the tiny damp bathroom he used as a vocal room. While 'Tramp' effectively flopped, San Francisco DJ Cameron Paul set about promoting the B-side he had first chanced upon in a club. He added to its unconventional structure, winding in a bassline and more keyboards to create a remix for his KMEL Bay Area radio show. When other stations started playing his mix, Next Plateau made it an A-side, in defiance of its creators' concern that its overt pop sensibilities would damage their street credibility. Not only did those fears prove unfounded, its addictive thrust helped usher in a fresh wave of female MCs.

### 'Put The Bone In'

Terry Jacks
GOLDFISH 1973
A-Side: 'Seasons In The Sun'

**Brel hitmaker in risqué mood.**

Beloved by David Bowie, Scott Walker and Marc Almond, the songs of Belgian chansonnier Jacques Brel rattled with sex, death, disillusion and bruised romance. 'Le Moribond' was a case in point — a satirical, bitter song from a doomed man giving a withering goodbye to his unfaithful wife and hypocritical friends. Translated into English by Rod McKuen in 1964, its original meaning was consigned to dust when Canadian producer Terry Jacks (who had previous in the Chessmen and Poppy Family) recorded a take with the Beach Boys for 1970's *Surf's Up*. Unfinished and deemed unsuitable for the Californian surf-pop gods, Jacks eventually decided to cut his losses and have a pop himself, bagging a huge transatlantic hit. If 'Seasons In The Sun' was way too saccharine and over-sentimental for most, self-written flipside 'Put The Bone In' was a whole new universe of bizarre throwaway pop. Jacks deployed the same slightly fluttering voice for its highly euphemistic plea for a pork bone — a rude entreaty he just about managed to fudge with the tale of a runover dog (and also notable for his barely audible "Aw man!" at the fade). It impacted on some impressionable minds, with straggly Minnesota rockers Soul Asylum reviving it jam-style as a 'bone-us' (sic) track on 1988's *Hang Time*.

**'The Rabbit Got The Gun'**

The JB's

PEOPLE 1971

A-Side: 'Gimme Some More'

**Rare funk dynamite from James Brown's band.**

Widely known as the 'hardest working man in showbusiness', James Brown revelled in his gutsy reputation. The bandleader born in a one-room tin shack in South Carolina was an instrumental prodigy (proficient on keys, guitar, bass, saxophone, trumpet and drums) and seriously demanding taskmaster, whose behaviour (and readiness to use his fists, if necessary) often toppled over into bullying. Band-less after a pay dispute, Brown assembled the JB's, drilling Cincinnati session outfit the Pacesetters into possibly the meanest, tightest funk ensemble going (even if its fractious line-up was endlessly passing through revolving doors). When the driving rhythms, popping basslines and crisp guitars of 'Gimme Some More' finely gained them traction on the US pop charts, flipping single buyers were gifted another slab of pristine, floor-filling funk. Predicated on the old southern saying 'It ain't no fun when the rabbit's got the gun', the B-side had the light feel of a cartoon chase scene, its Fred Wesley arranged horns careening around a track directed by Fred Thomas's rubbery bassline and the tight percussion interplay of John 'Jabo' Starks. Rarely mentioned and rarely played, it's one of Brown's best but least celebrated instrumentals.

### 'Rebel Without A Pause'

Public Enemy
DEF JAM 1987
A-Side: 'You're Gonna Get Yours'

**Politicised Long Island rhymers set new gold standard.**

The first Public Enemy song to truly capture their incendiary live energy, its creators were in a hurry to get 'Rebel Without A Pause' to the public. If the Long Island band's mastery of rhetoric and polemic about black America was unbalanced on 1987 debut LP *Yo! Bum Rush The Show* and the already dated DMX drum machine-driven A-side, a fresh creative approach, predicated on dense sample collage, quickly yielded wilder, more invigorating results. Inspired, in part, by the technical advance of Eric B. & Rakim's 'I Know You Got Soul' and based on a squealing saxophone motif from The JB's instrumental 'The Grunt', the B-side ramped the tempo of James Brown's 'Funky Drummer' to a sweaty, hot-stepping 109 beats-per-minute. Smashing in after a Jesse Jackson sample, Chuck D's deep, resonant rhymes baited broadcasters ("Radio!/Suckers never play me!") and riffed on their growing status as rap's Black Panthers, offset by hypeman Flavor Flav's urgent ad-libs and DJ Terminator X's scratched-up chorus (from Chubb Rock's 'Rock N Roll Dude'). A musical hand grenade that both upped the ante and finally nailed their sound (Chuck D was so elated he declared "I could die tomorrow" on playback), this hastily tacked-on B-side became an instant hit with their British fans — who took Public Enemy to their hearts long before America turned on — and naturally became their next A-side too. It cheer-led the way to the dissonant funky sample-fest of second LP *It Takes A Nation Of Millions To Hold Us Back*, then hip-hop's greatest long-playing epistle.

## 'Recurring Dream'

Crowded House
CAPITOL 1986
A-Side: 'Now We're Getting Somewhere'

**Kiwi pop craftsmen's shimmering guitar work-out.**

Architects of a pleasing pop/rock hybrid, Crowded House marked the start of a new chapter for former Split Enz singer/guitarist Neil Finn and drummer Paul Hester. Abetted by bassist Nick Seymour, 1986's self-titled debut was the perfect shop window to showcase Finn's authorial range — hopeful, sad and all points in-between, with moving middle-eights and more hooks than a Mr Jelly convention. Home to no less than five singles, how the percussively detailed power pop 'Now We're Getting Somewhere' failed to get anywhere in the charts remains a minor mystery (follow-up 'Don't Dream It's Over' proved the tipping point). It meant many listeners missed the unravelling majesty of 'Recurring Dream'. Among the oldest songs in Crowded House's repertoire, it rested on Finn's chiming guitar work (channelling a beefed-up Johnny Marr) and his sensitive, alluring voice as he packed mystery into two simple lines: "Within myself/There are a million things". It later found a wider audience on the soundtrack to Nadia Tass's 1988 film *Rikky & Pete* and was used as the title for (but not included on) 1996's greatest hits collection.

## 'Remember Me I'm Gone'

Motörhead
BRONZE 1982
A-Side: 'Iron Fist'

**Gnarly metal trio's back-to-basics burner.**

There was more than an air of *déjà vu* on the last Motörhead single to feature the classic line up of growling bassist Lemmy Kilmister, speedy guitarist 'Fast' Eddie Clarke and punky kickdrum stylist Phil 'Philthy Animal' Taylor. With its allusions to a 'snakebite kiss' and the 'devil's grip' it was highly similar, in lyrics and tone, to their biggest hit 'Ace Of Spades', marking the point where the after-effects of their enthusiastic intake of alcohol and speed finally started to show. The rougher, rugged thrills of its B-side got many fans more revved up. Opening with a vintage rockabilly riff, the hurt tone of its lost love lament was more than compensated for by a stomping boogie beat and an amazing Clarke solo that distilled his twisted restoration of vintage rock 'n' roll riffs. And while 'Remember Me I'm Gone' retains a powerful place in the stable of guaranteed Motörheadbanger B-sides — along with the motorcycle menace of 'Like A Nightmare' ['No Class', 1979], slow ascent of 'Over The Top' ['Bomber', 1979] and primal fornications of 'Dirty Love' ['Ace Of Spades', 1980] — it's also a fitting memorial to the louder-than-life trio, all now sadly gone.

**'Return To The Future'**
Jammer
JAHMEKTHEWORLD 2003
A-Side: Kano: 'Vice Versa (Boys Love Girls)'

**Grime rule-breaker shows instrumental prowess.**
An early grime poster boy, Jammer was instrumental in the music establishing its outsider edge. A precocious teenage beatmaker who diligently assembled a state-of-the-art studio in the basement of his parents' Leytonstone home, his skills helped launch several other figures from the local NASTY Crew. So it proved with the A-side here, Jammer's dark and dank beats a vibrant match for the quick-witted flows of East Ham freestyler Kano on his explosive first single. Those who snaffled up this rare self-issued white label 12-inch were rewarded with a more exotic side of his skills on 'Return To The Future', a svelte slice of eastern-inflected mystery whose emotive movements worked wonderfully unadorned, although it was hard not to imagine Jammer's scampering flow on top. Soon his basement would start to resemble grime's Abbey Road — a haven where Dizzee Rascal, JME, Wiley, Tinchy Stryder and Skepta all came to record — and became home to the influential DVD series *Lords Of The Mics*. Able to make a comfortable living bypassing industry norms, seven years elapsed before Jammer surfaced overground with *Jahmanji* — a more widescreen take on this B-side's mystic meanderings.

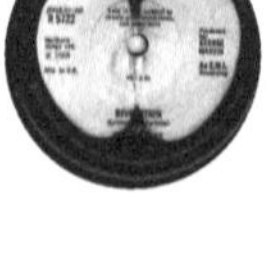

**'Revolution'**
The Beatles
APPLE 1968
A-Side: 'Hey Jude'

**Distorted 'masterpiece' vetoed by John Lennon's bandmates.**
The stakes were high when it came to issuing the Fab Four's first release on their own Apple label. In one camp was John Lennon, who wanted 'Revolution' — a song he considered "one of his masterpieces" — to take pride of place. A track that had already been recorded, and split in two, for their upcoming self-titled double LP (better known as *The White Album),* the more conventional first half ('Revolution #1') — about freeing your mind to achieve social change — ended just before it tripped into an experimental, loop-heavy slab of *musique concrète* ('Revolution #9', the album's most controversial offering). Written at a transcendental meditation camp in India, 'Revolution' was Lennon's response to calls for uprising in Europe and America. "I wanted to talk, I wanted to say my piece about revolution," he told *Rolling Stone* magazine, feeling that he'd previously been muted by their late manager Brian Epstein, who discouraged his charges expressing overt political views. Despite his readiness to speak, the song was deemed too slow as a single by Paul McCartney and the Beatles' producer/studio arbitrator George Martin, who both felt it wasn't a hit. Lennon would not be easily silenced. He persisted in recording a faster, heavier and, well, far more revolutionary version to try and sway his bandmates. He added an important lyrical shift too, emphatically saying "You can count me *out*!" of causing destruction. It mattered not. His fellow Fabs demurred and wistful McCartney singalong 'Hey Jude' — a good-hearted lullaby written for Lennon's young son, Julian — eventually got the A-side nod instead. Nonetheless many Beatles fans got a rude awakening when they flipped the single over. The sound of its wildly distorted guitars — plugged directly into the Abbey Road desk to deliberately overload the meters — even led some to return the record, imagining it was a defective pressing (the tight grooves of the 7:11 minute A-side, then the longest single to top the UK charts, also made the B-side play much louder). For many 'Revolution' caught Lennon at his zenith, with this startling B-side its definitive take.

**'Ride Easy'**
Asia
GEFFEN 1982
A-Side: 'Heat Of The Moment'

**Prog rock supergroup at their most adventurous.**

A throwback to self-important 70s prog supergroups such as Captain Beyond or Matching Mole, Asia was the brainchild of Geffen A&R man John Koldner. Built around the songwriting and vocal strengths of ex-King Crimson and Uriah Heep bassist John Wetton, he was abetted by two ex-members of Yes (florid keyboardist Geoff Downes, classically-edged guitarist Steve Howe) and drum royalty Carl Palmer (Emerson, Lake And Palmer). While its poppy A-side — a last minute addition to 1982's self-titled debut, written to order after Geffen requested a hit — did brisk chart business, rubbing shoulders with new romantics in the *Billboard* Top 5, the epic grandeur of 'Ride Easy' (a B-side in all territories bar the UK) became something of a connoisseur's anthem. One of Asia's earliest songs — an existential fable about going nowhere fast — it proved an ample showcase of its members' chops. Although Asia got too big too fast and were lost to internal recriminations a year later, 'Ride Easy' has retained its revered status.

**'Right Track Wrong Train'**
Cyndi Lauper
PORTRAIT 1983
A-Side: 'Girls Just Want To Have Fun'

**Post-punk thriller, full of vim and snarl.**

A decade in the wilderness, after the dissolution of new wave group Blue Angel, put flame-haired Brooklyn singer Cyndi Lauper in the last chance saloon. The 30-year-old had most of her solo debut *She's So Unusual* in the can when producer Rick Chertoff persuaded her to cover Robert Hazard's 'Girls Just Want To Have Fun'. Lauper baulked at first, uneasy at Hazard's ode to loose women, before rewriting it as a defiant anthem of female solidarity. Its contagious melody soon held sway, transporting it into a transatlantic number two with a helping hand from WWF star Captain Lou in its heavily rotated video. Not wildly dissimilar to early B-52s, 'Right Track Wrong Train' was more daring and far closer to Lauper's original vision for her LP, as she made the most of her four-octave vocal range over a propulsive punky rhythm and beat group backing vocals. A Lauper co-write with Ellie Greenwich (the Crystals' 'Da Doo Ron Ron', the Shangri-las' 'Leader Of The Pack'), it helped establish her incoming status as the queen of quirk.

**'Rite Of Man'**
Mike Oldfield
VIRGIN 1983
A-Side: 'Moonlight Shadow'

***Tubular Bells* creator's folk parody.**

The tortured teenage instrumental prodigy that inspired Richard Branson to launch Virgin Records finally let his hair down in the early 80s. Buffeted by continual sales of 1973's debut *Tubular Bells* — a one-track new age excursion synonymous with William Friedkin's horror film *The Exorcist* — he started balancing his longer instrumental forays with shorter, folkier pop songs. The Maggie Reilly-sung A-side epitomised the approach — an archaic sounding folk-ballad detailed with state-of-the-art synth wizardry that became a hit across Europe. There were distant echoes of Jona Lewie's Christmas cracker 'Stop The Cavalry' to B-side 'Rite Of Man', a track shamelessly loaded with squeezeboxes, Morris dancer beats and jingling tambourines. Its self-spoken words were clearly cocking a snoop though, Oldfield goading "Here's to another folk cliché" before it fizzled out. Given that mid-70s sets such as *Hergest Ridge* and *Ommadawn* had saddled Oldfield with a deeply unfashionable folk-rock image, it was a bold move and proof that this late developer — Oldfield became a regular Ibiza raver in his forties — was not as stony-faced as he had been portrayed.

**'Rock And Roll Friend'**
The Go-Betweens
BEGGARS BANQUET 1988
A-Side: 'Was There Anything I Could Do?'

**Seamless picture painting from hit-less critical faves.**

The misses had started to pile-up when Brisbane's finest indie troubadours recorded their sixth album *16 Lovers Lane*. A sumptuous power play on the bittersweet songwriting of the Go-Betweens' two frontmen, Robert Forster and Grant McLennan, their acoustic-led efforts were given a shimmering studio overhaul detailed with Amanda Brown's impactful strings. If the album's driving second single was a little gauche by their own high standards, B-side 'Rock And Roll Friend' was sublime. From its low-slung groove and evocative opening line to its chorus's unspecific but insistent pleas to "Do something about me!", it painted a rich portrait of a strained relationship and the tensions bubbling just below the surface. So good that Forster would revive it on 1996's solo outing *Warm Nights* — with producer Edwyn Collins treating it like a vintage soul tune — it also became the title of Tracey Thorn's 2021 memoir about her friendship with their drummer Lindy Morrison. The band's staunch division of labour — Forster and McLennan would routinely contribute five songs apiece to each album — inevitably spilled over into other enduring B-sides, see also: 'Karen' ['Lee Remick', 1978], 'This Girl, Black Girl' ['Man O'Sand To Girl O'Sea', 1983] and 'When People Are Dead' ['Right Here', 1988].

### '(We're Gonna) Rock Around The Clock'

Bill Haley & His Comets
DECCA 1954
A-Side: 'Thirteen Women (And Only One Man In Town)'

**Rock 'n' roll has lift-off.**

With his pot belly and kiss-curl, Bill Haley was rock 'n' roll's least likely breakout star. Having landed a surprise hit with the slang-blasted 'Crazy Man, Crazy', written by his bassist Marshall Lytle, the 30-year-old Michigan ex-country musician was keen to capitalise with a song that had ignited recent live shows. A co-write between Philadelphia songwriter Max C. Freedman and Haley's publisher James E. Myers (under the pseudonym Jimmy De-Knight), '(We're Gonna) Rock Around The Clock' was vetoed by Haley's Essex Records boss Dave Miller, whose longstanding antipathy to Myers enabled country vets Sonny Dae & His Nights to have first dibs. Haley finally got to play it *his way* after switching to Decca, who needed a B-side for the foot-tapping Dickie Thompson number 'Thirteen Women' — a game male fantasy about the aftermath of a nuclear bomb. Haley and his Comets had just 40 minutes to cut the B-side — time for just two takes. They fudged the first, playing so loud that Haley's vocals were almost inaudible. A second, more minimal version was then painstakingly spliced together with the first by Decca's in-house engineer. The single was only a minor hit and its B-side — defined as much by its gimmicky 12-bar flit around the clockface as it was by Danny Cedrone's lightning-speed guitar solo — totally forgotten about. Everything changed when Richard Brooks, director of B-movie *Blackboard Jungle*, heard its lead actor Glenn Ford's son play the song and decided to use it in the film's opening credits. Its invocation to "put your glad rags on" soon had teenagers dancing in the aisles, prompting Decca to re-release it as an A-side. If not exactly the first rock 'n' roll record, 'Rock Around The Clock' became its national anthem — a phenomenon that surged to the top of the US charts (and stayed there for two sticky summer months) before it took over the world.

### 'Rock Island Line'

Lead Belly
ASCH 1942
A-Side: 'Ol' Riley'

**Definitive take on 'work song' standard.**

Lead Belly was ahead of the curve. The singing, songwriting son of a Texas sharecropper had served several jail terms when he met folk anthologist Alan Lomax at Angola state prison. He was back at large, acting as Lomax's driver and field assistant, when they recorded the inmates of the Arkansas Cummins State Farm prison singing Clarence Wilson's work song 'Rock Island Line' in 1934. Later added to Lead Belly's live repertoire and altered extensively, he cut his own version in 1942 as B-side to slave song 'Ol' Riley'. Backed with just his tinkling acoustic guitar, Lead Belly was in distinctive voice as he narrated a train driver's role on the Chicago, Rock Island and Pacific railroad line, boasting how he gleefully lied — claiming he had livestock on board, instead of pig iron — to dodge paying the tolls. Covered by Woody Guthrie, Bobby Darin, Johnny Cash and three of the Beatles (only Paul McCartney resisted), Lead Belly's arrangement took on a new meaning when it was adopted by Lonnie Donegan in 1954. Recorded at a far fiercer tempo, backed by Chris Barber's trad jazz band, it launched the skiffle movement. Yet no one sung the choruses with the same potent intensity as Lead Belly — a blues and folk master who never received his dues in his lifetime.

### 'Rock Me'

Sister Rosetta Tharpe
DECCA 1939
A-Side: 'The Lonesome Road'

**Original soul sister pens first rock ballad.**

The godmother of rock 'n' roll set a high bar for the guitarists that followed her. The daughter of a travelling gospel missionary known as Mother Bell, Sister Rosetta Tharpe grew up within the Pentecostal rules of the Church of God in Christ. Encouraged to sing and use rhythmical musical expression, she had mastered guitar by age six. After coming to fame as the frontwoman for Lucky Millinder's swing band, Tharpe became an overnight sensation when she turned solo in 1939. That was largely due to the self-written 'Rock Me', the ballsy, confident B-side of her first single. With its powerful vocals, idiosyncratic electric guitar stylings and jazzy horns the suggestively titled song (lyrics adapted from Tommy Dorsey) was a lightning bolt that upset church audiences unused to the marriage of gospel with secular music. An enduring influence on Little Richard, Elvis Presley, Johnny Cash and Chuck Berry — the latter once claimed his career was just "one long Rosetta impersonation" — 'Rock Me' was astonishing for bearing rock 'n' roll's stylistic stamp nearly two decades before the genre's presumed arrival.

## 'Roland The Headless Thompson Gunner'

Warren Zevon
ASYLUM 1978
A-Side: 'Werewolves Of London'

**Excitable Boy's blood-seeped mercenary fable.**

There were several false dawns before Warren Zevon tasted success. The Chicago son of a professional gambler and a devout Mormon, Zevon was a hard-drinking satirist who played with Jackson Browne, Fleetwood Mac and the Everly Brothers before the world caught up with his scholarly brand of ironic detachment. While the slightly gimmicky A-side — written to order after a dare by Phil Everly — proved to be his breakthrough (and only) hit, its B-side's evocation of European mercenaries in Africa touched many fans much more deeply. Written in Costa Brava Irish bar the Dubliner alongside ex-mercenary David Lindell one hazy afternoon in 1974, its narrative told of a Norwegian mercenary in the Biafran War, whose success riled the CIA so much they blew off his head. Yet the headless Roland took his revenge, not just on his killer, but by stalking the world. When the hard-living Zevon received a diagnosis of terminal lung cancer in late 2002, talk show host and super-fan David Letterman turned an entire hour of *The Late Show* to the singer, insisting that he play this deeply political B-side (it proved Zevon's last live performance). Just as its folky piano figure faded, he offered up some parting advice: "Enjoy every sandwich."

### 'The Romance Of The Telescope (Unfinished)'

Orchestral Manoeuvres in the Dark
DINDISC 1981
A-Side: 'Joan Of Arc'

**Moody track signals synthpop duo's new direction.**

In late 1981 Orchestral Manoeuvres In The Dark (OMD) were at the peak of their success. Despite regularly tackling non-pop subjects — atomic bombs in 'Enola Gay', 'Joan Of Arc' on the A-side's ravishing synth waltz (the first of two consecutive hits about the doomed French saint) — the Liverpool duo of Andy McClusky and Paul Humphries' radio-friendly skills had won them a dedicated audience. The stately bars of this moody and cryptic B-side, all wavering brass and tremulous poetics, caught OMD at their most experimental and curiously moving. Along with 'Of All The Things We've Made' ['Maid Of Orleans', 1982] OMD considered it too good to leave as a B-side, and both songs resurfaced in remixed form on 1983's 4th album *Dazzle Ships* — a cold war treatise, summoned in the grip of writer's block, that nearly torpedoed their career. Nonetheless 'The Romance Of The Telescope' remains a band favourite. Not only did OMD open shows on their *Architecture & Morality* tour with it, they used it to close 2018's homecoming concert alongside the Royal Liverpool Philharmonic Orchestra.

### 'Roots'

Bob Marley & the Wailers
ISLAND 1977
A-Side: 'Waiting In Vain'

**Rare non-album flip from Tuff Gong skipper.**

Bob Marley made the most of his short time on earth. The Jamaica reggae superstar left behind a fearsome legacy that took in the 60s Studio One era, early 70s Trojan years and massive overground success with Island, whose label-head

Chris Blackwell often acted as co-producer. 'Roots', an unused outtake from sessions for 1976's *Rasta Vibration*, found Marley in confident if mellow form. Yet his gift for sounding laidback while making incisive observations remained intact, as he boasted about his dominance in reggae ("I and I are the roots") above "shoo-be-doo" female backing vocals and a knotty Wailers backdrop fashioned by engineers Sylvian Morris and Errol Thompson. It was recorded just a few months before a politically motivated attempt on his life — intended to stop him playing free concert Smile Jamaica — resulted in Marley performing with a bullet lodged in his arm. He flew out of Jamaica the next day and made a fresh start with 1977's London-recorded *Exodus* (home of yearning A-side 'Waiting In Vain'), a key text in the evolving Marley canon as he discovered fresh ways to relay the harshest truths.

**'Rose Room (In Sunny Roseland)'**

Benny Goodman's Sextet

COLUMBIA 1939

A-Side: 'Flying Home'

**Charlie Christian adds electric guitar chops to jazz.**

Benny Goodman did much to kick off the big band era. The distinctive Chicago clarinettist, widely dubbed the 'King of Swing', was a hard taskmaster who nonetheless launched many fresh jazz careers and was a steadfast promoter of smaller groups — interrupting big band shows with short sets from his Benny Goodman Trio (alongside drummer Jess Stacey and pianist Teddy Wilson). His late 30s sextet was something else. And while the A-side 'Flying Home' gave ample space to vibraphonist Lionel Hampton's chops it was its B-side, 'Rose Room', that went down in jazz history. A melodious Art Hickman tune dating back to 1917, the bandleader suggested Oklahoma guitarist Charlie Christian play the notoriously difficult number during his audition. Unknown to Goodman, Christian had learned how to improvise to the song and his solos proved so good that it eventually ran to over 40 minutes. While that was never captured on tape — the three-minute limit of 78 rpm discs precluded such wild abandon — the single version lacked nothing for its brevity. Meditative and bright, Christian's penchant for defined single notes and inventive phrases was an early example of how the electric guitar could sound at home on jazz recordings.

### 'Rose, Rose I Love You'

Frankie Laine
COLUMBIA 1951
A-Side: 'Jezebel'

**Old Leather Lungs' rare two-sided hit.**

Frankie Laine possessed a massive voice. Born into the LoVecchio family — Sicilian immigrants with genuine mob connections — the Chicago song-stylist once danced a marathon 3,501 hours over 145 consecutive days to create a world record before he scuffed his way through the singing ranks. Fame arrived relatively late, at 34, for the vocalist Bob Hope called "a foghorn with lips". The hits flowed thick and fast after 1947's 'That's My Desire' took off, with Laine seeming equally at home bellowing out the risqué, hyper-dramatic 'Jezebel' as he was showing a more delicate touch with his take on Yao Lee's Mandarin pop hit 'Rose, Rose I Love You'. Given fresh lyrics by British radio presenter Wilfrid Thomas (and widely purported to be about Malayan stripper Rose Chan), the B-side touched a chord with servicemen who had served in the east and helped Laine linger around the *Billboard* chart's zenith a little longer, landing just one place behind the A-side at number 3. It later showed up in Peter Bogdanovich's 1971 coming-of-age drama *The Last Picture Show*.

### 'Roxanne, Roxanne'

UTFO
SELECT 1984
A-Side: 'Hangin' Out'

**B-side that incited hip-hop's opening beef.**

There was no strategic powerplay to hip-hop's first public beef (that would come much later). Brooklyn quartet UTFO (UnTouchable Force Organization) were best known for gamely styling themselves as the 'Village People of rap' when the B-side to their unremarkable first single 'Hangin' Out' put them firmly on the map. 'Roxanne, Roxanne' was a slice of cynical one-upmanship that found rappers Kangol Kid, the Educated Rapper and Doctor Ice volubly chastising a 'stuck-up' girl for spurning their advances over Mix Master Ice's squelchy DJ cut-up of Billy Squier's 'The Big Beat'. It unwittingly incited the wrath of b-girls across New York. Not least fierce 14-year-old Marley Marl protégée Roxanne

Shanté, who launched her career with her uber-confrontational response, 'Roxanne's Revenge', directly over the original's beats. UTFO realised they were onto a good thing and issued an answer record to the answer record — enlisting Elease Jack to take on the role of 'The Real Roxanne' — which opened the floodgates for all-comers to pitch in. Efforts such as Sparky D's 'Sparky's Turn (Roxanne You're Through)' and Ralph Rolle's unforgettable 'Roxanne's A Man (The Untold Story)' stirred the pot further before the East Coast Crew put a polite full stop to the saga with 1985's 'The Final Word — No More Roxanne (Please)'.

## 'Ruby Red'

Kingston Trio
CAPITOL 1958
A-Side: 'Tom Dooley'

**US folk cheerleaders show their brighter side.**

The Kingston Trio spearheaded the late 1950s folk revival, their youthful exuberance breathing new life into an unfashionable scene. With their sparse guitar and vocal arrangements (sometimes enhanced with bongos), the nerdy Californian trio of Nick Reynolds, Bob Shane and Dave Guard made waves via a residency at San Francisco's Hungry I club. They became unlikely pop stars when 'Tom Dooley' — a plaintive take on an old folk ballad about the 1866 murder of Laura Foster — suddenly took off. Not only did it hang around the *Billboard chart* as 1958 turned into 1959, it allowed the likes of the Weavers, the Tarriers and the Limeliters to capitalise, even if Lonnie Donegan's sped-up skiffle take narrowly bested them in the UK charts. The vocal interplay on its rousing stop-start B-side 'Ruby Red' was every bit its equal. And while the object of their affection — a "priceless gem of perfection" — inevitably got away, the lyrics' rich references to rubies, diamonds, emeralds and sapphires showed her place in their affections.

## 'Running Scared'

Nick Cave and the Bad Seeds
MUTE 1986
A-Side: 'The Singer'

**Australian prince of darkness' twisty paranoiac fable.**

Nick Cave wasn't always a critical darling. The bug-eyed, backcombed ex-Birthday Party leader had, at best, a fractious relationship with the UK music press as he tried to evolve a solo career with the waifs and strays of the Bad Seeds. It was Cave's journalistic antipathy that inspired the biblical title to 1986's *Kicking Against The Pricks*, a rousing covers set that gave him an independent chart-topper with its lead single's purring take on Johnny Cash's 'The Singer'. That was roundly trumped, however, by its B-side's slow-building spin on Roy Orbison's 1961 rock ballad 'Running Scared'. Riding over new drummer Thomas Wydler's ominous thumps and Blixa Bargeld's sparse but incisive guitar, Cave sounded flustered and all at sea, trapped in a love triangle and convinced he was about to be jilted as the tension mounted. And while The Big O's trembling tones at least gave the song a hopeful ending, Cave chose the doomier option and abbreviated its final line. He further underlined his interpretative skills on the 12-inch, with a bellowing run-through of Lead Belly's work song 'Black Betty', while his stripped back version of 'Deanna' (on the 'Acoustic Versions EP', a free CD with initial copies of 1990's *The Good Son*) was notable for showing the bones of the song it gladly grave-robbed — Edwin Hawkins' gospel standard 'Oh Happy Day'.

**'Running Thin'**
Blancmange
LONDON 1982
A-Side: 'Living On The Ceiling'

**Electro-pop duo show their darker side.**

Among the most underrated duos to emerge during synth-pop's early 80s heyday, Blancmange stood out for their differences — lyrically luxuriating in their Englishness while managing a glitzy clash of musical styles. Breakthrough hit 'Living On The Ceiling' epitomised the dichotomy, singer Neil Arthur happily going "up the bloody tree" as Stephen Luscombe patched together traditional Indian instrumentation with cutting-edge synth technology. B-side 'Running Thin' was a much darker, starker prospect that could almost be mistaken for early Depeche Mode. Above a terse, claustrophobic Roland drum machine, Arthur's baritone resisted hysterics as he described "broken bodies whining" and "broken bodies twining" and the deleterious effects it was having on his temper.

He later told *The Herald* that "the record company probably thought it a tad dark door", which explained why the band lifted this B-side from a session for John Peel's BBC Radio 1 show. Arthur continued to perform it live when he reactivated Blancmange after 26 years in cold storage in 2011.

### 'Sabbath Bloody Sabbath'

Anthrax
ISLAND 1987
'I'm The Man EP'

**A little fan appeasement goes a long way.**

Anthrax started life as a conventional metal band until singer Joey Belladonna started to duck the standard clichés. Having established themselves as masters of fast, aggressive thrash on 1987's second LP *Among The Living*, this EP's title track (offered in three contrasting versions) was a wild gamble — a founding experiment with Def Jam-era hip-hop (that sampled both Run-DMC and Beastie Boys) seen as heresy by some of their more lunkheaded followers. A band never afraid to honour their roots — as covers of the Police, Boston, Joe Jackson, Rush and Thin Lizzy would prove — their B-side take on 'Sabbath Bloody Sabbath' succeeded through sheer force of will. It arguably bettered the original as the New Yorkers' controlled aggression reanimated the Tony Iommi riff said to have saved Black Sabbath and Belladonna out-witched Ozzy Osbourne with the depth of his conviction. And as with the off-piste live version of 'Caught In A Mosh', also included, it reassured wavering fans of Anthrax's status among the metal faithful. The eagle-eared would find a second cover lurking *within* its grooves — Anthrax bludgeoning their way through Stormtroopers of Death's bijou 'Taint' within its last five seconds.

### 'Safe'

The House of Love
FONTANA 1989
A-Side: 'Never'

**Hope amid the major label ruins.**

In 1989 the House of Love had the world at their feet. Signed to major label Fontana after an extraordinary series of cheaply recorded, quickly made records for Alan McGee's Creation label that peaked with 1988's 'Destroy The Heart' — a single that topped BBC Radio 1 DJ John Peel's Festive 50. The protracted sessions for their second album, using multiple producers and studios, compounded rumours that the partnership between stub-faced singer Guy Chadwick and mercurial guitarist Terry Bickers had fractured amid drug abuse, depression and nervous breakdowns. That disconnect was apparent on 'Never', a single issued against the band's wishes that failed to get out of first gear and stalled at number forty-one in the charts, despite their new paymaster's corporate muscle. A shred of hope was found on the single's other side. A one-off studio dalliance with Depeche Mode producers Daniel Miller and Gareth Jones, once mooted as a potential A-side, 'Safe' was everything 'Never' wasn't, its romantic plea not to settle for the easy life or take the road most travelled tapping into the same rock classicism as the House of Love's earlier work.

**'Samba Pa Ti'**
Santana
COLUMBIA 1970
A-Side: 'Oye Coma Va'

**Latin-rock guitar great finds his tone.**

With their show-stealing turn at 1969's Woodstock, Santana ushered Latin rock into the mainstream. The Californian band acted decisively on their second album *Abraxas*, replacing their debut's often improvisatory tunes with more song-driven affairs, including a cover of Fleetwood Mac's 'Black Magic Woman' and a full throttle version of Tito Puente's cha-cha-cha 'Oye Coma Va' that reputedly outraged its originator (until the royalties rolled in). Yet it was founder Carlos Santana's first truly memorable instrumental on the B-side that struck a more resonant chord. Recorded after a jet-lagged Santana watched a jazz saxophonist playing outside his apartment, it shifted gear from a slow samba over a Hammond B3 progression into a hook-laden head of steam that mangled Latin trills with blues thrills and established Santana's inimitable bell-like tone. Santana later told *MOJO* magazine it was the first time he felt truly able to express himself: "I get angry because, 'Why can't I say what I really mean?' Then

'Samba Pa Ti' comes out of me and everybody understands it." And although neither Santana nor Columbia considered it single material, it became his first UK hit when reissued as an A-side in 1973.

### 'Scary Movies'

Bad Meets Evil
GAME 1998
A-Side: 'Nuttin' To Do'

**Detroit dream team's Halloween parade.**

Eminem might have peppered horror references throughout his catalogue, but none hit quite as hard as 'Scary Movies'. An initially short-lived alliance with fellow Detroit rapper Royce Da 5'9", united by mutual friend Proof, Bad Meets Evil's self-titled duet for Eminem's *The Slim Shady LP* revealed an intense chemistry that didn't stint on invention. It was already in the can when the pair stopped off in New York to perform on the Lyricist Lounge tour. As soon as they landed, ex-*Source* magazine editor and Game label head Jonathan Shecter seized on a loophole in Eminem's Interscope contract to record this one-off single. Written and tracked at pace, along with its more traditionally structured A-Side, 'Scary Movies' was a fierce bout of MC interplay that found the pair spitting thunder above a dramatic sample flip of Shirley Bassey's 'If I Never Sing Another Song'. The duo fell out soon afterwards — evidenced by the dis tracks traded between Royce and Eminem's proteges D12 — until Proof's murder in 2006 proved a timely wake-up call. This B-side also accompanied the closing credits of Keenen Ivory Wayans' millennial horror comedy *Scary Movie*.

### 'Schizophrenia's Weighted Me Down'

Cat Power
MATOR 1996
A-Side: 'Nude As The News'

**Singer's Sonic Youth and Skip Spence mash-up.**

From the moment she emerged on New York's experimental scene in the early 90s, Cat Power was mad for sadness. That continued with the confessional tone of 'Nude As The News', a vibrating diary page that sensitively tackled abortion, and its hushed, intimate B-side. An acoustic meld of parts of Sonic Youth's 'Schizophrenia' (opening track of 1987's art-rock favourite *Sister*) with the chorus of ill-starred Moby Grape co-founder Skip Spence's 'Weighted Down (The Prison Song)' (from 1968's minimalist solo album *Oar*), the perpetually pouting Atlanta-born singer subverted their meanings as she inducted both into her uniquely tortured world. It was a fitting payback to Sonic Youth drummer Steve Shelley, an early supporter who first caught Cat Power supporting Liz Phair in 1993. Shelley played drums on her emotionally intense first two albums *Dear Sir* and *Myra Lee* (recorded the same day) and produced psychologically fragile parent album *What Would The Community Think*.

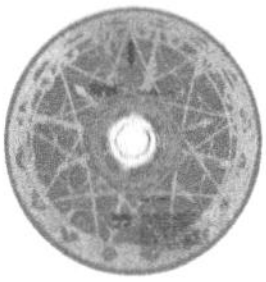

**'Scream'**
Slipknot
ROADRUNNER 2004
A-Side: 'Vermillion'

**Masked metal bogeymen's new spin on an old therapy.**
Iowa's most detested sons worked harder than most to shock their fans. With their identical jumpsuits and homemade death masks, Slipknot committed themselves to conveying horror with an industrial grind through metal, post-punk and rap spiked with furiously nihilistic lyrics. They walked as they talked it too — drummer Shawn 'Clown' Crahan would reputedly huff a dead crow until he vomited into his mask to get into the right onstage mindset. The success of 2001's breakthrough LP *Iowa* did little to temper their necromantic fury. While the restless ticks of the Rick Rubin produced 'Vermillion' showed them refining their terrifying schtick further, they tapped into something far more primal on 'Scream' — a hard-to find B-side beloved by their fan base of 'maggots'. After a deeply uncomfortable grindcore riff, 'Scream' took listeners through multiple mis-directions before its itchy, scratchy chorus allowed Corey Taylor to let rip, spilling out his guts with ornery dedication. Taylor's unique talent had fringe benefits too — his spine-tingling shrieks voiced the monster in 2015 *Dr Who* episode *Under The Lake*.

## 'See That My Grave Is Kept Clean'

Blind Lemon Jefferson
PARAMOUNT 1928
A-Side: ''Lectric Chair Blues'

**Influential Texas blues pioneer's finest hour.**

There was a haunted quality to Blind Lemon Jefferson's greatest track. Unsighted since birth, the Texas-born Jefferson became an itinerant entertainer in his teens, working the bars and brothels of Louisiana, Mississippi, Alabama, Virginia and his home state. One of the first blues singers to enter the studio, Jefferson's trembling, expressive voice captured the dread of execution (a prominent punishment in the Lone Star State) on its harrowing but largely forgotten A-side. It was surpassed by its topical flip. An adaptation of old blues spiritual 'Two White Horses In A Line' it wed his tender voice to poetically stark lyrics and a guitar accompaniment whose two sustained low notes imitated ringing church bells. It turned out to be prophetic — within two years Jefferson was dead at 35. Buried in an unmarked grave in Texas' Wortham Negro Cemetery, it took until 1997 for this request to be granted, after blues fans clubbed together to erect a new headstone inscribed with his signature song's refrain. Jefferson's famous B-side has been widely covered since — by Bob Dylan, B.B. King, Mavis Staples, Lou Reed — while Half Man Half Biscuit recorded the affectionate parody 'See That My Bike's Kept Clean'.

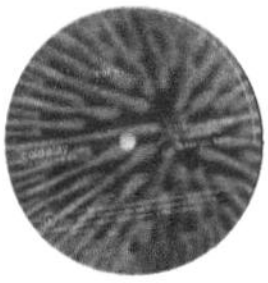

## 'See You Soon'

Coldplay
PARLOPHONE 1999
'The Blue Room EP'

**Simple and profound acoustic ballad.**

Long before they became aggressively-styled pop stars who counted Rihanna, Beyoncé and Brian Eno as collaborators, Coldplay were the misfits who gate-crashed the dying Britpop party. A fresh-faced quartet whose early press photos captured them in hoodies and trainers — with singer Chris Martin sporting the most voluminous brown corduroy trousers imaginable — it chimed with Creation boss Alan McGee's scathing quip that they made "music for bedwetters". And while this under-the-radar gem from Coldplay's first major label release is hardly rock 'n' roll Valhalla, it showed the tenderness and sensitivity that endeared them to them to the masses on their breakthrough hit 'Yellow'. Martin's yearning vocal and ambiguous lyrics (with its mentions of lost trust, bulletproof vests and telescopic lens) layered up the anxiety over Jonny Buckland's lovelorn acoustic guitar before a spare organ figure added an ethereal edge. Arguably better than most tracks on their moody debut *Parachutes*, it became a live favourite, particularly prominent on 2016's visually lavish *A Head Full Of Dreams* stadium tour.

## 'Sentimental Me'

The Knickerbockers
COLUMBIA 1925
A-Side: 'Manhattan'

**Double-sider by the pseudonymous 78s king.**

Ben Selvin was an American recording pioneer. After making his first public appearance at the Star Casino aged nine, the child fiddle prodigy became a fixture on the New York club scene, reaching wider ears with the success of his Novelty Orchestra's 1919 hit 'Dardanella' (said to have sold over five million copies). The son of Russian immigrants went on to become the 78s era's most recorded bandleader, signed to multiple labels (Paramount, Vocalion, Brunswick) under a slew of names (the Broadway Nightlites, the Columbians, the Harmonians) as he notched up more than 13,000 releases. Originally credited to the Knickerbockers, this 1925 single found him at his most mainstream as he put his spit and polish on a pair of Rodgers & Hart tunes from stage revue *Garrick Gaieties*. And while his take on 'Manhattan' shot to the top of the US charts, its super-swinging B-side 'Sentimental Me' (not to be confused with the Ames Brothers' 1950 hit of the same name) proved equally persuasive — it landed right behind it at number 2.

## 'Set The Ray To Jerry'

The Smashing Pumpkins
VIRGIN 1996
A-Side: '1979'

**Peak power Pumpkins in minimalist mode.**

Songs poured out of Billy Corgan when the Smashing Pumpkins were creating 1996's ambitious third album *Mellon Collie And The Infinite Sadness*. Arguably the last big record of the alternative rock era — a double LP, packed to the rafters with 28 big-screen efforts — many more of Corgan's compositions made up the multiple B-sides of its five spin-off singles. 'Set The Ray To Jerry' was one such affair, a track that harked back to the Chicago alt-rockers' more simplistic early recordings, dotted with some of Corgan's most direct yet oblique lyrics. Delivered in his uniquely raspy voice over a flurry of James Iha's phased guitars, it let drummer Jimmy Chamberlain's jazz roots shine through as he switched imperceptibly between 2/4 and 4/4 time during its choruses. For a band infamous for going OTT in the studio and using up to 60 guitar tracks within a single song, it was particularly sparse. It gathered serious fan kudos before long-stewing tensions started to rip the Smashing Pumpkins apart.

## 'Seven By Seven'

Hawkwind
UNITED ARTISTS 1972
A-Side: 'Silver Machine'

**Existential flip to the ultimate space-metal 45.**

Hawkwind were in a ropey position at the start of 1972. Practically skint, the counterculture's biggest band's funds had diminished through playing too many free shows. The Londoners suffered another blow when thieves stole a van full of equipment on the eve of the Bickershaw Festival. 'Silver Machine' single-handedly saved their bacon. Recorded live at a benefit concert at London's Roundhouse then heavily overdubbed in the studio, it witnessed future Motörhead bassist Lemmy Kilmister replacing their recently sectioned singer Robert Calvert's more distracted vocals. It had grazed the UK Top 20 when a filmed *Top Of The Pops* segment from Dunstable Civic Hall, that starred their stage dancer Stacia sprayed silver, blew impressionable minds and pushed it into the Top 3. Anyone who required further evocation of Hawkwind's existential darkness only had to play B-side 'Seven By Seven' for proof. A fragmented affair where seagull noises and minor key fingerpicking was subsumed by Dave Brock's jagged riffs, Kilmister's throbbing bass and wild layers of darting synths, it found the sci-fi obsessed Calvert pondering the gravity of living in a world of "timelessness and woe".

### 'Shadow Of Your Love'

Guns N' Roses
GEFFEN 1987
A-Side: 'It's So Easy'

**Driving flip captures Hollywood outlaws' raw energy.**

Guns N' Roses' reckless tales of Los Angeles low life redefined the heavy metal landscape. Four fifths of the band — Axl Rose, Slash, Izzy Stradlin and Steven Adler — also made up their earlier incarnation, Hollywood Rose, whose songs carried into their initial studio session with producer Mike Clink. 'Shadow Of Your Love' was the first to be tracked. "Axl was running up and down the walls screaming," drummer Adler later told musicradar.com, "I thought, 'This is the greatest thing ever.'" Written by Rose with childhood friend Paul Tobias, the song rifled along at breakneck pace and packed the same swagger and intensity as *Appetite For Destruction*, the debut LP that shifted the axis away from Motley Crue's preening hair metal. Mystifyingly cut from the track list, it finally surfaced on the 12-inch B-side of their first single (and later backed a cover of Wings' 'Live And Let Die'), albeit with overdubbed crowd noise. A remastered version corrected that when it belatedly became an A-side to promote an expanded edition of their debut in 2018.

### 'She's My Summer Girl'

Jan & Dean
LIBERTY 1963
A-Side: 'Surf City'

**Californian duo reap rewards of a helping hand.**

Part-time Californian college students Jan Berry and Dean Torrence lost their way after 1959's first single 'Baby Talk' went Top 10, but found kindred spirits in support band the Beach Boys. When their singer Brian Wilson asked Berry to help with 'Surf City', a song he was having trouble finishing, not only did it gift Jan & Dean their first number 1 single, it enraged Wilson's dad and manager Murry — who was convinced his son had wasted a potential Beach Boys hit. As well as doubling the lead vocal on 'Surf City', Wilson sang and co-wrote its B-side 'She's My Summer Girl' with Berry's long-time collaborator Don Altfeld. A full-blown evocation of the Jan & Dean sound from all-star backing band the Wrecking Crew — Hal Blaine, Carol Kaye, Earl Palmer, Leon Russell, Glen Campbell — the doo-wop nodding charmer teemed with summer romance, the naked regret of its last verse sweetened by "de-dumb-dumb-dumb-dumb" backing vocals. On a more trivial note, the single that immortalised the line "Two girls for every boy" featured two boys and a girl on its cover.

### 'Sheffield: Sex City'

Pulp
GIFT 1993
A-Side: 'Babies'

**Brutalist city tour packed with carnal possibilities.**

A chart miss at the first time of asking, 'Babies' became a quintessential part of Pulp's repertoire. Perhaps the luckiest band to be tarred with the Britpop brush — it took them out of sustained obscurity — the A-side's voyeuristic take on romance was raised several notches on its chorus-free, eight-and-a-half-minute B-side. A horny celebration of his brutalist birthplace it found singer Jarvis Cocker listing various Sheffield locales (Hackenthorpe, Shalesmoor, Wombwell, Catcliffe) while keyboardist Candida Doyle deadpanned a passage from Nancy Friday's sexual fantasy compendium *My Secret Garden*. A corrective to the Justified Ancients of Mu Mu's mocking 1991 club hit 'It's Grim Up North', 'Sheffield: Sex City' brought out the best in Cocker's Pulp bandmates, with Doyle's repetitious keyboard vamps and Russell Senior's treated violins snaking congo-like between Steve Mackey's steady bassline, given added subwoofer low-end by Warp in-house producer Zebedee. It was ultimately the Cocker show, however. So close-miked he could be whispering in your ear, his increasingly lurid entreaties, groans and gasps invoked a city-wide orgasm at one of Sheffield's signature high-rises.

### 'Shikako Maru Ten'

Can
UNITED ARTISTS 1971
A-Side: 'Spoon'

**Pioneering Krautrockers hit perfect groove.**

One of the late 20th century's most influential avant-garde bands, Can's improvisatory live approach leaned much more on careful editing when they were studio bound. That was instantly apparent on A-side 'Spoon' — a three-minute miniature commissioned for Francis Durbridge's TV mini-series *Das Messer* whose prominent drum machine rhythm, then relatively unheard of, helped it patter unexpectedly into the German Top 10. The first song the band recorded in their new studio just outside Cologne, B-side 'Shikako Maru Ten' was even more accessible and highlighted their under-sung ear for rhythmic hooks and grooves. Topped with two vocal lines from resident poet Damo Suzuki — one in English, the other Japanese — it let Michael Karoli's swooping guitar and Irmin Schmidt's textured Farfisa ride the magic rhythmic carpet of Holger Czukay's funky bassline and free-jazz drummer Jaki Liebezeit's clatters and bangs. They would cut 'I'm So Green' and 'One More Night', highlights of 1972's third LP *Ege Bamyası*, from a similar cloth.

**'Shout'**
Michael Jackson
EPIC 2000
A-Side: 'Cry'

**Ailing King of Pop's call-to-action.**

For a prodigious singles artist — serving up seven Top 10 US hits from 1982's all-killer no-filler *Thriller* alone — Michael Jackson was an almighty B-side curmudgeon, sometimes offering fans an inferior live version or remix for their support, often much, much less. 'Shout', only available as the B-side of UK single 'Cry', was something of a rare gift. First intended for 2001's *Invincible* — the lavish 77-minute album that reputedly cost $30,000,000 to record — it was replaced at the eleventh hour by a saccharine paean to his children, 'You Are My Life'. Above a jagged, recycled Teddy Riley beat (first road-tested on Guy's 'Do It'), the daring sensory assault of 'Shout' found Jackson showing off his little-used but not ineffective rap skills over a screaming guitar figure that recalled guest turns by Eddie Van Halen ('Beat It') and Slash ('Give In To Me'). Possibly intended as a socially conscious equivalent to Prince's 'Sign O' The Times', if its lyrics about conspicuous consumption, the nine-to-five, child-on-child homicide and drug-addicted babies seemed miles adrift from the pampered unreality of Jackson's life at Neverland, there was no doubt about his performative conviction. It was later covered live by Backstreet Boys.

## 'Shut Out The Light'

Bruce Springsteen
COLUMBIA 1984
A-Side: 'Born In The USA'

**Moving companion to fist-pumping A-side.**

'Born In The USA' might have made Bruce Springsteen a superstar, but it came at the price of being gravely misunderstood. A bitter critique of American foreign policy and lament for imperilled working-class identity, the A-side's message was all but lost behind a bombastic chorus and artwork replicating the American flag. If that became a hit for the wrong reasons, there was no mistaking the message of its B-side. An acoustic lament, written after reading Vietnam veteran Ron Kovic's memoir *Born On The 4th Of July*, 'Shut Out The Light' described the life of a returning Vietnam veteran in explicit terms — as he grappled with trauma and dislocation, haunted by visions and memories. Stark and restrained, detailed with gospel-tinged backing vocals and Soozie Tyrell's spare violin, its intimate lyrical details — the anxious wife who undoes an extra button on her blouse, the 'Johnny Welcome Home' banner, the polished chrome on his car — it accentuated how much his life had changed. Before he played this B-side at his Breathless in Paris concert in 1985, Springsteen revealed that he received his draft papers in 1969 but failed his medical due to concussion from an earlier motorcycle accident. A sort of Masonic handshake for true-blue Springsteen heads, 'Shut Out The Light' ranks alongside the punky 75-second concision of 'Held Up Without A Gun' ['Hungry Heart', 1980] and the Duane Eddy-styled retro thrills of 'Pink Cadillac' ['Dancing In The Dark', 1984].

## 'Shut Up'

Stormzy
MERKY 2015
A-Side: 'WickedSkengMan 4'

**Lyrical smackdown proves pivotal grime moment.**

The 'WickedSkengMan' freestyle series was the making of Stormzy. By the time the tall, confident Croydon rapper born Michael Omari had recorded its fourth iteration, word about his lyrical ambition and deep flow had spread beyond the grime scene's confines. 'Shut Up', originally a video shot in a South London carpark, further established his freestyle panache, his naturally deep rumble spewing out a scathing riposte to rumour mongers "chatting bare fucking shit" and calling him a "back-up dancer" over producer XTC's well-rinsed 'Functions On The Low' instrumental. Reputedly directed at Wiley's younger brother Cadell, Stormzy took over the bragging rights as he referenced his small-time drug-dealing past and contested: "I set trends/Dem man copy". After he performed this B-side during boxer Anthony Joshua's ring-walk at the 02 Arena in December 2015, Stormzy launched a campaign to take his viral sensation to number one at Christmas, ahead of *X-Factor* winner Louisa Johnson. Despite boasting over 35 million YouTube views, 'Shut Up' didn't quite make it, but still went one place higher than Johnson at number eight.

## 'Silence Is Golden'

The 4 Seasons
PHILIPS 1964
A-Side: 'Rag Doll'

**New Jersey doo-wop updaters' doomed romance.**

The Four Seasons specialised in old style pop of the sweetest hue. A band who'd been around the block several times, they scraped by on session fees before they hit big with 'Sherry' in 1962. The hits kept coming afterwards, mini-soap opera 'Rag Doll' making the most of lead singer Frankie Valli's falsetto with its dramatic octave shift at the close. A co-write between their Philadelphia producer Bob Crewe and singer/organist Bob Gaudio, its balladic B-side was written from the point of view of a man secretly in love with a woman already spoken for, one who watched from afar as her boyfriend deceived her and, to smite himself further, decided to mind his own business. Augmented with swooping harp glissandos and vibrato guitars, Valli's emotional intelligence helped make the most of a threadbare lyric culled from a 19th century German proverb. Covered by the Tremeloes, with guitarist Rick West gamely handling Valli's falsetto, the Essex beat outfit took 'Silence Is Golden' to number one in the UK in 1967.

### 'Silver Springs'

Fleetwood Mac
WARNER BROS 1977
A-Side: 'Go Your Own Way'

**Radio-friendly revenge, best served cold.**

Fleetwood Mac's monster-selling *Rumours* had a hellish back story. Recorded as the band's resident couples — Christine and John McVie, Stevie Nicks and Lindsey Buckingham — were on the verge of breaking up, Mick Fleetwood, founding drummer and fifth wheel, had to arbitrate between Buckingham and Nicks' songs about each other. They somehow rolled with the heightened tensions and made their private pain universal, creating a soft-rock blockbuster that became America's 4th best-selling album of all time. Considered too long and too slow to fit in (it was bumped it in favour of 'I Don't Want To Know'), 'Silver Springs' was Nicks' defiant personal response to Buckingham's break-up tale 'Go Your Own Way' — making this a rare single that tells two sides of the same story. Carefully structured so that its harmonised chorus has maximum impact when fully unveiled, Nicks later told *The Arizona Republic* that its stalkerish lyrics were deliberate — she wrote the song to tell Buckingham: "I'm so angry with you. You will listen to me on the radio for the rest of your life, and it will bug you." The radio part failed to materialise initially and Nicks even quit the band in 1990 when Fleetwood refused to let her include it on solo greatest hits LP *Timespace*. When Fleetwood Mac reunited in 1997 to record live album *The Dance* a cathartic version of 'Silver Springs', complete with video footage revealing Nicks-Buckingham's still confrontational stage chemistry, became a single in its own right and won Nicks a Grammy.

### 'Sing With Your Eyes'

Jon & Vangelis
ARISTA 1991
A-Side: 'Wisdom Chain'

**Long-in-tooth prog duo get emotionally direct.**

Jon & Vangelis's connections ran deep. The singer with prog-rock behemoths Yes and the Oscar-winning sound-tracker to *Chariots Of Fire* and *Blade Runner* first crossed paths in 1974, when the keyboardist (formerly in Greek outfit Aphrodite's

Child with Demis Roussos) stood in for the departing Rick Wakeman. Having enjoyed pop success together in the early 80s and written Donna Summer's hit 'State Of Independence' (whose bassline Michael Jackson allegedly slowed down for 'Billie Jean'), they attempted to repeat it on their 4th LP *Page Of Life*, only for Arista to sit on the master tapes for five years, destroying any lingering momentum. And while multi-voiced A-side 'Wisdom Chain' flopped, stuck in a grandiose bygone age, its non-album flip proved more passionate and direct as Vangelis' genteel piano refrain and Anderson's simple pledge of love swelled to a grand synthesised climax. A flop single, issued to little fanfare after their partnership had dissolved, it would later become much sought-after by fans.

### 'Sleeping Gas (Live)'

The Teardrop Explodes
MERCURY 1982
A-Side: 'Tiny Children'

**Fried version of Liverpool band's first single.**

"Every day we would wake up, take acid, then ride to the studio on our imaginary horses," recounted Julian Cope in his memoir *Head On* vis-à-vis a typical day in Teardrop Explodes as they set about recording second LP *Wilder.* Previously abstemious, Cope's wholehearted embrace of LSD would fundamentally shift the focus of his 60s psych-tinged band, derailing the chart trajectory that had given them a Top 10 hit the previous year with 'Reward'. Instant teenybop stardom sat uneasily on Cope's narrow shoulders, whose drug intake and growing megalomania saw him hiring and firing band members at will, not least keyboardist David Balfe. And while the returning Balfe's ethereal synths proved fundamental to its bruised, despairing A-side, the real grease was a nine-minute live version of first single 'Sleeping Gas', captured at Liverpool's Club Zoo the previous December. Introduced with a trademark bark of "Hey, hey what's that sound!" it quickly morphed into an audible trip as a deranged Cope dispensed with its verses before he barked like a dog and threatened to "savage the audience" as Balfe's organ and a hired horn section made merry around its motoric bassline. Two thirds in, Cope suddenly announced: "The people at the front are now witnessing a face solo", having convinced himself that the song was a plane that only he could steer back down to earth. Thrilling, out-there and off-the-map, it was a Just-Say-No campaign on wax and the antithesis of lazily filling up a B-side's grooves with a run-of-the-mill live take.

### 'Slippin' And Slidin' (Peepin' And Hidin')'

Little Richard and His Band
SPECIALITY 1956
A-Side: 'Long Tall Sally'

**Extravagant rock 'n' roll revolutionary at his peak.**

Raw, primal, sexualised, Little Richard was without precedence. The singer and pianist's onstage flamboyance gave conservative parents the collywobbles during the Eisenhower-era. His rise from humble beginnings in Macon, Georgia — where he was one of a church deacon's dozen children — was rapid as he leapt from an impromptu onstage performance with Sister Rosetta Tharpe to launching rock 'n' roll rallying cry "A wop bop a loo bop a wop bam boom!" on 1955's first single 'Tutti Frutti'. No expense was spared nailing the right take for its frantic, howling follow-up, 'Long Tall Sally'. Richard's rapid-fire vocal delivery was even more pronounced — somewhere 'twixt scream and holler — on its influential flipside 'Slippin' And Slidin''. A rousing soundtrack to many a teenage knee-trembler, it found Richard pounding madly away on the piano as a crack team of New Orleans' session players conjured brassy magic. While the B-side would prove to have complicated origins — Richard ripped its tune and most of the lyrics from Eddie Bo's 'I'm Wise' (itself an adaptation of Al Collins' obscure R&B number 'I Got The Blues For You') — his transformation rocketed it to number 33 on the US pop chart. Much covered (by Dickie Pride, Buddy Holly, Otis Redding) it was especially loved by the Beatles. And while John Lennon included it on 1975's covers album *Rock 'N' Roll* (where it was scheduled to be the B-side of 'Ain't That A Shame'), Paul McCartney's fondness for falsetto came directly from Richard — he taught him how to scream in tune at New Brighton's Tower Ballroom in 1962.

### 'Slow Down'

Larry Williams
SPECIALTY 1958
A-Side: 'Dizzy, Miss Lizzy'

**Fab Four-loved rock 'n' roll workout.**

Larry Williams was an unsung rock 'n' roll hero. On the hunt for another Little Richard — now retired from secular music and in his gospel phase — Specialty unearthed 19-year-old leg-shaking New Orleans heartbreaker Williams (previously a singer in California teen band the Lemon Drops) and devoted its energy into making him a star. If the A-side was a straight-up Richard pastiche, 'Slow Down' — a song that made you want to do the exact opposite — was something else. Williams was in his element throughout, his high-energy piano groove and ecstatic wails umbilically knotted within Earl Palmer's big-snare backbeat before they cleared the deck for Plas Johnson's tenor sax. Yet it failed to stop the A-side stalling at number 69 on the pop charts and brought Williams' chart career to a screeching halt. And while it led him into a life blighted by drugs, guns and prison (its nadir coming in 1977, when he threatened life-long friend Richard at gunpoint over a drug deal gone sour), Williams' proved a critical influence on the Beatles, who covered both sides during their long Hamburg residencies. Although essentially faithful, their studio reproductions — 'Dizzy, Miss Lizzy' on *Help!*, 'Slow Down' on the 'Long Tall Sally EP' — barely lit a candle to the originals.

**'So What?'**
Anti-Nowhere League
WXYZ 1981
A-Side: 'Streets Of London'

**Sneering misanthropy from punk second-wavers.**

Anti-Nowhere League set out their agenda on their first single. The Tunbridge Wells punks, fronted by no-nonsense growler Animal, proved nothing had changed for the better on the A-side's disgusted thrash through Ralph McTell's sobering tale of destitution. If that stated the obvious, its cheerfully offensive, stop-start B-side — a snarled riff on 'Nick Nack Paddy Whack' — made their name. Inspired by overhearing two men trying to out-do each other in drunken pub boasts, its first verse's genteel bants about going to Hastings, Brighton and Eastbourne were quickly supplanted by increasingly outrageous claims about fellating old men, goat-shagging, drugs, STDs and paedophilia, all with the chorus-payoff of "So what?/So what?/You boring little cunt." The single had climbed to number 48 in the charts when 5,000 copies were seized and destroyed by the Metropolitan Police's Obscene Publication Squad. Legally forbidden from including it on 1982's debut LP *We Are...The League*, the band capitalised with a headline 'So What?' UK tour alongside punk veterans Chelsea instead. Their best-known song by some distance, it became a B-side again when Metallica covered it for 1993's 'Sad But True', but effectively obliterated its crass bad taste.

**'Song To The Siren'**
This Mortal Coil
4AD 1983
A-Side: 'Sixteen Days/Gathering Dust'

**Folk cover redefines cult indie label.**

Ivo Watts-Russell's indie supergroup This Mortal Coil was borne from a simple premise. When Modern English, one of the mysterious 4AD label supremo's prestige acts, rebuffed his request to record a medley, he decided to do it anyway, vocal turns from Cocteau Twins' Elizabeth Fraser and Cindytalk's Gordon Sharp transforming the source material. Stuck for a B-side of the nine-minute, 12-inch offering, he asked Fraser to cover his favourite song — Tim Buckley's 'Song To The Siren' — with partner Robin Guthrie. A haunting ballad awash with oceanic imagery, it suited Fraser's ethereal voice to a tee, her trademark melasmas and Guthrie's echo-filled guitar transforming it into a weeping Gaelic hymn. Quickly re-released as a seven-inch A-side, 'Song To The Siren' was moored to the independent charts for two years and sold over half a million copies, prompting Watts-Russell to expand This Mortal Coil into an albums project. It led to an overdue reappraisal of Buckley's career (and a kinship between Fraser and his ill-starred son Jeff), plus defining big screen roles in David Lynch's *Lost Highway* and Peter Jackson's *The Lovely Bones*. In many ways it remains 4AD's defining release.

**'Sophia Loren'**
Sophie Ellis-Bextor
EBGB 2010
A-Side: 'Bittersweet'

**Lost banger from first lady of posh disco.**

After her millennial number 1 'Groovejet (If This Ain't Love)' with Spiller, Sophie

Ellis-Bextor refused to look back. The plummy-toned ex-singer with indie bedwetters Theaudience transformed herself from indie ingenue into an unlikely disco diva, albeit one happy to jump on prevailing pop trends rather than set the agenda. If the busy Freemasons-masterminded electro of 'Bittersweet' was prime serviceable fluff, a rare treat was hidden on its shuffling flip. From its opening handclaps and title chant, this co-write with Cathy Dennis and Chris Rojas screamed hit potential, its spare synth wallop and distorted guitar reverberating with Ellis-Bextor's enthused tales about living *la dolce vita* and riding Vespas. Once intended as lead single for Ellis-Bextor's slick 4th album *Make A Scene*, 'Sophia Loren' gradually slid down the pecking order before falling off it altogether. It was certainly superior to much of that album's supermarket pop-by-numbers and gained enough cult status to be resuscitated at Ellis-Bextor's Instagram kitchen discos during 2020's first COVID-19 outbreak.

**'Sorrow'**
The McCoys
BANG 1965
A-Side: 'Fever'

**Bowie-loved garage rock nugget.**

Indiana garage band the McCoys were still in high school when they topped the charts with 1965's elemental first single 'Hang On Sloopy'. Before the dust could settle, they cashed-in, retaining an almost identical sound for their gnarly take on Little Willie John's much-abused standard 'Fever'. A rare exception to their derivative formula came on its B-side 'Sorrow' — a slow-paced, countrified original penned by their producers Bob Feldman, Jerry Goldstein and Richard Gottehrer (core of Brooklyn hitmakers the Strangeloves). With its longing lyrics, soothing harmonies and haunted harmonica figure, it showed a subtler side of the band headed by sixteen-year-old guitar stylist Rick Derringer. An uptempo refresh by Liverpool Cavern Club regulars the Merseys blasted into the UK Top 5 the following year and it was reinterpreted again by David Bowie, as he retreated from his *Ziggy Stardust* persona, on 1973's covers set *Pin Ups*. Reworked with a fresh Mick Ronson string arrangement, piano countermelody by Mike Garson and Bowie's distinctive 12-string acoustic guitar, it went Top 3, bolstered by an extraordinary B-side cover of Jacque Brel's 'Amsterdam'.

### 'Sorry Sorry Pardon What'

Wiley
BIG DADA 2007
A-Side: 'My Mistakes'

**Eskiboy at his wild-roving best.**

Long before he wilfully trashed his career with anti-Semitic Twitter rants in 2020, Wiley made his name on UK garage crew Pay As U Go's freestyles on pirate radio station Rinse FM. A hyper prolific grime originator, with or without his subsequent Roll Deep crew, he was in full production mode when he came up with the skittish and abrasive 'Ice Rink' instrumental — possibly grime's signature beat. And while his Wiley Kat label pushed out two different EPs in 2003 with MCs such as Kano, Sharkey Major, Tinchy Stryder and Dizzee Rascal riding its minimalist riddim, Wiley held off attacking it himself until 2007. It was a genius move. A far more dextrous and advanced rapper by that point, his unrelenting lyrics bristled with composed aggression (worth it for the third verse's sustained riff on 'William' alone) either side of a sampled chorus hook lifted from Dizzee Rascal's version. A renegade from his infamous *Tunnel Vision* mixtape series refashioned into the seven-inch B-side of 'My Mistakes' — a single issued amid Wiley's empty threats to hang up the mic for good. Much graver errors of judgement would follow.

### 'Soul Makossa'

Manu Dibango
AFRICAN 1972
A-Side: 'Hymne De La 8e Coupe D'Afrique Des Nations'

**Lion of Africa creates early disco anthem.**

Cameroon jazz saxophonist Manu Dibango had started to make a dent on the world stage when he penned the A-side here — an optimistic tribute to his native football team as they hosted 1972's Africa Cup Of Nations. While that was a major flop so, at first, was its B-side. In Dibango's 1994 autobiography, *Three Kilos Of Coffee*, he revealed that people at first made fun of its stuttering refrain "Ma-ma-ko ma-ma-sa mako-makossa!" and were dubious about his soul and jazz doused spin on a popular Cameroonian dance style. 'Soul Makossa' (literal translation: I will dance) was forgotten about until New York DJ David Mancuso started to play it at his underground loft parties and WBLS DJ Frankie Crocker introduced it to the wider public. When Atlantic licensed it as an A-side in 1973 it became a Big Apple club hit and cracked the US Top 40, beating off a sharp cover by Los Angeles' studio chancers Afrique. Regarded, in some quarters, as the first disco record, it clearly inspired Kool & the Gang's 'Hollywood Swinging' and Michael Jackson's 'Wanna Be Startin' Somethin''. While the latter lifted its distinctive refrain wholesale (sampled, in turn, by Rihanna for 2007's 'Don't Stop the Music'), numerous rappers (including Kanye West, Jay-Z and Childish Gambino) have also plundered its good time vibes.

## 'Soul To Squeeze'

Red Hot Chili Peppers
WARNER BROS 1991
A-Side: 'Give It Away'

**Soulful side of LA's age-defying funk-rockers.**

Dark clouds gave way to light for Red Hot Chili Peppers at the start of the 90s. Having survived the tragedy of losing founder Hillel Slovak to a heroin overdose and successfully integrated new drummer Chad Smith and guitarist John Frusciante into the ranks, MTV started to back their increasingly commercial brand of bad boy funk. Recorded amid lengthy sessions for fifth outing *Blood Sugar Sex Magik* with Rick Rubin, they evidently didn't rate the relatively mellow 'Soul To Squeeze' and left it off the double album. An emotive look at singer Anthony Kiedis' struggles with heroin addiction and battle for peace of mind set to Frusciante's weeping guitar and a searching Flea bassline, it was arguably stronger than some of the ballads they retained. Dusted off again as one of multiple B-sides to their big breakthrough hit 'Under The Bridge', it became an A-side in its own right in 1993 in a tie-in with Dan Ackroyd's crude sci-fi comedy *Coneheads*. And while that rightly bombed, the single didn't, reaching 22 on the US charts.

## 'Southern Can Is Mine'

Blind Sammie
COLUMBIA 1931
A-Side: 'Broke Down Engine Blues'

**Country blues innovator's no-nonsense directive.**

The mystery and mythology of its outlaw bluesmen provided a necessary escape for Americans at the height of the depression. None more so than Blind Willie McTell. Whatever name he used on record — he also recorded as Georgia Bill, Red Hot Willie Glaze and, here, Blind Sammie — there was no mistaking the born rambler's unusually sweet, quivering voice, nor his discrete picking on his 12-string acoustic guitar. There was nothing sweet about the Georgia bluesman's growls about feeling ground down like an ageing automobile on the A-side, however, his woes compounded by gambling debts and female troubles. The jauntily played but outwardly hostile sentiments of B-side 'Southern Can Is Mine' took it up another notch. A succession of warnings that if his women wanted to "get crooked I'm gonna give you my fist", its violent threats soon piled up, with the blind singer improbably invoking house bricks and barbed wire fences as additional punishments. Yet given the dark dry wit of McTell's other material, it's possible his infectious-as-hell tune was rendered with his tongue in cheek. The White Stripes would go on to introduce it to a new generation on 2000's *De Stijl*.

**'Spirit'**
Sade
EPIC 1984
A-Side: 'Smooth Operator'

**Sophisticated soul aesthetes' hidden gem.**

Quality control was at the heart of the Sade franchise. Not just the singer they were named after (ex-model Sade Adu), the London band minted a soothing, mature sound as they fused soul, pop and jazz on a scene pivoted around Soho's Wag Club. It was hard to tell if their Nigeria-born singer Adu was celebrating or deriding the titular playboy of 'Smooth Operator' — a US breakthrough single initially frittered away on the 12-inch B-side of 'Your Love Is King' — although the longer album version provided a clue. An incredibly measured and decidedly non-prolific band, usually immune to doling out treats as B-sides, Sade bucked form here — not only offering a unique stand-alone but showing a new side to their talents. Clearly designed to move butts, the simple entreaties to go with the flow and keep the faith of 'Spirit' were offset by funky guitars that nodded heavily towards Chic and an indomitable bass groove. It stood apart from the barrel-aged sophistication of their debut *Diamond Life*.

### 'Spitting Out The Demons'

Gorillaz
PARLOPHONE 2007
A-Side: 'Feel Good Inc.'

**Virtual band's minimalist morning-after lament.**

By their second album, *Demon Days,* Gorillaz had morphed from a three-way collaboration between Damon Albarn, cartoonist Jamie Hewlett and hip-hop producer Dan The Automator into the erstwhile Blur leader's main gig. And if their chart-busting collaboration with De La Soul 'Feel Good Inc.' retained the light genre-fluid pop of their breakthrough hit 'Clint Eastwood', the vibe was much darker and more theatrically foreboding. Some of that darkness spilled into 'Spitting Out The Demons'. A song centred on ridding yourself of sin and bowing down to a higher power, it built momentum slowly, its twinkly keys overtaken by a distorted bass figure before woozy synth chords and flinty guitars joined the fray. It was seemingly going nowhere fast, stuck in a warm stoned haze, when Albarn's dark vocal chants kicked in, alluding to his dalliances with heroin in a delivery redolent of vintage Terry Hall. Albarn also performed the B-side live, speeding it up a little, when he toured 2014's first solo album *Everyday Robots*.

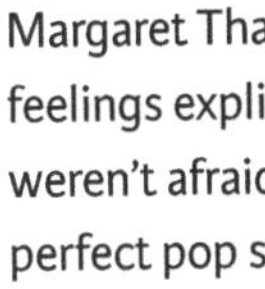

### 'Stand Down Margaret (Dub)'

The Beat
GO-FEET 1980
A-Side: 'Best Friend'

**Ska band protest milk-snatching PM.**

Margaret Thatcher had only been in office a year when the Beat made their feelings explicit on debut LP *I Just Can't Stop It*. The Birmingham ska outfit weren't afraid to throw their pork pie hats into the ring, fashioning a suite of perfect pop songs that blended the personal with the political. This single did the same. While driving A-side 'Best Friend' included a nifty line about narcissism (a preoccupation of chief songwriter Dave Wakeling? cf: previous single 'Mirror In The Bathroom'), its B-side's dub take on LP track 'Stand Down Margaret' (initially presented as a medley with Prince Buster's 'Whine And Grine') set its sights on 10 Downing Street's latest incumbent. Among the first anti-Thatcher songs to reach vinyl, the B-side mix maxed out on its dubby bassline and high-life guitars, flanging toaster Ranking Roger's vocals in and out with his references to her "cold grey hands" and premonitions of war proving particularly resonant. The Beat even smuggled its protest pop onto national TV. Given a coveted slot of children's game show *Cheggers Plays Pop*, saxophonist Saxa convinced host Keith Chegwin its title was the name an old Caribbean dance — an illusion quickly destroyed when they unzipped their jackets to reveal T-shirts that juxtaposed the Iron Lady's grim visage with a nuclear mushroom cloud. An alternative national anthem that paved the way for more overtly political pop hits from the Jam, UB40 and Heaven 17, it raised over £14,000 for CND.

### 'Standing Here'

The Stone Roses
SILVERTONE 1989
A-Side: 'She Bangs The Drums'

**Manchester band's mysterious two-parter.**

There were few obvious fault lines to the Stone Roses as the 80s shuffled to a close in ill-fitting Joe Bloggs flares. If the euphoric A-side here needs little introduction, 'Standing Here' seems to have eluded many pop historians. After a blast of John Squire's best Hendrix impression, the guitarist launched into a series of fluid blues licks that weaved in and out of bassist Mani and drummer Reni's rhythmic funk clatter as singer Ian Brown laid on the mystery with a stalker-ish short story addressed at an unwitting quarry. Just as it seemed content to play out one way, a fresh melancholic guitar figure tinkled in and Brown mysteriously murmured that he could "park a juggernaut in your mouth". Once earmarked as a potential A-side, this steady live favourite was reprised again for 2016's reunion tour. Along with fellow Manchester bands the Smiths and Oasis (who possibly lifted a bit of this flip's melody on 'Cloudburst'), the Stone Roses rarely short-changed fans on B-sides, whether spotlighting romantic betrayal on 'Where Angels Play' ['I Wanna Be Adored', 1989] or wilding out with xylophones, bongos and wah-wah pedals on 'Something's Burning' ['One Love', 1990].

## 'Stardust'

Hoagy Carmichael & His Pals
GENNETT 1928
A-Side: 'One Night In Havana'

**The 20th century's most enduring jazz standard.**

Hoagy Carmichael was a sophisticated, meticulous jazz craftsman. The suave Tin Pan Alley singer, composer and actor was studying law at Indiana University when he started whistling the melody to 'Stardust' while walking across campus. "I knew that I had something very strange and different," he later told the BBC, and rushed home to write it down. Soon afterwards the hot pianist and bandleader recorded the instrumental for the Starr Piano Company's Gennett label. With Carmichael on piano alongside Emil Seidel And His Orchestra, there was a rare elegance to the recording that bolstered its dreamlike dynamic. Yet Gennett had other ideas. Dissatisfied with the quality of the studio take, they considered destroying the masters before opting to put it on the B-side of slow foxtrot original 'One Night In Havana' instead (where they erroneously labelled it a 'stomp'). While the single barely sold out of its pressing, the B-side's wistful melody would evolve into a jazz standard after Carmichael published the song as covers by McKinney's Cotton Pickers and Irving Mills' Hotsy Totsy Gang paved the way for Bing Crosby's smash vocal rendition in 1931. Later recorded by Louis Armstrong, John Coltrane and Nat King Cole, among many others, Carmichael never ceased tinkering with his creation and returned to it throughout his career, often at its more familiar slow tempo.

## 'Stay Close To Me'

Bad Brains
BAD BRAIN 1980
A-Side: 'Pay To Cum'

**Hardcore innovators show chilled-out side.**

Bad Brains were a key part of an American hardcore scene that reimagined British punk rock during the 80s. The black Washington DC outfit weren't short of real chops, evolving from jazz fusion ensemble Mind Power after they heard Sex Pistols. Yet the Rastafarians' fiery marriage of punk and reggae, played at break-neck speed to better display their technical skills, was not an instant hit in their hometown, leading to numerous club bans and all but forcing their hand into a

DIY first single. In contrast to the fast, precision-etched 93-second A-side, 'Stay Close To Me' was a tender, punky tale of devotion that made best use of Bad Brains' musical arsenal, sauntering along to an almost 2-Tone ska beat before distorted power chords kicked into its chorus. While Bad Brains would finesse their blistering harness of punk velocity and reggae ideology on 1983's *Rock For Light* — a crucial screed that showed the way for 24-7 Spyz, Fishbone and Living Colour — this single helped the hardcore scene find its feet.

### 'Stop The World I Wanna Get Off With You'

Arctic Monkeys
DOMINO 2013
A-Side: 'Why'd You Only Call Me When You're High'

**Afterhours pop with a whiff of goat.**

In the lead-up to Arctic Monkeys' fifth album *AM*, singer Alex Turner upset some of his fanbase's more rank and file members by telling the *NME* their new album was "less like four lads playing in a room this time" and referencing Dr. Dre. While he was possibly overstating the set's rap bones, there was a certifiable G-Funk frisson to late-night booty-calling A-side here, brought out even further when Miley Cyrus tackled it on an *MTV Unplugged* special. Its similarly swaggering B-side took a slightly more romantic tack. It allowed Alex Turner's increasingly slick vocal to essay a party scenario, where he disliked everyone bar one and declared his frisky intentions over an up-and-down bass riff, jaunty piano figure and stuttering hip-hop beats. Even the rank and file seemed to dig it, the B-side garnering enough streams to propel it to number 74 on the UK charts. It joined a pantheon of affecting Arctic Monkeys' B-sides including the teenage dating traumas of 'Bigger Boys And Stolen Sweethearts' ['I Bet You Look Good On The Dance Floor', 2005] and surprise Dizzee Rascal duet 'Temptation Greets You Like Your Naughty Friend' ['Brianstorm', 2007].

### 'Strong As Death (Sweet As Love)'

Al Green
HI 1975
A-Side: 'Oh Me, Oh My (Dreams In My Arms)'

**70s soul goliath's best-kept secret.**

No singer was as seductive as Al Green in the 70s. The Arkansas star's superlative six album run — from 1970's debut *Green Is Blues* to 1975's *Al Green I Love*, American R&B chart-toppers all — was unmatched in craft, sound and success. Green was indebted to a critical hook-up with Willie Mitchell's Hi imprint and its inhouse Hi Rhythm Section — the slinky talents of brothers Charles, Leroy and Mabon 'Teenie' Hodges augmented by Stax drum legend Al Jackson, Jr. A welcome, if much darker companion to the A-side's blessed funk, 'Strong As Death (Sweet As Love)' caught Green at his most heart-rending as he compared the urges for love and death over aching strings, a sweet but sour guitar solo and some ghostly vibraphone work. Written for his on-off girlfriend Mary Woodson, Green recorded it hours before she threw a pot of boiling pot of grits over him for rejecting her marriage proposal. And while, as his 2000 autobiography *Take Me To The River* recalled, "my world exploded into a thousand splatters of pure agony" there was much worse to come than the 'egg-sized blisters' on his burned flesh. The next sound he heard was Woodson shooting herself dead with his gun. The incident changed the soul star's life forever — Green read it as a sign from god to enter the ministry. By 1976 he was presiding over the Full Gospel Tabernacle Church in Memphis.

## 'Sucker MCs (Krush Groove 1)'

Run-DMC

PROFILE 1983

A-Side: 'It's Like That'

**B-boy anthem announces hip-hop's second wave.**

Simplicity was at the core of Run-DMC's breakthrough first single. A trio of tight friends from the New York borough of Hollis, Queens, rappers Run, DMC and DJ Jam Master Jay caused a revolution in rhyme by stripping hip-hop right back to brass tacks. 'It's Like That' led the charge as the trio cast their magnifying glass over the state of their locale, and found it wanting, over a particularly blunt backing. The sheer raw energy of B-side 'Sucker MCs' proved the clincher. Among hip-hop's first dis tracks, it witnessed rappers Run and DMC denigrating their foes over handclaps and rock-hard Oberheim DMX beats (later sampled by Aphex Twin, Backstreet Boys and Drake). And while Run offered up standard boasts about his car and sex appeal, DMC was more relatable, proclaiming "I go to Saint John's University" and noting his dietary fondness for "chicken and collard greens" as their contrasting personalities shone through loud and clear. It blew up on radio and reset hip-hop's sonic template. In a stroke rap transformed from a disco offshoot into an urgent communique that reflected the thoughts of real street teenagers (Run-DMC made a virtue of dressing in the Kangols, chains, trainers and tracksuits their fans could relate to). It also excited multiple covers, with Wu-Tang Clan, Lordz of Brooklyn and UK rap satirist Pitman all having a pop.

## 'Sugar Mountain'

Neil Young
REPRISE 1968
A-Side: 'The Loner'

**Affecting rumination on lost youth.**

Written while Los Angeles' folk-rockers Buffalo Springfield were falling apart, Neil Young's first solo single proved that their lead guitarist and most esoteric songwriter was in it for the long haul. If the autobiographical, string-laden 'The Loner' exposed the fragility of Young's high-tenor voice, its noisy guitar leads also prefigured his future Crazy Horse antics. The single's B-side was much older, a first glimpse of the balladeer that would slay MOR hearts with 1972's 'Heart Of Gold'. Written after he quit first band the Squires on his nineteenth birthday, 'Sugar Mountain' focussed on leaving an idyllic childhood behind and crossing into the unknowns of adulthood, the premature nostalgia of its repeated evocations of county fairs, midway barkers, cotton candy and balloons stirring up deep emotions. Young had to violently edit its original draft of 126 verses down to just four when it was finally recorded four years later (he would repeatedly castigate himself onstage for its weak 3rd verse), during an intimate performance at Ann Arbor's Canterbury House. The song's over-the-hill-by-20 sentiments had such a powerful effect on Joni Mitchell that the Canadian singer-songwriter wrote 'Circle Game' as a more hopeful rejoinder. Young's long-time live favourite became a B-side twice when it was coupled with 1970's 'Cinnamon Girl'.

**'Sunshine'**
Uriah Heap
BRONZE 1973
A-Side: 'Stealin''

**Prog-metal forerunners shed mystical edge.**
When they checked into the plush confines of Château d'Hérouville, just outside Paris, to record their sixth studio LP *Sweet Freedom*, Uriah Heap were dead set on returning to the heads-down hard rock of their earliest releases. The London band named after the scheming lawyer from Dickens' *David Copperfield* had grown weary of the madcap attentions of US occultists, who took the lyrics of early 70s sets *Demons And Wizards* and *The Magician's Birthday* at face value. Although they managed it without losing their firepower, regret-riven A-side 'Stealin'' failed to chart in the UK despite boasting all the ingredients for a huge radio hit (which it was in faraway New Zealand). It meant fair-weather Heap-heads missed its rousing flip 'Sunshine' — a rare song from guitarist Mick Box and bassist Gary Thai, predicated on a wah-wah-powered central riff and screeching Hammond organ fills as singer David Byron displayed his impressive range. A great hulk of a B-side, it was left to wander around lost when Heap's heads-down strategy backfired.

**'Surfing And Spying'**
The Go Gos
IRS 1981
A-Side: 'Our Lips Are Sealed'

**California girls get their full surf-punk on.**
The Go Go's roots poked through 1981's big-selling debut *Beauty And The Beat*. The all-girl band that emerged from Hollywood punks the Misfits slowed their breakneck songs right down to emphasise their sweet pop hooks, at the insistence of veteran Blondie producer Richard Gottehrer, but still sprinkled dirty surf guitar riffs over its shiny surface. While Belinda Carlisle's exuberant vocal made the A-side — the silken pop gift of a brief affair between the Specials' Terry Hall and guitarist Jane Weidlin that yielded wildly contrasting hits for both writers — the unprepossessing 'Surfing And Spying' lived up to its descriptive title. Short and to the point, it let guitarist Charlotte Caffey show off her six-string smarts while

paying tribute to one of her favourite bands, the Ventures. The appreciation proved mutual. The pioneering surf-rockers both covered it and made it an A-side just a year later (with Carlisle's one-time roommate Pleasant Gehman plastered over its sleeve). Even when the Go Gos began to implode around 1984's *Talk Show*, amid rancour and addiction, this B-side remained an oven-ready live favourite.

### 'Susanne'

Weezer
GEFFEN 1994
A-Side: 'Undone — The Sweater Song'

**Geek icons' sweet heavy power-pop.**

'Susanne' ranks among Rivers Cuomo's sweetest moments. Having signed to Geffen in 1993 with great expectations, the Los Angeles' unlikely lads led by songwriter and Harvard student Cuomo were in limbo, bewildered by the protracted delays to the release of their Ric Ocasek-produced debut (self-titled but generally known as *The Blue Album*). It led him to pen 'Susanne', an open-hearted tribute to the Geffen A&R assistant who helped keep their spirits up, and made them brownies, during the wait. First performed a cappella in her Geffen office, a studio take found a fitting home on the B-side of 'Undone' — the first Weezer song to catch MTV fire thanks to its one-take Spike Jones video. And with its buoyant, romantic lyric, undulating Pixies bassline, crunchy guitars and Beach Boys harmony vocals, it seemed a natural bedfellow to their incoming crossover smash 'Buddy Holly'. Weezer's most-played B-side live, 'Suzanne' made its big screen debut at the end of Kevin Smith's muffled second movie *Mallrats* in 1995, just as Cuomo returned to Harvard to study classical composition.

### 'Suzy & Jeffrey'

Blondie
CHRYSALIS 1980
A-Side: 'The Tide Is High'

**NYC power-poppers' mysterious death disc.**

As the 70s closed Blondie were among the planet's biggest bands. The Big Apple sextet led by tough yet vulnerable ex-Playboy pin-up Debbie Harry were determined not to blithely press repeat on 1979's multi-platinum *Eat To The Beat* as they welcomed jazz, blues, hip-hop and reggae influences to cascade through their critic-confounding fifth LP *Autoamerican* (a streamlined alternative to the Clash's sprawling *Sandinista!)*. And while the A-side's sunny reframing of the Paragons' 1967 rocksteady staple kept them at the number one summit, flippers were given something much bluer and hauntingly beautiful to conjure with. Written with bassist Nigel Harrison, Harry took the names of a troubled young couple who had crashed through the wall of Blondie's studio to construct a great ultra-downer B-side, replete with intriguing references to Charles Manson's one-time residence Spahn Ranch, Orson Welles and the STD blood tests US states used to insist on prior to marriage. Harry was in peak deadpan form as she dispensed her detached tale of doomed romance, detailed with Jimmy Destri's siren-like synths, Chris Stein's twanging tremolo guitar and vintage sound effects.

**'Sweet Intuition'**

Björk

ONE LITTLE INDIAN 1995

A-Side: 'Army Of Me'

**Icelandic polymath reworks her song for Madonna.**

Madonna's desire to head in a new direction on 1995's sixth album *Bedtime Story* found her honing in on the talents of a new pop rival: Björk. Heavily inspired by the Icelandic army-of-one's 1993 album *Debut* and a swathe of recent British dance music, the singer's shared producer Nelle Hooper helped swing a deal for a Björk original. Initially nonplussed, the Reykjavík wildcard soon realised fun could be had putting words into the mouth of the best-selling female artist of all time. "I decided to write the things I have always wanted to hear her say," she told biographer Marj Pytlik before handing over 'Let's Get Unconscious' to Hooper and his production foil Marius de Vries. As hypnotic and different as the resulting (and retitled) 'Bedtime Stories' was, it still sounded a lot like Björk, who took listeners right under the bonnet when she reworked her demo as 'Sweet Intuition'. If its stuttering rhythm and ambient electronics were vastly similar, the lyrics were even further abstracted, only dovetailing on its middle-eight's cry of "Inside we're all still wet." A more peaceful live version was later captured at London's Royal Festival Hall for the B-side of 'It's So Quiet'.

# TO B OR NOT TO B

*That is the question when rustling up a B-side yields unexpected results...*

This book boasts many examples of B-sides that would outstrip their A-sides, both commercially and in the eyes of fans. Many of those happened unwittingly. But there are other times when the intended inferior track is clearly anything but.

There is little doubt that 'Kiss Him Goodbye', an unfinished song by early 60s doo-wop band the Chateaus, would not have become a cultural phenomenon were it not for the double-sided single. The band had long petered into dust when their ex-singer Gary DeCarlo signed to Mercury and set his sights on the charts with proposed 1969 single 'Sweet Laura Lee', a ballad by 'Rhinestone Cowboy' songwriter Larry Weiss. Needing a throwaway B-side, his producer (and ex-Chateaus pianist) Paul Leka suggested resurrecting it and enlisted co-writer Dan Frashauer to help out. Feeling it was too bad to bother paying session musicians for, they kept it in-house, and let Leka's piano ride a loop of Ange DiGeronimo's conga drums, lifted from another session entirely. They even papered over the song's dearth of words with a whole bunch of vocal vamping — its nagging, domineering "Na na na na, hey hey, goodbye" refrain.

To their shock, Mercury A&R man Bob Reno loved it and was adamant it should become an A-side. The bemused trio at first refused to put their names

on the record (if not its writing credits) and the single, now retitled **'Na Na Hey Hey Kiss Him Goodbye'**, was issued in late 1969 under fictional band name **Steam**. Scorned as bubblegum in more sniffy quarters, it knocked the Beatles' 'Something' off the US number one spot and sold more than a million copies in America alone. A regular 70s football terrace singalong and baseball anthem (after it was first embraced by Chicago White Sox), it became a hit all over again for Bananarama and the Nylons in the 80s.

Hard-rocking Dublin band **Thin Lizzy** were hitless and luckless when their

charismatic singing bassist Phil Lynott started improvising a take on traditional Irish drinking song **'Whisky In The Jar'** as they wound-up rehearsals in a Kings Cross hostelry. Thought to have evolved from a mid-16th century folk song about murderous highwayman Patrick Fleming, its most popular reading to that point had been served up by the Dubliners on 1967's alcohol-heavy *More Of The Hard Stuff* LP. Lizzy's manager Ted Carroll was unfamiliar with their banjo and tin whistle version, but liked what he heard and suggested his charges record it as the B-side for their forthcoming 'Black Boys In The Corner' single. They reluctantly agreed, bastardising it with guitarist Eric Bell's repeated refrain (based on an old Chieftains' bagpipe part) and skewing the lyrics so its unnamed protagonist let Captain Farrell have it "with both barrels".

At Decca's insistence it became an A-side in late 1972, hitting the UK Top 10 and topping the Irish charts, despite its makers' belief that it was something of an embarrassing novelty. Their misgivings were compounded when a stream of flops followed their instant St Patrick's Day favourite, until the unstoppable swagger of 1976's 'The Boys Are Back In Town' turned that rancour to dust.

By 1980 the **Jam** had finessed their tightly-wound combo of lyrical pissed-off-ness, high-energy Pete Townsend riffs, soul yelps and growled, incisive melodies. The increasingly popular Woking mod band that rode in on punk's coattails were now four albums deep and starting to stretch their muse out in less familiar directions. That was evident on their next A-side 'Dreams Of Children' — a spacey examination of adolescent high hopes, heavily infused with Beatles-inspired psychedelia and backwards instrumentation. Its intended B-side, **'Going Underground'**, played to known strengths — condensing all their finest attributes within three minutes. Written on an acoustic guitar by their 21-year-old songwriter Paul Weller late at night in his Pimlico flat, its firecracker chorus drilled home its politically intense and frustrated verses as Weller bit back against Thatcherism's empty charades.

Elevated to a double-A-side after a fortuitous pressing plant mix-up, the power pop thrills of 'Going Underground' became the radio DJs side of choice (few bothered spinning 'Dreams Of Children') and the single entered the UK charts at number 1. The Jam were so chuffed they abandoned a US tour and

*Concorde*-ed home for *Top Of The Pops*.

**Siouxsie & the Banshees**' powers were on the wane as the 80s drew to an end. The unlikely goth-pop pioneers, spawned from a gaggle of Sex Pistols' fans known as the Bromley Contingent, had defied their early critics to become a spidery post-punk *tour-de-force*. Yet the loss of their creative guitarist John McGeoch found them making do and mending, marking time in 1987 by issuing the covers set *Through The Looking Glass*. '**Peek-A-Boo'** emerged, almost unbidden, during these sessions after producer Mike Hedges accidentally played a sample from their cover of John Cale's 'Gun' backwards. Written around the resulting loop of sound — a bizarre but bravura Charleston-hop hybrid that tipped a lyrical wink to jazz standard 'Jeepers Creepers' — they added a lurching accordion, brass samples and one-note bass before Siouxsie Sioux's ever-morphing vocal arrangement, each line sung through a different microphone.

Initially earmarked for the B-side of their cover of Iggy Pop's 'The Passenger', they squirrelled its oddball charms away for 1988's *Peepshow* LP instead, and scored their first US chart hit in the process (and the premier number one on *Billboard*'s brand-new Modern Rock chart). The single so impressed Prince, he sent a note of appreciation.

A similarly inauspicious attempt to conjure up a club-friendly B-side in 1990 spawned arguably the most emblematic song of **Madonna**'s career. Inspired by a dance craze originated in Harlem's 'ball culture', voguing was popular in New York's underground gay club scene as dancers used hand gestures and poses to emulate their favourite Hollywood stars and cover models. Written alongside her favourite remixer and Sound Factory DJ Shep Pettibone (where Madonna first saw vogueing in action), its lyrics about dancefloor escapism also aced a film brief from Madonna's then-boyfriend Warren Beatty, who asked to her write a song to fit her character Breathless Mahoney in his *Dick Tracy* film.

Recorded, on a tight budget of $5000, for the B-side of 'Keep It Together' – the last US single from *Like A Prayer* — Warner Bros executives decreed **'Vogue'** was far too good for B-side status. They backed up that belief by spending considerably more on filmmaker David Fincher's accompanying black and white video, which caught Madonna coolly name checking her heroines (Greta Garbo, Marilyn Monroe, Grace Kelly, Rita Hayworth, Bette Davis et al) in a practically see-through sheer lace blouse, flanked by House of Extravaganza dancers. Even more resplendent in its revelatory 12-inch mix, 'Vogue' touched a nerve in the HIV/AIDS era and went to number one in thirty different countries, becoming the year's best-selling single (shifting over two million copies in America alone).

Knowing self-referential types not shy of putting out powerful B-sides — see the proto-trip-hop of the Q-Tee featuring 'Filthy' ['Only Love Can Break Your Heart', 1990] — **Saint Etienne** didn't always give them away. The trio masterminded by former music scribe Bob Stanley (who showed the depth of his devotion with 2014's extended love letter *Yeah Yeah Yeah: The Story Of Modern Pop*) alongside Pete Wiggs and Sarah Cracknell, bridged the gap between clubland's cutting-edge beats and yearning 60s pop classicism, their dance-tinged early output fizzing with knowing campness.

Allegedly knocked off in ten-minutes, their perky 60s beat-pop throwback **'You're In A Bad Way'** — a Herman's Hermits homage appended with a Moog bassline and fashion advice ("Don't you know that crew cuts and trainers are out again?") — was a nailed-on B-side to 1993's 'Everlasting' single until their manager, Creation Records big cheese Alan McGee, sensed it was a hit. Incidentally, 'Everlasting' defied its title and vanished completely, eventually surfacing on an expanded reissue of *So Tough* in 2009.

**Arab Strap** blearily announced themselves to the world with **'The First Big Weekend'**. Their ironically titled ode to transient happiness was a true short story of what a group of close friends got up to — canteen quizzes, clubs, drinks, drugs, cheese, *The Simpsons* — between June 13-17, 1996. A song that can be dated specifically thanks to its reference to a Scotland/England football clash at Saint Andrews (when Paul Gascoigne scored a wondergoal and Gary McAllister missed a penalty, allegedly due to Uri Geller moving the ball by psychokinesis), its arrangement set a blueprint for much of the band's subsequent material: Aidan Moffat's matter-of-fact spoken word monologues weaving above Malcolm Middleton's fingerpicked guitars and a drum machine's metronomic pulse.

The Falkirk duo already had their debut LP *The Week Never Starts Round Here* in the can when their label suggested coming up with B-sides for a lead single. Written and recorded in the same session, it was fast-tracked into an A-side and went on to dominate the late-night BBC Radio 1 airwaves helmed by Steve Lamacq and John Peel. It ended the year at number 2 in Peel's Festive 50 (after Kenicke's 'Come Out 2 Nite') and gained a second life via a Guinness advert.

**Radiohead**'s **'The National Anthem'** had a much more protracted genesis. First attempted and abandoned in 1994, it was revived as a potential B-side for one of the singles from 1997's third LP *OK Computer*. Tethered to a looping, repetitive bassline and the distinctive wavering sound of an Ondes Martenot played by guitarist Johnny Greenwood, Radiohead bussed in musicians from Saint John's Orchestra to play its Charles Mingus-inspired free jazz-brass section — directed to sound like a 'traffic jam' by Greenwood and singer Thom Yorke, the latter breaking his foot with stamping excitement during recording. It was taken up a notch further by Yorke's ambiguous lyrics about fear and holding on, distorted via a ring modulator and a final thirty seconds of transistor radio babble (that possibly inspired its title shift from the original 'Everyone').

The Oxford band decided their jazz-rock Frankenstein's monster was far too good to get lost in the crowd, and preserved their most energetic and out-there moment for 2000's crowd-splitting follow-up *Kid A*, using it as the curtain-raiser during every show of its accompanying live tour.

**LCD Soundsystem** registered one of the most discussed singles of the early 21st century. A self-referential piss-take of its creator's own cooler-than-thou credentials over a stuttering analogue synth and the bassline from Killing Joke's 'Change', **'Losing My Edge'** was the making of New York DJ turned engineer/producer and DFA label co-founder James Murphy. Recorded with longstanding collaborator Nancy Whang and Spank Rock's Alex Epton, his first foray into artistry was meant to be a one-off — the conversational sound of a petrified ageing DJ looking over his shoulder at the "kids are coming up from behind" armed with the power of Google. Their looming presence made his increasingly desperate I-was-there tales and namedrops (Suicide, the Fall, Can, Eric B & Rakim, the Sonics) sound more and more embarrassing before he unleashed his *coup de grace*: "But have you seen my records!"

Universally hated among his friends, it was pencilled in as the B-side to 2002's 'Beat Connection' right until it was due at the pressing plant, when Murphy decided "that should be the one I should sink or swim with". Swiftly vindicated, his self-aware musings turned into a post-modern millennial anthem, while LCD Soundsystem mushroomed from a back-of-a-beermat project into one of the early 00s greatest electronic bands.

As good as all these are, the most critical case of an intended B-side outstripping its intended fate harks right back to 1958 — when an undistinguished former skiffle band singer went solo. Columbia's A&R man and producer Norrie Paramor had already earmarked a whistling, doo-wop take on Bobby Helms' 'Schoolboy Crush' for **Cliff Richard and the Drifters'** first single — a song hardly set to rock the boat. In need of a B-side, rhythm guitarist Ian 'Sammy' Samuel came up with **'Move It!'** on his way home to Cheshunt on the 715 Green Line bus. After playing it to Paramor in his office, Paramor decided "Well, this is quite good. It'll *do* for a B-side" (or so he told Radio 2 documentary *Wired For Sound*). The producer had massively underestimated its impact. An adrenalized slice of rock 'n' roll that stacked up against its US predecessors, Richard's impassioned celebration of the "rhythm that gets into your heart and soul" was further inflamed by session player Ernie Shear's howling lead guitar breaks.

It was down to TV producer Jack Good to alter the course of history, after he insisted Richard perform 'Move It!' on his teenage show *Oh Boy!* instead of 'Schoolboy Crush'. Keen to capitalise on the exposure, Columbia swapped A and B-sides at the eleventh hour — gaining not only a number 2 hit single (held off from the summit by Connie Francis' 'Stupid Cupid'), but an instant superstar, widely hailed as the UK's answer to Elvis Presley. And although Richard's music quickly softened and he turned into a very different star after announcing his Christian beliefs in 1966, 'Move It!' underlined a very stark reality — had this intended B-side not been awarded top billing, there may well have been no Shadows, no Beatles, no Rolling Stones and no British rock 'n' roll.

### 'TV Baby'

Magazine
VIRGIN 1979
A-Side: 'Rhythm Of Cruelty'

**Atmospheric art-rock Mancunians let rip.**

As the art student who both organised Sex Pistols' near mythical show at Manchester's Lesser Free Trade Hall and issued punk's first DIY single with Buzzcocks, Howard Devoto was never likely to rest on his laurels. By 1979 the singer had shed punk's stylistic straitjacket for a more expansive sound with Magazine — a band that traded Bowie's Berlin trilogy sonics with the literary heft of Proust and Dostoevsky. There was a heightened tension during the sessions for *Secondhand Daylight* (the production debut of Bowie engineer Colin Thurston) that streaked through its only single 'Rhythm Of Cruelty' — a crunching mix of proggy dynamics and punkish concision. B-side 'TV Baby' was much looser. Written alongside keyboardist Dave Formula, it let Devoto indulge his love of Iggy Pop and the Stooges as his possibly improvised lyrics bestrode a pummelling Barry Adamson bass turn, Formula's old school electric piano and the otherworldly interjections of John McGeoch's wailing sax. It was the sound of a band with an overly-serious aura having under-rehearsed fun.

### 'Take A Chance'

Frank Sinatra
CAPITOL 1953
A-Side: 'Young At Heart'

**Ol' Blue Eyes at his upbeat swinging best.**

Frank Sinatra was on a sustained losing streak at the start of the 50s. Trouble came in threes for the judiciously connected New Jersey singer with the sudden death of his publicist George Evans, the end of his marriage to Nancy and his doomed tryst with Ava Gardner. Washed-up, broke and reputedly suicidal, the style-setting teen idol who rose to fame with Tommy Dorsey's big band was saved at the bell by his Oscar-winning turn as Private Angelo Maggio in *From Here To Eternity* and a career-changing studio relationship with Nat King Cole arranger Nelson Riddle. The zippy 'Young At Heart' showed his renewed mettle, just missing the US top spot but quickly turning into a standard. 'Take A Chance' proved his new direction was no fluke. From its striking opening line ("Love may be a gamble or a lead pipe cinch") onwards, there was a palpable sense that Sinatra truly believed you should grasp the great nettle of love and damn the consequences, as Riddle's evocative chart brought out a hitherto hidden vulnerability to his unmistakable gin-soaked burr. Their next stop was inventing the concept album with 1955's ode to loneliness *In The Wee Small Hours.*

### 'Take Me Home'

Spice Girls
VIRGIN 1996
A-Side: 'Say You'll Be There'

**Sultry slowie from empowering girl band.**

Spice Girls' rapid rise was unprecedented. It took the previously unknown 20-year-olds just one single ('Wannabe'), a mysterious phrase ("zig-a-zig-ah") and Johan Camitz' one-take video to knock ex-Take That singer Gary Barlow off his number 1 perch and show there were spikier new sheriffs in town. And while to more cynical pop observers it was just one manufactured group replacing the offshoot of another, Spice Girls' 'girl power' slogan resonated loudest in the Cool Britannia era through the fivesome's skimpy outfits, gregarious personalities and a clutch of singles snagged with implacable hooks. Only their second single, 'Say You'll Be There' added the sophistication 'Wannabe' lacked. 'Take Me Home' reinforced the distinction. Over a laid back, trip-hop-ish breakbeat, punctuated by a wah-wah guitars and sampled saxes and strings, Spice Girls demonstrated their vocal differences — Melanie C and Mel B doing the heavy melodic lifting as Emma Bunton filled in between and Victoria Adams and Geri Halliwell traded low-voiced come-hithers. Better than much of the assembly line dance-pop of first LP *Spice*, its member's differences would become more pronounced as they progressed.

### 'Take Your Time'

Lynyrd Skynyrd
MCA 1974
A-Side: 'Sweet Home Alabama'

**Southern rock royalty at bad-to-bone best.**

The Top 10 US success of 'Sweet Home Alabama' indicated Lynyrd Skynyrd were well on their way to stardom. The relatable hard rockers, renowned for having not one, not two, but three lead-guitarists, were Jacksonville high-school drop-outs who named themselves in mocking tribute to their high school PE teacher (the long-hair hating Leonard Skinner). Their natural gift for rebellion was scrawled across the A-side. A song that told Neil Young precisely where he could stick 1970's 'Southern Man', singer/songwriter Ronnie Van Zant's impassioned defence of the south bucked the usual clichés to create a sing-along that would long outlive his time in the band (he perished in a 1977 plane crash). Its B-side, ostensibly a demo, rode a much more relaxed groove. Over a honky-tonkin' piano boogie, Van Zant's tale of a penniless but natural born teenage lady-killer ("I take my time and I love 'em slow") proved totally believable, if something of a side show from the epic slide solo of third guitarist Ed King — a slippery thing that dipped and soared, wailed and roared with outrageous technique.

## 'Talk Show Host'

Radiohead

PALOPHONE 1996

A-Side: 'Street Spirit (Fade Out)'

**Slow-burner that made it to the big screen.**

Radiohead were in rude health when Britpop started its fall from grace. The Oxford outsiders were far too arty and aloof to be considered part of that gang, but risked being written off as one-hit-wonders if second LP *The Bends* didn't pass muster. It delivered in all respects, its purest offering 'Street Spirit' (a track singer Tom Yorke modestly claimed "wrote itself") smacking into the UK Top 5 alongside Jonathan Glazer's dream-like video treatment. B-side 'Talk Show Host' was another downbeat affair. Predicated on a haunted guitar figure and restrained, lightly daubed bass, there was a distinct air of unease as Yorke inhabited the role of its titular presenter, gearing up for a fight as he waited (with sandwiches and a gun) while Philip Selway's low-in-the-mix drums backgrounded queasily swerving synths. Composed at a fertile point in Radiohead's evolution, live renditions often became more protracted, with a much longer, guitar-driven ending. Nellee Hooper made it even scarier and sparser when he remixed it for Baz Luhrman's *Romeo And Juliet* soundtrack the following year.

## 'Teacher'

Jethro Tull
CHRYSALIS 1970
A-Side: 'The Witch's Promise'

**Cautionary fable from prog-folk mavericks.**

When it came to recording third album *Benefit*, Jethro Tull had found their defining sound — a *sui generis* meld of folk and rock spiked with sardonic wordplay. The sessions yielded a glut of material for the oddball Blackpool band named after an English agriculturist, with enough left over for this non-album single. While 'The Witch's Promise' was a foretaste of the naturalist prog-folk to come, the more commercial-sounding 'Teacher' harked farther back to their beginnings, essaying a satisfying blues with outgoing bassist Glenn Cornick adding strident Hammond organ licks. A crisply-sung warning about worshipping gurus, it found their heavily bearded leader Ian Anderson decrying the fakes supposedly leading disciples on a spiritual path to enlightenment. "They would suck in people. And a lot of the time, of course, it was just about getting your money and driving around in a big, white Rolls Royce," Anderson told *Rolling Stone*. A completely different take and arrangement of 'Teacher' — prominently featuring Anderson's flute and recorded with US radio programmers in mind — was included on American pressings of *Benefit*.

## 'Tear It Down'

Def Leppard
MERCURY 1987
A-Side: 'Animal'

**Sheffield pop-metallers' thumping epic.**

DIY pioneers of the New Wave of British Heavy Metal movement just under a decade earlier, Def Leppard embraced mainstream metal clichés with greedy force in the early 80s. Chief to their rapid rise was a hook-up with songwriter/producer Robert John 'Mutt' Lange, whose pop-styled metal hybrid — a playful marriage of earworms and bludgeoning riffs — hit multi-platinum heights on 1983's *Pyromania* and 1987's *Hysteria*. While A-side 'Animal' initiated a ten-song run of US Top 40 hits and finally broke them on home turf, its self-produced B-side welcomed new fans to their grittier roots. Worked up during live rehearsals and centred around a rousing twin-guitar riff, Joe Elliot's yearning paean to a seductress with the "look of a howlin' wolf" was topped with an anthemic group chorus and typically fleet solo from resident axe hero Steve 'The Riffmaster' Clark. An instant live favourite that was re-worked for 1989's *MTV Music Video Awards* — Clark's final show with the band — Def Leppard would wind up re-recording and vicariously over-polishing 'Tear It Down' for 1992's fifth LP *Adrenalize*.

## 'Teen Angel'

Donovan

PYE 1968

A-Side: 'Hurdy Gurdy Man'

**Scottish songwriter in sublimely stoned mode.**

Donovan enjoyed a gilded run of forward-thinking late 60s pop singles. UK Top 10 hits such as 'Sunshine Superman', 'Mellow Yellow' and 'Jennifer Jupiter' took the working-class Glaswegian from the folk movement's margins into the epicentre of London's flower power pop scene, assisted in his increasingly psychedelic quest by producer Mickie Most. Most's skills shone heavily on the trippy 'Hurdy Gurdy Man'. Written while on holiday with the Beatles in Rishikesh, India, and reputedly recorded with future Led Zeppelin bandmates Jimmy Page, John Paul Jones and John Bonham, the song tapped into Donovan's new fascination with transcendental meditation and the teachings of Maharishi Mahesh Yogi. Its B-side was a more sensitive gem. A mellow folk love song with his acoustic strums detailed with pattering hand-drums, distant piano licks and non-intrusive bass, its understated backing was all the better for catching the yearn in Donovan's quavering voice. 'Teen Angel' was later resurrected by raspy New Jersey songstress Sharon Van Etten for 2015 tribute album *Gazing With Tranquility*.

## 'Teenage Love Affair'

Showaddywaddy

BELL 1976

A-Side: 'Trocadero'

**Rare original from Leicester rock 'n' roll revivalists.**

Merging local Leicester groups Choise and the Golden Hammers,

Showaddywaddy rose to almost improbable fame on ITV talent show *New Faces* and scored an instant hit with 1974's self-penned Gary Glitter-like stomper 'Hey Rock And Roll'. Togged out in colourful velvet-trimmed drape jackets, drainpipe pants and white brothel creepers, the easy-on-they-eye teen stars increasingly found that covers (Eddie Cochran's 'Three Steps To Heaven', Buddy Holly's 'Heartbeat') outstripped their originals in the charts. 'Trocadero' proved the point. The title track to their third album stalled at number thirty-two in the UK, despite a strong performance on *Top Of The Pops*. Its flipside 'Teenage Love Affair' fell under the radar too. Written by singer Dave Bartram and guitarist Trevor Oakes for the Bay City Rollers during their imperious pop phase, its staccato beat and building verses seemed to ace the brief. When it was rejected Showaddywaddy reworked it with producer Mike Hurst, but slightly nullified the demo's harmony-heavy charms in their haste. After scoring their first number one with Curtis Lee's 'Under The Moon Of Love' later that year, Showaddywaddy's reliance on the covers conveyor belt became an inter-band bugbear. And while they addressed it on B-side 'One Of These Days' ['Dancin' Party', 1977] their protests went unheeded.

## 'The Tennessee Waltz'

Patti Page
MERCURY 1950
A-Side: 'Boogie Woogie Santa Claus'

**World's first 'one-woman quartet' gets tearful.**

The Oklahoma-born singer dubbed the 'Singing Rage' often double-tracked her distinctive alto voice. Discovered by Jimmy Joy bandleader Jack Rael after hearing her sing on Tulsa radio station KTUL, the pair's joint innovations brought sustained 50s chart success. Having first tried double-tracking on 1947's debut single 'Confess' as a fiscal necessity (their budget did not stretch to backing singers), Page and Rael made hay with the four-part harmonies of 1950's 'With My Eyes Wide Open I'm Dreaming' (its label memorably read: "Vocals by Patti Page, Patti Page, Patti Page and Patti Page"). In need of a song to back long forgotten seasonal novelty 'Boogie Woogie Santa Claus', Page hit upon Pee Wee King and His Golden West Cowboys' 1946 country song 'The Tennessee Waltz', one of her father's favourites. Her label happily acquiesced. "Mercury wanted to concentrate on a Christmas song and they didn't want anything with much merit on the flip side," Page later revealed. In the event, DJs didn't even bother with its festive A-side, preferring Page's distinctive self-harmonising ballad and buying into her tremulous heartbreak and Rael's soothing string accompaniment, detailed with a mellow trumpet solo at the bridge. 'The Tennessee Waltz' would eventually settle in for a thirty-week chart run (spending thirteen weeks at the top of *Billboard*'s Most-Played in Juke Boxes chart) and become the decade's biggest-selling single, lagging just behind Bing Crosby's 'White Christmas' in the all-time rankings. It was later officially adopted by the Volunteer State.

### 'Tequila'

The Champs
CHALLENGE 1958
A-Side: 'Train To Nowhere'

**Latin-tinged liquor jam goes loco.**

The Champs were the freakish outcome of Challenge Records' bid to launch Dave Burgess as a rockabilly sensation. With the bluesy uptempo 'Train to Nowhere' already in the can, the assembled session musicians spent less than ten minutes getting its throwaway B-side match fit. Centred on a honking dirty sax riff that Danny Flores played with his trio before the intermission on club dates, it was paired with Buddy Bruce's rhythm and Burgess' picked guitar as Gene Alden essayed a Cuban mambo beat on his cymbal and Flores hollered "Tequila!" with lustrous force. Its creators first twigged the B-side had eclipsed the A-side when east coast sax player Eddie Platt's cover started to enjoy regional success. It prompted Challenge to issue instructions for radio DJs to "turn the record over". They followed the diktat and it shot up the US charts, reaching number 1 within three weeks and winning Flores a Grammy. The Champs became a real band *after* the song's success, openly pastiching themselves on 'Too Much Tequila' and 'Tequila Twist' while similarly styled instrumentals 'Limbo Rock' and 'La Cucaracha' became minor hits. A Flores live staple, up until his death in 2006, numerous covers followed (Wes Montgomery, Bad Manners, Dr Feelgood) as its distinctive rallying cry featured in *Happy Days*, *Breakfast At Tiffany's* and *Pee Wee's Big Adventure*.

## 'That Girl Is A Slut'

Just-Ice
FRESH 1986
A-Side: 'Put That Record Back On'

**Shock treatment paves way for porno rap.**

Early hip-hop B-sides allowed their creators to spit and spout unfiltered, much like they would perform at early block parties. Just-Ice, an intimidating Brooklyn ex-bouncer with a full set of gold teeth, laid down a marker with the unremittingly filthy rhymes of 'That Girl Is A Slut', recounting a night of sexual misadventures over the Original DMX's heavy human beat-boxing and Kurtis Mantronik's distinctive production (his meticulously programmed beats lit up the A-side). And while there were inevitable hints of Doug E. Fresh and the Get Fresh Crew's great B-side 'La Di Da Di' in its sing-song combination of drama, sex, shock value and no-holds-barred rhyming, this B-side briefly made Just-Ice the talk of the neighbourhood — a reputation that grew when police in Washington D.C. arrested him on suspicion of murdering of a drug dealer. Fellow controversy-mongers N.W.A would later appropriate elements of its second verse twice, for their B-side 'Just Don't Bite It' ['100 Miles And Runnin'', 1990] and on 1991 *Efil4zaggin* LP track 'She Swallowed It'.

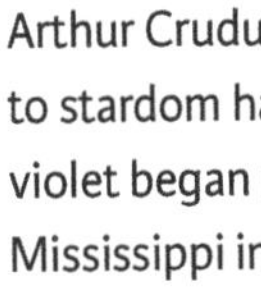

## 'That's All Right'

Arthur 'Big Boy' Crudup
RCA VICTOR 1947
A-Side: 'Crudup's After Hours'

**Mississippi blues man sets controls for rock 'n' roll.**

Arthur Crudup's role in launching a certain swivel-hipped sharecropper's son to stardom has long eclipsed his talents as a bluesman. The non-shrinking violet began paying his trade as a blues one-man-band around Clarksdale, Mississippi in the 30s, dropping anchor in Chicago in 1939 after first visiting as a member of rotating gospel outfit the Harmonizing Four. He barely made ends meet as a street singer and was living in a packing crate when producer Lester Melrose made moves to capture his brisk, unpolished, guitar-driven sound for RCA Victor. Moderate R&B hits followed with 'Rock Me Mama', 'Ethel Mae' and the lonesome 12-bar woes of 'Crudup's After Hours', crafted alongside bassist

Ransom Knowling and drummer Judge Riley. Raw and frisky, the Crudup original on the latter's B-side was barely noticed at the time, despite liberally borrowing its chorus from Texan country blues legend Blind Lemon Jefferson's 'That Black Snake Moan' and boasting one of the first recorded lead guitar breaks. It was not until Tupelo teenager Elvis Presley, a devoted Crudup acolyte, began messing with 'That's All Right' in the studio with guitarist Scotty Moore and upright 'slap' bassist Bill Black in 1954 that Sun boss/producer Sam Phillips intuited its true hit potential and recorded an unfussy live take as Presley's first single. "Damn. Get that on the radio and they'll run us out of town," Black opined on playback. And while it became the initial tremors of a legend, Elvis' popularity was strictly regional at first. Sometimes called the 'father of rock 'n' roll' for launching Presley's career, Crudup never got the royalties he was due, allegedly receiving just $100 and a promise of greater rewards that never materialised. He died in abject poverty and relative obscurity in 1974.

## 'That's My Impression'

Pet Shop Boys
PARLOPHONE 1986
A-Side: 'Love Comes Quickly'

**English synth duo do it themselves.**

If the sign of a great band lies in the strength of their B-sides, Pet Shop Boys can rest easy. Whether the devastating ballad 'Do I Have To?' ['Always On My Mind', 1987], disco-drama of 'Bet She's Not Your Girlfriend' ['Where The Streets Have No Name (I Can't Take My Eyes Off You)', 1991) or 'Hell' and its infectious denouncement of evil politicians ['Leaving', 2012], Neil Tenant and Chris Lowe have rarely let the side down. "We've always used the B-side as a way of learning to produce," Lowe explained in the sleeve notes to 1995's B-sides compilation *Alternative*, "... the B-side was where we learned to do things ourselves. So it wasn't a throwaway, ever. It's been fundamental to how we progress." And while 'That's My Impression' was their first full self-production, it served them well — setting down the panning percussion, arpeggiated bass and choral melody lines that would define their first decade. Tenant also sounded less mannered, almost plaintive on its middle eight, his tone slightly embittered as he searched London's Hyde Park for his straying lover — in contrast to the more studied melancholia to come. A more-than-worthy B-side whose 12-inch Disco Mix made it into the Top 10 of the US Hot Dance Club Play chart, it suggested Pet Shop Boys were in it for the long haul.

### 'Theme From Q'

Objekt

OBJEKT 2017

A-Side: 'Needle & Thread'

**UK techno producer's ever-morphing club banger.**

One of this book's more recent B-sides was not all it first seemed. Presented as a full-on tribute to Berlin's Basement Q club, the closed down Schöneberg venue's soundsystem was said to be instrumental in forming the musical identities of Objekt creator TJ Hertz and his collaborator Call Super. While Hertz used his technical nous to condense a typical Thursday club night into its nine-minute A-side 'Needle & Thread', its B-side's reinterpretation of DJ Bogdan's supposedly unreleased anthem 'Love Inna Basement (Morning Dub)' was better still. Its combination of warped breakbeats, eerie atmospherics, bulbous basslines and infectious synth hooks struck a chord with the Ibiza crowd which seriously elevated Objekt's profile. Although their heartfelt tribute to a shuttered idyll proved to be a delicious ruse (one they perpetuated into 2019, when a white label of Bogdan's mythical original surfaced), it failed to stop 'Theme From Q' being anointed *Mixmag* magazine's Best Track of 2017. It also allowed Hertz to quit his day job to focus on music full-time.

### 'Theme Music From BBC TV's Dial M For Murder'

BBC Radiophonic Workshop

BBC 1974

A-Side: Norrie Paramor and the Midland Radio Orchestra: 'Ricochet'

**Proto-techno from in-house BBC sonic sorcerers.**

Curators of the world's biggest vinyl and sound recording archive, the BBC's offshoot label proved one of the most off-beam, unpredictable imprints of them all. Take the A-side here. A cover of the theme of one of Radio 2's first stereo shows — a thriller about an investigative journalist with deep connections in the criminal underworld — that sprinkled gunshot effects across it in the hope of airplay (and was doubtless vetoed by DJs for precisely that reason). Its B-side was even more off-the-wall, the theme to a BBC anthology of crime stories loosely based on Alfred Hitchcock's *Dial M For Murder* by arch tape manipulator John Baker (part of BBC Radiophonic Workshop, best known for the *Doctor Who* theme and the show's spooky sound effects). Just as Baker had once made a futuristic jingle for Radio 4's *Woman's Hour* by splicing the sound of a glug of water with the pop of the cork, this theme was created by recording the parts of a dismantled telephone. Baker crammed as many weird noises as possible into his abstract piece, later dubbed "a pre-Detroit slice of British techno" by exotica expert Jonny Trunk.

**'There Ain't Half Been Some Clever Bastards'**
Ian Dury & the Blockheads
STIFF 1978
A-Side: 'Hit Me With Your Rhythm Stick'

**Chameleonic punk poet's display of geezer-ish wit.**

Ian Dury was one of a kind, as both sides of this number one demonstrate. With its 16-notes-to-the-bar bassline and highly suggestive lyrics, 'Hit Me With Your Rhythm Stick' corralled funk and disco to Dury's despicable ends, its exotic groove matched by the polio-afflicted art teacher turned punk godfather's linguistic merry-go-round, dipping into French and German with relish along the way. Its B-side — the talk of playgrounds up and down the UK for its title alone — was arguably more audacious. An off-kilter cockney knees-up, it witnessed his super tight backing band the Blockheads summon some lightly skanking music hall for the man once dubbed 'the Count Dracula of vernacular' to pay tribute to Noel Coward, Van Gogh and Einstein in his inimitable fashion (praising the "lucky bleeders" and wishing for "lots more to come"). Aware of the A-side's commercial potential, Dury chose this B-side with care, aware that its royalties could give a serious boost to co-writer Russell Hardy, his old mucker in pub-rockers Kilburn and the High Roads.

## 'There For Me'

Mariah Carey

VIRGIN 2001

A-Side: 'Never Too Far/Hero Medley'

**Power ballad to the big guy upstairs.**

2001 was Mariah Carey's annus horribilis. Having accrued more number 1 *Billboard* Hot 100 hits than any other solo act, the octave-hurdling New Yorker was suddenly in the midst of a very public crisis. Intense battles with her new label Virgin (after signing the most lucrative album deal in history) and terrible reviews for vanity movie *Glitter* led to a full-on physical and emotional breakdown that saw her sectioned. Carey had recovered some of her poise and was back on the promo treadmill as the year ended, appearing the very image of showbiz glamour as she promoted a medley for the Heroes Fund charity in the wake of September 11's terrorist attacks. Fans who kept the faith were rewarded with an exclusive B-side (first recorded for 1999's *Rainbow* album). A message to a higher power, 'There For Me' was understated by Carey's histrionic standards, although she still couldn't resist making its closing chorus as rousing as possible. Unlike most stars of her magnitude, Carey has slipped out a brace of glittering prize Bs, from the gritty soul of 'Do You Think Of Me?' ['Dreamlover', 1993] to the lustrously smooth R&B of 'Slipping Away' ['Always Be My Baby', 1995].

## 'There's No Love Left'

The Isley Brothers

TAMLA 1966

A-Side: 'This Old Heart Of Mine (Is Weak For You)'

**Break-up beast with a complicated lineage.**

A good B-side often shows another dimension to an artist. This was particularly true with Motown 45s. While many of their A-sides were aimed squarely at the dancefloor, their balladic flips reflected the quality of the team players boss Berry Gordy insisted on. Considered something of a star signing, ex-Ohio gospel outfit the Isley Brothers enjoyed a brief mid-60s flirtation with Motown offshoot Tamla at the precise moment the pens of Holland-Dozier-Holland blazed with hits. Authors of both sides here, the floor-filling A-side was dominated by Ronald Isley's soaring lead vocals and the sound of house band the Funk Brothers in full swing. 'There's No Love Left' had a more complicated history. A re-reading of an old Four Tops LP track that was earmarked for the Supremes, the Isley Brothers got there first and made it their own, Ronald's wounded falsetto weaving between brothers O'Kelly and Rudolph layered harmonies to declare "She don't love me no more" with sheer heartbroken force.

### 'These Days'

Joy Division
FACTORY 1980
A-Side: 'Love Will Tear Us Apart'

**Last single proves fitting full-stop.**

Ian Curtis had been dead a month when the tragic yet danceable pop of 'Love Will Tear Us Apart' emerged in a Peter Saville sleeve that resembled a gravestone. It was an atypical Joy Division track in many ways, given the suffocating murk that engulfed studio albums *Unknown Pleasures* and *Closer*. Final B-side, 'These Days', also deviated from the standard songbook. While Peter Hook's tightly-coiled bassline and Stephen Morris's rattling drums half anticipated the dancefloor reinvention of the surviving members' next incarnation as New Order, Bernard Sumner's spidery guitar figure and thrashy chorus chords keep it strictly JD and wordlessly evoked the cold war era. As with the A-side, matters of the bleeding heart were conveyed in Curtis' disconnected deep croon, although a glimmer of hope rested in its parting question: "Can you stay for these days?" Whether a plea to his long-suffering wife Deborah or his reputed lover Annik Honoré, it alchemised the singer's distress into something of deep beauty, before those days finally became too much. Life imitated art when the A-side's title was later inscribed on Curtis's memorial stone.

### 'These Days'

Powderfinger
UNIVERSAL 1999
A-Side: 'The Passenger'

**Brisbane band tackle fate's creeping hand.**

Their unfussy brand of heartfelt classic rock turned Powderfinger into one of

Australia's most popular bands. The Brisbane outfit named after a Neil Young song were writing their 4th album (confusingly titled *Odyssey Number Five*), when film director Gregor Jordan asked them to write something to accompany a scene in his comedy crime drama *Two Hands* (breakthrough movie for Heath Ledger and Rose Byrne). Singer Bernard Fanning responded with the gloomy 'These Days', but nearly let it lie when he failed to come up with a suitable second verse (he ended up repeating the first). While its lyrics bolstered Fanning's unwanted depiction as an antipodean misery guts, particularly to his singing nemesis Ben Lee, he had the last laugh when the B-side topped Australia's Triple J Hottest 100 chart (A-side 'The Passenger' came in at 100), a poll voted by the radio station's listeners, and won Song of the Year at 2000's *Music Critics Awards*. It even made the English curriculum in a smattering of Australian high schools.

### 'Those Eyes, That Mouth'

Cocteau Twins
4AD 1986
A-Side: 'Love's Easy Tears'

**Otherworldly treasure that acted like a warm embrace.**

By 1986 Cocteau Twins were on a creative roll. The unlikely dream-poppers that seemed to emerge fully formed from the shadowy imagination of 4AD label boss Ivo Watts-Russell (but actually hailed from Scottish port-town Grangemouth) were refreshed from some rulebook ripping-up. Singer Liz Fraser and guitarist Robin Guthrie had gone drum-free on duet LP *Victoria* while bassist Simon Raymonde helped on the second coming of Watts-Russell's vanity project This Mortal Coil. All three had then played slightly against type on *The Moon And The Melodies*, a collaboration with pianist Harold Budd. 'Love's Easy Tears' was a restatement of core strengths — its programmed beats, murmuring basslines, heavily flanged guitars and Fraser's uniquely ethereal voice provided a scintillating distillation of their artfully constructed sound world. Bigger and more uplifting than its lead track, 'Those Eyes, That Mouth' doubled down on their darkly romantic assets. Even Frazer's upfront declaration of "Yes I'm in love" seemed much more about the up and down rhythms of her voice than the words themselves, until its exultant chorus made that notion a lie.

### 'Through My Eyes'
The Creation
POLYDOR 1967
A-Side: 'Life Is Just Beginning'

**Slow jam from missing link in British psychedelic canon.**

The Creation never got their dues. The Hertfordshire band that emerged from the ashes of the Mark Four failed to shake their previous incarnation, whose lengthy stints playing Wilhelmshaven's Big Ben Club made them much bigger in Germany than they were at home. With a young gunslinging manager in Robert Stigwood and a pedigree producer in Shel Tamy (the Who, the Kinks), 1966's spunky first single 'Making Time' soared to number 5 in Germany. Yet the quartet managed just one minor UK hit with 'Painter Man', notable for guitarist Eddie Phillips' innovative use of a violin bow (a gimmick later borrowed by Jimmy Page). Phillips' patience was wearing thin when the zig-zagging strings and chanted mantras on their 4th single 'Life Is Just Beginning' joined their run of flops. Perhaps even more so given the doomy charms of its deeply atmospheric B-side. A resonating slab of modish psych, whose ghostly massed vocals echoed singer Kenny Pickett's invitation to take a trip as Phillips' bludgeoning solo showed his bespoke approach to feedback. Covered by Sex Pistols during early rehearsals, 'Through My Eyes' was equally loved by ginger impresario Alan McGee, who not only named his Creation label in homage, but his band Biff Bang Pow! too (after the B-side to 'Painter Man'). The Creation's influence was also manifest in the slow, steady power-dynamics of early Oasis.

### 'Time Warp'
Eddy Grant
PORTRAIT 1983
A-Side: 'Electric Avenue'

**Hypnotic proto-house banger.**

Eddy Grant led one of the UK's pioneering multi-racial bands, the Equals, before a 1971 heart attack checked his progress. The Guyana-born, London-raised all-rounder reinvented himself as a solo artist with the muscular funk of 1979's 'Living on the Frontline', a string of successive hits enabling Grant to emigrate to Barbados. He nonetheless reflected on his old home in 'Electric Avenue, 'whose declamatory "Oi!", revved motorcycles and references to the 1981 Brixton riots were slightly let down by its kitschy 80s beat. If that dated badly, B-side 'Time Warp' was still light years ahead of the curve. A Grant song that went even further back — it first appeared on the B-side of 1977's 'Nobody's Got Time', a single credited to the Coach House Rhythm Section (in-house band at his recording studio) — it was one of the earliest examples of minimalist house. Widely bootlegged due to its rarity, its pure groove would make it a DJ favourite, equally popular in Chicago and New York. Its influence was explicit on Gorillaz' 2010 collaboration with Bobby Womack and Mos Def, 'Stylo', with Grant breaking cover to accuse them of ripping off 'Time Warp'. "My song sits almost note to note with their release," Grant frothed to *The Guardian*. "I am outraged."

**'To Sir With Love'**
Lulu
COLUMBIA 1967
A-Side: 'Let's Pretend'

**Tetchy producer buries movie ballad.**
When Lulu struck a production deal with producer/impresario Mickie Most, he wasted little time repointing her towards the pop mainstream. A distinctive star since 1964's unforgettable cover of the Isley Brothers' 'Shout', the bee-hived Glaswegian teenager was still best known for earthy R&B turns when she landed the part of callow student Babs, opposite Sydney Poitier, in James Clavell's 1967 film *To Sir, With Love*. Written by Lulu's friends Mark London and Don Black, the lusciously stringy title song (give or take a comma) sounded like a great lost James Bond theme as Lulu tenderly essayed Black's lyric about the bittersweet transition from adolescence to adulthood. Even though he produced it, Most was resistant to its charms and, in an act of supreme petulance, refused to let it be released as a UK A-side, burying on it on the back of the less effectual 'Let's Pretend' because he only wanted Lulu to score hits *he* had selected. Lulu must have questioned Most's control freakery when it topped the US charts and made her only the second British female artist (after Petula Clark) to reach that milestone.

### 'Together We Are Beautiful'

Fern Kinney
MALACO 1979
A-Side: 'Baby, Let Me Kiss You'

**Session voice joins one hit wonder club.**

Mississippi singer Fern Kinney had spent most of her career knocking on the door in vain. After appearing in Dorothy Moore's 60s girl trio the Poppies, Kinney juggled housewifery with studio stints backing Irma Thomas, Freddy Fender and James Brown prodigy King Floyd before she turned solo in the late 70s. Having put a winning disco spin on two of Floyd's keepers — 'Groove Me' (his only Top 10 US hit, originally B-side of 1969's 'What Our Love Needs') and 1971's 'Baby, Let Me Kiss You' — to very little noise, she was shaken when radio DJs unexpectedly went a bundle for the latter's super slinky B-side (penned by the composer of TV cartoon *Doctor Snuggles*, Ken Leray). Over a laid back disco beat and sweeping strings, Kinney's vulnerable and reigned-in child-like vocal had an anesthetising effect that helped it slink to the UK's number 1. Energy company EDF later paired it with interactive bot mascot Zingy across a series of 00s TV ads.

### 'Top Billin''

Audio Two
FIRST PRIORITY MUSIC 1987
A-Side: 'Make It Funky'

**One of hip-hop's most sampled songs.**

Audio Two were hip-hop addicts long before its first records were pressed. Brothers Milk Dee and DJ Gizmo scoured the streets for DJ mixes and bootlegs in their Brooklyn locale before resorting to DIY techniques to record their first demos. It led to many happy accidents as they dabbled with basic bits of studio kit. None more so than on 'Top Billin''. Dee used a Roland TR-707 drum machine to trigger the kick, snare and hi-hat from the Honey Drippers' 'Impeach The President', sampled using a Boss foot pedal (sample capacity: two seconds) to create a stuttering yet undeniably funky vibe that would become one of hip-hop's most imitated beats. Add in a supremely confident vocal (referenced by everyone from Dr. Dre, Jay-Z, 50 Cent to Run the Jewels since) and a classic was born. Albeit a slow-burning one. Having ignored the pleas of their producer,

Daddy-O, to make it top billin' over the more obvious 'Make It Funky', the B-side spent eight long months in the wilderness before Juice Crew DJ Marley Marl alerted the faithful. Among the first hip-hop tracks to be covered in full — their half-sister MC Lyte refired the original instrumental in 1998 — it alone explains Audio Two's vaunted position in the hip-hop history books.

**'The Trick'**
The Prodigy
XL 1996
A-Side: 'Breathe'

**Rhythmic bliss from fire-starting Braintree outsiders.**

The Prodigy became a dominant pop force in the mid-90s. Ever since the BBC Public Information Film-sampling hit 'Charly' — once ridiculously accused of 'killing rave' — brought them into public consciousness, nearly all the dysfunctional Essex quartet's singles had been hits. They had also sidestepped their novelty rave origins to create bustling dark-toned tunes wreathed in elements of rap and hard rock that spoke to the breakdancing past of their musical mastermind Liam Howlett. If that worked a treat on the claustrophobic Wu-Tang Clan and Thin Lizzy sampling A-side 'Breathe', its speaker-smashing big beat instrumental B-side 'The Trick' was also well up to snuff. Centred around a dense rhythm and overly distorted bass figure, Howlett cascaded in a gothic piano refrain for the choruses. As brilliant as it was, it reeked of missed potential — a well-timed vocal turn from Kool Keith or their underused in-house MC Maxim Reality could have taken it stratospheric. It mattered not; parent album *The Fat Of The Land* broke the Prodigy in America — a goal many of their retro-fixated Britpop contemporaries could only fantasise about.

**'The Twelfth Of Never'**
Johnny Mathis
COLUMBIA 1957
A-Side: 'The Chances Are'

**Showman's velveteen croon defines 50s pop.**

Johnny Mathis risked being left behind by rock 'n' roll. The Texan-born singer was an exceptional athlete who forsook a college scholarship to sing soft romantic ballads under the tutelage of Columbia's rock-hating A&R man and producer Mitch Miller. That move seemed to pay off spectacularly when A-side 'The Chances Are' jinked its way to number one. DJs also went a bundle for its simpler, more minimally orchestrated B-side, adapted from folk staple 'I Gave My Love A Cherry' by film songwriters Jerry Livingston and Paul Francis Webster. Although Mathis was a reluctant suitor at first — "I didn't like it because it was all so repetitious, and nothing seemed to happen," he told radio documentary *Pop Chronicles* — the hot-to-trot singer gained a new affection for it when it became his next *Billboard* Top 10 hit. Tackled by Glen Campbell, Cher, Nina Simone, Dolly Parton and Elvis Presley since — with Donny Osmond hitting the UK top spot in 1973 — none have quite matched Mathis' quivering emotional reach or the sustained emotive power of his heavy vibrato.

### 'Twilight Alehouse'

Genesis

CHARISMA 1974

A-Side: 'I Know What I Like (In Your Wardrobe)'

**Proggers' eight-minute epic hits the sauce.**

Tensions were running high when Genesis promoted their fifth album, *Selling England By The Pound*. Members of the public school-formed Surrey prog-rock band feared that singer Peter Gabriel's increasing penchant for outlandish stage costumes — flower, vicar, fox — was undermining the serious import of their music. Some of that snobbery extended to elements of Genesis's fanbase. Accustomed to long, epic songs, they took against the A-side's tale of an eccentric groundsman and his lawnmowing life, feeling its relative brevity was something of a pop sell-out. Its double-length B-side, part of their repertoire since the early 70s, sent the same fans into excited raptures. Previously issued on a free flexi disc with *ZigZag* magazine, the dark theatrical drama about a loner seeking solace in "the magic power of wine" cut a similar jib to *Trespass* LP cut 'Stagnation' with its moody mash-up of rock, classical, folk and psychedelic motifs detailed by Tony Banks' ornate organ runs, Steve Hackett's chiming guitars and Gabriel's fluttering flutes and husky voice. Few observers had any idea how prescient the A-side would prove. Before the year was out singer Gabriel had quit the band to spend more time tending his Cotswolds vegetable patch.

### 'The Twist'

Hank Ballard and the Midnighters
KING 1959
A-Side: 'Teardrops On Your Letter'

**Bawdy original launches 60s biggest dance craze.**

As soon as he wrote it, Hank Ballard realised 'The Twist' could be his ticket to fame. The Detroit songwriter had already enjoyed some good fortune. Overheard singing on the Ford Motor Company assembly line in his teens, he became lead singer for doo-wop group the Royals. He gradually steered them away from romantic harmony songs towards an earthier version of R&B (cf: 1953's 'Get It') and changed their name to the Midnighters. While 'The Twist' cleaved to the same raunchy style, Ballard's producer at King, Henry Glover, didn't share his enthusiasm. "I couldn't give that song away," Ballard later told *The Los Angeles Times*. "I rewrote it and added another groove. My record company *still* didn't like it." Glover eventually decreed it could be used as B-side to slow, piano-laced ballad 'Teardrops on Your Letter', a song he'd written himself. And while his instincts were vindicated with a US Top 5 R&B chart hit, word that a new dance was evolving to its B-side had reached *American Bandstand* presenter Dick Clark. Clark decided Ballard's song was too bawdy and too risky (shorthand for 'too black') for his show, but didn't want to miss out. So, he persuaded one-time chicken-plucker Chubby Checker, whose voice closely resembled Ballard's, to re-record it. Introduced on Clark's Saturday night show, Checker's almost note-for-note reading went supernova, topping the charts accompanied by a more sanitised version of its dance moves (which toned down the pelvic thrusting). Ballad was not in the least bit bitter — a sudden rush of royalties helped — and fully vindicated when 'The Twist' was re-released as an A-side in his name in 1960.

### 'Two Pints Of Lager And A Packet Of Crisps Please'

Splodgenessabounds
DERAM 1980
A-Side: 'Simon Templer'

**Highly relatable barroom blues.**

Chaotic prank-playing Peckham punks Splodgenessabounds' B-side struck a chord with anyone who had queued in a British pub at last orders and vainly tried to catch the barman's eye. The simplest of constructions — a driving bassline and a nifty back-and-forth guitar riff — allowed singer Max Splodge's increasingly frustrated requests and terse asides ("I'm getting very thirsty... Listen, I'm getting impatient, John") to ramp up the theatricality before time was called. Unsurprisingly, it was inspired by a real-life encounter. "One night I rushed into the Crown in Chislehurst waving a pound note, trying to buy two pints of lager and a packet of crisps," revealed singer Max Splodge in Chris Welch and Duncan Soar's book *One Hit Wonders*. "The bell rang and the bloke wouldn't serve me." Issued on the B-side of a speedy run-through of TV show theme *The Saint* alongside the best-avoided fart-fest 'Michael Booth's Talking Bum', it took off when Radio 1 DJs John Peel and Mike Read started playing it. While the punk cabaret circuit would soon beckon for its creators, Splodgenessabounds' best-known track also inspired a 00s British sitcom starring Ralf Little and Sheridan Smith.

### 'Unchained Melody'

The Righteous Brothers
PHILLES 1965
A-Side: 'Hung On You'

**Blue-eyed soul duo's much-abused tear jerker.**

Their partnership was short-lived, but The Righteous Brothers' made a definitive impact. Contrasting baritone and high tenor singers Bill Medley and Bobby Hatfield joined forces from respective Californian groups the Paramours and the Variations in 1962 to become the first white vocal act on wall-of-sound producer Phil Spector's Philles imprint, hitting gold two years later with 'You've Lost That Lovin' Feelin''. Allowed a solo song apiece on their albums, both Medley and Hatfield had designs on 'Unchained Melody' — an Alex North number used as the theme to 1955 prison film *Unchained* — and tossed a coin for it in the studio. Hatfield won. Medley played its understated piano part and produced it, approximating Spector's orchestral ambience in the process. He also insisted Hatfield take a second stab at its soaring final falsetto final line ("I need your love") and dared him to do it better — Hatfield's emotive second take would give him the chills. It was one of the reasons DJs chose to ignore Gerry Goffin and Carole King's 'Hung On You' and play the romantic throwback B-side instead. Spector was irate. Renowned for his deliberately disposable B-sides, he called radio stations directly to protest but failed to stop it rising to the top. Famously used during a pottery scene in 1990 blockbuster *Ghost*, Simon Cowell's favourite song has been butchered multiple times by TV talent show wannabes ever since he masterminded Robson & Jerome's 1995 cover smash.

### 'Uncle Salty'

Aerosmith
COLUMBIA 1975
A-Side: 'Sweet Emotion'

**Bruised blues from excess-all-areas rockers.**

By the mid-70s Aerosmith's outlaw brand of bluesy raunch ruled the US stadium circuit as they mastered the fine art of making heavy music that concealed polished pop hooks. The one time Boston bar band finally breached the US charts with the groovy, riffy 'Sweet Emotion' (later used to devastating effect at the start of Richard Linklater's 1993 comedy *Dazed And Confused*) from their third album *Toys In The Attic*. The multi-layered sentiments and sad double-entendres of B-side 'Uncle Salty' went deeper, digging into their blues and country roots as singer Steven Tyler outlined a tragic tale of child abuse and prostitution. It was contentious subject matter for a toxically inclined band whose open pursuit of sex and drugs was unremitting (Tyler convinced the parents of a 16-year-old Portland groupie to give him guardianship so she could live with him in Boston later that year). Thematically in line with 1989's Grammy-winning hit 'Janie's Got A Gun', 'Uncle Salty' was twice the song, debunking Tyler's claims that Aerosmith made their best music sober.

### 'The Undisputed Champs'

Del Tha Funky Homosapien
ELEKTRA 1994
A-Side: 'Wrongplace'

**Ice Cube's cousin goes for delf.**

Del Tha Funky Homosapien's first album *I Wish My Brother George Was Here* was a flash in the pan. A slightly goofy trawl over the P-funk samples his cousin and producer Ice Cube effectively imposed on him, a more three-dimensional artist emerged on follow-up *No Need For Alarm* as Del opted for a jazzier, almost east-coast sound allied to a much more serious-minded, combative lyrical approach. Tucked away on the B-side of second single 'Wrongplace' was a posse cut whose three-way display of bragging rights won underground hearts. A song that got better verse by verse, little known Hieroglyphics rapper Peplove warmed up the crowd before A Tribe Called Quest's Q-Tip casually fired off some lyrical clips and Del let rip with "lyrical lacerations" that showed he could "maim foes metaphorically" as he casually took out suckers over its dusty double bass loop. Among the rapper's own favourite B-sides, its distillation of lyrical skills marked him out as a survivor, someone who would still be creating innovative, gimmick-free records, solo and with Gorillaz and Deltron 3030, long into the future.

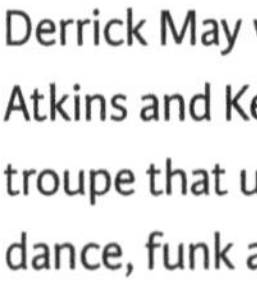


### 'Untitled'

X-Ray
TRANSMAT 1986
A-Side: 'Let's Go'

**Detroit innovator's little heard techno banger.**

Derrick May was instrumental in the birth of Detroit techno. Alongside Juan Atkins and Kevin Saunderson, the Belleville High School students formed a troupe that united their passion for European electronic music, hip-hop, Chicago dance, funk and legendary Detroit radio DJ The Electrifyin' Mojo. When they started releasing singles in the mid-80s they maintained a unified DIY vibe, May launching his Transmat imprint hot on the heels of Atkins' Metroplex. The label's first single, 'Let's Go', found all three messing around with old school electro, a bit drunkenly by all accounts, with May confessing to *DJ* magazine: "I was quite upset with that record because I didn't think it was me." After a trippier, reverb-drenched dub mix its B-side included an uncredited hidden track that sounded defiantly like the future and foretold why May would be considered techno's answer to Miles Davis. Created with just a Roland TR-808 drum machine and two synths, its pulsing beats and searching, celestial keys foreshadowed exactly what would be exciting global dancefloors in the early 90s. Rarely spoken of and little known, 'Untitled' hinted at the greatness to come.

### 'Untitled (How Does It Feel?)'

D'Angelo
EMI 1999
A-Side: 'Left & Right'

**Neo-soul star's hyper sensual Prince homage.**

D'Angelo shifted the scope of R&B on its axis with second album *Voodoo*. Lengthy sessions at Electric Lady Studios with producer Questlove, hip-hop fusion crew Soulquarians and beat scientist J Dilla yielded one of greatest, most game-changing synthesises of hip-hop and R&B. Issued three months earlier, 'Left & Right' was a light and teasing affair, the Virginian singer dodging in and out of Method Man and Redman's jolly rhyme-offs. B-side 'Untitled (How Does It Feel?)' was a more substantial hint at what lay ahead. A sparsely orchestrated, slow-burning cross of Prince and Al Green whose carefully contained swells of brass, Fender Rhodes and guitars underlay intensely sexual lyrics before D'Angelo's falsetto built to a screaming, wordless climax. The A-side's relative failure proved to be a blessing in disguise. On January 1, 2000, 'Untitled' was rebooted as D'Angelo next single alongside a Paul Hunter directed video that had an instant cultural impact. Simply but powerfully shot against a black backdrop, it showed the tattooed, toned and lubriciously baby-oiled singer dramatising the lyrics slow build towards ecstasy (exciting scurrilous rumours that D'Angelo was being fellated during the shoot). The video not only brought him an instant legion of female fans, it helped *Voodoo* debut at US number one three weeks later and won him Best Male R&B Vocal Performance at 2001's Grammy Awards.

## 'Urge For Going'

Joni Mitchell
ASYLUM 1972
A-Side: 'You Turn Me On, I'm A Radio'

**Confessional singer-songwriter at melancholic best.**

After emerging in the late 60s folk revival, Joni Mitchell became a singularly influential force, known for her poignant, personal songs. Sarcastic A-side 'You Turn Me On...' was something different — a naked attempt to pen a radio hit, written solely to appease her paymasters. Worked up with a collective of smooth Los Angeles session players, Mitchell's instincts proved spot-on and it took her into the US Top 40 and Canadian Top 10 for the first time. Its B-side was much more personal. Written during her first marriage and covered by singer-songwriter Tom Rush (on 1968's *The Circle Game*), Mitchell finally attempted it acoustically during sessions for *Blue* in 1971. An extended metaphor about the cycling seasons inspired by the extreme winters in Saskatoon, where she grew up, her warbling paean to escape and the great unknown cut to the core when captured with such minimalist passion. Tellingly, Mitchell included 'Urge For Going' as the opening track on 1996's first compilation *Hits*, rather than its more experimental companion *Misses*.

## 'Vacuum Cleaner'

Tintern Abbey
DERAM 1967
A-Side: 'Beeside'

**Short-lived Londoners' rare psychedelic jewel.**

Named after a William Wordsworth poem and managed by teenage multi-millionaire Nigel Samuel, Tintern Abbey could have been contenders. All they needed was a hit. Fitted up with Carnaby Street's latest mod threads and sent to Cornwall to write an album, their first studio dalliance spawned the confusingly titled 'Beeside' — a mysterious ode to the honey-making insects whose tinkling pianos and swarming mellotron lines reminded of the Moody Blues. It lacked distinction though, unlike its groove-based B-side. Written after the band hoovered up all their drug paraphernalia amidst a police raid, David MacTavish's heartfelt lyrics about not fitting in rubbed up against Stuart McKay's staggered bass, John Dalton's jazzy drums and Don Smith's unearthly bowed guitar solo. Tintern Abbey's opening number during the few gigs they played — MacTavish dramatically accompanied by his pet honey buzzard — it got lost in the Christmas market and a planned follow-up was axed. After being anthologised on 1981's *Chocolate Soup For Diabetics* compilation, original copies started selling for four-figure sums — a hefty fee for a 'Vacuum Cleaner' that doesn't suck.

### 'Valentine Girl'

New Kids on the Block
COLUMBIA 1990
A-Side: 'Step By Step'

**Edgy boy band show harmonising skills.**

New Kids on the Block (NKOTB) blazed the way for a new generation of boy bands. The quintet of clean-cut New England teenagers were treated with open disdain when 1986's self-titled signature track boasted: "We're the funky MCs of the hip-hop craze." Proof that the band recruited by New Edition impresario Maurice Starr really had a winning edge came with 1988's precision-tooled rock/rap/pop amalgam *Hangin' Tough* — a hit-streaked set that set the route for Backstreet Boys, NSYNC and One Direction to follow. While the lush, string-filled Motown-lite 'Step By Step' caught NKOTB at their creative high, its super syrupy B-side 'Valentine Girl' showed them at their most vulnerable. A simple song in praise of a beautiful girl, with a rare falsetto vocal lead from in-band choreographer Danny Wood, it was played nearly as much as the A-side and gained extra ubiquity as the incidental music in the band's short-lived cartoon series on ABC. Originally intended as an airplay-only track, it became a Japanese single and a staple of NKOTB shows when they reformed in 2008.

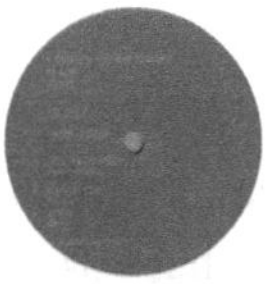

### 'Velocity Girl'

Primal Scream
CREATION 1986
A-Side: 'Crystal Crescent'

**82-second jangle pop masterclass.**

Bobby Gillespie was still better known as the stand-up drummer in the Jesus and Mary Chain when Primal Scream's second single emerged. Having hung up his drumsticks, few would have predicted a future as maximum rock 'n' rollers from 'Crystal Crescent' — a brass-blasted Rickenbacker jangler with a whiff of Teardrop Explodes. Its B-side came to the rescue. Recipient of one of Gillespie's fullest vocals, its tale of a glamorous yet sensitive young woman shooting speed to block out the world gave dreaminess a seamy edge, while its blend of strummed and picked guitars set the template for the Stone Roses to carve out 'Made Of Stone'. The opening track on the *NME*'s influential *C86* compilation, this B-side's impact was clear when it came in at number four on John Peel's Festive 50. While Primal Scream would later kick back against any indie scene associations ("They can't play their instruments and they can't write songs," Gillespie scathed), 'Velocity Girl' became the name of a Washington D.C. indie band and inspired an affectionate B-side cover from Manic Street Preachers ['Australia', 1996].

### 'Velvet Goldmine'

David Bowie
RCA 1975
A-Side: 'Space Oddity'

**Glammy and lascivious *Ziggy Stardust* outtake.**

'Velvet Goldmine' spent three years wandering lost and lonely before it was appended to David Bowie's first UK number 1 single. Originally recorded in the sessions for 1972's 5th studio LP *The Rise And Fall Of Ziggy Stardust And The Spiders From Mars* — the album that made the mercurial green/blue-eyed Londoner a star — it was dropped late on after RCA demanded Bowie write a hit single (he reciprocated with 'Starman'). It was later intimated that more censorious forces were at play. The song's provocative lyrics were deemed too risqué and salacious even after Bowie watered them down (another potential inclusion 'Sweet Head', was scrapped altogether for the same reason), its description of a groupie's feelings towards his fictional star offset by Mick Ronson's music hall eight-bar guitar/piano and the thumping interplay of rhythm section Trevor Bolder and Woody Woodmansey. Bowie loved the song but was reputedly upset that he never got to approve the B-side's mix. Later used as the title for Toddy Haynes' 1998 film homage to the glittering 70s (although Bowie nixed the filmmaker from using his music), it joins a relatively short list of B-sides that made the Thin White Duke's singles worth buying. These include the classic modisms of 'The London Boys' ['Rubber Band', 1966], wordy yet enticing 'Conversation Piece' ['The Prettiest Star', 1970] and his decadent cover of Jacques Brel's 'Amsterdam' ['Sorrow', 1973].

### 'Vigilante Man'

Woody Guthrie
KING 1940
A-Side: 'I Ain't Got No Home In This World Anymore'

**Folk legend's resonant migration fable.**

Woody Guthrie was immersed in the ballads and blues of America's past. The charismatic Oklahoma folksinger was a committed class warrior who used his art to depict the real lives and struggles of oppressed people while compulsively turning his back on success. Both sides here played to his gruff yet emotive strengths. While the A-side was a rewrite of the Carter Family's 1932 recording 'I Don't Feel At Home In This World Anymore', Guthrie rejected their hopeful assertion that life's struggles would be repaid in the next life, instead narrowing his sights on the greedy banks, businessmen, landowners and politicians he viewed responsible for society's inequities. He again borrowed the Carter Family's melody — this time from 1936's 'Sad And Lonesome Day' (itself based on Blind Lemon Jefferson B-side 'See That My Grave Is Kept Clean') — for the equally agitated 'Vigilante Man'. A take-no-crap denouncement of the corrupt railroad bosses that threw hobos off of trains, hired thugs to crush labour movements and forcibly chased off Midwestern farmers the Okies, its fifth verse detailed the murder of Preacher John Casey from John Steinbeck's realist novel *The Grapes Of Wrath* (published the previous year), something he'd return to again on the two-part 'Tom Joad'. Covered since covered by Ry Cooder and Bruce Springsteen, the eerie authenticity of Guthrie's original still resonates the loudest.

### 'The Wagoner's Lad (Loving Nancy)'

Buell Kazee
BRUNSWICK 1928
A-Side: 'The Butcher's Boy (The Railroad Boy)'

**Kentucky Baptist pastor in progressive mode.**
Buell Kazee was well-versed in traditional song. The Kentucky balladeer started playing banjo at five and refined his precise clawhammer style at Georgetown University, where he used his training to transcribe and update old oral traditions. After his regular shows at the University of Kentucky lured Brunswick to the table, Kazee ventured to New York to record a string of singles that showed off his prodigious five-string skills and lonesome Appalachian singing. There was a peculiar thematic unity to his eleventh single, 'The Butcher's Boy'. While its A-side told the tale of a jilted young girl who committed suicide, the flip 'The Wagoner's Lad' found Kazee essaying heartbreak from a female perspective. And while it was highly unusual to hear lyrics about women being "controlled by their parents" and becoming "slaves to their husbands" from a rural southern pastor's mouth, it spoke volumes about Kazee's progressive stance. Although Kazee devoted himself more thoroughly to his ministry after the Great Depression, fresh interest arrived when both sides of this single appeared on Harry Smith's *Anthology Of American Folk Music* in 1951.

**'Wait For The Sun'**
Supergrass
PARLOPHONE 1995
A-Side: 'Lenny'

**Cartoonish Britpoppers show hidden depths.**
When they sashayed into public consciousness in an effervescent blur of Chopper bikes, mutton chops and sparkling pearly whites, Supergrass had youth on their side. The teenage Oxford trio of Gaz Coombes, Mick Quinn and Danny Goffey also had a backpack stuffed with sharp but nuanced pop songs in the tradition of Buzzcocks, Madness and the Kinks, epitomised by the spiky charms of first Top 10 hit 'Lenny'. B-side 'Wait For The Sun' showed there was more going on below the fluffy barnets than many first thought. Based around a 12-string Byrdslike guitar jangle, it found Coombes wailing towards the "white budding sun" before his compatriots joined in for a sweeping psychedelic coda strangely redolent of Led Zeppelin in acoustic mode. It was a snapshot of the more textured band they would unveil on 1997's *In It For The Money*, having sidestepped the easy pigeonholing of their biggest hit 'Alright' and rejected

an approach from Steven Spielberg to make a Monkees-styled TV series. Such maturity was less apparent on the single's other B-side, 'Sex!', the less said about which the better.

### 'Waitin' Guilty'

The Black Crowes
ATCO 1980
A-Side: 'Hard To Handle'

**Twangy thriller from swaggering southern revivalists.**

Fearlessly retro in their approach, the hip-shaking Black Crowes drew heavily on source material from another era. The famously combustible Georgian throwbacks to the soul/blues-drenched rock of the Rolling Stones and the Faces stood out a country mile at a time when hair metal still held its precarious sway. First considered as filler and throwaway, their kicking take on 'Hard To Handle' (the B-side of Otis Redding's posthumous 1968 single 'Amen') succeeded where their original first single ('Jealous Again') had flopped and set them on the road to stardom. On its B-side they let loose 'Waitin' Guilty', a twangy southern rocker whose muscular guitars and Hammond-blasted riffs tipped the wink to Memphis and Muscle Shoals — ideal for Chris Robinson's searching vocals. Slightly out on a limb from the more streamlined thrills of debut *Shake Your Money Maker*, this B-side rarely made their early live sets. Nonetheless Black Crowes gave it a much rootsier treatment when they revived it for 2013 live LP *Wiser For The Time*.

### 'Wake Up Screaming'

Queens of the Stone Age
INTERSCOPE 2003
A-Side: 'First It Giveth'

**Californians' wild-eyed punk turn.**

Among rock's last remaining outlaws, Queens of the Stone Age found their true metier on *Songs For The Deaf*. The desert-dwelling Californian band looked back to move forward on their third album, channelling Black Sabbath and David Bowie on a driving doomy set that saw Dave Grohl put his Foo Fighters commitments on hold to helm its backline. His power plays were all over 'First

It Giveth', as the celebrated stoners questioned the validity of taking drugs to make music, and a B-side that ladled on the heaviosity with glee. A cover of Subhumans' 'Wake Up Screaming' (a little-known track from the Wiltshire punks' 1983 LP *From the Cradle To The Grave*), it started quietly, before lulling listeners into an evolving nightmare of ever-quickening riffs and pummelled drums punctuated by frontman Josh Homme's blood-curdling shrieks. Clearly a fun studio turn alongside outgoing bassist Nick Oliveri, their chemistry was also evident on B-side covers of the Kinks' 'Who'll Be The Next In Line' ['Feel Good Hit Of The Summer', 2000] and the Cramps' 'Most Exalted Potentate Of Love' (on the UK second CD single for 'First It Giveth').

### 'Walk Right Back'

The Everly Brothers
WARNER BROS 1961
A-Side: 'Ebony Eyes'

**Close harmony siblings' tender tearjerker.**

The Everly Brothers were in such a hurry to get 'Walk Right Back' down on tape, they repeated the sole verse its budding writer Sonny Curtis had showed them at a meeting in Hollywood. And while the future singer and guitarist for the post-Buddy Holly Crickets mailed them the second verse post-haste, they declined to alter the recording. It was easy to understand why. Singing brothers Phil and Don were riding high from a superlative string of late 50 singles for Cadence that paid equal mind to the B-sides — see 'Bird Dog' ['Devoted To You', 1958] or 'Claudette' ['All I Have To Do Is Dream', 1958] — when they were lured to Warner Bros and continued where they left off. Underscored by a fantastically twangy Gibson acoustic guitar, the heartbreak of 'Walk Right Back' was enhanced by a telling pause in the verses, before their fraternal harmonies gave the chorus the heart-rending yearning only they could dispatch. A hopeful rejoinder to 'Ebony Eyes' — a death disc about a doting lover waiting in vain for his bride at the airport — when the sides were flipped *Walk Right Back* fared one place better in the *Billboard* Hot 100 at number 7. Covered by Perry Como and Andy Williams in the 70s using Curtis's second verse, it became a huge country hit for Canadian Anne Murray in 1978, who copied the Everly's format to the letter.

## 'Warm Leatherette'

The Normal
MUTE 1978
A-Side: 'TVOD'

**Founder's icy electronics launch Mute label.**

The Normal brought a punk aesthetic to electronic music. Disillusioned that you needed to learn three chords to be in a punk band, London film editor Daniel Miller concluded you only needed to press one key on a synthesiser instead. Miller bought a MiniKorg 700S, the first mass-produced monophonic machine, and used it to chilling and minimalist effect on both sides of his home-recorded first single. While its jerky A-side predicted a dystopian future where TV viewers plugged the signal directly into their skin, 'Warm Leatherette' distilled the themes of a screenplay Miller had written based on J.G. Ballard's sci-fi novel *Crash* (which imagined a freaky sexual zeitgeist of people turned on by car crashes). A menacing beast whose repeated bass figure and detached monotone vocal felt subversive, the single quickly sold out its initial 2,000 run, with Miller using the proceeds to develop Mute as an independent electronic titan (home to Fad Gadget, Depeche Mode, Erasure and more). The robotic momentum of 'Warm Leatherette' has since been replicated by Laibach, Duran Duran and Suzie Quatro, although Grace Jones' dub reinvention with Sly & Robbie remains the high watermark.

## 'We All Fall Down'

Take That
POLYDOR 2007
A-Side: 'I'd Wait For Life'

**Reunited 90s boy band find new wings.**

Take That left a trail of broken hearts when they split in 1996. While songwriter Gary Barlow brazenly used their parting press conference to announce his solo career, that crashed and burned as ex-bandmate Robbie Williams mutated into Britain's most bankable pop performer. Relations with Williams were still frosty when Take That issued 2006's comeback LP *Beautiful World*. It found the foursome making a decent fist at classic rock and pop hybrids, epitomised by comeback hits 'Patience' and 'Shine'. While lachrymose third single 'I'd Wait For

Life' felt like a bad throwback and ended a winning streak of six consecutive number 1s (reaching a lowly 17), you could have got decent odds on a 7th successive chart-topper had they picked its B-side instead. A rousing full band co-write with songwriter Steve Robson, 'We All Fall Down' was sunshine in a glass, detectable shades of Electric Light Orchestra permeating its two hooky choruses and relatable sentiments about reaching the place you belong. And if its confusing basement/pavement metaphor was a little bizarre (see also: the slowly rolling cannonball of Oasis's 'Champagne Supernova') it failed to stop it becoming Take That's most persuasive deep cut.

**'We Are So Fragile'**

Tubeway Army

BEGGARS BANQUET 1979

A-Side: 'Are 'Friends' Electric?'

**An electronic star is born.**

Bathed in stark white floor lights, at his insistence, Gary Numan's first ever *Top Of The Pops* performance became an instant talking point. Sandwiched between Roxy Music and Donna Summer, he held his own, the humming discord of 'Are 'Friends' Electric?' launching a shy Londoner caked in Max Factor foundation and Revlon eyeliner into the world's first mainstream electronic pop star. The very dark and gloomy Philip K. Dick future it imagined, where robot prostitutes and rape machines held sway, hypnotised the nation as it made a slow crawl to the top. Almost the antithesis of the A-side (two songs that weren't quite working bolted into one), the pulsing 'We Are So Fragile' was a much more straightforward synth-pop track in line with Tubeway Army's self-titled debut earlier that year (punk songs refitted with synths after Numan stumbled across a Minimoog Model D in the studio control room), with glammy distorted guitars and handclaps driving its radio-friendly, four-to-the-floor stomp. While Numan sneered disconnected modern world ennui ("They could give us a war just to keep us amused") he was serially savaged in the music press as some sort of hideous Bowie android. A suggestion of ska skank and the bass riff from Numan's next number 1 'Cars' were added when Scottish pop-punkers Bis covered it for 1997 tribute LP *Random*.

**'We Got The Power'**
Dropkick Murphys
HELLCAT 2003
A-Side: 'Walk Away'

**Boston rabble rousers salute the power of a union.**

Dropkick Murphys' rowdy hybrid of oi!, US hardcore and traditional Irish folk won them a devoted following. Politicised and upfront about their allegiances ('Worker's Song (Fuck Capitalism)' gave a clue), they spent the late 90s and early 00s crafting fist-punching, spittle-flecked class anthems delivered in the deep gargled growls of bassist Ken Casey and frontman Al Bar. Far better than the A-side's generic Celtic punk sing-along was a tattered trawl through the politricks of 1919's Boston police strike, when members were denied the right to unionise with the American Federation of Labor by the city's police commissioner. Over bruising guitars its flag-waving call-and-response revealed how "19 men were tried and fired... For violation of rule 35" after Governor Calvin Coolidge sent the Massachusetts militia in (the republican's OTT role in the strike ultimately led to his presidency). Unlike many who talked the talk, Dropkick Murphys backed their words with actions, setting up charitable foundation the Claddagh Fund to help locals battle drink and drug problems.

**'Wee Wee Hours'**
Chuck Berry and His Combo
CHESS 1955
A-Side: 'Maybellene'

**Lonesome blues shuffle with potentially sinister edge.**

Chuck Berry's wild playing, out-sized personality and showmanship gave rock 'n' roll its early frisson. The duckwalking 'father of rock 'n' roll' set his stall out on his first single's bouncing hot rod tale 'Maybellene' (adapted from the traditional country fiddle tune 'Ida Red'), a rulebook-ripping vehicle for his electric guitar flash in its 24-bar solo. The first mainstream black rock record's B-side was its polar opposite. A much more traditional 12-bar blues, written in under an hour using Big Joe Turner's 'Wee Baby Blues' as inspiration, it found the Missouri-born Berry recalling an unrequited teenage crush on Margie, a girl he met at a United Services Organizations' dance. He even played the back, letting fleet-fingered pianist Johnny Johnson take all the leads. There was method to his madness. The ever-savvy Berry thought it had much more chance of winning a deal with blues label Chess than 'Maybellene' when he submitted his home-recorded demos. Although he was proved wrong, the B-side nonetheless became a Top 10 R&B hit and a live regular, among Keith Richard's selections for *Desert Island Discs* in 2015. And while 'Wee Wee Hours' took on a whole new meaning when Berry settled a $1million class action in 1990 for allegedly using hidden cameras to film women using the bathroom at his restaurant in St. Louis, other early B-sides were invariably top-notch — from the powerful pro-black sentiments of 'Too Much Monkey Business' ['Brown Eyed Handsome Man', 1956] and high energy licks of 'Reelin' And Rockin'' ['Sweet Little Sixteen', 1957] to his astute dissection of marital strife 'Memphis, Tennessee' ['Back In The USA', 1959].

**'The Weight Of The World'**
Roxette
CAPITOL 2002
A-Side: 'A Thing About You'

**Swedish pop phenomenon's prescient ballad.**

Sweden's second biggest pop export after ABBA, Roxette joined forces on the whim of record executive Rolf Nygren. Convinced their talents would combine — singer Marie Fredriksson had a middling solo career, songwriter and multi-instrumentalist Per Gessle's band Gyllene Tider was falling apart — the Halmstad-based duo proved him right, becoming a high-gloss, shoulder-padded pop phenomenon whose sleek English language hits 'The Look', 'Joyride' and 'It Must Have Been Love' arrived with a streak of sexual tension. Roxette's world turned upside down when Fredriksson was diagnosed with a cancerous brain tumour in 2002. And while the feelgood A-side was didn't waver from their efficient pop formula, the world weariness of its piano-detailed flipside — as Fredriksson described hiding in bed on a rain-drenched Sunday morning — seemed to tap into her new uncertain state. Despite being a leftover from 2000's *Room Service* LP, both members named it as a personal favourite. Roxette would defy medics and continue to tour until 2016.

## 'Well, Git It!'

Tommy Dorsey and His Orchestra
VICTOR 1942
A-Side: 'Somewhere A Voice Is Calling'

**Red-hot instrumental that got clubs jitterbugging.**

Tommy Dorsey's orchestra hit their peak during the early 40s. A regular chart-topper during the late 30s and RCA Victor's biggest-selling artist before Elvis Presley, the smooth-toned Pennsylvanian trombonist was blessed with great sidemen, top drawer singers (Jack Leonard, Frank Sinatra, Edythe Wright) and forward-thinking arrangers (Bill Finegan, Sy Oliver). And while the overly sentimental Sinatra-sung A-side was clearly aimed at the pop jugular, its big fat swinging B-side 'Well, Git It!' showed the true power and sass of Dorsey and his meticulously arranged sidemen. Written by Oliver and based on old jazz standard 'Bugle Call Blues' (later popularised by Benny Goodman), its 16-bar blues gave Dorsey's players plenty of solo shine, swaggering turns from Don Lodice's tenor sax, Heinie Beau's clarinet, Dorsey's unmistakable trombone and Milt Raskin's rampaging piano kept together by the incessant swinging rhythmic pulse of Buddy Rich. It was the big finale that slayed the dancefloor though — a fierce trumpet trade-off between Ziggy Elman and Chuck Peterson that remains one of the swing era's most iconic and thrilling sequences. It was a rare glint of hope in a challenging year as World War II heavily impacted on Dorsey's fortunes as a bandleader and bebop lurked around the corner.

## 'What It Is'

Amy Winehouse
ISLAND 2003
A-Side: 'Stronger Than Me'

**Doomed singer's acoustic confessional.**

Tracked down by Island over a period of months, after her backing vocals on a Lewinson Brothers' demo tape became a heightened source of fascination, Amy Winehouse was at the peak vocal power when she made her first solo moves in 2003. The Brit School graduate's extraordinary larynx — mysterious and rich, seemingly supplanted from someone older and more experienced — was more contained on its Ivor Norvello-winning A-side, as she lamented an older lover in need of constant reassurance (and bluntly enquired: "Are you gay?"). It might have only been her first single, but its B-side didn't hold back either, as Winehouse poured out the woes of a relationship running low on steam. "I don't know you anymore," she sideswiped at the 'Mr Ultrasensitive' who had suddenly become very distant, over increasingly broken-nailed downstrokes on her acoustic guitar. Essentially a demo that caught a moment of reflection, false notes and all, Winehouse's raw talent and charisma came through clear. It remains one of her few demos to survive — Island decided to destroy Winehouse's unfinished recordings after poor reviews for 2011's odds and sods compilation *Lioness: Hidden Treasures*.

### 'What Rap?'

Too $hort
JIVE 1990
A-Side: 'The Ghetto'

**West coast rap pioneer details his craft.**

Both sides of this single disproved the notion that Too $hort was a one-trick phoney. Best known for delivering raunchy but relaxed X-rated lyrics over a smooth bed of 70s funk, he switched formula completely for 'The Ghetto', riffing off Donny Hathaway's soul standard of the same name to discuss the crack epidemic in his native Oakland. Solely featured on the American B-side and hard to come by since, 'What Rap?' witnessed Too $hort opening up about his chosen profession and breaking down what it was really like to be an emcee. It was a rare glimpse behind the mask for an artist that almost imperceptibly moved from selling tapes out of the back of his car in the mid-80s to collecting platinum plaques in the early 90s, thanks to his wildly exaggerated pimp persona. Success, however, came at a price. In a candid 2012 interview with website Hip Hop DX, Too $hort contended that Jive prevented him from releasing the more positive songs he wanted to counterbalance his self-styled 'freaky tales' with. He also accused its president Barry Weiss of reneging on a verbal deal to do a socially conscious sequel to 2000's no-holds-barred *You Nasty*.

## 'What Will Death Be Like?'

Momus

CREATION 1986

A-Side: 'Murderers, The Hope Of Women'

**Erudite evocation of everything but the end.**

After a failed attempt to break into the indie jangle scene with ex-members of Josef K as the Happy Family, Bowie-obsessed Scot Nick Currie decamped to London and reinvented himself as louche and literate singer-songwriter Momus (named after the Greek god of mockery). After skewing Biblical history on his scholarly debut *Circus Maximus* and re-translating Brel during a fleeting stint for Mike Always's boutique él imprint, he caught up with modern life on his first single for Creation. While the A-side cribbed its title from Oskar Kokoschka's highbrow expressionist play and made much of the misery of modern marriage and its other B-side ('Eleven Executioners') toyed with German cabaret, 'What Will Death Be Like?' was the big revelation. Over seven minor-key minutes, Momus showed he was more than just a master of the unexpected chord change as he outlined an exhaustive itinerary of everything *not* waiting at the final curtain while the acoustic fingerpicking of Paul Inder (son of Motörhead's Lemmy) ran rife. And while its tightly-written mix of history, myth and real life came with an exhaustive cast list — Marquis de Sade, Tennyson, Wittgenstein, Sartre, Tolstoy, Lugosi etc. etc. — the literary showboating was tempered by its affecting beauty, as Currie used quick-fire repetitions to build towards an unexpected climax.

## 'When A Blind Man Cries'

Deep Purple

EMI 1972

A-Side: 'Never Before'

**Hard rockers' bluesy plaintive lament.**

Already one of the UK's genre-defining hard rock bands, Deep Purple made a definitive statement with sixth studio LP *Machine Head*. While the album was rapturously received — considered part of an English hard rock holy trinity alongside Black Sabbath's *Paranoid* and *Led Zeppelin IV* — the distinctly commercial feel of its lead single 'Never Before' won the Hertfordshire band no chart favours. It meant a paucity of listeners for 'When A Blind Man Cries'. A touching blues ballad that married Jon Lord's minimalist organ with Ian Gillan's emotive pondering in the wilderness, its second verse's oblique reference to "a cold month in that room" was a nod to their makeshift studio at Montreux's Grand Hotel after Montreux Casino burnt to the ground (inspiring the album's best known track/riff 'Smoke On The Water'). Although Ritchie Blackmore's tremulous solo won over floating voters, the highly capricious guitarist took against the song and this B-side was never played live on his watch. Later iterations of Deep Purple acquiesced, however, and it went through the Metallica mill for 2012's *Re-Machined* tribute LP.

### 'When I Had Your Love'

Marvin Gaye
TAMLA 1966
A-Side: 'One More Heartache'

**Unheralded ditty captures Gaye at his most soulful.**

Arguably Motown's greatest male solo star, Marvin Gaye had to work his way through the ranks. Having transitioned from singing in his father's church choir in Washington D.C. into a shy and withdrawn Detroit session musician, it fell to songwriter/producer Smokey Robinson to transform him from a practiced jazz crooner in thrall to Nate King Cole into a vibrant R&B performer and pop star. The infectious beat of 'One More Heartache' didn't hurt, supplying Gaye with his 12th US Top 30 hit. Some of its very subtle but undeniable eastern influences also seeped into the B-side. After the plonky piano of its Siamese intro, Gaye provided a vocal masterclass in tackling love lost over its unusual start-stop meter — reminiscing how he was once "a king" with precision and control, before a slightly hoarse "Now you're gone" showed the depth of the ache in his heart. Gaye would inspire countless soul singers before his tragic death at his father's hand in 1984, but this Robinson co-write (with Bobby Rogers and Pete Moore) stands alone from any other Motown song of the era.

**'Whenever You Breathe Out, I Breathe In (Positive Negative)'**
Modest Mouse
SUB POP 1996
A-Side: 'Broke'

**Cold-eyed slacker indie dirge.**

Modest Mouse were among the least likely candidates for mainstream stardom. The perpetually grumpy Seattle trio, named after a Virginia Woolf quote about ordinary people, rose to notoriety for their pained tales about the loneliness and isolation of small-town life, standing out for their eccentricity and often shambolic delivery. They were still in their infancy when this B-side emerged, Isaac Brock's slacker drawl capturing maximum ennui ("I haven't hung out with anyone/If I did, I'd have nothing to say") over an ever-spiralling guitar figure. Its resigned tone and power to capture the numb reality of depression cut through, making it a rapturously received live staple. Sly masters at making the painfully personal feel universal, Modest Mouse's charms even won over ex-Smiths guitarist Johnny Marr, who joined their ranks just before they topped the US charts with 2007's more upbeat yet still introspective *We Were Dead Before The Ship Even Sank*.

**'Where Did Our Love Go?'**
Soft Cell
SOME BIZZARE 1981
A-Side: 'Tainted Love'

**Supremes re-reading comes at a heavy cost.**

Soft Cell's ascension from likeminded Leeds Polytechnic art students to glittering chart-toppers was as swift as it was unexpected. Originally drawn together so synth wizard Dave Ball could soundtrack Marc Almond's theatrical productions, their demos caught the attention of Some Bizzare supremo Stevo, who helped mastermind their first hit. Something of an offbeat choice for a single, their twisted electronic revamp of old Gloria Jones' old B-side turned northern soul standard 'Tainted Love' ['My Bad Boy's Comin' Home', 1965], punctuated by Ball's distinctive double beep, then merged into a slower, more emotive reading of the Supremes' 1964 US number 1 smash 'Where Did

Our Love Go?' that the pair improvised in the studio, to a degree of head-scratching from producer Mike Thorne. While the original take was preserved on the nine-minute 12-inch A-side, it was chopped in two for the seven-inch single — a naturalistic move they would rue forever. And although Soft Cell didn't skirt on quality B-sides as their career progressed — excelling on the reflected solitude of 'Facility Girls' ['Bedsitter', 1981], deep club thrills of 'It's A Mug's Game' ['Where The Heart Is', 1982] and melancholia of 'Barriers' ['Numbers', 1983] — the fact 'Tainted Love' reached number 1 in 17 countries, spent a record-breaking 43 weeks on the *Billboard* Hot 100 and became the biggest-selling hit of 1981 hurt its creators — still living in a small housing association flat in Leeds — heavily in the pocket. "This was the biggest mistake we ever made," Almond lamented to *The Guardian*. "Having a cover version on both sides meant we didn't get any songwriting royalties."

**'Whisper'**
Marv Johnson
TAMLA 1959
A-Side: 'Come To Me'

**First Motown single introduces its forgotten star.**
Marv Johnson was the first artist ever heard on a Motown single. The Detroit singer and songwriter, discovered by label boss Berry Gordy playing a carnival with doo-wop group the Serenaders, helped mint Motown's classic sound alongside fledgling house band the Funk Brothers and the choral power of the Rayber Voices (headed by Berry's second wife, Raynoma Liles). A local hit in the Midwest, 'Come To Me' was so successful that Gordy's fledgling set-up couldn't cope with demand, with United Artists licensing the future US Top 30 hit. For many the traditional doo-wop of B-side 'Whisper' was its more compelling turn, making the most of Johnson's high emotive tenor and pleading tones over echoed backing vocals and a simple piano figure. Not only did it pave the way for the Miracles' slow ballads, it established Motown's formula of an uptempo A-side and a slow, moody B-side. And while Johnson's hitmaking tenure for the label would fade within a few years, he enjoyed success as a writer, penning hits for Tyrone Davis, Johnnie Taylor and the Dells.

## 'Who Scared You'

The Doors

ELEKTRA 1969

A-Side: 'Wishful Sinful'

**Los Angeles rockers' foray into bluesy funk.**

Chaos, both internal and external, swirled around the Doors when they came to record their 4th album. Ever since snake-hipped singer and self-styled 'Lizard King' Jim Morrison had been accused of inciting a riot at a Connecticut show in late 1967, the police had been on his tail and he was in the process of appealing a conviction for indecent exposure after a drunken onstage incident in Miami. A largely failed experiment in chamber-rock, the wistful Robbie Krieger-penned 'Wishful Sinful' flailed where its predecessor 'Touch Me' had thrilled, with Morrison's unconvincing croon proving a turn-off for some fans, who accused the Doors of softening the edges of their lysergic mantras and selling out. Those that did invest in this minor hit were rewarded with a superior flipside that welcomed additional instrumentation into the party. Predicated on Ray Manzarek's lumbering organ figure and Krieger's neat guitar riff, John Densmore's ever-shifting groove was lifted by atypically austere Morrison poetics and some very tastefully arranged horns. A conspicuous hit at 1969's Madison Square Garden show, it was the best of the paltry three non-album B-sides the Doors sanctioned, alongside the Manzarek-sung Willie Dixon cover '(You Need Meat) Don't Go No Further' ['Love Her Madly', 1971] and post-Morrison 'Treetrunk' ['Get Up And Dance', 1972], with many fans regarding it as the gilded fruit of *The Soft Parade* sessions.

## 'Who'll Be The Next In Line'

The Kinks

PYE 1965

A-Side: 'Ev'rybody's Gonna Be Happy'

**North Londoners' riffy paean to heartache.**

The Kinks established a tradition for B-sides as good as or better than their A-sides, as they knocked out singles (many of them non-album affairs) at a breakneck pace during the 60s. Chief storyteller Ray Davies' carefully crafted missives spoke to a generation while blurring the lines between pop, R&B,

blues and what would soon be known as hard rock. The catchy, insistent 'Who'll Be The Next In Line' was an exuberant example of the London band's skills. A passive-aggressive song about broken hearts, its nagging melody mainlined its way into consciousness over Dave Davies' nervously misshapen riff long before its premature fadeout. Those who argued the B-side had more hit potential than the one-dimensional lead — which broke a run of three consecutive UK Top 10 hits — were vindicated when it was became an A-side hit in America four months later (boosted by an appearance on Dick Clark-produced afternoon TV show *Where The Action Is*). Covered, in contrasting fashion, by both Francoise Hardy and Queens of the Stone Age, it joined other memorable shows of B-side largesse including 'It's All Right' ['You Really Got Me', 1963], 'I'm Not Like Everybody Else' ['Sunny Afternoon', 1966], 'Mr Pleasant' ['Autumn Almanac', 1967], 'She's Got Everything' ['Days', 1968] and 'Berkley Mews' ['Lola', 1970] — songs many bands would give their eye teeth to write.

**'Why'**
Avril Lavigne
ARISTA 2002
A-Side: 'Complicated'

**Tender side of skate-punk phenomenon.**

Long before she became the obsession of the travelling salesman in Nick Cave's secondnovel *The Death Of Bunny Munro*, skate punk-styled Canadian songstress Avril Lavigne was trying to find her place in planet pop. While Cave's creation rabidly fantasised about her "Valhalla of all vaginas", the devout Christian signed at 17 by Arista CEO Antonio 'LA' Reid was bucking against the Sheryl Crow-like country stylings first foisted on her in favour of spikier, guitar-driven power pop. If that was epitomised by the surly rebellion of first single 'Complicated', B-side 'Why' showed the raw talent lurking below the bombast ladled on by Los Angeles production allies the Matrix. Stripped back to just Lavigne bashing away on an acoustic guitar, it revealed a capable songwriter with persuasive vocal chops, its hurt-sounding refrains unbowed at the pain of love, yet resilient with it. Better than some of the filler that clogged-up Lavine's debut *Let Go*, 'Why' was a rare jewel whose wider commercial potential seems to have gone untapped.

## 'Why Can't I Touch It?'

Buzzcocks
UNITED ARTISTS 1979
A-Side: 'Everybody's Happy Nowadays'

**Progressive punks hit a new groove.**

Within two years of inventing indie pop with 1977's self-issued EP 'Spiral Scratch', their only studio recording with Howard Devoto, Buzzcocks inducted fans on a crash-course in pop perfection. With Pete Shelley taking over vocal and songwriting duties, the Mancunians embarked on a bruising run of singles (anthologised on *Singles Going Steady*) that reshaped the chart landscape. And while the band behind the busy fingers of 'Orgasm Addict' never issued a wanky B-side (see also: 'Oh Shit!' ['What Do I Get?', 1977], 'Noise Annoys' ['Love You More', 1978] and 'Lipstick' ['Promises', 1978]) the atmospheric sprawl of 'Why Can't I Touch It?' was both a heady contrast to the jaunty chart assault of 'Everybody's Happy Nowadays' and a vault onto a different plain. Pivoted around Steve Garvey's loping bassline and John Maher's precise drums, Steve Diggle's spidery fretwork jagged hard against Pete Shelly's slashing guitar figure and a heart-breaking vocal partly inspired by Captain Beefheart's 'Kandy Korn', with Shelly not so much caught in lust's clammy clutch as longing for transcendence. A relative marathon by their fleeting standards, its six-and-a-half minutes showed a hidden mastery of groove that pointed the way to more experimental third LP *A Different Kind Of Tension*.

## 'Why?'/'Friday Night, Saturday Morning'

The Specials
TWO TONE 1981
A-Side: 'Ghost Town'

**Double B-side reproves Coventry ska band's genius.**

The Specials caught the grim reality of Margaret Thatcher's Britain on one single, its three songs tackling societal malaise from different perspectives. Much has already been written about 'Ghost Town', a haunting, lyrically stark affair whose desolate effects and dub wizardry took its writer, Jerry Dammers, a year to get just-so. Written allegorically about the state of the band, it didn't so much catch the wider mood of despair as precipitate a wave of riots (in Birmingham,

Manchester, Liverpool and London) that showed the perilous state of the nation. Both its B-sides were equally pertinent. A sincere plea for racial tolerance, 'Why?' was a slab of easy-to-digest pop ska protest borne from bitter experience — its author, Lynval Golding, was taken into intensive care after being on the receiving end of a violent racist attack the previous year. Singer Terry Hall's 'Friday Night, Saturday Morning' tapped into the same line of social commentary as Alan Sillitoe's similarly titled 1958 novel about working class weekends. Hall's milk-thin deadpan effortlessly evoked the hen and stag parties at local Coventry dancehall the Locarno, as his narrator walked home alone with a chip shop pie rueing his romantic failures ("Wish I had lipstick on my shirt/Instead of piss stains on my shoes"). And while 'Ghost Town' was justly crowned Single of the Year across the UK's big three music papers, its imperious B-sides proved what a crucial band the Specials were, even as they were irreparably falling apart — Hall, Golding and Neville Staple announced they were quitting minutes before they performed their second number one on *Top Of The Pops*.

### 'Wilder, Wilder, Faster, Faster'

The Cramps

BIG BEAT 1991

A-Side: 'Eyeball In My Martini'

**Menacing rockabilly lovers in full trash mode.**

The Cramps were one of a kind. Although the ghoulish, high camp Californian rock 'n' rollers rarely deviated from formula, their frantic buzzsaw blend of Hammer Horror, sexploitation and B-movie imagery usually hit the mark, epitomised by guitarist Poison Ivy's intense riffage and Lux Interior's unhinged storytelling on 'Eyeball In My Martini'. Its driving B-side, doubtless titled with Russ Meyer in mind, offered something a little different. While Interior's frantic exhortations about "daring damsels", "teenage sickos", "psycho slaves" and "flagellating flabbergasters" cleaved to a back-to-basics guitar vamp, they broke from its quick-fire verses to chuck in a barrage of sound-effects (squealing brakes, revving motorcycles, rat-tat-tatting tommy guns). Better still was the unexpected announcement: "Hear The Cramps sing 'You've Got The Blues'" — followed by a single bar of this otherwise unknown song — to ape old 50s movie trailers. Clocking in just shy of five minutes, 'Wilder, Wilder, Faster, Faster' was longer than virtually all the Cramps' other songs and came with a built-in censorious ending: "Under 18 not admitted without an adult."

### 'Wilhelmina'

Thunderclap Newman
TRACK 1969
A-Side: 'Something In The Air'

**One-hit wonders' hit peak psychedelic whimsy.**

Assembled by Pete Townshend to show off his ex-chauffeur Speedy Keen's songwriting smarts, Thunderclap Newman was an all too brief marriage of convenience. Envisaged as a chart-friendly vehicle for Keen's skills after he penned 'Armenia City in the Sky' (the psychedelic opening to 1967's *The Who Sell Out*), Townsend was fully hands-on as mentor. Not only did he produce, arrange strings and play bass (using the pseudonym Bijou Drains) on the A-side's flower power call-to-arms, he also pulled in his jazz pianist friend Andy 'Thunderclap' Newman and unknown teenage guitarist Jimmy McCulloch. Newman was the dominant force on B-side 'Wilhelmina', taking lead vocals and playing full-on honky-tonk piano below its nursery rhyme-like lyrics about a strange "plump and round girl," with hints of the Bonzo Dog Doo Dah Band, Monty Python and Syd Barrett-era Pink Floyd. It was punctuated by a dramatic psych solo from McCulloch, hinting at the precocious invention he'd later bring to Paul McCartney's Wings.

### 'Winterlong'

Pixies
4AD 1990
A-Side: 'Dig For Fire'

**4AD misfits hymn a hero.**

While Pixies rarely skimped on supplying VFM with their plentiful B-sides, one of their best just happened to be a cover version. The oddball Boston proto-grungers had quickly burned through three albums in three years that fully established their loud-quiet-loud modus operandi (soon to be emulated by Nirvana), before exploring stranger tones on 1990's *Bossanova* (epitomised by brazen Talking Heads A-side homage 'Dig For Fire'). First recorded for 1989 tribute album *The Bridge*, their cover of Neil Young's 'Winterlong' was a duet between bassist Kim Deal and guitarist Black Francis flush with dreamy longing as Pixies enhanced Young's elemental greatness with Joey Santiago's searing guitar lines. Among the best Pixies' B-side covers going — although cases could be made for their live take of *Eraserhead* highlight 'In Heaven (The Lady In The Radiator Song)' ['Gigantic', 1988] and their *other* Young cover 'I've Been Waiting For You' ['Velouria', 1990] — Pixies showed just how much this personal Francis favourite meant by playing it at 2009's comeback turn at the Isle of Wight festival, minutes before Young hit the stage.

**'Wipe-Out'**
The Surfaris
DFS 1963
A-Side: 'Surfer Joe'

**Instant surf rock standard.**

Callow Southern California high school students the Surfaris saved and borrowed to record their first single 'Surfer Joe', the sole original song in their short canon. Pressed into action by the engineer at Pal Recording Studios in Cucamonga — who reminded the quartet that a single had *two* sides — they quickly rustled up 'Wipe-Out' in under ten minutes (and nailed its recording in the space of three takes). Partially inspired by the rhythmic thrust of Preston Epp's 'Bongo Rock', its straightforward but detonating 12-bar blues (named after the term for a bad surfboard fall) was distinguished by Jim Fuller's up-and-down guitar figure and an energetic tom-tom riff (effectively a paradiddle) that spoke loudly of Ron Wilson's previous tenure in a tartan marching band. Initially pressed in a short edition of 100 on manager Dale Smallin's teeny DFS label, it was picked up by Princess and then major label Dot, who quickly flipped sides — preferring to promote a cut that started with a strange cracking noises and maniacal laughter to run-of-the-mill vocal pop. Dot were vindicated when 'Wipe-Out' caught a giant wave and spent over thirty weeks on the *Billboard* Hot 100, peaking at number two. And although the Surfaris would part ways within three years, 'Wipe-Out' became one of rock's most memorable instrumentals, a staple of movies (*Meet The Parents*, *Runaway Bride*, *Wayne's World 2*) and a US number two once more via 1987's unlikely alliance of the Fat Boys and the Beach Boys.

## 'Wishful Thinking'

Big Punisher
LOUD 1997
A-Side: 'I'm Not A Player'

**Bronx big rap dog shows off cypher skills.**

The first solo Latin hip-hop artist to go platinum, Christopher Lee Rios emerged from a life of problems. The hefty Puerto Rican coped with a turbulent childhood defined by parental drug problems, homelessness and depression by eating too much — to the point where it endangered his life. None of that stopped the 600 pound-and-then-some MC becoming a larger-than-life star. There was no doubting his skills on the B-side to his first single (a *Billboard* Top 30 hit after a pop remix in 1998), a posse cut that made the most of a stringy sample from Uri Geller's 1974 spoon-bender 'Velvet Space'. After allies including Cypress Hill's B-Real, Fat Joe and Kool G Rap (whose nimble compound rhyming style Pun clearly admired) went first, Pun slayed the final verse of 'Wishful Thinking'. The song gained added emotional resonance when it was revealed that his vow to "Make my wife forget the tears" was based on chilling fact — posthumous 2002 documentary *Still Not A Player* showed footage of the rapper slapping wife Liza Rios in the face with a gun, captured on his own home security cameras.

## 'Worried Life Blues'

Big Maceo
BLUEBIRD 1941
A-Side: 'Texas Blues'

**Chicago blues pianist's weary standard.**

Big Maceo's cultural impact belied his bijou catalogue. While the devil was briefly on blues legend Robert Johnson's side, as he recorded twenty-nine tracks that helped define the genre, the self-taught Chicagoan Maceo, hailed as the 'king of the blues piano', cut just one less at just twenty-eight. It wasn't by design though — Maceo only got to record his first single 'Texas Blues' at the relatively past-it age of thirty-eight. It was backed by 'Worried Life Blues', the first song captured in his first recording session as Maceo mined the framework of Sleepy John Estes' 1935 single 'Someday Baby Blues'. He also eclipsed it, his wearied vow ("I ain't gonna worry my life no more") undercut by booming left hand piano figures and a sympathetic guitar turn from Tampa Red. A sophisticated take that belied his apprenticeship in southern juke-joints and sporting houses, it quickly became Maceo's signature tune, covered by Sonny Boy Williamson, B.B. King, Ray Charles, John Lee Hooker and the Animals. It was inducted into the Blues Foundation Hall Of Fame in 1983, thirty years after he suffered a fatal heart attack.

## 'Wrath Of Kane'

Big Daddy Kane
COLD CHILLIN' 1989
A-Side: 'I'll Take You There'

**Hip-hop's original lover man in battle mode.**

While Big Daddy Kane's debut LP *Long Live The Kane* showed off his battle-hardened microphone skills, he was quick to branch out into different styles on the sequel *It's A Big Daddy Thing*, embracing social commentary, love ballads, house and new jack swing. Yet the hard-knock Brooklyn rapper whose stage name was an acronym for King Asiatic Nobody's Equal went right back to his roots on the B-side of its 4th and final single. Over producer Marley Marl's brilliantly stripped back beat — a rhythmic union of Ricky Williams' 'Discotheque Soul Part 2' with The JBs' 'Givin' Up Food For Funk' — and DJ Mister Cee's avid scratching, Kane boasted "I'm only twenty-one and untouched by anyone" with a flow that seemed on another planet from the competition. One of the few MCs who could switch from smooth fly guy to verbal assassin in the blink of an eye, his album's live version (captured at Harlem's Apollo Theatre) showed Kane's talent for whipping crowds into a frenzy, but couldn't match this B-side take.

# YOU CAN'T B SERIOUS!

*Ever had the feeling you've been cheated? B-sides that really scrape the barrel...*

How low can you go? From the post-modern joke to the backstage barney via locked grooves and drunken blatherings, the other side of your most cherished hit has always been open to abuse.

It's an art that **Dickie Goodman** was intimately well-versed in. The novelty hitmaker pre-empted sampling by pioneering the 'break-in' on 1956's 'The Flying Saucer'. Posing as an excitable reporter, Goodman used short clips from pop hits to answer his questions. Lawsuits inevitably followed, but he fended them off by claiming his creations were burlesques, unique unto themselves. By the mid-70s Goodman's records regularly tapped into public fears — communism, UFOs, student unrest, Watergate — as he refined his discrete craft further, borrowing from Brownsville Station, Stevie Wonder, Elton John and Wings on the A-side here. Aptly titled, **'The Mistake'** ['Energy Crisis '74', RAINY WEDNESDAY 1974] was a botched test pressing that the record plant sent out featuring just the first few seconds of the A-side (Goodman saying "Mister President, the crisi...") followed by two minutes of silence. Goodman persevered with it anyway, although later editions featured guitar instrumental 'Ruthie's Theme' instead.

Inspired by a particularly hectic Black Wire gig in Leeds, **Kaiser Chiefs**' 'I Predict A Riot' catapulted the long-in-tooth band from the indie toilet circuit to the Top 40. A limited seasonal gift, **'I Predict Some Quiet'** ['You Can Have It All (Light Orchestral)', B-UNIQUE 2005] arrived with the inscription: "Play this side for a bit of peace this Christmas". A completely silent flip, it joined a long tradition of mute tracks stretching from John Cage's infamous '4 33 ' to John Denver, Crass and Afrika Bambaataa.

Tattooed teen heartthrob **Harry Styles** may have raced ahead of his boyband peers with the trippy gospel-laced R&B lead single from his second album. But **'Do You Know Who You Are?'** ['Lights Up', ERSKINE/COLUMBIA 2019] wasn't so much taking the piss as giving it away. Another fan special, this time a limited seven-inch issued for Record Store Day — possibly the first vinyl record many of his fans would buy — it was a locked groove containing a 14-second snatch (its "La-di-da-la" part) of the A-side. While some of the ex-One Direction star's most committed fanbase took the A-side as proof of the cross-dressing singer's alleged bisexuality, its flip marked him more as a cad.

Anyone who parted with good money for **Alvin and the Chipmunks**' singles — and many did — was aware that their B-side's titles often spoke for themselves. **'Mediocre'** ['Alvin's Harmonica', LIBERTY 1959] was no exception, songwriter Ross Bagdasarian doubling down on the A-side's deliberately offkey harmonica solo with a bit of easy-come piano music hall and the jokey sign off "Wait a minute! I can't publish that, it's mediocre," on a long chortle to the bank.

**'Sticky, Sticky'** ['1, 2, 3, Red Light', BUDDAH 1968] was cut from a very similar cloth. It found pioneering bubblegum collective the **1910 Fruitgum Company** inverting the super slick sheen of the irresistible, million-selling A-side with a simple piano vamp and a barrage of handclaps, topped with increasingly unhinged shouts of its title. It was more easy money for Buddah's in-house producers Jerry Kasenetz and Jeffry Katz, the brains behind the Ohio Express, the Lemon Pipers and the Music Explosion reproving their knack for keeping 45-buyers on their toes

Masterminded by Coventry jingle kings Rob Woodward and Nigel Fletcher, **Lieutenant Pigeon** was riding high on the success of wobbly ragtime instrumental 'Mouldy Old Dough' when they cut the hyperreal dada of **'Opus 300'** ['Desperate Dan', DECCA 1972] to back a near-identical A-side to their last. Whether that was an art prank or not, said avant-garde flip — backwards noises, eerie drones, a distorted

martial beat and a calypso bridge that advised "get your shoes from the menders and don't be late" over maniacal chuckling — was no laughing matter.

A fleeting presence on the late 60s psychedelic circuit, the out-of-body sounds of mysterious Minneapolis music makers the **Calico Wall** had been largely lost before this A-side's addictive repetitive riff was rounded up on the *Pebbles* anthology series. It made no concessions for **'Beep'** ['Flight Reaction', TURTLE 1967] though. The ultimate psychedelic trip-side, it was a one-second beep followed by three seconds of silence, repeated over six minutes — ambulance chasers unite. Similarly minimal, Gong's Tim Blake backed his one-off solo single as **Saratoga Space Sound** entirely with birdsong on **'Saratoga Space Messengers'** ['Surf', ISADORA 1967].

"We can't hear the backing track," moaned John Lydon at the start of **Public Image Ltd**'s most difficult B-side. While Lydon's sneering brilliance ignited his comeback single's vituperative attack on the press and his old band over 17-year-old Jah Wobble's thudding bassline, the drum-free cacophony of **'The Cowboy Song'** ['Public Image', VIRGIN 1978] — all scratched vinyl, sound effects, disembodied basslines and Lydon coughing — clearly failed in its attempt to rip-off the theme from *Bonanza*. Long-suffering Sex Pistols fans, who also had to endure the similarly challenging 'Fodderstompf' on PiL's debut LP *First Issue*, had every right to wonder whether they had just been fleeced.

Fainthearts would do best to avoid industrial ne'er-do-wells **Revolting Cocks**' endurance test **'(Let's Talk) Physical'** ['(Let's Get) Physical', WAX TRAX! 1989]. Having already rewritten the words to Olivia Newton-John's panting 1981 hit, to dodge a lawsuit, the B-side stretched a loop of a single snare drum hit and Chris Connelly seemingly screaming the word "talk" into infinity (well, for nearly seven minutes, which was more than enough).

"We thought we'd break a precedent and just say hello to everybody," schmaltzed Sonny Bono at the end of **'Hello'** ['But You're Mine', ATCO 1965] — the sound of the hippy husband and wife duo **Sonny & Cher** idly chit-

chatting over Bono's plinking piano chords. Drummer on many Phil Spector productions for the Philles label, Bono evidently picked up on the producer's antipathy for a B-side with a cat in hell's chance of challenging the A-side for supremacy. Essentially a fan club message with Bono admitting "There is no song", 'Hello' broke a precedent alright.

Radio 1 DJ Mike Read's decision to play moral guardian and yank off **Frankie Goes to Hollywood**'s first single live on air was the gift the Liverpool band desperately needed. Banned entirely by the BBC two days later, 'Relax' [ZTT 1983] shot to number 1 and stayed there for five weeks, the start of Frankie fever and a year of chart dominance in defiance of AIDS hysteria and a hectoring prime minister riding high on Victorian values. Its seven-inch B-side **'One September Monday'** took the soggy biscuit — one channel playing slowed down stems of the A-side, the other replaying a conversation between a slightly worse-for-wear singer Holly Johnson and dancer Paul Rutherford. A testing listen, they did it all again on their next B-side 'One February Friday' ['Two Tribes', 1984].

No B-side was written for **Band Aid**'s single to address the famine in Ethiopia when its starry rollcall entered Trevor Horn's SARM Studios (also the birthplace of 'Relax'). So **'Feed The World'** ['Do They Know It's Christmas', PHONOGRAM 1985] made do by rehashing the A-side's instrumental overlaid with festive greetings from the likes of Bono, Simon Le Bon, Paul Weller, Banarama, Big Country and Frankie Goes to Hollywood's Holly Johnson (the latter literally phoning it in down a crackly line). While Paul McCartney nearly stole the limelight with his motormouth skits, David Bowie's to-the-manor-born address supplied the necessary Christmas ham.

A bitter protest against the heavy commercialisation of the Xmas season, 'I Believe In Father Christmas' [MANTICORE 1975] — lyrics by poet Peter Sinfield, music based on Prokofiev's *Lieutenant Kijé* suite — ironically became **Greg Lake**'s biggest cash cow. Held off the coveted yule number one spot by Queen's 'Bohemian Rhapsody', the ex-King Crimson bassist clearly didn't lose much sleep over its B-side **'Humbug'**. A light-as-snow near-instrumental, laced with plum-voiced repetitions, festive flutes and trombone trippery, Lake still complained to *The Guardian* that he didn't earn "quite enough to buy my own island in the Caribbean".

While even diehard Beatles fans were split on the ding-donging merits of **Paul McCartne**y's solo festive smash and pension topper (said to have netted its author over £15 million — surely enough for a sun-lit archipelago?) few could mount a solid defence for **'Rudolph The Red-Nosed Reggae'** ['Wonderful Christmastime', PARLOPHONE 1979]. It was what it said on the tin — a violin-led quasi dub of the Xmas standard. While never going to trouble King Tubby, it was the latest manifestation of a reggae obsession that harked all the way back to the ska middle eight of the Beatles' 'I Call Your Name'.

This single's A-side may have been hastily tacked onto Pete Townshend's rock opera *Tommy* at the eleventh hour to appease critic Nik Cohn, but **'Dogs Part 2'** ['Pinball Wizard', POLYDOR 1969] really ramped up the lunacy in the **Who**'s strange universe at the time (deemed their "wanking off period" by singer Roger Daltry). Partially credited to Keith Moon, a lover of great danes, his OTT rhythms drove this rocking near instrumental (an unrelated sequel to a flop Part 1 A-side the previous year), although co-writers Towser-Jason — Townshend's spaniel mix and John Entwistle's Irish wolfhound, respectively — stole the show with their barking leads. Let's hope they spent their royalties wisely.

A re-arranged version of a 1950 Rosemary Clooney single **'Teddy Bear'** ['D.I.Y.', CHARISMA 1978] remains a true outlier in the **Peter Gabriel** catalogue. One of the first songs the ex-Genesis singer ever performed — aged six — he regularly used it to open dates on his second self-titled album's tour. After introducing "someone who has been a huge influence on me", Gabriel would plop a lark pink teddy bear on his piano — much like a solo Phil Collins would later place a paint pot on his — and play its childlike tune. He also added the line "We've got no hair/We don't care"

to reflect his new image, a sharp, controversial buzzcut.

Seasoned forgers of experimental B-sides from Midlands' murder mecca Northampton, art schoolers **Bauhaus** used the surrealist's exquisite corpse approach — an audio form of *Consequences* — to back their most stringent stab at a Top 40 hit. **'1. David Jay 2. Pete Murphy 3. Kevin Haskins 4. Daniel Ash'** ['The Passion Of Lovers', BEGGARS BANQUET 1982] witnessed each member take a minute or two to essay a part recorded in isolation, linked only by the same synthetic drumbeat. Pete Murphy's over-dramatic ode to fishcakes and Daniel Ash's backwards mutterings about whisky proved the regular press whipping boys — once challenged to an onstage duel by *Melody Maker* scribe Steve Sutherland — weren't as po-faced as their detractors claimed. Bauhaus repeated the concept, as 'Exquisite Corpse', while closing out that year's third LP *The Sky's Gone Out*.

It's a moot point whether **Squeeze** took any ques from those departed goth overlords, but they certainly applied the same solo collage approach to **'Suites From Five Strangers'** ['Last Time Forever', A&M 1985], grandly billed as "the most unusual record of all time ever made". While Gilson Lavis and Glenn Tilbrook opted for jokey instrumentals and Keith Wilkinson veered into the avant-garde, Chris Difford saluted a clarinet player and Jools Holland paid speaker-panning spoken word homage to the fictional Big John Gooley without anyone's sides splitting.

No one in the **England World Cup Squad '70** was laughing when the defending champions lost to their old nemesis West Germany in extra time of the quarter final of that year's World Cup in Mexico. At least it saved the agony of hearing them back a humdrum A-side by Eurovision specialists Bill Martin and Phil Coulter with a bizarre beat song about watching a girl in a café sucking a **'Cinnamon Stick'** ['Back Home', PYE 1970], with all the innuendo that implies. It sounded even more creepy for its delivery, as the squad's massed tones pronounced "See that twinkle in her eyes?" England's failure to qualify for West Germany in 1974 and Argentina in 1978 spared tender ears from more of the same.

A B-side test — try to keep a straight face listening to two members of

**Iron Maiden** going at it hammer and tong, airing their dirty linen in public on **'Mission From 'Arry'** ['2 Minutes To Midnight', EMI 1984]. An immaculate slice of real-life *Spinal Tap*, it caught aggrieved bassist Steve Harris and put-upon drummer Nicko McBrain having a full-on, no-expletives-spared barney after McBrain fell out with a roadie sent to instruct him to extend his drum solo during a show in Allentown, Pennsylvania. The pair had already been at it for a good twenty minutes when singer Bruce Dickinson intervened, stoking up the tension by asking McBain: "What would happen if he tried to tell you the lighting truss was going to fall on your head?" The argument restarted, covering similar ground, only this time Dickinson covertly caught the pair's frank exchange on tape.

## 'Yellow Ledbetter'

Pearl Jam
EPIC 1992
A-Side: 'Jeremy'

**Seattle grunge pretenders' lyrically obtuse ballad.**

Alongside Nirvana, Pearl Jam were the public face of grunge. Seasoned performers, with pedigree in ill-starred hard rockers Mother Love Bone, the plaid shirted Seattle band boasted an earnest, charismatic singer in Eddie Vedder — the more sensible schoolgirl's crush over the issue-riven Kurt Cobain. Pearl Jam also had supporters at MTV. While the influential cable channel played the mawkish A-side 'Jeremy' into the ground (despite being about teenage schoolboy Jeremy Delle's very public suicide), fans became hooked by its emotive B-side — among the most debated songs in Pearl Jam's repertoire. While theories raged over whether its title referred to an old friend of Vedder's from Chicago, the tongue-twisting effects of saying "yellow better, red better" as fast as possible, a tribute to blues legend Huddie Ledbetter (Lead Belly) or someone receiving a letter about a war fatality (sent in a yellow envelope), its mumbled, obtuse lyrics failed to elucidate further. Improvised on the spot by Vedder, its vague anti-war message (informed by the unfolding Gulf War) was allied to a melancholy Mike McCready guitar lick practically lifted from the Jimi Hendrix handbook (with close similarities to 'Little Wing'). Despite the ambiguity, Vedder's soaring delivery would wind its way onto US rock radio, the B-side peaking at number twenty-one on *Billboard*'s Mainstream Rock Tracks chart. Used in the final episode of *Friends*, 'Yellow Ledbetter' was a live favourite the band changed and morphed to their will, often closing shows with it.

### 'You Remind Me Of Gold'

The Human League
VIRGIN 1982
A-Side: 'Mirror Man'

**Intelligent post-*Dare!* electro-funk pop.**

Sheffield electronic pioneers the Human League travelled a long way in a short time. Just three years after recording first single 'Being Boiled' for the princely sum of £3 in a disused apple factory, they had shed half the band (founders Martyn Ware and Ian Craig Marsh becoming Heaven 17) and struck chart gold with *Dare!*, an album of linear electropop perfection overseen by producer Martin Rushent. The super squelchy, dancefloor primed synth lines of 'You Remind Me Of Gold' nodded to Kraftwerk's 'The Robots' and were the ideal backdrop for Phil Oakey's rich remembrances and Joanne Catherall and Susan Ann Sulley's backing coos. If anything, it harked right back to 1980 single 'Boys + Girls', suggesting it hailed from earlier times (the Human League made few bones about the writer's block that followed their success). Much more trenchant than the lightweight Motown pastiche of 'Mirror Man' — apparently written by a concerned Oakey about Adam Ant's mental health — this B-side might well have succeeded as an A.

### 'You Sexy Thing'

Hot Chocolate
RAK 1975
A-Side: 'Blue Night'

**British soul band's enduring signature tune.**

Hot Chocolate had a UK hit in every year of the 70s. The multi-racial London band, nominally discovered by John Lennon, forged a chart-busting partnership with production taskmaster Mickie Most — brains behind the RAK hit factory. Written by singer Errol Brown about his wife Ginette, 'You Sexy Thing' was first given away on the back of 1975's bruised, keening slow jam 'Blue Night' — a rare glitch in their chart matrix — because Most considered it too lightweight to be a hit. He evidently had a change of heart and radically remixed it as 1975 drew to a close. Built on a complex percussive groove (achieved by putting congas through a wah-wah pedal), deeply overdriven guitar riff and taut violins, its unusual bedrock chimed with Brown's impassioned croon and high-pitched screams. An undeniable juggernaut of hook-laden pop disco, it was held off the UK top spot by Queen's 'Bohemian Rhapsody' but became a Top 10 hit thrice (again in 1987 via a Ben Liebrand remix and after soundtracking the striptease scene in 1997 film *The Full Monty*). A hit in over fifty countries, 'You Sexy Thing' was a game-changer that effectively set the pop-disco template for the remainder of Hot Chocolate's career

### 'You'll Want Me Back'

The Impressions
ABC-PARAMOUNT 1963
A-Side: 'It's All Right'

**Crying soul from the pen of Curtis Mayfield.**

Few could tap into melancholy as beautifully as Curtis Mayfield. A key architect in the Chicago Sound and latter-day civil rights activist, the prolific Mayfield wrote and produced for the likes of Gene Chandler, Major Lance, Jan Bradley and Billy Butler while working hard to establish a signature sound — bridging gospel techniques with R&B and pop — for his band the Impressions. A lovely contrast to the horn-charged uptempo Chicago pop-soul of 'It's All Right', their most successful single, 'You'll Want Me Back' was a forlorn lover's lament against a hostile partner, with Mayfield's wounded falsetto, vowing to make his lover "cry, cry, cry" against supporting harmonies, wild flutes and a throbbing churchy organ. Little heralded at home, the B-side enjoyed a glittering second life in Jamaica after the Impressions toured the island in 1966. Not only did 'You'll Want Me Back' become one of the island's most popular riddims, acts such as the Paragons, the Wailers and the Heptones all drew heavily on the push and pull of the Impressions' unique vocal arrangements.

**'You're A Better Man Than I'**
The Yardbirds
COLUMBIA 1966
A-Side: 'Shapes Of Things'

**British blues abusers get philosophical.**

After featuring in Michelangelo Antonioni's era-defining arthouse movie *Blow Up*, the Yardbirds were at the forefront of progressive pop. Best known for their self-styled 'rave-ups' — galloping, high-energy sprints that made the most of their lead guitarists' widdling skills and singer Keith Relf's harmonica freestyles — the dandified London band that spawned, in their brief five-year tenure, three guitar greats (Eric Clapton, Jeff Beck and Jimmy Page) were in philosophical mode on both sides of this feedback-laden single. While the pure psych of 'Shapes Of Things' pondered the state of the human race, the wistful 'You're A Better Man Than I' condemned prejudice on all levels. A heartfelt plea not to judge another person by their appearance, religion or race, it was taken to a higher plane by Beck's mind-bending guitar solo (an indelible influence on David Gilmour's style). First issued as the opening track on the group's second US album (odds and sods compilation *Having A Rave Up with...*), it was heavily referenced in Aerosmith's 1993 hit 'Livin' On The Edge'.

**'You're My Favorite Waste Of Time'**
Marshall Crenshaw
WARNER BROS 1982
A-Side: 'Someday, Someway'

**Power-pop maestro's home demo takes off.**

Detroit singer songwriter Marshall Crenshaw enjoyed a circuitous route to success. The wannabe pop star had landed a plum role as understudy to John Lennon's character in Broadway musical *Beatlemania* when he started writing songs using a four-track recorder. He was still in the musical when 'You're My Favorite Waste Of Time' emerged — a tongue-in-cheek tribute to his wife. One of the first tracks he recorded alone, playing all the instruments himself, Crenshaw kept its charming homemade rawness intact when he slapped it on the B-side of the more sophisticated guitar pop of 'Someday, Someway', his first major label single. While that became his only hit, the B-side's huge chorus hook kept him out of the gutter in the lean years that followed. Royalty-spawning covers from Bette Midler, Ronnie Spector, Matthew Sweet & Susanna Hoffs plus fellow one-hit wonder Owen Paul — who made it a Top 3 UK hit in 1986 — proved its author's contention: "That song has really had staying power".

### 'You've Got The Power'

Van Morrison
WARNER BROS 1972
A-Side: 'Jackie Wilson Said'

**Belfast Cowboy's Stax-inspired slow jam.**

Although he made waves fronting bullish R&B bruisers Them in the mid-60s, Van Morrison came into his own when he turned solo, spinning the dial between loose jazz abstractions and radio-friendly blue-eyed soul. His exuberant homage to American R&B star Jackie Wilson didn't hurt his burgeoning popularity in the States, while a similarly soul-shouting, enlivened outtake from the sessions for 1972's 6th solo album *Saint Dominic's Preview* sustained the heightened levels of jubilation. Built around bassist Bill Church and drummer Gary Mallaber's irresistible groove, it found Van the Man at his soulfully sweaty best, bouncing off Jack Schroer and Jules Broussard's twin sax breaks and Tom Salisbury's swirling Hammond organ. And although it had the feel of a loose jam — its chord sequence was tried and tested, some of Morrison's key phrases ("Baby with your saint-like smile" and "Set my soul on fire") had surfaced before (on 'Sweet Thing' and 'I've Been Working') — the sheer chemistry was hard to deny. Hailed by Morrison biographer Peter Mills as "one of the best examples we have of Morrison's voice working in a fully integrated way with the superb band", this B-side has retained its rarity status and never been officially released elsewhere.

### 'Your Arms Too Short To Box With God'

Lakim Shabazz
TUFF CITY 1989
A-Side: 'Black Is Black'

**Five Percenter's lyrical blows to the jaw.**

New Jersey rhymer Lakim Shabazz was the first voice heard on DJ Mark The 45

King's signature cut '900 Number' in 1987. Heavily linked with the producer's Flavor Unit crew (alongside Apache, Latee, Chill Rob G and Queen Latifah), Shabazz's authoritative microphone command was allied to an unwavering sense of purpose — the member of the Nation of Gods and Earths (the Five-Percent Nation) littered his rhymes with references to their teachings and lessons. And although King's love of dusty funk and soul samples coursed through the A-side's call to action against a corrupt system (replete with *de rigueur* Malcolm X samples), its fat-free flipside was arguably the better cut. A rare studio dalliance with producer Louis 'Louie Louie' Vega (not the house DJ), its spare beats, crowd noise and echoing horns were all Shabazz needed to let rip a sequence of lyrical roundhouses that showed the power of his message. Referenced by name in Eminem's 2013 statement of technical mastery 'Rap God', this true hip-hop pugilist somehow slipped through the cracks.

**'Your Love Is Wonderful'**
The Four Tops
MOTOWN 1968
A-Side: 'Walk Away Renée'

**Redemptive keeper from steadfast Detroit quartet.**
With their regular songwriting foils Holland-Dozier-Holland out of the picture (and in financial dispute with Motown), the Four Tops had to scour harder for hits as the 60s ended. It found them reaching outside their comfort zone into MOR covers. Although it felt something of an oddity at first, their take on the Left Bank's baroque 1966 hit 'Walk Away Renée' improved on the original — thanks to the lead singer Levi Stubbs' yearning delivery. Many felt putting the more traditionally Motown-sounding 'Your Love Is Wonderful' on its B-side was a missed opportunity. Written by label staffers Ivy Jo Hunter and Jack Alan Gogo, it was just a small notch down from the high watermark of 'Reach Out, I'll Be There', its powerful melody, sinuous bass and uptempo strings all grist to the mill of Stubbs' gospel-strained baritone, one minute down in a hole "with all my bridges burned" the next bristling with unexpected exaltation. The Four Tops performed for over four decades without a change in personnel, but watched their chart fortunes fade when they bailed from Motown in 1972.

## 'Zing Zing — Zoom Zoom'

Perry Como
RCA VICTOR 1950
A-Side: 'If (They Made Me A King)'

**Mr C's simple tune with magical powers.**

Between the end of the big band era and the rise of rock 'n' roll, Perry Como's laidback style made him one of America's leading crooners. Born into a large Italian-American family, the one-time Pennsylvanian singing barber proved a cut above the rest when he started touring with Freddie Carlone and Ted Weems, parlaying a role hosting CBS radio show *Supper Club* into his own network TV variety vehicle and a solo deal with RCA Victor. Como even wore his barber coat when he performed A-side 'If', already the US number one, on *The Frank Sinatra Show* in early 1951, his easy, dreamy baritone showing just why he was sometimes dubbed Mr Relaxation by industry insiders. Its breezy B-side 'Zing Zing — Zoom Zoom' was a slice of unassuming whimsy that advised listeners to "vocalise" its silly title with supposedly magical results (said to be capable of opening "matrimonial doors") as Como's warm tones floated above Sigmund Romberg's jaunty string arrangements. Among the better of the light novelty songs Como increasingly turned to in order to sustain his fame, however much he personally despised them (see also: 'Bibbidi-Bobbidi-Doo', 'Hoop-Dee-Doo' and '(A Hubba-Hubba-Hubba) Dig You Later'), Como's career — and the rules of pop — changed forever when 1956's career nadir 'Hot Diggity (Dog Ziggity Boom)' was knocked off its number one perch by Elvis' 'Heartbreak Hotel'.

# ACKNOWLEDGEMENTS

A huge thank you to David Kerekes and all at Headpress for taking a punt on *B-Side*. It could never have become a reality without the critical mentorship of Chris Hunt — whose leap of faith really started this journey — and Colin Larkin, the real-life musopedia who expanded my horizons a thousand-fold. Thank you to my MOJO Editors past and present: Jenny Bulley, Danny Eccleston, Ian Harrison, Andrew Male, John Mulvey, Phil Sutcliffe. To everyone at Cambridge Public Health and the University of Cambridge's Primary Care Cancer Group, especially Louise Lafortune and Fiona Walter. Endless daps to everyone in the HHC posse, but with extreme gratitude to Nihal Arthanayake, Angus Batey, Martin Cook, Al-Rashed Dauda, Andrew Emery, Paul Hampartsoumian, Phillip Mlynar, James McNally, Normski, Barry Sugarman and DJ Yoda. For love, support and friendship: Kid Acne, Matt Beeke, Johny Brown, Tom Brown, Juan Calvillo, Luis Cowan, Klaus Cowan, Gary Crowley, James Cumpsty, John Dyer, Richard Ecclestone, Chris Elwell-Sutton, Mansel Fletcher, Bruce Godfrey, Ian Howell, Philip Kane, Sean Kelly, Paul Kurzeja, Mike Lewis, Kevin Lowery, Ian Madgin, Emma Rainbow, Samantha Smith, Emmanuel Stamatakis, Paul Whitbread, Joy & Harry Wilkin, Stephen Worthy. Special 'fanx' to my A1 wrecking crew: Alan Beeson and David Houghton. Thank you Mum and Dad for everything. Last, but far from least, Karen, for her love, patience and forbearance. Without you I'm just a man going mad in a shed.

*B-Side* is dedicated to David Denny and my number one band in heaven: Tim Dixon, Michael Leonard and Mark Pickstone.

# INDEX